HEAD SHOT

HEAD SHOT

Quintin Jardine

headline

First published in 2002
by HEADLINE BOOK PUBLISHING

10 9 8 7 6 5 4 3 2 1

British Library Cataloguing in Publication Data

Jardine, Quintin
  Head shot
  1. Detective and mystery stories
  I. Title
  823.9'14[F]

ISBN 0 7472 7447 9 (hardback)
ISBN 0 7553 0059 9 (trade paperback)

Typeset by Avon Dataset Ltd, Bidford-on-Avon, Warks

Printed and bound in Great Britain by
Mackays of Chatham plc, Chatham, Kent

HEADLINE BOOK PUBLISHING
A division of Hodder Headline
338 Euston Road
London NW1 3BH

www.headline.co.uk
www.hodderheadline.com

This is for Kyoko and Allan

The author's thanks go to . . .

Tom Lewis, my nephew, for putting me right about the US of A,

Jim Glossop, who knows who he really is,

J D Singh, of Toronto, for sharing with me the true recipe for a Martini,

Bill Massey, for his constant encouragement,

Jimmy Scott, Van Morrison and Diana Krall for most of the musical accompaniment, and as always,

Eileen, for putting up with it all. Yes, okay, honey, I'll turn the music down a notch . . .

Size matters . . .

'I didn't appreciate how big it was, not until the very moment when he brought it out.'

She looked up into his twisted, anguished face. 'I mean I've seen that calibre of gun before,' she added, 'but I've never actually held one.'

'It's quite a cannon,' he admitted. 'I'll give you that.'

'Yes, but I'm not just talking about its weight, or its smoothness, or any physical thing, I'm talking about a sheer sense of potency; I just seemed to feel it flowing into me. It scared me, yet thrilled me, at the same time.' Her voice was matter-of-fact; he realised the depth of her hysteria and that scared him more than anything.

He threw his head back and exhaled, a great breath hissing through his teeth. He could feel the tension gripping him, bunching the muscles behind his neck, puckering the scars of battle that he had picked up over the years. That roar of anger and frustration swelled up inside him again, and again he held it back.

He gazed at the weapon as it lay at her feet; a huge old-fashioned nickel-plated automatic, which he recognised as a 45 calibre Colt, with a long black silencer fitted to the end of the barrel. 'So . . .' He ground out the word. 'Gripped by this sudden surge of omnipotence, you . . .' Again he cut himself off short. 'Is that what you're saying?'

The emotion within him seemed to bring her to her senses, or to somewhere close by; yet still, she looked at him as if he was a stranger. 'No,' she said evasively, her whisper barely audible even in that still, silent room. 'That's not how it happened. I was frightened; he was mocking me.'

'If he'd laid down the fucking gun, and you had picked it up, why were you frightened?'

There was a long pause; he felt his heart-rate rise, and a strange, cold feeling ran through him. 'Come on,' he snapped, at last, forcing her to answer.

'It was the look in his eyes; he was sneering at me. He thought he was so dominant; he was just so damn confident. He was playing with me as

1

if I was his slave. He had me there, at his mercy, about to be killed and there was nothing I could do about it.'

'Did he speak?'

'Oh yes,' she said, her voice strengthening. 'He spoke, all right. He explained to me in great detail what it would do to me . . . after he was finished with me, that is . . . how the bullets were soft-nosed with a mercury core to flatten them on impact. He didn't have to, though. I've seen how they work.'

'Too bloody right you have,' he grunted, absently.

She gave no sign of having heard him. 'Then he told me he was going to shoot me in the back of the head. It would blow my face away, he said, make a mess that would be a message as well. He said that he wished he could be there when they found me.'

She took a deep breath. 'He laughed at the thought of it. That's how sure he was of himself; he laughed as he got down on me, and then he put it on the floor as he undid himself, he laid it right beside my face. He invited me to look at the means of my own destruction, to understand it, to feel its power. I remember thinking he was crazy, and looking at him, too scared really to understand what he was saying. He was smiling, all the time smiling. "Don't worry," he said, when he was almost ready. "The best is yet to come."

'But he had got it wrong. He thought I couldn't move, but when both his hands were busy, when he was . . .' She paused for breath. 'I made a grab for it. I almost dropped it: that's how badly I was shaking, that's how frightened I was. But I managed to keep hold of it, and to put it up against his head, and to tell him to get off me.'

He looked down at her, waiting for her to finish. She was still perched on the edge of her seat, her naked body shining silver in a shaft of moonlight that flowed through a narrow gap in the curtains.

'And then . . . okay, I suppose you could be right . . . then, I felt it: I felt the power that it gave me, power over him for a change. My hands had stopped shaking, completely. I could hold the gun steady. I saw the safety catch on the side, and I saw that it was off.

'He stopped laughing then. I pointed it at him and it was his turn to be terrified. And yes, you're right, I wasn't frightened at all; not by then. I just felt so angry, so tremendously, overpoweringly angry, at what he'd done to me, and been going to do. I couldn't stop myself; I didn't want to stop myself, and so . . .'

He finished for her. '. . . You blew his fucking head off. You had him under control, but you fucking well shot him.'

Suddenly he bent and picked up the great gun from the floor; releasing the magazine, checking it, then slipping it back into its housing in the butt.

He knelt down beside the body, feeling the queasiness which always overtook him when he confronted death, close up. He was glad that he had switched off the light as he looked at the leavings of the man, lying face up on the floor, in a dark puddle that had soaked into the rug on which he had fallen. 'He wasn't kidding about the ammo,' he said. 'You don't use this stuff to inflict flesh wounds. Shoot someone in the arm with one of these shells and you'll blow it right off.' He glanced over his shoulder, back towards her.

'You made a good job of it,' he said. 'You shot him right in the face; took out his right eye and the bridge of his nose. No, this bastard will not be bothering you again.'

He saw a shiver run through her shoulders; he knew that soon, she would need sedation.

'This leaves us with only one small problem,' he continued.

'What's that?' she whispered.

'What the hell are we going to do with him?'

1

The skull's empty eye-sockets seemed to be looking up at him from the white card, which the cabin attendant had given him. 'Welcome to Malaysia,' he murmured.

A significant part of Bob Skinner's police career had been spent pursuing the drug dealers who had threatened the social fabric of Edinburgh, the city that lay at the heart of his force's territory. The bigger they were, the more he hated them, with his strongest venom being reserved for those who peddled the most addictive substances in the most vulnerable areas, the places where the poverty trap was at its tightest, and where the perceived respite offered by spoon, flame and needle was, for some, an irresistible lure.

The heavier the sentences the Scottish High Court had handed down to those convicted, the wider had been his smile. But even he thought that the Pacific countries were going too far in imposing the ultimate penalty on the peddlers. At the same time, he recognised that much of the global supply of hard drugs originated in the area, and that at least the regional governments were showing the rest of the world that they took the problem seriously.

His difficulty with their policy was that, invariably, the people who fell through the trapdoor were the couriers, the mules, the foot soldiers, but never the generals. In any war, the great majority of the casualties come from the Other Ranks; in the global battle against narcotics the story was just the same.

The Deputy Chief Constable planned to say as much in his speech to the plenary session of the international conference at which he was representing the police service in Scotland. He knew that his view would not be popular with his Malaysian hosts, but that would not deter him from putting it forward.

'They spell it out, sir, don't they,' said Detective Chief Inspector Mary Chambers. 'A red skull and crossbones and "Death penalty for drug trafficking", stamped on your landing card. That's a bit unnecessary, heading in this direction, do you not think? There can't be a hell of a lot of smack smuggled from Heathrow to the Far East.'

Skinner glanced sideways at her, taking in the plain, square face, the forehead defined by close-cut dark hair which offered not a hint of personal vanity. 'She looks more like a copper than any bloke I've ever seen,' Andy Martin had said after her interview, and, the DCC had conceded, he had been right.

'Maybe not,' he agreed, 'but a lot of the traffic into Kuala Lumpur stops over at other airports in the region where consignments might be loaded.'

'I hadn't thought of that, I suppose.' The woman spoke with a pronounced Glasgow twang, a voice with muscles in it; her accent was not unlike Skinner's Lanarkshire dialect, but it was rawer, not dimmed as his had been by twenty years of East of Scotland life.

'I understand that,' he said. 'You've worked at the sharp end of the business until now, just as I did, once upon a time. Operating in Strathclyde you haven't had the bloody time to consider the global aspects of the trade; you've been too busy dealing with the problems on the streets. But believe me, it helps to have that broader understanding. The supply chains are long, but always they're interlinked, from the poppy to the needle. The more of us who share our knowledge and experience, the better chance we have of tracing each one right back to source and shutting it down for good.'

'Is that why you brought me with you on this trip? Not to learn; just to tell tales about pinching pushers in Paisley?'

He looked at her, laughing at her boldness. 'Why I brought you? It's why I recruited you in the first place. Did you think I brought you through to Edinburgh just on Willie Haggerty's say-so? Hell, no. I've been watching you since well before he was appointed to our command corridor.'

'Is that so?' She looked surprised. 'I just assumed that ACC Haggerty had put a word in for me.'

'Oh, don't get me wrong,' said Skinner, quickly, 'he did. But only after I asked him about you.'

Chambers frowned. 'And it was as easy as that, was it?' she mused.

'What? You asking if Strathclyde were happy to let you go?'

'Well . . .'

'Not a bit of it, Mary, I promise you. Your chief was pissed off; make no mistake about that. But I'm not without clout, and I'm playing a long game just now.'

'What do you mean?' she asked.

6

'You'll find out, when it's time,' he answered, intriguingly. 'But not just yet.'

'Cabin crew, seats for landing.' The captain's instruction through the small loudspeaker above their heads seemed to emphasise that all discussion was at an end.

2

PC Charlie Johnston hated this sort of night-shift work; sure, his colleagues told him he was daft, complaining about the cushiest job of them all, but he couldn't help it. He knew his limitations as a copper, yet he was never happy unless he was in a position to explore them. In his case that meant crowd control at football matches; being on patrol in shopping malls to deter and when necessary pursue thieves, or to come down on the occasional wee toe-rags who thought it was funny to harass and alarm respectable folks.

What he did not like was being sat on his arse in a decrepit sub-office like Oxgangs for hours on end, catching calls, which in practice rarely came in, dealing with theoretical evil-doers who were, in practice, tucked up in bed. It was not unusual for night-watch guys to spend their entire shift reading the *Evening News*, and listening to the insomniacs' programmes on Radio Forth, envying the disc-jockeys for the fact that at least they had someone to talk to, envying the guys and girls in their panda cars, just for the fact that they were out there. No, what Charlie did not like was sheer bloody boredom.

Yet, when the phone rang, at first he failed to hear it. He was on the verge of solving a tricky clue in the *Sunday Express* crossword . . . or, at least, he thought he was. It sounded four times before it made its way through to his consciousness. He scowled, and picked it up. 'Oxgangs police office,' he barked.

'Hello there,' said a female voice. 'Sorry to wake you.'

'That's okay, dear,' he responded, his weariness in contrast with her chirpiness. 'I was away for a hit and a miss.'

'Lucky it wasn't a day and a night. Listen, this is Nicola Ford; I'm a paramedic, and I'm at the doctor's surgery just down the road from your station. There's a dead man here.'

Johnston frowned. 'Aye, well, that happens. Doesn't it?'

'Not in places like this, in the middle of the night, it doesn't. Surgeries are usually closed at two in the morning. Our night time call-outs are either to houses, pub fights or road accidents. This man's had a heart attack, here at the doctor's.'

'So? What do you want us to do about it?'

'I want your lot to attend.'

'What for? Is there no' a doctor there?'

'Yes, but this is an unusual case. Dr Amritraj says the man called him at home, bypassing the normal emergency service. He was complaining of mild chest pains. The doctor says that he offered to call an ambulance right away, but the man refused. He wanted a home visit. Normally, Dr Amritraj would have referred him to the night service, but he says that he knew him quite well, so he went round to see him.'

Charlie Johnston stifled a yawn. 'Aye, so? How did he get to the surgery?'

'I was getting to that. The doctor says he was a bit concerned by his symptoms. He wanted to take him to A&E at the Royal, but the patient became agitated at the suggestion. He said that he had a phobia about hospitals and he refused point-blank to go there. The doctor has an ECG machine in his surgery, so he decided that he would take him there for a proper check-up, and that if he was having a heart attack, he'd sedate him, put him under, like, then call us.

'The patient agreed to that and they came here, but before Dr Amritraj even got him hooked up to the ECG, he took a cardiac arrest. The doctor tried to resuscitate him; he shocked him, gave him atropine, all the usual procedures, but it was no use. So he called us to take him to the mortuary.'

'That's fine, hen, but what do you need us for? There was a doctor in attendance when the man died, so we don't need to be informed.'

'That's what Dr Amritraj said, but there's the next of kin,' the paramedic answered, a little less chirpily than before. 'The man lived alone. The surgery has no other family members on its books, and no clue as to where they might be. It's your job to trace them, not ours. We can't stay here all night; we've got to shift him.'

'Aye, all right,' said Charlie. 'I'll get a panda round as soon as I can. Haud on a minute.' He laid the phone on the counter of the office, and turned to the radio transmitter. 'Any car in the Oxgangs area, come in please,' he said, into the microphone.

There was a crackling sound. 'Aye, Charlie?' a male voice answered.

'Need an attendance at the doctor's surgery in Oxgangs Road. There's a body there, and next-of-kin needin' advised.'

'Cannae do it, man. We've got a domestic here. Bloke's thumped his wife; we're having tae arrest him.'

'What about Jenny?'

'Her car's down the bypass at a road accident.'

'Aye, okay.' He flicked the mike off, and picked up the phone.

'Listen, hen,' he said. 'All our cars are occupied, so I'll have to come myself. I can do that; I just have to put my phone on divert and let divisional HQ know why. I'll just be a couple of minutes.'

Excited at last by the prospect of escaping from his nocturnal prison, the clerk, dispatcher and occasional jailer made his arrangements, slipped on his uniform tunic, with its utility belt, and made ready to step out into the fresh night air. As an afterthought, he took the office's Polaroid camera from the desk where it was kept.

3

He liked the spring; 'the renewal of God's promise' he called it, even though he had never been devoutly Christian. Few things appalled him more, in fact, than his country's religious right, and their active involvement in the electoral process ensured that he was an ever-present at the polls, voting the straight Democrat ticket whatever the personal failings of its candidates.

Indeed in the previous fall he had been proud to play his part in ensuring that party kept its grip on the New York State senatorial seat, beginning in the process a career which he hoped would lead the new incumbent to the White House in her own right. How the First Gentleman would take that would be something else again, but what the hell, he had had his eight years.

He approved of women in public life. *Just as well, Goddammit*, he thought, with a smile, *with the wife and daughter I've got.*

He had been an active politician himself once upon a time, forty-five and more years back, a young man not fresh from law school, but forged thereafter by bloody action in Korea. A short spell in the public defender's office in New York City had been enough to light the spark. He had seen men die in battle and had accepted it as something that came with his birthright. But the sight of one of his clients, a young black boy barely out of his teens, being dragged, screaming, to the electric chair, strapped down and virtually burned to death, had made him physically sick on the spot.

He was elected to the State Senate and served for a total of six years, through the cold dark years when Eisenhower was president, Nixon was scheming to succeed him, and John Foster Dulles, and his spymaster brother, ruled the country. With the rise of Kennedy, friends of his from Massachusetts persuaded him to put his own political career to one side for a while, to work on the young senator's presidential campaign team. There had been a promise of national office at the first electoral opportunity, but in the immediate aftermath of the narrow triumph, his reward had been a post as second assistant attorney general, in Bobby Kennedy's team.

He and the new president's aggressive, ambitious brother were at odds from the start, and relations between them had worsened when he had discovered that the New York senatorial seat, which he had been told would be his in time, was in fact earmarked for Bobby.

And so, a mere six weeks before the fall of the elected King Arthur, he had accepted an offer to become a senior partner in what was then known as McLean and Whyte, the largest legal firm in Buffalo, in his home state. In the same month, he had made an offer of his own, one of marriage to Susannah, a young teacher he had met in Washington.

Yes, he had seen a few springs since then, he mused, as he gazed out through the trees, across the glassy Great Sacandaga Lake, its waters catching the last rays of the evening sun. There had been thirty-eight of them, to be precise, every one memorable in its own way, every one marked by increasing success, professionally and privately. Where once he had dreamed on a national scale, dreamed without limit for a brief period, so caught up had he been in the seductive atmosphere of Camelot, now he reflected on the success he had made of his life, materially and spiritually.

Most of all there had been his daughter, a special girl from the outset. As she had grown, blooming in her intelligence and her beauty, he had looked at her, looked at his wife, and at himself, far more of a golden family than any branch of the doomed Kennedy clan, and he had wondered that he had ever been so weak that he had been seduced by their promises of joy. Why had he ever sought to bask in their glory, when such light had lain within himself, waiting for its moment to shine?

He leaned back in his rocking chair on the wide wooden terrace under the eaves of their log cabin, enjoying the shimmering colours of the lake before him. A brassy piece of Aaron Copland sounded from inside, and he caught the aroma of brewing coffee. 'Couldn't get any more American, could we?' he said aloud, and wondered what his son-in-law would think if he could see him lounging there.

He frowned as he thought of his son-in-law; now there was an individual who would have given them pause for thought, back in the sixties. There was still time for him to do that, even now. Yes, he had plans for his son-in-law. He had to see him, and soon, for there was something he had to discuss with him, something very serious . . .

The familiar creaking board sounded behind him; Susannah's footfall as she carried out the supper tray to lay upon their table. He made to rise, stiffly as always these days. And then he felt the cold, sharp thing whipping suddenly round his neck, tightening so fast, with a faint, peculiar twanging sound. He had no time to think, only to feel his tongue swell in his mouth and his eyes bulge in their sockets, to hear the roaring in his ears and to see the evening burst for an instant into sudden flaring light, and then go black.

The man held the strangling wire tight for some time after the old man's still-muscular body had gone limp, after his bladder had given forth its own signal. Finally, he released it, letting him slump down into his chair; and then he turned, and went into the isolated, lonely wooden house.

4

'So, Willie, how are you finding the air through here?' Sir James Proud asked his assistant; his deputy in Bob Skinner's absence.

'Pure and clear, gaffer,' Haggerty replied. 'So fuckin' pure that every so often it makes me dizzy.' The Chief Constable's left eyebrow twitched slightly; he realised that the dining room waitress was behind him, and had overheard. 'Excuse my French, Maisie,' he apologised.

'That's a'right, sir,' she said, as she laid a bowl of thick pea soup before him. 'Ah'm frae Glesca myself, originally. Ah know yis are a' linguists through there.'

Still, thought Haggerty, as she laid a salad before Detective Chief Superintendent Andy Martin, *this is another king's court I'm in now . . . even if the prime minister is away.*

Proud Jimmy scratched his chin. 'You know, gentlemen,' he mused, 'as an Edinburgh man, born and bred, I'm bound to say that I'm beginning to feel like an outsider in my own force. There's Bob, there's you, Andrew, and now you, Willie; west of Scotland men all of you, all my senior team. Mind you, the balance will swing back in my favour in a couple of weeks.'

'Aye,' Haggerty grunted. 'The Tay, the Tay, oh the silvery Tay,' he quoted. 'Long may it flow from Perth to Dundee. You looking forward to it, Andy?'

Martin shrugged his broad shoulders; green eyes flashed. 'Sure. On the whole, I am. It'll be a wrench though; I've been in this city for all of my police career so far.'

'Which is exactly why you had to go for the Tayside job, son,' the Chief interjected. 'It's the way things are; you can't be a one-force man any more, not if you have aspirations to command rank.' He glanced at Haggerty, reading his mind. 'I'm no example to quote either, before you do. I'm the last of the dinosaurs. Yes, I've been here a long time; too damned long, a few of our councillors have been heard to say. They think I'm just hanging on to spite them; I'm not, though.' He smiled, wickedly. 'We've got plans, Bob and I. A couple of years will see them through to fruition, then I'll be off.'

The outgoing Head of CID managed with some difficulty to keep his surprise from showing on his face. He had discussed the future with Bob Skinner, his closest friend as well as his immediate boss, but he had never heard Sir James anticipate his own retirement. He guessed that his imminent departure for assistant chief constable rank in the Tayside force had raised him to another level of confidence.

'So,' Haggerty murmured, pausing in his determined consumption of his soup, 'the balance is swinging back, is it? Is that still a secret?'

Proud Jimmy sat back slightly in his chair. 'It never was, Willie, not from you. I'm sorry, I thought you'd been informed. It was decided before you arrived, but I had to wait for the man at the centre of it to get back from holiday. He did, today, and we told him. Dan Pringle will succeed Andy as head of CID, when he goes in two weeks.'

'Big Dan, eh. He'll be pleased.'

'He's like a dog with two tails, Willie; like a dog with two tails.'

Martin grinned. 'You should have seen him,' he told the ACC. 'Pringle's such a phlegmatic bugger; I don't think I've ever known him to get excited, before this. When he was passed over last time, he thought that was it for him. He thought that Brian Mackie would be appointed, out of all the divisional CID commanders.'

'So did I,' Haggerty confessed. 'Either him or Maggie Rose, at any rate.'

'Bob and Andy thought it was too soon for either of them,' the Chief explained. 'Besides, Pringle's done a fine job over the last few months in sharpening up the Borders Division. We all agreed that he deserved it. Actually, the truth is it's very much an interim appointment; Dan's not that far away from retirement.'

'So who's going to the Borders?'

'Mario McGuire,' the DCS told him. 'He's done his Special Branch stint; he's earned a move as well. So he's off on promotion to a divisional CID command, as a detective superintendent just like his wife, and big McIlhenney's going to the SB job.'

'Which leaves a vacancy as Bob's executive officer,' Haggerty mused.

'Indeed it does,' the Chief agreed. 'That'll be decided after Bob gets back from his conference. Incidentally, he and I have been discussing that subject more generally. After all the fuss we had with Ted Chase, we've decided that you should have the opportunity to appoint your own assistant. Sergeant rank: think about it, eh?'

The new ACC leaned back from the table as the waitress took away his soup bowl and laid a plate of braised beef, carrots and chips in its place. 'Can I have Maisie, here?' he joked. 'She's doing a great job so far.'

Proud Jimmy shook his head. 'The needs of the senior officers' dining room supersede yours, William.'

The Glaswegian laughed; yes, the Edinburgh air was different, but it was fresh and it suited him. He had been astonished by Bob Skinner's phone call, asking if he would be interested in the job, in the wake of the appointment of his predecessor, Ted Chase, to the office of the inspector of constabulary. The bluntness of the question had taken his breath away. He had felt himself to be in a rut, his career path at its end, marked down as too rough a diamond for the command floor, an unlikely choice, as a confirmed thief-catcher, to be given charge of uniformed policing.

'Apply for it, Willie,' Skinner had said. 'The job's yours if you do; Jimmy and I'll make sure of that.'

'But why me, for fuck's sake?' he remembered croaking the question.

'I'm having no more Ted Chases in here, pal. It's as simple as that. Aye, we want new blood, but this time I'm going to make sure I know what type it is. You're my choice; and besides, it'll be a damn good career move for you. The Dumfries and Galloway post will be coming up in a few years; that'd be a nice place to command.'

'Jesus wept, you think long-term, don't you?'

'I've got fuck all else to do in this job; other people catch the thieves and murderers now. When Jimmy said he'd make a politician of me, he didn't know the half of it. I don't like the breed, Willie, based on bitter experience. But they exist, so I'll play their game . . . only I'll make up my own rules.'

So he had applied, and Skinner had kept his promise, despite what Haggerty had regarded, privately, as the worst interview of his career.

He glanced around the headquarters dining room, at the heavy silver braid on the uniforms. *Yes indeed*, he thought. *A different air from Glasgow.*

He had almost finished his beef when Martin's mobile rang. The Chief gave a slightly tetchy frown; he had a firm belief that there should be sanctuaries in which the telephone did not ring.

'Sorry, boss,' the Head of CID apologised, but he answered its call nonetheless.

'Andy?' The word was a sob. The voice on the other end of the line was so contorted that it was almost unrecognisable. At first, he supposed it was Karen; the fear of a miscarriage rushed into his mind. Then he looked at the number shown by the phone's LCD display, and he knew who it was.

'Sarah?' A muffled, gasping sound was her only answer.

'What's wrong?'

'Andy.' It seemed to be all she could say.

'Sarah, what is it? Are you ill? Is it one of the kids?'

'No,' she moaned. 'Andy, can you come out here? I need you. I can't get through to Bob.'

'Sure, I'll come. But what is it?'

He heard her sobbing intensify. 'I can't talk about it over the phone,' she whispered, through her tears.

'Okay, okay. I'm on my way.'

He ended the call. Proud and Haggerty were staring at him; and not only them. He realised that the urgency in his voice had brought all conversation in the dining room to a halt.

'What is it?' asked the Chief.

'I don't know,' he answered. 'She couldn't, or wouldn't, say. I'm off out to Gullane; that's where she was calling from.'

He rose from the table and turned towards the door. Before he reached it, it swung open and Detective Inspector Neil McIlhenney came into the room, shock and concern written across his face. 'Andy,' he said, his voice low, 'I've just taken a call from a guy who said he was the county sheriff, in Buffalo, New York. He was looking for the Boss, but the message was about Sarah . . .'

5

Detective Superintendent Maggie Rose was still on a high; the phone call from Mario had come as a complete surprise. She knew that the Special Branch posting usually carried a reward thereafter, but she had not expected that her husband would have jumped straight from his secretive office to the status of divisional CID commander.

'How long have you known?' she had asked him, with more than a hint of suspicion, once the initial delight had subsided.

'I didn't; not until this morning, when the Chief called me in and told me. Honest, love, it's the truth. Do you think I could have kept something like that from you?'

'After all that time in Special Branch? Too bloody right I do. But I'll take your word for it. So what's happening to Dan Pringle? Early retirement?'

He had hesitated for less than a second, but she had picked it up. 'Far from it. He's the new Head of CID.'

Thinking back, she had felt not even a twinge of disappointment; no, her instant reaction had been one of relief. 'Good for Dan. He's earned it.'

'Aye, sure, but . . .'

'I've told you, Mario. I've gone as far as I want for now. That job's about half a step below executive rank; I don't have the experience for it. Besides, I've out-ranked you for long enough.'

'You think we'll make the papers? Husband and wife team and all that?'

'Are you kidding?'

'TFR, I'm kidding. The Chief said he wants that aspect played down; the press guy's under orders not to mention it.'

But someone would, she mused, as she stared out of the window of her small office, all but deaf to the bustle of the Haymarket traffic. Sooner or later, some wag would decide to run a feature on the Nick and Nora Charles of Edinburgh CID, and for all of Alan Royston's contacts and negotiating skills, it would happen.

She was brought back to the present by a knock on her door. 'Come,' she called, sharply. It opened, with its familiar squeak, and a fresh-faced probationer constable came into the room. He was carrying a brown folder; she noticed that his hand trembled slightly as he held it out to her.

Christ, she thought, *is that how the youngsters think of me?*

'Yes, Constable?' she greeted him, deliberately softening her tone and offering a smile.

'I'm sorry, miss . . . eh, sorry, ma'am, but . . .'

She interrupted him. 'That's at least one "sorry" too many, son. You're new here, yes?'

'First month, ma'am.'

'What's your name?'

'PC Haddock, ma'am.'

Poor lad, she thought. *You're going to have to be good.*

'When they sent you up here, PC Haddock, did the lads tell you that I eat probationers for lunch?'

'More or less, ma'am.'

'They're right.' She paused. '. . . But not in their first few weeks. I prefer them a bit more seasoned. Now; what have you got for me?'

Pink-cheeked, the tall, gawky young man looked down at her. 'Chief Superintendent English called in, ma'am.' She nodded; English was the senior officer in the division, the top uniform. 'He's been detained up at headquarters; the meeting with Mr Haggerty's going on into the afternoon. So he asked if you'd take a look at the night-shift reports.'

Inwardly, Maggie bristled. Manny English was pushing his luck; the night-shift reports were pure bloody trivia puffed up by the panda patrollers to make it look as if they had been rushed off their feet. They could have been checked by a sergeant, but the Chief Super was a procedural paragon. In addition, he liked to keep in touch with everything that happened on his patch. Still, palming off uniformed officers' reports to the CID commander, as the next senior officer, was taking it a bit far.

Outwardly, she smiled again at Haddock, and took the folder from him. 'Of course I will,' she said. 'Anything for Mr English.' He stood there, uncertain of what to do. 'You can go,' she told him. 'I'll send them down to his office when I'm done.'

'Very good, miss . . . eh, sorry, ma'am.' The constable left the room much more quickly than he had entered.

Shaking her head as the door closed on him, Maggie opened the folder. By divisional standards, it looked like a light load. A false alarm at a chemist's shop in Fountainbridge, three assorted brawls, two domestic call-outs which turned out to be no more than loud arguments, and one in which a husband had been arrested and charged with assaulting his wife.

'Rubbish,' she muttered, and was on the point of closing the folder when her eye was caught by the last report; there was a photograph clipped to it. She slipped it out and looked at the Polaroid. It had been taken clumsily, and showed only the top half of a man's body, lying flat on a table. He was dressed in a heavy grey woollen jerkin, with a short zip, opened, at the neck. He looked to be in his fifties; he was bald, with a heavy, grizzled beard. Despite his weather-beaten complexion, from the blueness of his lips and cheeks, the Detective Superintendent could tell at once that he was dead.

She picked up PC Charlie Johnston's report and read carefully through his police-speak prose. The man had been identified by Dr Amritraj, who had certified his death, as Magnus Essary, of 46 Leightonstone Grove, Hunter's Tryst, Edinburgh, single, aged forty-nine. Using keys found on the body, Johnston had gained entry to the house and had searched thoroughly for any references to family, or next of kin; thoroughly, the constable insisted, but without success. There was nothing to be found, and the neighbours, delighted, Rose guessed, to have been wakened by a policeman at that hour of the morning, had all described him as a quiet, polite man who kept to himself. The report ended with the simple statement that its author had been unable to trace anyone who could be contacted and asked to take responsibility for the body.

'This is daft,' the Detective Superintendent muttered as she finished the report. 'This man cannot have been a complete loner. He lived at a fairly posh address; he must have had some sort of business life. Even if he didn't have any friends, there must be colleagues. We can't just let the guy lie in the mortuary.'

She picked up the telephone and called Oxgangs office; she was put through at once to the duty inspector, Laurence Gray, an ex-CID colleague. 'Laurie,' she began, 'I've got a report here on a sudden death on your patch in the middle of the night; man called Essary. It was written up by Constable Johnston.'

'Oh aye, our Charlie,' Gray growled, with a faint chuckle. 'I've been half expecting the Chief Super to call me about that one. Johnston's a book operator . . . the trouble with him is that he hasnae finished reading the bloody book yet.'

Rose relaxed. 'So you're following it up, not just giving up on it.'

'Come on, Maggie. I was in CID long enough not to be doing that.'

She accepted the reproof. 'Sorry. I should have known better.'

'Indeed, ma'am,' the inspector rumbled. 'As it happens, the thing's sorted. Mr Essary was in the wine importing business, in partnership with a woman called Ella Frances. She called Fettes this morning, and they put her in touch with me; I told her to go up to the Royal. She did; they called to let us know she's confirmed the identification and claimed the body. She's had it uplifted from the mortuary already. File closed.'

'That's good. No thanks to Johnston, though. It's just as well for both of you that the Chief Super was tied up.'

'Ach, don't blame Charlie. He didnae make any mistakes; he just focused a bit too hard on his finishing time, that's all. You know what the night shift's like. Short spells of action mixed in with long periods of near-terminal boredom.'

'You're right there. But you wait till you're in my job. There isn't a minute of your life you can call your own completely, with no fear that the phone'll ring.'

'It'll be double for you from now on then, wi' your man's promotion.'

Maggie Rose was rarely surprised. 'How did you know about that so soon?'

'Hah! You think e-mail's fast? It's got nothing on the force grapevine. Be sure to congratulate Mario for me, will you?'

'Of course. Thanks, Laurie.'

She hung up, slipped the report and photograph back into the folder, and leaned back in her chair, musing on the curse that Alexander Graham Bell had visited on mankind.

6

She was calm by the time she heard the big Dodge Caravan crunch its way up the gravel driveway. She opened the heavy front door to greet them; three of them, Andy Martin, Neil McIlhenney, and his wife, Louise, picked up on the way to Gullane.

The two women embraced. 'Neil called to tell me what had happened,' Lou murmured. 'He and Andy thought you might welcome a woman's company, and since Bob's daughter is working on secondment in London . . .' Her voice faltered for a second. 'Oh, I am so sorry,' she exclaimed, hugging her again.

Sarah felt herself begin to go again, but held on to her composure, steeling herself not to fold in front of the two men, however close to her and Bob they might be.

'Thanks, Lou,' she replied. 'Come on through to the conservatory.' She led the way from the entrance hall of the modern bungalow, towards the big glass-walled room, which looked out over the Forth estuary, drab and grey in the dull spring day.

'Can I do something?' asked Louise, making a conscious effort not to sound as if she wished she was somewhere else. 'What about the children?'

Sarah gave her a weak smile. 'They're fine. Mark's at school, James Andrew's dismantling his toys in the play room, and Seonaid's having her afternoon sleep. Tell you what, though; you could pour the coffee. I've made some in the filter.'

'Of course. What does everyone take in theirs?' She glanced at Martin.

'Nothing. Black, please.'

'Right now, I'll take brandy,' said Sarah. 'You'll find the cooking stuff in the cupboard above the coffee pot.'

'That's a done deal.' She turned and walked through to the kitchen; she had visited the Skinners on several occasions and knew her way around.

Left with Sarah, the two detectives looked from one to the other. It was she who broke the awkward silence. 'Sorry I was useless when I called you, Andy. But the phone call came as such a shock; it just floored me. I did the little woman thing, went into complete hysterics, and upset the kids in the process.'

'Okay,' he murmured. 'Now sit down, and tell us exactly what happened.'

She nodded and settled into one of the cane-framed conservatory chairs. 'It happened just after one o'clock. I was clearing up after lunch with the kids when the phone rang . . . It's Trish the nanny's day off,' she added, irrelevantly.

'It was the New York State Police. A gruff-sounding guy asked me if I was Sarah Grace, the daughter of Leopold and Susannah Grace, of Buffalo, New York. The sound of his voice was enough to scare me right there. I said I was and he went right into it.' Her accent seemed to roughen. 'No messing about. "I'm sorry to have to tell you, ma'am, that I'm at the scene of a double homicide, at your folks' lakeside cabin. It appears they've been murdered."

'I didn't say anything for a long time; I remember holding on to the kitchen table, and hearing the guy ask if I was all right. Eventually I said that I was far from all right. I asked him to repeat what he'd just said, and he did. I asked if he was sure of the identification, and he said "Yes, ma'am." He suggested that I should maybe call a doctor. I shouted into the phone, "I am a doctor", and hung up. That was when I folded up. I was just scared witless, Andy. I tried to phone Bob, but I got all confused by the international dialling code. So I called you on your mobile.

'Once I knew you were on your way, that helped. That and James Andrew; he just begged me to stop crying, so I did.'

'What did you tell him?'

'I said I'd had a nasty phone call from a bad man.' She shuddered. 'He frowned at me, with the same expression Bob has when he's angry, and said, "He'll be in trouble when Dad gets home." The look on his little face was almost as scary as the phone call.'

She glanced up at them. 'Could you call them back for me? Could you find out exactly what's happened?'

McIlhenney shook his head. 'We don't have to call them, Sarah. They've already been in touch with us. I guess the guy who called you was a detective. He also reported in to his headquarters and they passed the news to the local police force in Buffalo.'

Sarah nodded. 'That would be the Erie County sheriff's department,' she murmured.

'It was reported to the sheriff himself,' the inspector continued. 'He knew your father well and he knew all about you. So he called the office, looking for the Boss; he wound up speaking to me.'

He paused, as Louise returned with the coffee pot and cups, on a green plastic tray. She caught the moment and laid it on the glass table without a word. 'I'm sorry,' her husband continued. 'But there really is no doubt about the identification. They were found in their cabin, just before seven a.m., local time. They had been strangled, both of them.

'Going by the information that Sheriff Dekker had from the men at the scene, it looks like a robbery. The cabin was ransacked, money, credit cards, watches, jewellery all taken. The investigation's still in its early stages, of course. A technical team from Albany were on their way there when Dekker called.'

'Strangled, you said.' Her voice was a whisper.

'Yes. Expertly, according to the sheriff. He spoke on the phone to the ME while she was still at the scene; she told him that there were no signs of a violent struggle, which indicates that they were both taken by surprise. Your father was killed on the veranda of the cabin, your mother in the kitchen. The doctor said that a ligature was used . . .'

'What type?'

Neil hesitated; he wanted to avoid the detail, but one look at Sarah's face told him that he could not. 'Wire. They were both garrotted, from behind. It must have been over in seconds; your father didn't even make it out of his chair. They don't know how many perpetrators there were, but the police at the scene said that from the disposition of the bodies and the strength required, they're looking, at least, for a tall man.'

Her mouth, normally soft and sensual, seemed no more than an opening carved into her face. 'For a few dollars and a few baubles . . .' she hissed. 'Let's hope they try to fence them. I have a date with these people, whoever they are; I plan to be there when they strap them on to the execution table. However long it takes, however many years the appeal process drags on, when they inject the bastards, I'll be there. If there's a place worse than hell, I'll send them there.' Her voice cracked and she leaned forward in her chair, her face buried in her hands, her shoulders shaking.

Andy Martin dropped to a crouch in front of her, and put his arms around her. 'Okay, love, okay,' he said, softly. 'Let it out, there's a girl.' He waited, until her sobbing began to subside. 'Listen, why don't you take some time on your own. Take a sedative and lie down for a bit. Neil and I will phone Bob; he needs to be told.'

She nodded, and rose from her seat; Louise slipped an arm around her waist and walked her out of the room.

'You got that hotel number?' asked Martin, taking out his cellphone. McIlhenney nodded, took a piece of paper from the breast pocket of his jacket and handed it over. He watched as the Chief Superintendent keyed it in, then waited.

'Hello,' he said at last. 'I want to speak with one of your guests, Mr Skinner. Yes, I'll hold.'

The voice that sounded in Martin's ear a few seconds later was wide awake, if more than a touch irritable. 'Yes?' it barked.

'Bob? It's Andy.'

'What's up?' The testiness vanished, replaced by concern.

'Some very bad news, I'm afraid.' Speaking carefully, almost formally, he told his friend what had happened to his parents-in-law, setting out the detail of McIlhenney's conversation with Sheriff Dekker. When he was finished, there was silence. For one of the few times in his life, Bob Skinner was lost for words.

'How's Sarah?' he asked eventually, sounding strained and older, Martin thought, than he had ever heard him. 'How's she taking it?'

'As you'd expect; she's devastated. I'm at Gullane now, with Neil. Lou's here, looking after her.'

'And the kids?'

'They're okay. Mark's at school, Jazz is being man of the house and the baby's asleep.'

He heard Skinner take a deep breath; when he spoke again it was as if he was at a crime scene himself. 'Right,' he said. 'This is what's going to happen. I'm on the first flight out of here to New York, whether there's a seat on it or not. Tell this man Dekker that I want to be met at JFK, either by the State police or his guys, and transported straight to the cabin. After that I want to be taken to Buffalo, to meet with him and with the officer in charge of the enquiry.

'If it sounds to you like I'm pulling rank here, Andy, well, that's because I am. Just to reinforce that, I want you to call my FBI pal Joe Doherty in Washington and brief him. Joe'll smooth the way if it's necessary; I want to be at that scene within twenty-four hours and I do not want anything to be touched that doesn't have to be. I'll call Dekker once my travel arrangements are made.'

'What will you do about the conference?'

'Fuck the conference! Mary Chambers can read my paper. She's sound and she's not the nervous type; I trust her to do that, no problem.'

'Okay. Do you want to speak to Sarah?'

'Let her rest for a bit. I'll call her in a couple of hours, maybe from the airport, if we can move things along that fast.'

'Right.' Martin paused. 'You know, Bob, I thought Sarah's parents lived in Florida.'

'They did, for a while; at least, they had a condo there, as well as the house in Buffalo. But Susannah didn't like the climate in Florida, so last autumn they sold the place and bought the cabin in the Adirondacks National Park instead. It was going to be a surprise for the kids next time Sarah took them over. Shit; some surprise!'

His anger seemed to flow down the phone. 'I tell you one thing though, Andy; it'll be nothing on the shock this man has coming . . . however fucking tall he is. Oh boy, does he have grief heading his way!'

7

'You know,' said the newly promoted Detective Superintendent Mario McGuire, 'we should do this more often.' He glanced along the length of Umberto's Restaurant, surprisingly busy for a mid-week evening. 'For a dinky couple, we definitely do not put ourselves about enough.'

His wife shot him a puzzled look. 'Dinky?'

'Come on. Dual Income No Kids.'

'Ah,' she exclaimed. 'You mean we've moved up in the world from being Yuppies?'

'Nah. We've just got too old. The acronym game keeps moving along, and personally I'm looking forward to being a Bobo.'

'What the hell's a Bobo?'

'Burnt Out But Opulent. I've always fancied making it to that level.'

She chuckled softly as she sipped her Chablis. 'We're well on the way to the opulent bit now, with two superintendents' pay packets coming into the house, not to mention two superintendents' pensions at the end of the day. We'll be the envy of every copper on the force . . . apart from Big Bob and the Chief, who're both filthy rich anyway.'

'Aye, I suppose we will be. Mind you, I'd still chuck it just to be able to ditch the second part of dinky.'

Maggie frowned at him across the table. 'Well that's not a runner, is it, so don't brood about it.'

'Sure I know, but . . .'

'Makes you feel less of a man, does it?'

'Something like that,' he muttered.

'Well don't let it, for it's nonsense. That's a fine piece of ordnance you've got there, officer; it's not your fault that it shoots blanks. It's not a sin not to have babies, you know. Looked at from a certain angle it's an advantage; we can plan our future in the knowledge that it's only the two of us on the payroll and always will be. Plus, we can concentrate on making life miserable for the bad people. Who knows? Maybe that's what we were put here for.'

The arrival of their starters forestalled his answer. He sat in silence as

27

the waiter set a warm goat's cheese salad before Maggie, and served his pasta and bean soup from a tureen.

'. . . Put here for?' he exclaimed, as the young man headed back to the kitchens. 'This is Planet Earth calling Superintendent Rose. This is Houston calling Maggie. In case you've forgotten, I became a copper because if I didn't there was a fair chance that I'd have ended up on the other side of the fence, or at the very least in regular skirmishes with the VAT man, like the rest of my family.'

'Come on,' she retorted, 'your family's very respectable, specially your mother. If you weren't a police officer you'd probably be in her business.' The light smile left her face, and her eyes flickered down for a moment. 'The fact is I've always envied you your family.'

He caught something in her expression, and in her tone. 'Sure, because they're alive . . . but why do you say it like that? Mags, you've been iffy for a couple of days. Have you got a problem?'

She opened her mouth to reply, then stopped, staring at the table as if she was considering something very important. Finally she looked up and into his eyes. 'I've had a letter from my sister,' she told him. 'She's had a birthday card from my father.'

'Your father?' he exclaimed, astonished. 'You told me your father was dead.'

'Oh how I wish . . .' The words came out in a long, malevolent hiss. 'I thought he was,' she continued. 'No, I hoped he was, I prayed he was, and eventually I let myself believe he was. Now it turns out . . .'

'But why?' he asked her. 'What was so bad about him?'

'You don't want to know.'

'I bloody do, and you're going to tell me.'

She glanced around and over her shoulder, checking for anyone who might be within earshot. 'If you insist,' she said, quietly, her eyes narrowing with her frown.

'You know why I really became a copper, Mario?' She hesitated for a second or two then leaned toward him, her voice dropping even lower, until he had to lean himself to catch it. 'I did it to get even with guys like my old man.

'You ask me what was so bad about him? "Bad" doesn't cover it, not by a long way. That bastard abused my sister and me . . . damn it, no, he raped us. And as if that wasn't enough, he beat my mother bloody when she found out about it.

'I'll tell you something I've never told you or anyone else before, Mario. I felt guilty for years after that; not just because of what happened between my old man and me, but because it was me who got her that tanking. When I told her what he was doing to us, do you know what happened? The first thing she did was to beat the daylights out of me!' She glanced again at the nearest occupied table, but the couple there were too far away to overhear.

'That's right. When I told her she knocked me right off my feet. So I got up and showed her the bruises he always left on me. She hit me even harder, she actually knocked me out. So I showed her the same marks on my wee sister. When my father came in from the pub, or the bookie's, or wherever he had been, she confronted him, and it was her turn for a thumping. I hate to think what would have happened to Eilidh and me if we'd stayed in that house, but I hauled her out of there and screamed bloody murder at the door of the woman downstairs.

'She took us in, and her husband, a great big man who'd been a boxer or something, went up and stopped my father. Yet no one called the police. It never occurred to them to do that. It just wasn't part of their culture. What went on between husband and wife was their business, until the kids got hurt; then, the community usually took care of it. That's what happened in our case.

'My dad left, for good, that very night. We were actually better off, for my mother had always been the breadwinner; he never had a regular job that I knew of, although he was always out and about. As far as I could see he just leeched off her. After he went, we never spoke about what had happened, not even when Eilidh and I were grown up. It was always there, though, hanging like a curtain between my mother and me, something unspoken that we knew nonetheless.

'It stayed that way, until she was dying. She developed breast cancer; she had a big lump but she kept quiet about it until it was way too late. The afternoon before she died, I went in to see her. I was a probationer then; she didn't approve of my joining the police, and she didn't hide that from me.

'She couldn't speak above a whisper at that stage, but she beckoned me close to her, and she said to me, "I never could forgive you, Margaret." And I said, "For what, Mum?" And she said, "For telling me. I loved your father." And that was the last thing my mother ever said to me.

'Oh, how I hated him then; far more than ever before. The fact is, I don't think I really did hate him until that moment; not even when he was doing all those things, because he was my father and I didn't know any different and I didn't understand, until someone at school said something and it all rushed in on me.

29

'What it all comes down to is this. What I said back there was only partly true. I joined the police because of my father, but not just because of him. I joined because I wanted to change the culture I grew up in, the notion that even in the direst circumstances, the police are somehow the enemy of the working class. I wanted to be an accessible copper, to be the sort that people would rush up to in the street.'

She frowned, a deep dark frown, which pained him for her. 'Yet somewhere along the line I lost that; I became a control freak, an authoritarian, the sort of copper kids run away from in the street. And now, my junior colleagues see me as some sort of dragon, and maybe, that's what I am.'

He waited, until he was sure that she had finished, that she had drained whatever well had overflowed inside her and brought her to spill out the deepest, darkest truths that she had withheld even from him, until that moment.

'Why haven't you told me all this before?' he asked her quietly, when it was time.

'I suppose I've been afraid you'd look at me in a different light. Now you know why I'm ambivalent about the kids thing. The truth is, there are times when I'm positively glad we can't have any.'

'Why? Because you'd be afraid to trust me with our daughters?'

He put the question gently, yet still her hand flew to her mouth in horror. 'No! Not for a second! No, it's because of me. I never had a proper, natural relationship with my mother; I'm plain scared that I wouldn't know how to begin to build one myself.'

He shook his dark head. 'Of course you would. I'll tell you something else; you're no bloody dragon either. You're a good, a better than good copper.'

'You might not say that if you'd seen a thing that happened this morning.'

'What was that?'

'Something very simple, but I can't get it out of my head. A young probationer came into my office, and he was shaking. The boy was scared, Mario, of me, and that's not right.'

'Course it is,' he laughed, making light of it. 'The traditional function of the probationer is to crap themselves when going into the super's office.' She did not return his smile.

'Look, Mags,' he told her. 'You have to believe this. You are an exceptional, dedicated police officer; Bob Skinner picked you out as that, and shot you up the ladder because of it, and that's all the

30

commendation you need. If you joined the force to be cuddly and nice, you were fooling yourself, for we can't be like that, especially not in CID. You are what you should be, and you are where you should be. Whether it's in spite of your background or because of it doesn't matter any more than a single bean in my rapidly cooling soup.'

He grinned at her as he picked up his spoon, and this time, she smiled back, weakly.

'This birthday card your sister received; did she say where it was posted?'

'London.'

'And it arrived out of the blue?'

'Yes.'

'Did he put an address on it?'

'No. What concerns me is how he found out where she is.'

'The Internet, maybe,' Mario suggested. 'She has a website, doesn't she, with her design business, and she has an unusual name. That would do it.'

'Maybe. Anyway, she's scared and she wrote to me to warn me.'

'And are you worried?'

She snorted. 'Me? Just let him come near me.' She stopped. 'Now, please; I've told you; can we talk about something else, at least till we get home.'

Mario nodded. 'Sure What did that lad want this morning anyway?'

'Nothing. He brought me Manny English's night-shift reports, that was all.'

'What the hell for?'

'You know Manny. He was away, and he's so bloody rank-conscious that only the next senior officer would do to check them over.'

'A load of crap, were they?'

'Yup. There was a funny one where someone had died in a doctor's surgery, but that was all.'

'Death happens, wherever. There more than in most places, I guess.'

'Yes, but not . . . Ach, let's forget it. Enough shop. Have you had many "well done" calls since the press notice went out?'

Mario nodded. 'A few . . . and one that took my breath away. My Uncle Beppe phoned me. He and my mother want to have a family party to celebrate.'

'Jesus. Your godfather called you? What did you say?'

'What could I say? I said okay. I had to; my mum and my nana might have been upset otherwise.'

31

'Am I invited?'

'Course you are.'

'Will I have to learn Italian songs and dances and such?'

'Hardly,' he laughed. 'However he acts, my Uncle Beppe was born in Newhaven, not Napoli.'

8

This time, Sarah was awake when the phone rang. 'How're you doing?' he asked.

'Better,' she answered, not because she was, but because it was what he wanted to hear. In reality she felt cold and shivery, slightly out of touch with the planet. The initial shock had worn off, to be replaced by a stunned disbelief that what had happened actually involved her, and a feeling that instead she was a spectator looking in on someone else's nightmare.

'That's good,' said Bob, knowing that she was putting on a front, but going along with it. 'You were zonked when I called earlier. Lou said you'd taken a couple of pills.'

'Yes, on top of a couple of brandies; not such a good idea.'

'It was if it did the job.' He hesitated, and background noise flooded into her ear. 'My love, I'm so sorry,' he blurted out. 'I wish I was there with you. Maybe that's where I should be. I'm at KL airport, but I haven't picked up my tickets for the States yet. If you want, I'll cancel them and come home instead. I sort of went off at half-cock earlier, when Andy called and told me what had happened.'

'No,' she said, quickly, almost sharply. 'You go to New York. I might want you here, but I need you there. I'll come over as soon as I can, once I've had a chance to make arrangements for the kids. Meantime, please, you take care of everything that needs doing . . . and make damn sure that the police throw everything into the investigation.'

A quiet chuckle sounded down the line. 'Hey, this isn't just someone else's force, it's someone else's country. I'll need to tread softly there.'

'You don't know how to do that,' she exclaimed. 'I mean it, Bob; keep them on their toes.'

'I'll do what I can,' he promised. 'Do you know this man Dekker?'

'The county sheriff? No, I don't; I've heard my dad mention his name, though. He's been around for a while; he's an elected official and he's part of the civic furniture in Buffalo.'

'Is he a talker or a doer?'

'You'll have to make up your own mind on that one.'

'I will, don't worry. I'll see him soon enough.'

'What time is it with you?'

'Around three a.m. It'll be the middle of yesterday afternoon in New York right now, so I should get there early this morning . . . I reckon.'

'What time does your body think it is?'

She heard him chuckle again. 'My body doesn't have a bloody clue, love. I just have this strange feeling that when I get to the States I'll be a day younger.'

'Lucky you!' she muttered, instinctively, unable to keep the bitterness at bay. 'I feel about ten years older.'

'Hey, I'm sorry. Look, it's still not too late. Shouldn't I come home first?'

'How many times do I have to say it?' Her voice rose; he had never heard her sound so strained, not even at the worst of times in their marriage. He knew how tough she was, but he understood that this had to be the worst day of her life.

'Okay, okay. I'll go straight there. I'll call you again from Buffalo.'

'Is that where you're going first?'

'No. I've asked to be taken straight to the crime scene. They'll fly me from place to place. My US geography's crap, but as I understand it the Adirondacks are a couple of hundred miles east of the city.'

'Then call me from the cabin.' She sounded calmer, and he sensed her need to be involved.

'If that's what you want.'

'It is. Where are you planning to stay in Buffalo?'

He paused. 'I haven't given that any thought. I suppose I'll check into a hotel.'

'No. I want you to stay in my folks' house. Get it ready for me. I'll be over as soon as I can. I'll arrange for Trish to live in, and ask Lou, or Karen Martin, to look in every so often, just to see that the kids aren't giving her too much trouble. I can't just sit on my ass here; it'd drive me crazy.'

'Are you alone now?'

'No. Lou's here; the men have gone, but she's going to stay over tonight. With her having lost her dad last month, we're sort of good for each other.'

'Sure. Just watch the brandy, the pair of you. Alcohol's a depressant.'

'But like you said, it also helps you sleep. Don't you worry about your Remy Martin, though; we're not going to touch that.'

'That's good.'

'No. We plan an evening on the Martinis, American style.'

'What, as in wave the vermouth lightly over the gin?'

'No, that's too much. I'm going to make them my dad's way. He believed that the gin and the vermouth could be allowed in the same room, but only for a few moments, that's all.'

9

They lay in the dark, silent but awake. They had finished their celebration meal in a sombre mood, had come home and gone straight to bed. They had made love, intensely, passionately, as if each had something to prove to the other, only neither was sure what it was.

Maggie rubbed the flat of her hand over the ridged muscles of her husband's abdomen. 'Not bad,' she whispered, 'not bad.'

'Hard enough for you?'

She slid her hand down and held him. 'Not any more.'

'Give it time.'

She eased closer to him, her head in the crook of his arm. 'Isn't it good,' she said, suddenly. 'You don't have to call me ma'am any more.'

'I wonder how long that'll last.'

'For good, I think. I reckon my only way up the ladder is to go for Manny English's job in a few years, when he chucks it . . . but I won't do that. I'm tied to CID; it's what I do best.'

'Don't be so inflexible,' he cautioned. 'You put down English, but we're all in the same job.'

'What? Would you leave CID?'

'I will if I have to. I don't feel tied to it at all. For example, I fancy commanding the city centre unit some day.'

'From what I hear, you'll have to shoot Brian Mackie if you do. He's next in line for that job, so they say.'

'Yeah, I know,' he conceded. 'But still, we're living in times of change, with Andy going to Tayside and Haggerty in from Glasgow.'

'Yes, that was a surprise.'

'Which?'

'Haggerty's appointment. Not Andy; I know exactly why he's gone to Tayside, and I know who put him there.'

'Who? The Chief?'

'No. Big Bob.'

'Why? So he can bring him back, eventually, as his deputy?'

She laughed softly, almost in his ear. 'You surely have been locked away in Special Branch for long enough; you're out of touch with the politics. No, the whisper is there's another plan being drawn up.'

'Such as?'

'We'll all know that when it happens. But don't underrate Andy Martin; he's his own man. He was never going to live all his life in Bob Skinner's shadow . . . any more than you were in mine.'

'I'm happy to be in your shadow, my love. The prince consort, that's how I've always seen myself; three paces behind, hands clasped behind back.'

'Bullshit.'

He gave a mock sigh. 'Aye, okay. Bullshit.'

The silence returned, but neither felt remotely like sleep. 'Your Uncle Beppe,' Maggie began, taking a guess at his thoughts. 'Why don't you get on with him?'

'Because he's a tit.'

'There's more to it than that.'

'Well, okay,' he conceded. 'It's not that I don't get on with him; it's more the other way round. When I was a kid, my Papa Viareggio, my grandfather, and I were very close. I worshipped that old man, and he trusted me with his confidence, in a way he never did with my cousins Paula and Viola; they were that bit younger . . . and also, they were girls. Beppe didn't like that; he had always disapproved of my mother marrying a non-Italian . . . Catholic or not . . . even though my papa and my nana were both fine about it.

'When I was a wee boy, he called me a fucking half-breed once, in front of my papa. The old fellow carried this stick . . . he didn't need it, it was just for effect . . . and he cracked Beppe right across the shoulders with it, whipped him as if he was a kid.

'That didn't help things, but the real problem was that Beppe was afraid of me. He was scared that Papa would leave me control of the family business, the cafés, the delicatessen chain, the properties, the lot. He might have too, only he died, and in the will that he left Beppe was to be in control of the trust which is the legal owner of all the family businesses.'

'Yes,' said Maggie. 'I knew that. You told me, but why have things still been cool between you, since Beppe is in charge?'

She felt his shoulder twitch in a slight shrug. 'I suppose it's to do with a clause in the will. I try not to think about it, because I don't like it any more than Beppe does.'

'What clause? You never told me about that.'

'Like I said, I don't like it myself. You see, Beppe inherited control of the business all right, but it's not as simple as that. There are two trustees; him and my mother, but he has the casting vote. But when my mother dies, becomes incapacitated, or just plain decides to retire, the old man's will says that I take her place. When Beppe dies, Paula, the older of my cousins, succeeds him, but control passes to my mother, and through her to me.'

She sat bolt upright. 'What!'

'Like I said, it's the evil day I try not to think about. I love the force, Mags; no way would I want to have to leave it.'

'Well, when the time comes, can't you just decline, abdicate, or what have you?'

The silence returned. 'Well?' she insisted.

'It's not as easy as that,' he murmured. 'This is what my papa wanted; it's a family thing. It's an obligation, and it's in my blood . . . the Italian cells in it, at any rate.'

'Oh, come on.'

'I'm serious. Beppe might have let it run down a bit, but . . . okay I go on about him, but it can't be that bad or my mum would have done something about it years ago . . . it's still the business my papa built up, and if I walked away from it, I'd be snubbing him. Plus, I don't know if I could just hand it over to Paula.'

'Why not? Is she that thick?'

'Oh, Paula's not thick. She's anything but.'

'Does she work in the business? I've never been sure.'

'Oh yes, she's involved. She runs the deli down in Stockbridge. But she has other interests.'

'Such as?'

'Saunas.'

'You mean brothels?'

Mario grunted. 'You might say that, but I couldn't possibly comment. She owns three licensed saunas in central Edinburgh that belonged originally to Tony Manson; she bought them when his estate put them on the market. You know the way those places run.'

'She bought them with what? Family money?'

'No. Neither my mum nor I would have stood still for it if she'd done that.'

'How could you have stopped it?'

'We'd have raised hell with Beppe, and if that wasn't enough, we'd have got my nana to veto it. My uncle would never disobey her. No,

38

Paula used her own dough to buy those businesses . . . but I don't know where she got it.'

'Are you saying that your cousin's dodgy?'

'I'm saying that when I was in Special Branch, I went so far as to keep a private file on her. There's nothing in it to prove that she's bent, but I've been a copper long enough to worry about her. I like Paula, you see; she's got a wildness about her, same as I used to have, till I met you. What she's doing just now is within the law as it stands. I keep tabs on her so that if she ever looks like stepping across the line, I'll be there to haul her back.'

She settled back down beside him. 'Have you spoken to your mother about this?'

'I don't need to. She's got her eye on the ball, and on Paula as well.'

'Hmm,' she murmured. 'So why this family party, I wonder?'

'Dunno. Maybe it's my nana's idea. Could be; her word's still law. For all she's eighty-seven, Uncle Beppe still jumps when she barks. Anyway, we'll find out on Wednesday. That's when it is.'

'Have I got to go?'

'Like I said, you're specifically invited, my dear.'

'Yes. But have I got to go?'

She could sense his smile in the dark. 'I'd like you to. With that lot, I might need a witness.'

10

Bob Skinner's mobile phone stored ninety-nine numbers; he flicked through the index until he found number sixty-six, then pushed the rapid-dial button.

The call was answered, on the third ring, by a woman. In that instant, the policeman was taken by surprise; his friend was single . . . or had been the last time they had spoken. 'Is that the Doherty residence?' he asked.

'Sure. This is Philippa; Dad's watching the ball game.' Of course; he had forgotten that Joe had a daughter, the same age as Alexis, his own first-born.

'I'm taking my life in my hands, in that case. Could you tell him that his friend from Scotland is calling.'

'Just one minute, please. Dad!'

In fact it took less than thirty seconds for Joe Doherty to come on line. 'Hey, Bob. What gives? Your man Martin called me this morning; told me what had happened. This fucking country I live in . . .' He broke off. 'Where the hell are you, anyway?'

'I'm still in Malaysia. There's been a delay on my flight, but I should be on the move soon. Sorry to come between you and the Lakers, or the Bulls or whoever . . .'

'The Wizards, buddy,' said Doherty. 'Always the Wizards, for my sins.'

'Basketball's a closed book to me, mate; those two names, plus Michael Jordan, are the only ones I know.'

'What about Magic Johnson?'

'Played for Glasgow Rangers, as far as I know . . . at least he did every now and again.' He drew a line across the sporting exchange. 'How's the new job going?' he asked.

'Great, so far. Truth is I'm glad to be back where I belong.'

Skinner had known Joe Doherty since the American's spell as the resident FBI man in the US Embassy in London. The election to the White House of an old college chum had led to his being plucked from

Grosvenor Square to an exalted post with the National Security Council. The change of tenancy in Washington had brought that to an end, but the new incumbent had been sufficiently impressed to send Doherty back to the Bureau as second-in-command and, as most insiders saw it, director-in-waiting.

'Andy told you the story about Sarah's folks, then.'

'Yeah. I'm really sorry, man. Of course I've done what he asked, and a little more. Two of my people, rather than the police, will meet you at JFK, and arrange your onward transport. We'll fly you upstate in one of our aircraft.'

'Hey, Joe, I didn't mean for you to get the Bureau involved in ferrying me about.'

'Don't worry about that for one second. We know who our friends are, especially since last September, and I'm sending a clear signal to the cops on the ground that you are one of them. Now, what else can I do for you? I know you didn't just call to improve your working knowledge of the NBA.'

Skinner laughed lightly. 'All knowledge is power, mate; I thought that was your lot's motto. But you're right; I was wondering if you'd get someone to look into that legendary computer of yours and see if you can come up with a list of unsolved homicides where robbery was the motive . . .'

'Jesus, Bob, it'll take a lot of paper to print that out!' Doherty interrupted.

'Humour me on this, eh?'

It was as if he could hear Doherty's brain click into gear. 'Okay. You want anything else while we're in there?'

'Yes. Can you also print me out a list of murders, also unsolved, where a wire ligature was used?'

'I guess we can manage that too. But I hope you got a good-sized document case with you.'

'A Zero Halliburton attaché, my son. The strongest there is.'

'We'll fill it for you; you can bet on that.' Doherty paused. Skinner heard a click and guessed that he was lighting a cigarette.

'Haven't you chucked smoking yet?' he asked.

'Say that in a soprano voice and you'd sound just like Philippa. Have you any idea how many people around the world rely on guys like me to keep them in a job?'

'Sure. I've met several; all of them were either oncologists or cardiologists.'

'I prefer to think about the little guys in the tobacco plantations and on the production lines. But whatever way you look at it, I'm performing a public service. Anyhow, what are you going to do with all this stuff I'm going to get for you?'

'Me? Nothing. I just want to help the investigating officers all I can, that's all.'

'Sure. By shoving firecrackers up their asses . . . I know you.'

The Scot chuckled again. 'If they're not doing it already I'm sure they'd get round to it eventually. I just thought we could help the process along, that's all. Kid gloves, Joe; I'll wear kid gloves, I promise you.' He paused; for a second or two, Doherty thought they had lost the line. 'He never did say it in the movie, you know,' he resumed, at last.

'Uh?'

'He never did say it.'

'What?'

'Play it again, Sam.'

Skinner could almost hear the American's bewilderment as he ended the call and headed for the boarding gate.

11

Still, sleep failed them. They made love again, but again, the usual drowsiness did not follow. There was something there still, something unsaid, a question begging to be asked. And so, eventually, Mario did.

'When was the last time you saw him?'

'I told you. When I grabbed Eilidh's hand and hauled her out of that kitchen. The last time I saw my father was twenty-three years ago, and he was battering blood and snot out of my mother.'

'Never since then?'

'Never.'

'Have you ever felt the need to find him?'

'Never. Why in God's name would I want to do that? The man was a beast.'

'How does Eilidh feel?'

'I don't know, because I've never talked to her about what happened. She was very young; to this very day, she might not have realised what happened to her.'

'What if he does turn up, out of the blue?'

'Then you deal with him. Okay? I really mean it; if I confronted him I don't know what would happen.'

'Okay.'

She jumped out of bed and went into the en-suite bathroom. Returning, she slid in beside him once more, face down, propped on her elbows, looking at him in the dim crystal light of their beside alarm. 'There's guilt there, Mario; so much of it. I feel guilt over what happened to my mother. If I'd kept quiet it would have saved her all that pain. On the other hand, I feel guilt about not waking up sooner to what was happening, to the fact that there was something terribly wrong about our "wee secret", my dad's and mine. If I had, maybe I could have prevented it from happening to Eilidh.

'And even now, when you ask me whether I want to trace him, I feel guilt because I don't. What if he found another woman? What if he had more daughters? What if he still has? By doing nothing, I'm shutting my

43

eyes to that possibility. The truth behind it all is that I don't think I've got the guts to face him.

'I just hoped he was dead, Mario. And now I find out that he isn't.'

'What's his first name?' he asked, quietly.

'Jorge,' she answered, pronouncing the name in the Iberian fashion. 'Jorge Xavier Rose: my grandmother was Portuguese, and he lived in Lisbon for the first few years of his life. His father decided to see out the war there. That's where the Christian names came from.' She guessed the reason for his question. 'Listen, if you're planning to do anything about this, I don't want to know,' she whispered.

'Okay.'

She leaned across and kissed him. 'Now can we get some sleep?'

'Unlikely, I'd have thought,' he murmured, cupping her right breast in his big hand. 'Not without tiring ourselves out a bit more.'

They did, until finally, the drowsiness overtook them.

12

DC Alice Cowan was in the office when McIlhenney stepped into the small Special Branch suite. 'Morning, sir,' she said, with just a shade of caution in her voice.

'And a good morning to you, Constable,' he greeted her. 'If you haven't heard, I'm the new broom.'

'Yes, I had heard, sir. Mr McGuire told me yesterday afternoon.'

'Told you, but has he asked you yet?'

'What do you mean?' she asked, still in a cagey tone.

'You know damn fine. Has he asked you whether you'll go to the Borders with him? I know he rates you.'

Her cheeks turned a delicate pink. 'Yes. He's asked me.'

'So?'

'So I told him that I'd like to stay here. That's if you want me,' she added. 'I know that Special Branch commanders sometimes like to bring in their own people.'

'Their cronies, you mean? Their yes-men, like the guy you replaced, Tommy Gavigan? Relax, Alice; that's not my style. If my friend McGuire rates you, that's all the more reason for me to want to keep you.'

He nodded towards the door of the inner office, which would soon be his. 'Is he in yet?'

She shook her head. 'No. He's a bit late; it's not like him.'

'Ah, he and Maggie'll have been out on the razzle last night.'

Bang on cue, the door swung open, and a slightly bleary-eyed Mario McGuire strode into the room. 'Sorry, Alice. Sorry, Neil,' he boomed. 'Traffic.'

'Traffic, my bottom,' McIlhenney grunted. His marriage to Louise had resulted in a moderation of his language that had surprised his friends, male and female alike. 'If you can't make it to Fettes on time, how are you going to manage the commute down to the Borders?'

'Mags and I were talking about that over breakfast,' he said. 'We might move further out; maybe to somewhere near the city bypass.'

'As long as you don't actually have to go on the thing!' In common with most Edinburgh car-owners, the big inspector regarded the constantly overcrowded ring road round the capital as a bad joke.

'How much time have you got?' McGuire asked him.

'The rest of the day, more or less. I've gone through the Boss's mail and there was nothing spectacular. Plus, he's up in the sky somewhere over the north Pacific, so I won't be getting any surprise phone calls.'

'Any progress on that, by the way? Have the Americans caught the guy who did it?'

'Not that I've heard. They'd better get their acts together, though. They'll be under scrutiny in a few hours.'

'I just hope they're taking it as seriously as he thinks they should.'

'I'm sure they are; Sarah's old man was quite a local heavyweight. Anyhow, apart from that, I'm clear. If anything unexpected crops up, Ruthie knows where I am.'

'Fine. This isn't going to be a short hand-over. The mysteries of Special Branch are many and complex; I've got to teach you all the secret handshakes and code words, and of course the safe combinations . . . which you'll have to change once I'm gone, so I don't know them any more.'

He led the way through to the inner office. 'So what's it really like, this Special Branch?' McIlhenney asked.

His friend looked him in the eye. 'The truth, as between buddies?'

'Of course.'

'It's a fucking anachronism, most of it; a hold-over from the Cold War days. In some ways it's a wonder we're still here, because you would not believe how amateur this place used to be back in the fifties and sixties. Tommy Gavigan told me a story about a guy back then, name of McGinley, the bloke he followed into the job, who actually used to go around local newspaper offices offering to pay journalists for private reports on Communist Party meetings . . . who was there, who said what and so on.

'Some of the stuff he got's still on file, and it's rubbish; it's obvious to a blind man that the journos just took the piss out of him, and took the money as well. Mind you, a couple of the informants are interesting. Back then they were juniors on local papers, but now they're senior guys, one in newspapers, the other in telly.'

McIlhenney smiled. 'Do they know you know?'

'Too fucking right they do. When I found the file, I went to see them both and gave them back the reports they had sold McGinley. They were both deeply embarrassed, I can tell you. And of course, since they can't be a hundred per cent sure I didn't keep copies . . . although I told them I didn't, and that's the truth . . . I now have two bloody good contacts as a result. So that money turned out to be a long-term investment.

'I'll give you their names and contact numbers; you might like to pay them a call when you've settled in.'

'I will do. Okay, where do we start?'

'I'll brief you on the Special Branch network around the country; you'll know some of the names through your job with the Boss, but I'll give you the inside on them. But first, I've got a bit of private enterprise to do while I'm still here. You never heard any of this, okay?'

McIlhenney nodded. 'As long as it's not treason, fine.'

McGuire unlocked a door in a pillar of his desk, and took out a drum-like object, which his colleague recognised as an old-fashioned Rolodex. 'This thing is the Bible,' he said. 'All sorts of surprising people are in this box. It's been part of this office for donkey's years and soon, my boy, it will be yours.' He spun it until he found a card, and dialled the number printed on it.

'DSS,' he whispered, as he waited.

'Ron?' he said at last. 'Mario McGuire. I need a favour. Usual thing; I'll give you a name; I need to know if he's still alive and if so, where he is. How soon? End of the week will be fine.

'Okay? The guy's called Jorge Xavier . . .' He spelled out both forenames '. . . Rose. UK national, Portuguese mother. Last known address, Wellington Street, Leith, in the mid to late 1970s. He'll be early sixties now; too young to be drawing a state pension.

'Good. Thanks.' He paused. 'Oh you saw that, did you? Yes, I'm off soon. DI Neil McIlhenney's going to be my successor. What's he like?' He glanced across the desk and winked. 'Imagine, if you can, a grizzly bear with haemorrhoids.'

The big inspector gazed at him as he hung up. 'Okay, I never heard any of that. But if it's who I think it is, why do I doubt that, if you find him, you're going to invite him to your place for Christmas?'

McGuire shot him a mournful look, and shook his head slowly. 'What I'm going to do, mate, is make sure that he never turns up at our place . . . at any time of year.'

13

Although it hurt her to be thought of as forbidding, nevertheless only one person ever came through her office door without knocking, and then only under special circumstances. So, when it swung open, she looked up, automatically expecting to see Bob Skinner on the warpath.

Just as she remembered that he was en route for America, a man in a grey double-breasted suit swept into the room. He was squat, and ruddy-faced, with greying crinkly hair, which swept back in a 'v' from his high forehead. She frowned at him, and the short fuse to an explosion started burning inside her, until she saw his smile and realised that there was something familiar about him.

'Hello there, Superintendent,' he boomed, in an unmistakable Glaswegian accent. 'Aye, you've come up in the world since the last time I saw you. Mind? A few years back when we were chasing thon bloke that was chopping people up all over Edinburgh.'

Of course, she remembered. They had never been introduced, but she had seen him with Skinner, after they had cornered their suspect in his suburban villa. Willie Haggerty, the rough-edged detective from Strathclyde; the new ACC whose appointment had surprised everyone when Andy Martin had announced it at his weekly meeting of divisional CID heads, the same gathering at which he had confirmed the open secret of his own impending departure for Tayside.

'Good morning, sir,' she said, formally, rising from her chair.

'Sorry if I disturbed you,' Haggerty continued, beaming. 'They said you were on your own, and I like to make an entrance. Stupid of me, really; just to march into a female officer's room like that. Christ, you could have been adjusting your dress or anything.'

Although she was careful to keep her face straight, she smiled inwardly. There was something unreconstructed about the man, an innate charm that overrode the most outrageous comments and behaviour. More than anyone, he reminded her of her husband. 'Or touching up my make-up?' she suggested. 'That sort of girlie stuff?'

She could have sworn that his face turned a slightly deeper shade of red. 'That's me sorted, eh,' he chuckled. 'Oh, by the way, don't be "sirring" me, when there's no troops around. The name's Willie.'

'And mine's Maggie, in the same circumstances.' She allowed her smile to break loose, as she settled back into her chair. 'So, Willie, why the surprise visit?'

'Just getting to know everyone,' he answered, taking the seat opposite her. 'The senior officers' dining room's all very well, but by and large it's only the headquarters brass that goes there. And that's no' where a police force is really run.'

Rose understood at once why Bob Skinner had such a liking for the man. 'Your predecessor held a similar view,' she commented.

'So how come he pissed everyone off so fast?'

'Who says he did? Mr Chase was promoted.'

'Promoted my . . .' Haggerty snorted. 'It's all right, Maggie; when he was moved into the inspectorate after only a few months, every copper in Scotland got the message. So, between us, what was his problem?'

She hesitated. 'I'm not privy to what goes on in the command corridor,' she began, cautiously, considering her words. 'But I do know there was resentment in the divisions over the way he went about things. He didn't just drop in for a chat in civvies, he turned up in full uniform and staged snap inspections. Okay, an ACC Operations has the right to do that, but when he started using Inspector Good, his exec, in his place, that annoyed quite a few people.'

'Ahh,' Haggerty murmured. 'That explains it.' He glanced at Rose. 'I've been told I can have an exec,' he said, 'but the Chief was very careful to specify sergeant rank. Tell me . . . you've done that job for Bob, I know . . . d'you think I should appoint someone?'

'Depends how you work,' she answered. 'If you have a personal assistant, you have to keep him, or her, occupied. Ted Chase appointed Jack Good as a sort of status symbol, because Mr Skinner has Neil, but very soon he had to invent things for him to do, and that's where a lot of the trouble started.'

'Mmm. That's what I was thinking. Maybe I should hold fire for a while.'

'Maybe you should.' She looked him in the eye. 'So, Willie, is that the real reason why you dropped in on me? Just to ask me that? I mean, you could have spoken to Neil, right there in your office. He'd have given you the same answer. Nah, there's more to it than that.'

He gave her an innocent look. 'Like I said to you when I came in; I'm just getting to know the divisional offices and the people in them.'

'Sure you are. But why me? I'm CID. You're ACC Operations; you're not in my chain of command. I report to the Head of CID and through him to the DCC.'

'Maybe I just heard so much about the great Maggie Rose I wanted to meet you for myself.'

'Flattery and bullshit smell exactly the same. I don't fall for either.'

Haggerty laughed out loud. 'Big Bob wisnae kidding about you, right enough. You don't mess about. I did want to meet you though, that much was true. I wanted to size you up, get to know you, like.'

'Why?'

'Because I'm on the lookout for a potential divisional commander. No names, no blame and all that, but there's one that's past his sell-by date, and I've decided that I'm going to paint him a rosy picture of life after the polis. You interested in filling his slot?'

Maggie shook her head. 'I want the Head of CID job when Dan Pringle retires.'

'Even if it means kicking your husband into touch? You and he are on the same rung. In CID, there's only one move up. Are you saying to me you'd tramp on his fingers if you had to?'

Her eyes dropped from his and she shook her head. 'No, of course not.'

'It might come to that, though, if you set your heart on that job. Anyhow, that's only a chief super post too, and it's a while off. And also, what's so great about it? Do you no' fancy my job?'

'ACC?'

'Why not? These are volatile days, Maggie; unpredictable too. It might come up sooner than Pringle's.'

She looked back up at him. 'The truth is, I've never seen myself as a contender for chief officer rank. I've come through CID fast, but that's because I'm good at it. I'm under no illusions that I'm cut out for anything else.'

'Well, hen, other people seem to be. But the thing is, if you decide yourself you want to get there, it would be in your best interests to broaden your experience.'

'You've been sent to tell me this, haven't you.' It was a statement, not a question.

He shot her such a look of mock offence that for a second or two she took him seriously. 'Nobody sends Willie Haggerty,' he exclaimed.

'Oh sorry. Let me put it another way; someone's suggested it to you.'

The grin was back in an instant. 'Well. Now you mention it, Bob

Skinner might have said something along those lines. Oh aye, and the Chief might have agreed with him an' all.' He looked at her, wholly serious for the first time. 'I'm not saying that this is going to happen tomorrow, but it pays to be ready. All kidding aside, I've been doing my homework since I got here, as well as listening to what Bob and Sir James tell me. You got me in one, this wee chat's a sort of informal interview, and it's confirmed what they say.'

She looked at him with raised eyebrows. 'You're easy to please.'

'I make up my mind about people on the spot. It's the old CID thing; evidence is nice, but trust your instincts. In this case I've got both. So please, Maggie; think about it. And if it's just a matter of worrying about no' looking nice in the uniform shirt . . .'

Her laugh interrupted him. 'Another girlie thing?'

Once more, he flushed slightly. 'See me? See political correctness? We're strangers to each other. Let me put it another way, if you're one of the many detectives who've got out of the way of wearing the blue serge, you're like me. I keep it to the minimum and I let others do the same.'

'Another reason why you and Mr Skinner get on,' Rose remarked. She took a deep breath. 'Okay, I'm duly flattered; and I will think about it, if for no other reason than that it'll get me out of the same loop as Mario.'

'Pleased to hear it,' the ACC said. 'You've made my day.' It was his turn to pause. 'In that case, to help you make an informed decision, I want you to sit in for Manny for a week or so. There's a situation in Strathclyde that's needing investigation by senior officers from outside forces. I've been asked to provide one and I've nominated him.

'I briefed him on it yesterday; that was why he was late back. He's off through there as of now, and I want you to take temporary charge of the division. Before you ask, I've cleared it with Andy Martin and Dan Pringle. I'm not asking you to do the job actively in the way Manny does; delegate as much as you can, just take the command decisions, and keep me in touch as necessary. You game for that?'

She scratched her chin. 'Well,' she answered, thoughtfully, 'we seem to be winning the battle against crime for the moment, so . . . I'm game.'

14

'You've been on the command corridor long enough to know what I'm talking about,' said McGuire.

'Sure,' McIlhenney agreed. 'Special Branch still keeps an eye on the bogeymen; it's just that the accents have changed.'

'Come on, man, that's too simplistic, even for you. The end of the Cold War changed what we do, sure, but less so than people think. The Irish problem didn't go away . . . still hasn't . . . there are other international terrorist threats, as the folk in Lockerbie know too well, and there are the general nuisances we watch just in case. But on top of all that we've got a role to play alongside the mainstream police in tracking major or organised crime, and in gathering information on unusual domestic situations, when they might threaten the national interest.

'Those fuel demonstrations were a good case in point. The first time the government was caught with its drawers round its ankles, and the word went out that it wasn't to happen again.'

'I know about that,' McIlhenney chuckled. 'I saw some of the correspondence that came our way at the time.'

'Aye, of course you did. I reckon that was a real sea change in our remit . . . which has always been, in effect, "Do what you're fucking told but don't let anyone find out about it." For the first time, it got us involved in keeping tabs on ordinary people, folk who aren't political, or organised in any meaningful way. They weren't threatening the country as such, just the government, yet we were brought into the act. 'I don't think I like that.'

'It's a good time for you to be going, then.'

'You approve of it?'

'No, but the answer lies in the ballot box . . .'

McGuire threw him a glance askance. 'Do you actually believe that?'

'No, but fortunately it also lies in the hands of people like you and me and Big Bob, using our common sense.'

'Don't let the people in the Home Office or up the Mound hear you say that.'

'Worry not, pal. I'll be a conscientious spook; I'll just do it my way, like the Boss told me to. Right; let's get into these files.'

McGuire was reaching for his keys when his direct line telephone rang. He glanced at the panel on the instrument before he picked it up. 'Hello, Ron,' he said. 'You really should block your number, you know, especially when you're phoning people like me . . . not that it would do any good.' He waited. 'Yes? Excellent. I'm impressed. Hang on, let me grab a pen.'

As his successor designate watched, he made rapid notes on a pad on his desk. 'That it? Fine, thanks. Sure, our debt to you is duly recorded.'

He hung up, tore off the note, and put it into his pocket. 'Well?' McIlhenney asked, heavily.

'He's alive; more's the pity, because he's bloody well here. There's a gap of twenty years in his UK Social Security record; during that time, he was living in Portugal and apparently paying contributions there. He came back to Britain three years ago. He spent a short time in London then moved back up to Edinburgh, only, according to my pal, he now calls himself George Rosewell. He lives in Newhaven Road.'

'Why would he change his name? Does he think we might still be after him for wife-battering?'

'God knows. Maybe the Portuguese police were after him; maybe someone else was.' An anxious look crossed the big detective's face, taking his friend by surprise. 'Listen, Neil,' he muttered. 'You're my best pal. You, and only you, know about Maggie's father knocking ten bells out of her mother and leaving them all. That's the way it's got to stay, okay?'

'Of course. I'm huffed that you should even say that.'

McGuire winced. 'Sorry, mate; I should have known better. It's just that she started talking about him the other night, which she's never done before. It came out the blue; something trivial happened at work and just seemed to trigger it off. Lots of stuff she'd never even hinted at, that had been bottled up in there. You think Mags is controlled? You don't know the half of it.

'I won't go into detail, Neil, but the guy was a real fucking monster, worse than I ever suspected. I just had to sit there . . . in a bloody restaurant, it was . . . and let her get it all out, doing my best to keep calm, when inside I'm exploding, wanting to kill the bastard. I can't do that, of course, I can't touch him. It all has to stay in the past for her

53

sake. Still, I had to find out at the very least whether he's still alive; hence my call to Ron. But now I'm in a real quandary.'

'Howzat?'

'Because of what he does for a living. Mr George Rosewell is the janitor in a primary school, right here in Edinburgh; right here in Maggie's division.'

15

It was just after midday, yet Skinner had to force himself not to think about the weariness which gripped him. He had been such a short time in Kuala Lumpur that his body had not even begun to catch up with the time change, before he had flown on to the United States. Three-quarters of the way around the world, and he had never been able to sleep on board aircraft. His Mont Blanc watch, still set on UK time, told him that the jet lag should be no more severe than if he had flown across the Atlantic, but his biological clock ticked out a different message.

'Round the next bend, there should be a turn-off to the right,' said the FBI agent with the map. They had been driving for twenty minutes since they pulled off the highway, along a road on the west side of the Great Sacandaga Lake which was little more than a forest track. The trees were mature and even as early in the growth cycle as they were, the woods on either side were dark and deep. He thought of Robert Frost and his horse as he looked at them, and wondered what they would be like in winter.

The two agents, Isaac Brand, the navigator, and Troy Kosinski, the driver, had been waiting for him at JFK, as Doherty had promised. He had spotted them at once; they looked the part, fit, lean and sharp-eyed. They had whisked him across the airport to a small executive jet, which in turn had whisked them all to a local landing strip near Saratoga Springs, in what had seemed to Skinner, after his two marathon flights, to have been no time at all.

'Okay, there it is,' Brand called to his partner. 'That should take us directly to the crime scene.' The Scot glanced at the agent. He had a cynic's view of the modern FBI agent, seeing them in his mind's eye either as short, feisty women, or as square-shouldered, clean-cut guys, and he was quietly pleased that this one was an exception to his rule. His fine features gave him a vulnerable look, although the DCC knew that he must have passed the toughest physical examination to have earned his seat in their car.

Kosinski, who did fit his mental stereotype, made the turn; the road narrowed and at once, the day grew darker. 'Fucking hell,' Skinner exclaimed. 'Either of you guys seen *The Blair Witch Project*?'

The driver looked in the rearview mirror, catching his eye. 'We can't comment on that, sir,' he said in a lazy drawl. 'It's the subject of a continuing Bureau investigation.'

'Sure,' Zak Brand chuckled. 'There's an X-File on it. We could arrange for you to meet Scully, if you'd like.'

'No thank you, gentlemen,' he answered. 'She's too short for me.' He was grateful for the banter; it kept his mind off what was waiting at the end of the track. All the way from New York, they had exchanged only pleasantries and platitudes. The FBI men had asked no personal questions, nor had they referred to the reason behind his visit. But finally, they were almost there.

'Do you know the people who'll be meeting us?' he asked.

'No, sir,' said Special Agent Kosinski, glancing in the mirror once again. 'We're New York City operatives; this is not territory where we'd normally be deployed, unless an interstate crime was involved.' Skinner nodded; he knew enough about American policing to understand the rivalries between the agencies. 'This is the jurisdiction of the New York State Police Department homicide squad. The local county police department is very small; they don't have a detective division, so when they run across something like this, they call for help, damn quick.'

Ahead, the gloom seemed to lighten, and the track widened out. 'Almost there, sir.' The agent slowed the car, a big General Motors off-roader, as he approached a small clearing. A black Pontiac saloon, with State Police markings, and a Ford Explorer were parked at its edge, on either side of a mailbox, which was set on a pole. He leaned out and read the name on it. 'Grace. Yup, this is it.'

The three men climbed out of the vehicle. Skinner saw that there was a path behind the box; through the trees he could make out the broad shape of a single-storey, chalet-style house. He sniffed the air; it was crisp and fresh, and in the distance he heard water lapping and birds crying. They set off, Brand and Kosinski taking the lead on the narrow walkway.

One crime scene looks like any other, Skinner thought as, finally, he reached his destination. *We follow the same rituals, with the tape and everything . . . as if that's worth a damn out here.*

'Hey there in the house,' Brand called out as they stepped around the side of the cabin. 'FBI!'

The front door creaked as it opened, and two men stepped out; as he looked at them, the Scotsman found himself thinking in American football terms. A quarter-back and his minder. They were both blond and clean-shaven; one was around six feet tall, wide at the shoulders, narrow at the waist, probably in his mid-thirties, the other a few years younger, and enormous, his body looking as if it was fighting its way out of his clothes. About six eight, Skinner guessed, weight at least three hundred pounds. He wondered how he had squeezed into the Pontiac.

'Hi,' the smaller man greeted them, as he walked down the steps from the porch. 'You didn't need to tell me you were the Bureau guys. I'd have known you by those suits. I'm Dave Schultz, lieutenant, State Police Bureau of Criminal Investigation . . .' He directed their eyes behind him with his thumb. '. . . And this is Detective Toby Small, one of life's great ironies.' The giant gave them an amiable grin.

Schultz looked at Skinner. 'So you, sir, must be the victims' son-in-law. Deputy Chief Skinner, is that right?'

The Scot nodded, reaching out a handshake; there was enough in the lieutenant's tone to tell him that, alien or not, his rank was going to count for something.

'Did you have a good flight from Scotland, sir?'

'No. I had a long flight from Malaysia.' He decided that a little more personal information would do no harm. 'I was due to address an international drugs conference there.'

'You got that problem too?' asked Small, as if to prove that he could speak.

Skinner glanced up at him. 'Detective, everyone has that problem. In our case we have one of the largest unprotected coastlines in Europe. So every comedian with a boat thinks he can stuff his ballast tanks with hashish, sail it up to Wester Ross, offload it and get away clean. More often than not he's right, as well.'

His eyes snapped back on to Schultz. 'Okay. Let's get something out of the way. Was it either of you guys who phoned my wife?'

The New York policeman seemed to recoil slightly; he held up a hand as if to ward Skinner off. 'No, sir,' he said, vehemently. 'It was not. We heard about that and we apologise that it happened. It was one of the local guys, playing detective before we got here. Don't worry, he's had his balls fried.'

'Well make sure he's kept out of my way, or I'll make him eat them.' He caught Small gazing at him with an expression that he had seen once in the eyes of a police dog as it looked at its handler.

'Okay, gentlemen,' he continued, 'if I can have a look at the house. Are your technicians finished up here?'

'Yes, sir,' the lieutenant answered. 'They're all done. As you requested we've left the scene as close as we could to the way it was when we got here ... apart from the bodies, of course. They've been taken to the morgue in Loudonville, our regional headquarters. After we're done here, the coroner would like you to go there: he prefers for a family member to make a formal identification. We've put a hold on the autopsies till you've done that.'

Skinner shivered inwardly; outwardly he nodded briskly, as he headed up the short flight of steps, on to the veranda. The New York detectives followed him up, but his Bureau escorts stayed below, anxious, he guessed, not to offend local sensibilities by intruding on to their scene. 'How were they found?' the DCC asked Schultz. 'That part of the story was pretty vague.'

The lieutenant pointed out towards the expanse of lake, which could be seen from where they stood. As he did so, Skinner noticed a jetty, with a small powerboat moored against it. 'A neighbour of Mr and Mrs Grace was out in his cruiser, getting set for some dawn fishing. He saw that the porch light was on, and that the front door was open. He came ashore to check the place out and found them. He called the nearest police office, in Edinburg.'

Skinner's eyes screwed up as his momentary bewilderment registered on his face. 'Where?' he asked.

'Edinburg,' Schultz repeated. 'It's the nearest township, although it's barely big enough to warrant a dot on the map.'

He shook his head wondering whether it was simply coincidence, or whether it had been the name that had first attracted Leo to this remote place. 'I see,' he murmured. 'This fisherman guy: he's been checked out, has he?'

'Yes, sir. We're satisfied that's how it really was. The guy's over seventy; even if he had a grudge against the Graces, he couldn't have killed them like that.'

'No, I guess he couldn't. Time of death?'

'Around 9 p.m., the coroner reckoned; give or take an hour, he said. It was very cold through that night.'

Skinner looked down at the rocking chair, at rest now on the wide porch, to the left of the front door as he faced it. A chalk circle had been drawn around it. There was a cushion on the seat, untethered but still in place, the shape of its occupant's buttocks still showing clearly in it. 'Nothing's been touched? That cushion's as it was found?'

'Yes, sir. You'll see the crime scene photographs, but the old man was sat in his chair just as if he had died in his sleep. That's what Mr

Southern, the neighbour, thought at first, till he went inside.'

The DCC nodded and walked indoors, into a big living room, with a great hearth, filled with the grey ashes of a log fire. He looked around; the place looked as if it had been turned over by an expert in a hurry. Most of the cushions of the leather suite stood on end, left in those positions by whoever had searched under them. The drawers and doors of a big farmhouse sideboard lay open. Books had been stripped from their shelves, flipped open, he guessed, then thrown on the floor. His father-in-law's flap-front desk, which he remembered from the den in his Buffalo house, had been ripped open. The chisel which the killer had used lay beside it. The whole scene, furniture, books, every loose object in the room was covered in white fingerprint powder. 'You've been thorough,' Skinner murmured.

'Yes, sir,' the lieutenant agreed. 'We always are.'

'Did you lift any prints?'

'Nada. We got prints of Mr and Mrs Grace, Mr Southern, and the cleaning lady, plus one or two wild ones, but we don't think that any of those belong to the perpetrator. They were in the wrong places for him.'

'One perpetrator?'

'There's no indication that there was more than one perp. There are creaking boards all over the deck outside, yet Mr Grace was taken completely by surprise; my gut feeling is that this was a lone burglar.'

'Did he get anything, do you think?'

'We'll need you or someone else to do an inventory, but as far as we can tell he got money, cards, watches, rings, other valuables: everything you'd expect in a robbery.'

The big Scots policeman shook his head. 'Not everything, Lieutenant Schultz, not everything.' He picked up a book from the floor, and held it out. 'See this? It's a first edition of *Moby Dick*, and it's signed by Herman Melville.' He looked at the volumes on the floor and selected another, then turned to the flyleaf. 'That signature? James Thurber. If you root around here for long enough you'll find first editions signed by Mark Twain, Ernest Hemingway, Margaret Mitchell and God knows who else.

'I'm no expert, but there's thousands of dollars, no, tens of thousands, lying on the floor here. Yet this guy looks through them all, for some reason, then just leaves them here. And this, you tell me, is a professional thief, who's prepared to kill . . .'

He broke off. 'Where's the kitchen?' he asked, sharply.

'Through there,' said Small, pointing to a door to the left of the hearth.

59

Skinner walked across and looked inside. The inevitable outline was chalked on the floor; there was blood too, a lot of blood, around where the body had lain, streaking the pine doors of the wall cupboards, and splashed across one of the work surfaces. 'Bastard!' he murmured.

'The guy cut through an artery with the strangling wire,' Schultz explained, unnecessarily. 'It must have been over in seconds, though.'

Bob thought of his gentle parents-in-law as he pictured the scene. His head swam, and for an instant it was as if he had been there, and he could see it all happening. He felt himself sway, and grabbed hold of the nearest worktop to steady himself. He knew that he could not postpone sleep for much longer.

As far as he could see, neither detective had noticed his moment of weakness. He led them out of the kitchen and out of the house. As he stepped out on to the wide porch, his cellphone sang out. Joe Doherty was on the line. 'Where are you?' he asked.

'At the cabin; by the lake. I've seen what was done and how. Thanks for Brand and Kosinski, by the way; they've been great. Right now they're down below, practising diplomacy.'

'What you got?'

'A shit-awful mess. The officer in charge here feels there was only one killer, and I agree with him. Leo and Susannah were clearly killed by the same person, expertly at that. If there had been more than one, they'd probably have taken one each.'

'Where you going next?'

'We're going back to Saratoga Springs, to see the coroner and do what's necessary there, then your guys are going to take me on to Buffalo.'

'Fine. Let me know when you get there. By the way,' Doherty added, just when Skinner thought he was going to ring off, 'did you get that stuff I sent you?'

'Yes.'

'What did it tell you?'

'What I thought it would.'

He heard a heavy sigh. 'Okay, I give in. What's with the "Play it again, Sam"? What did you mean by that?'

Skinner chuckled, but grimly, without a trace of a smile. 'It's my suspicious mind at work; the whole thing made me think of *Casablanca*, my favourite movie. Remember where Bogart says, "Of all the gin joints in all the world, she had to walk into mine"? Well, my friend, tell me this. Of all the vulnerable lakeside cabins in the great United States of America, why did this guy have to walk into Leo Grace's?'

16

The chief superintendent's office was bigger than hers, but the view from the window was no better. Rose gave it only a brief glance and then turned her gaze back to the uniformed officers sat at the meeting table; two superintendents, clearly bristling that she was chairing the meeting, and three chief inspectors, of whom at least one was enjoying their discomfort.

'That's the way it is,' she said, briskly. 'You've all seen the ACC's memo. Anything you would normally bring to Mr English, you bring to me in his absence; otherwise it's business as usual. I know that the Chief Super is in the habit of holding Monday morning meetings with this group. I'll continue that practice, except that for the duration of this arrangement, which hopefully will not be long, they'll be on Friday afternoons. The Monday timing clashes with the head of CID's weekly briefing, and I have to be there.'

She caught the look of surprise on one superintendent's face, and shot the group a brief glance. 'Yes, gentlemen, I'm doing two jobs. So please: don't take the piss. Don't go bringing me decisions that you would normally take yourself.'

The two senior officers stared back at her, unblinking. She would have welcomed Haggerty's presence to underline his message, but she knew that this was part of the test.

'CID's going through a quiet spell just now,' she continued, 'but the hooligans don't work to a timetable, so that could go pear-shaped at any moment. To make sure that I'm always contactable, I'm going to have a go-between, a runner; PC Haddock, one of our young probationers, will be my contact. He will know where I am at any given moment.'

'Hope he's up to the job,' grunted Superintendent Davie Halliday. 'Back-watching calls for a bit of experience.'

Rose looked at him, evenly. 'I don't see why it should in this case,' she said. 'I have every confidence in my fellow officers.' Everyone in the room, Halliday included, read the warning in her words.

She stood up, ending the meeting. 'Okay, gentlemen, that's all. Barring crises, I'll see you here at three o'clock on Friday, when we can run through the programme for next week. If anyone does need me, I'll be in my own office. I'm not moving in here.' She ushered them to the door, then went back to her own room. Back in familiar territory, she called the front office and asked for Haddock.

'And don't scare the boy this time,' she added, pointedly.

No more than a minute later, there was a knock on her door. Haddock was less nervous that on his first visit, but still eyed her cautiously as he stood, all teeth and sharp elbows, in front of her desk. 'You sent for me, ma'am?' he ventured.

'Obviously. What do they call you, Constable Haddock? What's your Christian name?'

'Harold, ma'am,' he answered. 'But everybody calls me Sauce. Ye ken, like in brown sauce, like you put on a fish supper.'

Rose wrinkled her nose. 'You might: I certainly don't. But Sauce it will be, if that's what you're comfortable with. Right, here's why I wanted you.'

She explained the duties she had in mind for the young officer. As she spoke she fancied his chest puffed out a little, and he began to look a little less awkward. 'Okay, Sauce, have you got that? Whenever I leave the station, I'll tell you where I'm going and how I can be contacted. If you see me heading out the front door and I haven't told you, stop me and ask me.'

Haddock nodded, his face telling her that he hoped it would not come to that.

'Good; you are now my official temporary gopher. You can start right away; you'd better get me those bloody night-shift reports.'

17

The bedside phone sounded at five minutes past seven; Sarah snatched it up on the second ring. Normally, at that hour, it would have wakened her, but Seonaid had done that already. Having claimed her mother's attention, in the manner of infants she was asleep once more, on the pillow on Bob's side of the bed.

She knew who was calling before she heard his voice. 'Hi,' she answered softly. 'Where are you?'

'I'm in Buffalo. I'm sorry I didn't call you from the scene like you asked, but I just couldn't, with those guys around.'

'I understand. How are you?'

'I'm fine.'

'You don't sound fine; you sound tired.'

'If I do, it's because I am. I fell asleep at seven o'clock yesterday evening and I woke up an hour ago.'

'Poor love. You at the house?'

'No, not yet. I checked into a hotel for the night; the Hyatt Regency in Fountain Plaza; I just told the guys to take me anywhere. I was so damn knackered I didn't think to look for keys at the cabin, and anyway, I don't know the alarm combination. To make it hassle-free, I called the security company that looks after the place. They've got everything I'll need to get in. My FBI nursemaids are taking me to meet them there at midday tomorrow. Hopefully I'll have had some more kip by then.'

'Have you seen Sheriff Dekker yet?' she asked, speaking urgently, yet quietly at the same time, for fear of waking her daughter.

'Gie's a break, love. I spent most of yesterday with Little and Large, the State coppers.'

'How was the cabin?'

'Upside down, ransacked; just as I was told I'd find it.'

'And where else did they take you?'

He could hear her hesitancy. 'They took me to the morgue; I've done the formal identification and given the coroner signed authority to proceed with the autopsies. He's doing everything by the book.'

63

'How . . . how were they?'

He had been waiting for that question. He could still see their faces; he always would. Leo's eyes had been bulging almost out of their sockets, and Susannah's head had been all but severed by the wire garrotte. 'Peaceful. They'd barely have known a thing,' he told her.

'When can we have the funerals?'

'The coroner said he'll open an inquest, then adjourn it indefinitely. After that, he's prepared to release the bodies. Shouldn't be more than a couple of days. I'll contact an undertaker, and get things under way. Be prepared for a big turn-out, love, and not just of family and friends. This is big news in the media here. It's all over television and the papers. I was filmed going into the coroner's office in Loudonville; I didn't want to speak to anyone so Schultz and Small, the local guys, took me out the back way after I was done.'

'I thought you said they were called . . .' She stopped. 'Sorry. My humour switch is still off.'

'No, I'm sorry. But you should see Small. I thought Lennie Plenderleith was big, but this bloke; Jesus.' He whistled.

'Anyhow,' he continued. 'That's where we are. My Bureau escorts are collecting me at eleven. We'll get the house opened, and then I'll go and see Dekker, although I'm not quite sure why, in the circumstances.'

'What do you mean?'

'I mean that the investigation has sod all to do with him. The crime happened a hell of a long way from here, and it's state jurisdiction, quite clearly; my seeing him is really no more than a courtesy call.'

'Well just remember, be courteous. We set great store on that in the USA.'

'Yes, dear, I'll be nice, I promise. I might even call him Sheriff.'

She heard him stifle a yawn. 'How are the kids?' he asked.

She looked at Seonaid, and saw that she was awake, and peering back at her, curious. 'One of them's right here,' she answered. 'Say hello to her.'

18

Looking at it from the street, Mario McGuire could see that Hargreen Primary School had grown over the years, and had changed rapidly in the process. Back in the days when Colinton village really was a village, it had probably boasted three or four classrooms in a small stone building, and would have been perfectly adequate for its purpose, given the standards and methods of the day.

Happily not for decades had its pupils been crammed into classes of fifty, cowed, and frequently thrashed, into obedience and attention. The original school was still there, but a brass plate on its door indicated that it was now the administration block. A big modern structure seemed to burst out from it, enveloping it in grey concrete, and a second block, of roughly similar design, had been added at some later point. The architecture was definitely not Frank Lloyd Wright, but neither was the surrounding area.

The detective checked his watch. It was twenty-five past one, and the playground was empty; the Hargreen Primary pupils were back at work after lunch. He opened the green wooden door of the administration block, and stepped into a small vestibule, its only furniture an umbrella stand, well used on that showery day. It opened out into a slightly larger hall, its walls lined with the work of children.

Straight ahead, facing him, there was a door with the word 'Janitor' printed on a burnished metal plate. As he walked up to it McGuire took a deep breath, then turned the handle and pushed it open. The room was empty.

He looked around. It was furnished with a steel-framed desk and chair, a small fridge, a grey filing cabinet, a coat-stand and a small table on which were a kettle, a jar of coffee, a box of tea bags and a jar of sugar. A big white mug sat beside them, with the word 'Jannie' emblazoned in big blue capital letters. A Day-Glo yellow tunic and a crossing warden's hat were hanging on the stand and a tall traffic lollipop stood in the far corner. He noticed a grey metal wastebin beside the desk. He was about to look in it when an insistent female voice sounded behind him.

'Excuse me. Didn't you see the sign?' it asked, as he turned. 'All visitors to the school must first report to the office.'

'No,' he answered, untruthfully. 'I didn't see it.' He looked at the woman; grey well-cut hair, plump, peach-coloured woollen sweater, mock-tartan, mock-tweed skirt, brown tights, sensible shoes, inky fingers. He guessed at once who she was, but he asked his question out of politeness. 'Are you the head teacher?'

As she smiled and gave a self-deprecating shake of her head, he knew that he had been right, and that he had made a friend. 'Oh no,' she said, 'I'm only the school secretary. Mrs Dewberry's the head teacher; she's in her room. Would you like to see her? I take it you're a parent.'

McGuire shook his head. 'No, I'm not a parent; I'm a policeman. Detective Superintendent McGuire.'

The woman gave a small gasp. 'Ohhh. You'd better see Mrs Dewberry, then. Just hold on a minute.' As she bustled across the hall, and down a corridor leading off to the right, McGuire glanced into the wastebasket; it was empty. Quickly, he tried the desk's only drawer, but it was locked. He stepped out of Rosewell's room, closed the door behind him and followed the secretary into the corridor.

At once, his eye was caught by a big display panel, along the wall on his left. It bore the heading 'Hargreen Primary — Our Staff', and carried individual head-and-shoulders photographs of the teaching complement. Top, front and centre, an attractive woman in her thirties smiled out; oval face, glowing chestnut hair, the sort of eyes that won your confidence at first sight.

'Mr McGuire?' He turned and the woman was looking at him in real life, but without the smile. 'I'm Pat Dewberry, the head teacher. Come into my office.' She held the glazed door open for him, and followed him inside. As he entered, the secretary gave him a quick smile, then slipped out.

'Take a seat, please,' said Mrs Dewberry. He followed her pointing finger and settled on to a chair; it was soft, but for him, uncomfortably low. She sat facing him, with a final tug on her shortish skirt. He took out his warrant card, and showed it to her; she looked at it, nodded, and handed it back.

'A superintendent, eh,' she began. 'And in plain clothes. We usually have uniformed sergeants in here.' She paused. 'Mrs Barnard's bringing us coffee. I assume that's okay with you; I never met a policeman who didn't drink coffee.'

'You've still got a hundred per cent record, then,' he chuckled.

Her eyes stayed cool as she looked at him. 'So what brings you here, Mr McGuire? And what are you? You're not a community policeman, that's for sure.'

He decided to volunteer a little of the truth. 'Not in the sense you mean. I'm Special Branch.'

Highly predictable body language normally followed that disclosure. The other person would draw back slightly, and would throw him a look that registered either consternation or fear, and sometimes both.

Pat Dewberry simply raised an eyebrow. 'Really?' she exclaimed. 'I didn't think that existed any more. You've made my day; it's not often you get to meet a genuine anachronism.' She caught his surprise. 'Stop it, Pat,' she chided herself.

'Sorry to be so flippant,' she continued, 'but my grandfather was an old-fashioned communist, through in Glasgow; one of the Red Clydesiders. He knew Shinwell very well; he was in court with him, although the sheriff decided he was too young to go to jail. I grew up to tales of the Special Branch: Grandpa used to think of them as his regular companions. In fact he was quite friendly with some of them.

'I just thought that when his Party disappeared, so did you.'

'I wish we could,' said McGuire, 'but there really are dangerous people still in the world, and they have to be watched.'

'And in here?' she asked, showing a trace of impatience. 'Have I got a terrorist on my staff?'

He shook his head. 'I doubt it. No, I didn't walk into the janitor's office by mistake. I was looking for him.'

'George Rosewell? What's he done?'

Mario looked the woman in the eye, and decided that she could be trusted with more of the truth. 'Recently? Nothing that I know of; he's my father-in-law.'

'Ahh,' she exclaimed. 'There I go getting my conspiracy theories sorted out, and it turns out to be a family matter. As it happens, I'm looking for the old devil too. He hasn't turned up for work this week, and he hasn't called in sick either. I phoned him, but I got no reply. I suspect you'll find him in the pub, or in the betting shop. When you do, tell him he's in bother and send him back in.'

Mrs Dewberry stopped abruptly as the door opened and Mrs Barnard returned, with a smile for McGuire and coffee for them both. When she had gone, she picked up her mug and glanced at the detective. 'But why do I sense that this isn't really a family visit?'

'Because you're a perceptive lady, that's why. Rosewell . . . or Rose, to use his real name . . . walked out on his family more than twenty-five years ago. He lived abroad for most of that time. I've only just learned that he's back in Scotland.'

'So you've come to arrange for him to be reunited with his long-lost daughter?'

'Not quite.'

'Should I be looking for a new janitor?'

'That might be no bad idea. After I've spoken to him, he might not want to stick around.' He drank half of his coffee in a single swallow. 'Tell me, Mrs Dewberry, have you ever had any complaints about him?'

'What kind?'

'Any kind.'

'From parents or children?'

'Either.'

'A mother complained about him once; she said that he had frightened her daughter. I investigated, of course, but it came to no more than George having spoken sharply to the girl because she was slow in getting back to her class after the break. I told him to leave that to the teachers in future. Since then, I've had no bother.'

She looked keenly at him, as if for the first time he had really interested her. 'You're not trying to tell me he's on a register somewhere, are you?'

'If that was the case, it would have been reported to the education authority at once. No, I'm not trying to tell you anything. But, to come back to your earlier question, I'll come off the fence; yes, you should find another janitor, because I'm going to make absolutely certain that George Rosewell never works in this or any other school again, under that or any other name.'

The teacher nodded, and drank more of her coffee. 'I won't ask how you're going to do that,' she said. 'I'll just report his unexplained absence to the directorate, and insist that he be replaced. I've been here for a while; that will happen automatically. He isn't a union member either, so that won't be a problem.'

McGuire glanced into his mug; his Italian blood rebelled against finishing what was in it. He raised himself from his low chair. 'Thanks for your confidence,' he murmured.

'Thanks for yours. Don't worry, none of this leaves this room.'

'If I was worried about that, none of it would have come into it.'

'What will you do?' she asked. 'Go to see him at home?'

'Yes, first chance I get, although that won't be today. Listen, if he does turn up for work in the morning, would you give me a call? That's my direct line number. If I'm not there, you can leave a message with Inspector McIlhenney or PC Cowan.' He handed her a business card.

'I'll do that.'

She opened the door for him, and accompanied him along the corridor. As they reached the display panel he stopped and looked at the photographs. There, on the bottom row, he saw him; looking a good deal younger than his years, clean-shaven, his face and bald head heavily tanned, gazing out at him with eyes that were chilling in their familiarity. He would have known him even without the name printed below.

'Can I have that?' he asked.

'You might as well,' she said. 'It's no use to me now. It's a good likeness.' Carefully, she prised it from the board and handed it to him. 'There. Will you show that to your wife?'

'Good question, Mrs Dewberry; good question.'

19

Bob Skinner stood at the foot of the driveway and looked up at the big house on Stanford Avenue. It was white-painted, two-storey, with a pillared front and a terrace, which seemed to run all round the house at the level of the upper floor. 'Neo-colonial,' his father-in-law had called it. 'Flashy,' had been Skinner's description.

He shuddered at the thought of Leo and Susannah in that small-town morgue, he with those terrible bulging eyes, she with a towel draped over her savaged neck by a considerate attendant, although his policeman's training had forced him to remove it, to see for himself what had been done to her.

He had been very fond of Leopold Grace and his wife. They had never treated him with anything other than affection, even when he and Sarah had gone through their estrangement and when he had gone to the States to visit his son, and to see whether there was any ground on which they might build a renewal. His father-in-law's legal career had made him tolerant and non-judgemental, and while their conversations at that time had been frank, he had never come away from one without feeling at least understood.

The representative of the security company, which monitored the alarm system, was waiting for him at the front door as he approached, with the dutiful Brand and Kosinski at his heels. She was tall and long-legged, around the thirty mark, and dressed in a pale blue business suit. With her shoulder-length auburn hair, she looked vaguely like Sarah. 'Mr Skinner?' she asked, her hand outstretched. He nodded and shook it.

'I'm Kelly Lance. Do you have the court order?'

'Yes.' He took an envelope from his jacket pocket; it held confirmation from a probate judge of the district court that he and Sarah were joint executors of Leo's will. 'You'd better have a look at it,' he said.

She glanced at the official stamp on the outside. 'That's okay.' She unclipped a slim leather case and looked inside, eventually producing a thick, folded document.

Setting the case at her feet, she unfolded the sheet and held it out for him to see. 'This is a plan of the alarm system. It's wired into the nearest police precinct; they guarantee two-minute response if it lights up.'

'Have they had any incidents in the last couple of days?' Skinner asked.

'No; at least none they've told us about, and they would have, since we hold the keys to the property.'

'So where's the control box?'

'In the usual place, just inside the front door. The first sensor has a programmed delay, so that once the owner unlocks he has thirty seconds to key in the code number and disable the system. Shall we go in?'

He nodded. 'Yes; let's get on with it. What's the code?'

Kelly Lance glanced at the plan. 'Eight, nine, two, and seven,' she read. *Fine security*, he thought. *Leo's birthday.*

She handed him the keys, as they stepped up to the big, solid, white-painted door, indicating which two from the bunch he would need. One was a simple Yale, but the other was for a five-lever, double-locking mortise. He unlocked them both and opened the door, seeing the sensor light flick on as he did so. He saw the small control panel at once, and flipped back the lid covering the number pad. He looked at the indicators, then at Kelly Lance.

'This isn't active, is it?'

She shook her head. 'No. If it was there would have been an audible signal as soon as the sensor picked you up.'

Skinner frowned as he stepped into the big, familiar house, in which his wife had grown up, in which he had spent happier times himself. 'How long had they been away?' he asked the woman.

'They advised us last Saturday week that they were driving up to the Adirondacks for a month. We have their telephone number at the lake on our files, for use in the event of an incident.'

'But you haven't had one.'

'No. Everything's been silent since then. But it would have been, wouldn't it, since Mr Grace didn't set the alarm.'

'I know they have a cleaning woman. Is it possible that she could have been in and forgot to reset the pad when she left?'

'That's possible, but unlikely. We require our clients to give us the names of all key-holders, even those who might only have access for a few days. There's no one on their list other than Mr and Mrs Grace themselves, and Dr Sarah Grace Skinner, their daughter.'

'. . . Who has definitely not been here in the last ten days.' He looked over his shoulder and called to the FBI agents, who were waiting outside. 'Come on in, lads.'

Kosinski stepped into the entrance call, with Brand close behind. 'Everything okay, sir?' he asked.

Skinner shook his head. 'No. My brain's not working very well. Have you got a number for Lieutenant Schultz?'

'Yes, sir.' He dipped two fingers into the breast pocket of his jacket and drew out a business card.

The Scot's cellphone was in his hand as he took it from him. He glanced at it to make sure that he was tuned into a network, and dialled the number shown. 'New York State Police, Loudonville,' drawled a nasal operator.

Schultz was in his office. 'Deputy Chief Skinner,' he said. 'What can I do for you?'

'You can find the guy who killed Leo and Susannah. Failing that, tell me something. Before I got there yesterday, were there any personal effects removed from the house? Specifically, I mean keys.'

'No, sir, none at all. That was in accordance with your request. However, since your visit we have removed certain valuable or sensitive items; the books, for example. And keys will be among those; let me check, please. This may take a moment. Would you like me to call you back?'

'No, I'll hold.'

As it happened, Schultz was gone for less than a minute. 'I have them here, sir. I'm looking at all the keys that were recovered from the cabin.'

'Okay. I'm looking for a brass five-pointed key, with no manufacturer's name, and for a Yale-type latchkey, again without a manufacturer's name.'

'They were supplied by my company,' Kelly Lance whispered to him. 'As part of our security they are unmarked in any way.'

'No, sir,' Schultz replied, in a slow, deliberate tone, after a few seconds' perusal. 'I have nothing like that here. I two Chubb keys, and two mailbox keys, and that's all.' He paused. 'Can I ask what this is about, sir? Do you have a problem in Buffalo?'

'I think we might have. In fact, I think your investigation's just moved about three hundred miles west.'

'We'd better get there, in that case. I'll clear it with my boss.'

'Put a hold on that for a bit,' said Skinner. 'I'll have a look around here; after that we'll get back to you.' He ended the call and turned to the two special agents. 'Leo Grace might have been over seventy,' he told them, 'but he was as meticulous a man as I ever met. No way did he call

Ms Lance's office to report that he was leaving town, then forget to set his alarm.

'Somebody's been in here.'

'Impossible,' Kelly Lance protested.

'No it isn't,' snapped Skinner. 'Nothing's perfect, nothing's foolproof. How do you keep your records?'

'On computer.'

'All of them?'

'Yes.'

'And if someone hacked into it, would you know?'

'Yes, we'd know straight away . . .' She hesitated. '. . . If the system was in use.'

'Exactly. But if it wasn't you'd have to check back to know that it had been accessed. Do that; call your office and have them do it now.'

His eyes flashed back to the FBI men. 'Whose bloody jurisdiction are we in now, out here in the suburbs?'

'This still belongs to the Erie County Police Department,' Brand answered.

'Okay. I want them here, now. I'm not going to see Sheriff Dekker; in the circumstances I think it's better that he comes to me.'

20

'Ah bet you thought I'd have cotton wool stuffed in my cheeks.' Beppe Viareggio's voice boomed around the room, drawing sharp glances from his mother and sisters. The look that Maggie gave him was a mixture of genuine bewilderment and forced tolerance. From the moment he had stuffed an envelope full of cash into her hand at their wedding reception, she had never cared for Beppe.

Hopefully he looked at her, eager for the slightest sign that she understood his joke. 'Marlon Brando, ken?' he offered, finally giving in. 'In *The Godfather*? That's how he was able to mumble like that; he had his cheeks stuffed with cotton wool.'

Mario laid a hand on his uncle's shoulder. 'Okay, Don Beppe,' he said quietly, with a grin and a mock Italian accent. 'I come to you and I ask you humbly for your aid. I ask you to do me a small favour, as my godfather and as my friend. Please to knock off the Mafia patter. You know it really annoys my nana, and my mum looks none too happy either.'

Beppe shrugged his shoulders. 'Okay, my boy,' he mumbled. 'I will do you this favour; but one day I may ask you to do me a small service in return.'

The policeman shook his head as he ambled away, before casting his eye around the living room of Beppe's penthouse, the biggest flat in a new development looking across the water to the offices of the civil servants who served the Scottish Executive. There were ten members of the clan at the party in addition to Maggie and himself. His gaze took them all in: his nana, his mother, his Uncle Beppe and Aunt Sophia, his unmarried cousin Paula, her younger sister Viola, with her husband, Stanley Coia, and their children, Ryan and David ... Stan was a Manchester United fan ... and finally the venerable Auntie Josefina, Papa Viareggio's ninety-four-year-old sister. Brought by Beppe from her nursing home, she sat in a chair by the window, sipping from a glass of dark Amarone, having forgotten at least half an hour before where she was or why she was there.

Taking his wife's arm, Mario led her over to his grandmother. 'Honest to God,' the old lady muttered glowering across at her son. 'Sometimes I wonder how that one manages to get up in the morning, wi' the little brain he's got. If your papa had heard him talk that nonsense.'

She looked at Maggie. 'I'm sorry, lassie. We don't get together enough as a family, but I can hardly blame the two of you for steering clear of that son of mine.'

Nana Viareggio may have been eighty-seven years old, but her back was still ramrod straight, and she carried herself with the air of a woman in her seventies. She was tall and slim, with piercing brown eyes and silver hair, which was always bound tight in a bun, and she dressed predominantly in black. From Mario's earliest memory of her, she had never seemed to change; indeed, there were moments when he fancied that she was growing younger. Her Christian name was Marla, he knew, but he had never heard anyone other than his grandfather address her by it; she was 'Mama' to Beppe and Sophia, and to Christina, his own mother, and 'Nana' to everyone else. She and her only grandson had been close before Papa Viareggio's death and they had grown closer since. He and Maggie saw more of her than of Christina, and visited her for lunch on the first Sunday of every month.

She frowned at Beppe once more. 'Listen to him,' she muttered. 'You know, son, for all that big bog-Irish father of yours . . . God rest his generous soul . . . you're more Italian than your uncle ever was or ever will be. When they named you after your papa, I think much of him passed into you. You understood him, and you still value the things he did. Like your dad, he died too soon, or a lot of things might have been different.'

She put a strong hand on his elbow and drew him into a corner. 'That's what we want to talk to you about, your mother and I,' she said, quietly.

'What do you mean?' As he spoke, he realised that Maggie was no longer by his side; Aunt Sophia had taken her off to meet the two boys, who were dressed, inevitably, in Manchester United shirts. As he glanced across at them, his mother moved towards him, as if answering a private summons by Nana. Christina McGuire was tall and handsome, like her mother, and like her she was a one-man woman, who regarded her widowhood as a period not of mourning, but of waiting.

'I mean,' Nana continued, reclaiming his attention, 'that there's family business to be talked about.'

'Such as?'

'Such as your part in it,' his mother answered, pausing for a moment to let her words sink in.

'I've made a decision, Mario; I'm retiring. I'm selling my share of the business to Rachel and Bert.'

Christina McGuire was an Edinburgh player in her own right; she had trained as a personnel manager after leaving university, and had worked in industry, until, two years after Mario's birth, and with backing from her father, she had set up a recruitment consultancy. She had begun by specialising in finding staff for the financial services industry, and she had shared in its success and expansion. Over the years the scope of her business had broadened, taking in new sectors, including law and accountancy, and adding on a training division. Christina had refused several offers for the company, preferring to control her own destiny with the support of the two partners who had joined her in the eighties, Rachel Dawson and Robert Ironside.

Her son stared at her in surprise; through all of his life, her consultancy had been part of her. When his father, big Eamon, had died of cancer ten years earlier, it, more than anything or anyone else, had helped her deal with the tragedy.

'You serious?' he exclaimed.

'Never more so,' she assured him.

'You realise that as soon as you're gone those two'll sell out?'

'Good luck to them if they do. I'm happy with my deal.'

He put his hands on her shoulders and kissed her on the cheek. 'In that case, good for you, Mum. If it's what you want to do, I couldn't be more pleased for you.' He frowned, suddenly. 'But what the hell's it got to do with me?'

'I'm not just retiring from the consultancy, son,' Christina answered. 'I'm going away. I've bought a house in Florence, and I'm going to live there. I want to study fine art, I want to paint, and I want to listen to music till my head's completely filled with it. I'm selling my flat in Northumberland Street; whenever I come back I'll stay with Mama or with you and Maggie.'

He blew out his cheeks. 'You're taking my breath away; but again, if this is what you really want, then go for it.'

Christina had never been a demonstrative woman, but she pulled her son to her, and hugged him. 'I'm so glad you feel that way, all things considered.'

Gradually, the rest of the truth began to dawn on him, and he understood the real reason for the family gathering. 'Wait a minute . . .'

he exclaimed. On either side of him, the two women smiled.

'You've got it,' said his mother. 'I'm retiring from all my business, including the family trust. And in that event, my place as a trustee passes to you.'

'Oh bloody hell, Mum,' he protested. 'I can't take that on, not now. I've just been given a division to run. Surely to Christ, you can still do that from Italy.'

'No,' she answered, adamantly. 'I want my life back, Mario. I'm sixty-two years old, and I still have things to do. I've been a trustee since Papa died, and I've run my own business at the same time. Now it's your turn.'

'But . . . Come on, the paperwork can be couriered out to you, you can fly back for trustee meetings.'

'No!' Nana Viareggio snapped. It was the first time she had spoken sharply to him in thirty years. 'Your mother has made her decision,' the old woman declared, in a judicial tone. 'You've always known this day would come, lad. Just you be thankful it hasn't been forced on you by Him upstairs. And anyway, I know quite well that you've been keeping an eye on things all along. I told you, you've got your papa's blood in you.

'He needs you, I need you; it's time.'

Backed into a corner, Mario looked from one to the other. 'What the hell is this?' he grunted. 'There might be only two witches here, but I still feel like bloody Macbeth!'

'You can't avoid what's for you,' said his grandmother. 'Besides, there's a job needs doing that only you can do; it's beyond Beppe. He's not a bad man; but he's a fool to himself and he's not up to this on his own.'

'What's that?'

The old lady nodded, almost imperceptibly, across the room. Maggie and Aunt Sophia had been joined by another striking Viareggio woman; she was only an inch or two shy of six feet tall, olive-skinned, with dark eyes and lustrous hair which had turned silver, prematurely. She wore it undisguised, with pride, and to some it made her look around forty, although in fact she was only thirty-two.

'That one there,' murmured Nana. 'You have to keep a very close eye on your cousin Paula. She's my granddaughter, as much of my blood as you are, so it pains me to say it, but I do not trust that girl.'

She patted him on the shoulder. 'Now, Mario, son; you call everyone to attention. Your mother has her announcement to make.'

21

Bob Skinner looked at Bradford Dekker and thought of his own chief. Where Sir James Proud was silver-haired, massive and statesmanlike in his uniform, a man of gravitas, his counterpart in Buffalo was sleek, sharp-suited, around his own age, and looked more like a stereotypical car salesman than a policeman.

This was not unnatural since he was a politician first and foremost. On Skinner's first visit to Buffalo, Leo Grace had told him about a former sheriff of Erie County, Grover Cleveland, who had gone on to become president of the United States. As he appraised Dekker, he tried to imagine him taking the oath of office on the Capitol steps; he tried, but he failed.

Whether it was prompted by the murdered Leo Grace's standing in his home town, or by courtesy to a fellow police officer, the Sheriff had come to the house on Stanford Avenue without the faintest sign of annoyance at the summons. He stood in the hall, at the foot of the broad flight of stairs which led to the upper floor, with Skinner, Brand and Kosinski, Kelly Lance having been sent back to her office to check how often her company's computer had been accessed within the last few weeks, and whether all of these searches had been authorised. The two uniformed officers who had brought him to the scene were on guard at the open front door, staring grimly at the few neighbours who had been attracted out by their car to see what might be going on.

'How well did you know my father-in-law, Mr Dekker?' Skinner asked.

'I knew him very well,' the Sheriff replied. 'I was an intern in Mr Grace's law firm twenty years ago. He took an interest in me, and directed me towards criminal work. Then when my internship was over, he pulled a couple of strings to get me a post in the state attorney's office.'

'You must have impressed him.'

Dekker gave him a slightly sheepish look. 'Maybe, but I had clout with him too. He and my father were colleagues in the Democratic Party; as a matter of fact, my dad nominated Mr Grace for the State senate. Of course, he wouldn't have gone to bat for me if he hadn't thought I was up to it, but he reached out to the people in Albany because of their history.'

'He still had contacts twenty years ago?'

Dekker glanced at him from beneath a raised eyebrow. 'Bob, your father-in-law still had contacts last week. Mr Grace told everyone that he gave up politics a long time ago, but that wasn't exactly true; shit, it wasn't at all true. He was a kingmaker among Democrats, and privately, through his contacts, he raised a lot of money for the Party. When the new US senator started angling after the nomination, he was the second person she came to see, straight after she saw the incumbent. He must have approved of her, because without the support of Leopold Grace . . . well, to say the least, she'd have found things a whole lot more difficult.'

'Mmm,' Skinner murmured. 'That's a side of the man that I never knew at all. Mind you, I have a natural antipathy towards politicians; maybe he read that and kept it from me.'

'That would have been just like him,' Dekker agreed. 'Other than in the courtroom, or in negotiation, he never forced his views in anyone's face. He was a very considerate, very polite man; and you won't find anyone in Buffalo to disagree with that opinion . . . not even our Republicans.' The Sheriff's jaw set in a firm line. 'That's what makes what happened to him and Mrs Grace so hard to take. Be sure, my friend, the killings might have taken place outside my jurisdiction, but I'm leaning pretty hard on the State police to get results.'

'In that case,' said Skinner, slowly, 'you won't be unhappy if I bring the investigation on to your doorstep.'

'Uhh? How you gonna do that?'

He glanced around the hall. 'Someone's been in this house, Sheriff; after Leo and Susannah were killed. The cabin by the lake was trashed, and the usual money, cards and valuables were taken to make it look like a robbery. But . . . the keys to this place were taken too.

'When I opened the house with the woman from the security firm, the alarm had been de-activated.' He paused for a second. 'Let me ask you something. Knowing Leo as you did, would you agree that it would have been unlike him to call the company to tell them he was leaving town, then forget to set the thing?'

The Sheriff nodded, vigorously. 'I sure would. He was just about the neatest man I ever met. And he didn't just phone the security people when he left; he always phoned the precinct office as well, to tell the desk sergeant there.'

'Could you call him to confirm that he did the same this time?'

'Sure.' He moved towards the hall table. 'I'll use this phone.'

'No,' said Skinner sharply. 'Use this one.' He took out his cellphone and gave it to the police chief. Dekker gave him a puzzled look, but took the phone and dialled, turning his back to the three others as the call was answered.

After a couple of minutes, he rang off and handed the phone back to the Scot. 'Not only did he speak to the precinct,' he told him heavily, 'he told the sergeant not to worry, that he was about to set the alarm. That tears it; you're right, someone's been in here.'

'I knew that for sure anyway,' Skinner confessed. 'We had a quick look round before you got here. Don't worry, we touched nothing, just looked. The house looks immaculate, but it's been searched. Look at that hall table, and at the dining table, and you'll find thick layers of dust on them both. Then go into Leo's den and look at his desk, and his filing cabinet. There's hardly any to be seen. Someone's given it an expert going over. But God knows what he was looking for; as far as I can see, nothing's been taken.'

'Shit,' Dekker hissed. 'In that case we better get the hell out of here and call in a scene-of-crime team.'

'Yes,' said Skinner, 'your people, certainly, but also, of necessity, the same team who went over the cabin in the Adirondacks. They need to look for forensic matches. You might want to send for the State detectives too, Schultz and Small; this thing has to be co-ordinated.'

'Shit again. A territorial war with the State cops is just what I do not need.'

'That may be over-ridden,' said Skinner.

'What do you mean?'

As if in reply, the big DCC handed him back the cellphone. 'First you give those orders, then we'll take it back to your office and I'll explain.'

The Sheriff nodded and made two calls; one short, to his own specialist unit, the other longer, to the head of the State Police Bureau of Criminal Investigation. Returning the phone to Skinner, he retrieved the key to his car from one of the patrolmen on the door then headed towards it, beckoning the three to follow him.

The journey into the centre of Buffalo took no more than twenty minutes. The Graces' house was in an eastern suburb of the small lakeside city, and as they drove westward the surroundings became first more industrial, then, as they passed the football ground, more commercial. The day was clear and cool; sitting in the back of the car that the FBI men had hired, Skinner wound down the window to enjoy the fresh air, and to listen to the universally familiar sound of the Lake Erie gulls.

Dekker's office was on the top floor of the low-rise headquarters building on Delaware Avenue, in the business heart of Buffalo; the city had always reminded him of Edinburgh, inasmuch as it appeared to be a tight-knit community, where everyone probably knew everyone else.

'No calls,' the Sheriff barked, brusquely, to his secretary as he ushered his three companions into his spacious room. He pointed them at a small conference table, and took a seat at its head. 'Okay, Bob, I ought to call the chief of my criminal investigation unit, but something tells me I should hold on that. Let's hear what you've got to say first,' he said.

Skinner laid his big silver document case on the table, opened it and took out a pile of computer print-outs, which Brand had given him when they had met at JFK, and which he had begun to study on the flight upstate. He separated them into two bundles, then looked Dekker straight in the eye. 'Do you know how many burglary homicides we have in Scotland in a year, Brad?'

'I have no idea.'

'None. Don't get me wrong, we have an endemic burglary problem, and we have our share of murders. Sometimes, in fact, it seems to me that in Edinburgh, we have more than our share . . .' he flashed an ironic grin '. . . at least when I'm around. But our thieves just do not break into people's homes, not even rich people's homes, with the intention of killing then robbing. Is it all that much different here?'

The Erie County Sheriff shook his head. 'No, I can't say as it is. Our homicides tend to be gang things, or family things.' He paused. 'But we're not talking about Buffalo here; we're talking about the Adirondacks. That's a whole different country.'

'Maybe so; but rural New York State actually has a lower homicide rate than you do. In fact it hardly has any. It also has a very low incidence of burglary. The place where Leo and Susannah were killed is remote, in terms of this part of the eastern United States at any rate; and that's true of most of the communities like it. From what I've been told by the BCI chief many of them barely are communities, just a collection of cabins gathered around lakesides, many of them empty for much of the year, furnished sparsely, with no valuables left there. Who's going to travel upstate to rip off a TV set and a few cheap knives and forks?

'Answer, no one. So let's get real, the guy who killed my in-laws went there to do just that.' He tapped the larger of the bundles before him. 'This stuff's from the FBI computer,' he said. 'Country-wide, in the last three years there have been fewer than ten genuine burglary homicides which match this one even remotely. So let's forget that theory. This was murder; first and foremost.

'If you want me to convince you, let's look at the way Leo and Susannah were killed. They weren't completely in the back of beyond, out there. The nearest cabin is half a mile away, and that lake is fished from dawn till midnight; there's always some bugger out in a boat. Sound travels, especially over water; the guy couldn't exactly have walked in with a sawn-off and blown them all over the fucking place. So he didn't: instead he strangled them with a wire garrotte. Why? Because he was a pro, and because that was his method of choice. I'd guess he watched them for a couple of days, saw Leo sit on the porch around suppertime, and chose that as his moment. The old man was taken completely by surprise, and so, I guess, was Susannah, since she was still in the kitchen when she was killed.

'Let's go on. How many murders have there been in the entire United States in the same three-year period in which the victims have been garrotted in the same way; that is, in which the killer has used a wire ligature?'

Dekker shook his head.

Skinner ruffled the smaller bundle on the desk. 'The answer, according to the great big computer, is twenty-five. Of these, twelve took place in Miami, Florida, and were the trademark of a gang called the Toledos, who chose to use lengths of razor-wire and to strangle their victims slowly. They were distinguished by the amount of blood at the scene; most of the poor bastards bled to death, in fact.

'Of the remaining thirteen, nine were domestic crimes, in which the victims . . . as it happens, they included five wives, one grandfather and three mothers-in-law . . . were related to the murderer. All of the perpetrators are now in jail, other than one who refused to appeal his death sentence and was executed three months ago.

'That leaves four, not counting Leo and Susannah. In every one of those cases the victim was murdered at home; two of them were Italians, known to have been involved in organised crime, and two of them were Colombians, a husband and wife, drug dealers who had been ripping off their suppliers.'

'Okay, I agree,' said the Sheriff. 'But how does that tie in with what you said back at the house, about jurisdiction over the investigation?'

Finally, Skinner smiled, the big broad smile of a card-player laying down a winning hand. 'On the journey upstate, and in my waking hours in the hotel, I've been through all of these burglary homicide reports.

They're very detailed; it says a lot for the FBI computer, ask it a specific question and you'll get an answer. It took a while, but eventually, I found two files which, set together, make interesting reading.

'One homicide took place in a suburb of Las Vegas two weeks ago. The victim's name was Sander Garrett; he lived alone in a big new luxury development on the outskirts of the city. He was found dead in his kitchen, cause of death a single gunshot wound to the head. His house had a security system, which Garrett normally set at night, but when the cops arrived they realised that it wasn't activated. There were no signs of forced entry.

'The other murder was committed five days later, in Helena, the state capital of Montana. Again the victim was a lone male, Bartholomew Wilkins. He was found dead in the den of his home by his wife, RoseAnne, when she got back from the shopping mall. The autopsy showed that he'd been killed by a single blow from a slim, stiletto-type blade, driven into his brain with great force.

'In each case, cash and other items were taken from the scene of the crime, and it was written up as a burglary in which the victim had disturbed his killer.

'Until now, that is.'

The big Scot leaned forward across the desk, his shoulders hunching in the jacket of his dark suit.

'You see, Sheriff, there are three very remarkable coincidences in these two cases, which tie them right to the murders of Leo and Susannah. Both victims were retired lawyers. Both of them were or had been active and prominent Democrats. Both of them, early in their careers, had spent time in Washington, at the same time as Leo Grace.'

Dekker looked at him across the table, and let out a long slow whistle. 'Fucking-A,' he murmured, with a deep frown creasing his forehead. Brand and Kosinski sat silent, their slightly stunned expressions offering proof, if any had been needed, that they had not sneaked a look at the documents before handing them over.

Skinner put the files back into his attaché case. 'I was asked . . . informally, I stress . . . by my friend Joe Doherty, the deputy director of the Bureau, to report to him on what I found at the lake.' He glanced at the two agents. 'Correct me if I'm wrong, gentlemen, but when a crime goes interstate, it becomes your responsibility, yes?'

Brand nodded, firmly. 'That is correct, sir.'

'In that case,' said the Scot, glancing back at Dekker, 'to come back to what I said earlier, you may not need to worry about a turf battle with the

State police. I suspect that the FBI may want to take charge of this one.'

The Buffalo Sheriff's expression was one of pure, unadulterated relief; he looked more than ever like a politician rather than a policeman. 'Do you want to call your friend, Bob,' he asked, 'or will I?'

22

'Seriously though, Andy, is this job not what you choose to make it?' asked Dan Pringle, with a trademark tug at a corner of his heavy moustache.

The outgoing Head of CID looked across the desk at his successor, as if trying to determine whether he was serious. 'That depends entirely on the level of your ambition, my friend. If your main objective is to maximise your pension and get the hell out of here at the earliest opportunity, you would certainly approach it in that frame of mind.

'If, on the other hand, you do not fancy having your door kicked in every other day by a deputy chief constable waving worsening clear-up figures in your face, you'll approach it with just one single objective, that being to make sure that for as long as you're sat in this chair, every CID division is working at its maximum efficiency.'

'Aye,' said Pringle, a slow grin spreading across his face. 'That was more or less what I supposed. So every time you chewed us out at the Monday morning meeting, it was because Big Bob had given you a doing?'

'Not invariably,' Andy Martin answered. 'Most of the time it was to make sure that he didn't give me a doing. Chief Super or not, you do not want his boot on your neck; so, as of next week, when you're sat in this chair you'll find yourself concentrating very hard on avoiding that possibility.'

Pringle gestured over his shoulder with his thumb. 'By kicking the crap out of the likes of Mario here, you mean?'

'Exactly.'

'Give me a break!' McGuire protested, from his seat against the wall. 'I'm not even in the job yet and you're getting at me. Give me a chance to make mistakes before you take me to task for them.'

'Why? Have you got any in mind?' asked Martin.

'One or two; just for openers, I was thinking of head-butting my new boss for pinching the best detective sergeant in the division.'

Pringle looked at him, all innocence. 'Big Jack McGurk, you mean? Christ, and here was me thinking I was going to get away with that without you noticing.'

'Think again then. You're a fucking asset-stripper . . . with respect . . . sir.'

'I was going to tell you, Mario, honest. I just haven't had an opportunity until now. I know McGurk's good; that's why I took him to the Borders Division in the first place, and that's why I want him in my office when I move up here. There's more to it than that, though; there's his marriage as well. If I leave him down there, that's done for. They've tried hard, but it's just not working just now.'

'What? Are you a social worker, too?'

A flash of real annoyance showed for a second in the older man's eyes. 'No, but I've been long enough in my rank to have become a decent man manager. We all have to learn that skill; mostly the hard way, like you with that bloody Tommy Gavigan. Aye, I could leave big Jack down there and he'd do a good job for you, but if I give him a chance to patch things up with his missus, he'll do a better job for me.

'Anyhow, don't get your Calvin fucking Kleins in a twist, you're getting a first-class substitute. Young Sammy Pye's going down to take his place.'

McGuire looked at Martin. The Chief Superintendent nodded. 'That's the game plan,' he confirmed. 'Sam's been here long enough, and he's every bit as good an operator as McGurk. You can take my word for that.'

'That's fine, Andy, but am I going to find myself with another domestic situation there, like Dan did with Jack?'

'What? With Sammy and Ruthie McConnell, you mean? No, not at all; they're getting married in the autumn, and they're going to live in Gorebridge. They can both travel to work easily enough from there.'

Pringle nodded in confirmation, then glanced at Martin. 'What are you and Karen going to do about that, Andy?' he asked. 'Are you two moving house?'

'No choice,' the DCS answered.

'How's Karen doing?' asked McGuire, blowing them away.

'Great,' Martin replied. 'First-rate, blooming, glowing with health and all that stuff . . . now that she's well past throwing up every morning, that is. She's decided that we're moving to Perth, rather than Dundee. We're going to look at houses there at the weekend; we've got to sort it out sharpish, either that or put it off for a bit. She's due in a couple of months.'

The big superintendent laughed softly. 'How are you going to get a baby chair into the MGF, Andy?'

'Sore point. The sports car's going down the road; as of next week it's turning into a new Mondeo.'

'Bloody hell! What happened to the Andy Martin we knew, and a thousand women loved?'

'Same as happened to you, McGuire. He met the right woman. Oh aye, and that reminds me. Willie Haggerty asked me for the okay to have your Maggie stand in for Manny English while he's away investigating Strathclyde. It came as a bit of a surprise, even to me, when he told me she's agreed.'

'It was a surprise to her too; ACC Haggerty must be a persuasive bugger. It's only a temporary thing, though; just to let her get the feel of the job.'

Martin grinned. 'So now she's responsible for everything that goes on in the division. Every crime, every public nuisance, every waif and stray.'

'Aye,' said McGuire heavily. 'And that could be a bit of a problem.'

23

Joe Doherty, sallow-faced as ever, drew on a cigarette as he looked around Bradford Dekker's conference table. He was the only person there who was smoking, and the fixed expression on the face of the Erie County Sheriff made it clear that in his view that was one too many. 'I mean it. Those things will kill you one day, my friend,' murmured Bob Skinner, sat on his right.

'You keep telling me that,' replied the American, quietly, 'but living does that in the end, any way you go about it. Look at your father-in-law; I bet he never smoked in his life.'

'You lose,' said Dekker, close enough to overhear. 'Mr Grace loved a Monte Cristo after dinner.'

'That's true,' Skinner agreed. 'He always had a supply handy, wherever he went. The Dominican Republic variety, of course, never Cuban,' he added with a faint grin, which vanished as quickly as it had appeared. 'Shit!' he whispered, then glanced along the table. 'Lieutenant Schultz, can you remember; did you find any cigars at the cabin? I don't remember seeing any.'

The New York detective frowned as he searched his memory, then opened a folder on the desk before him and looked through several pages. 'I don't recall that, sir,' he answered, finally, 'and there's no mention of them on the inventory.'

'So? Could that be the first thing we know about this killer: that he's a cigar smoker, and couldn't resist taking them with him?'

'Unless the first guys on the scene found them,' said Schultz, quickly. 'Those boys out there can be a touch . . .'

'I resent that, Lieutenant,' snapped Dekker, cutting across him, 'on behalf of county police forces everywhere. You State people . . .'

'Resent all you like, Brad, but it's a valid point.' The only female voice in the room belonged to Superintendent Barbara Weston, the head of the New York State Police, a severe-looking woman in her early fifties.

Doherty's presence at the hastily called morning conference in Buffalo had attracted a top-drawer turn-out from the agencies involved. There

88

were nine people at the table; three FBI: the deputy director, Brand and Kosinski; three from the State police: Weston, Schultz and Small; Dekker and his chief of detectives, Eddie Brady, and Skinner himself. The DCC had been invited by Doherty, with Dekker's agreement, to attend the conference as an observer, although his presence had caused the superintendent to raise a disapproving eyebrow.

'Yes, it probably is, Barbara,' Doherty drawled. 'It might have been more tactfully put, that's all. We will check it out . . . discreetly, I promise. If Bob and Brad are certain that there should have been cigars in the cabin, that may be significant. As Deputy Chief Skinner points out, at the moment we know nothing about this man other than he's a professional. If he took the damn things, that's item number one in his personal profile. He's hardly going to fence them, is he; no, he's gonna smoke 'em.' He smiled. 'Trust me on this.'

He paused, stubbing out his cigarette in the heavy glass ashtray which Dekker's secretary had found for him, then taking a mouthful of coffee from the mug before him on the table. 'Okay, let's cut the trivia, end the inter-force sniping and get this discussion on the road. What are we looking at here?'

With barely a break, he answered his own question. 'Four homicides, one of them a double, in three different states, all within the last month. Common factors are as follows. We have three men and one woman, all retired and aged over sixty . . . over seventy in the case of Mr Grace. We have three incidents reported initially as burglary-related homicide, and accepted as such by the responsible jurisdictions.

'Common factors, the men's profession, their political allegiance, and the fact that they all worked in Washington at the time of the Kennedy administration.'

Skinner raised a hand. 'Common factors that we know of, Joe.'

'Three's enough for me, buddy.'

'Maybe, but should it be?' Barbara Weston broke in. 'They have crime everywhere, even in Asshole, Montana, or wherever. And the three locations are hundreds, even thousands of miles apart. Okay, three retired lawyers are burglarised; lawyers are rich, so they get robbed. Okay, so they're all Democrats. Democrats get killed every day in this country; so do Republicans. Okay, so they all worked in Washington. It's just about before my time, but in the early sixties, it's my understanding that every ambitious young Democrat lawyer wanted to be there, and that a hell of a lot of them made it.'

'Leo Grace wasn't an ambitious young lawyer, Barbara,' Sheriff Dekker interjected. 'He was a senator in this state's legislature for six years before he joined the Attorney General's office under Kennedy.'

'Okay, strike out the young lawyer part, but don't tell me that he wasn't ambitious.' Her gaze switched to Doherty. 'And what about Garrett and Wilkins? Do we know whether they worked in the same area as Senator Grace? In fact do we know if they ever even met?'

'No, we do not,' the Deputy Director admitted, his face showing his impatience. 'Their files aren't complete, we only know that they worked in DC, not what they did there. Come on, Superintendent, spit it out. Say what you're leading up to.'

'If you insist, Mr Doherty. Frankly, I think that the Bureau's grounds for showing up here are at best questionable and at worst contrived. Our friend from Scotland . . . your friend . . . shows up here and is given instant access to material it would take me weeks to screw out of you. Next thing we know he's used it to weave a fanciful conspiracy theory and you're jumping in to back him up, to the extent of letting him take part in a conference that he has no business even observing.

'He sees a hit-man rubbing out retired Democrats; I see a single burglary homicide on my territory and I see no reason why Lieutenant Schultz and his team shouldn't be allowed to clear it up. As for your friend, I sympathise with his loss, but I'd advise him to bury his father-in-law and get the hell back home.'

Doherty's eyes narrowed. 'I hear . . .'

Skinner put a hand on his shoulder, looking past him, along the table. 'A second please, Joe. Superintendent, I know that you're a career police officer, but you're appointed by the governor, and the state senate, so let me ask you something. Have you ever in your life worked as a member of a criminal investigation team?'

Barbara Weston hesitated for a second too long.

'No,' he said, fixing her with an icy, unblinking glare, locking eyes with her so powerfully that it seemed that however hard she might try, she could not look away. 'I didn't think so; your type of copper exists the world over.

'Well, madam, I have dirtied my hands with crime for nearly all my professional career. I've chased villains of all shapes and sizes: serial killers, gangsters, thieves, terrorists, drug pushers and all the rest, and do you know what? I've caught nearly all of them; apart from the ones that the competition got to before I did.

'I haven't done that by being lucky, or weaving fanciful theories. I've done it by being a bloody good analytical detective. If Joe Doherty's invited me to sit at this table, he hasn't done so because he's my friend. He's done it because he thinks I can contribute something. And what I'm telling you is this; these four murders are linked. That isn't supposition; at the least, it's a probability flowing from the facts as they exist. And in my experience there's a very fine line between probability and certainty.

'Oh yes, and one more thing. If you want me to go home before this crime is cleared up, you may have to deport me . . . but I don't think you have the clout to do that.'

He released the Superintendent from his glare and nodded to Doherty. 'I'm sorry, Joe. You were saying?'

'You just said it,' muttered the Deputy Director, tersely, and turned back to Weston. 'You want me to give Bob status, Barbara? Okay, as of now he's a special adviser in this investigation which will . . .' he leaned on the word '. . . be co-ordinated by the Bureau. We can do this one of two ways; either we take things over completely, or we work in co-operation with your department, using the skills and local expertise of Schultz and Small, partnered with Special Agent Kosinski.'

He glanced along at Dekker. 'Same would go for your department, Brad, given that we're certain the killer came to Buffalo also.

'You two people up for that or would you rather butt out now?'

'I'm more than happy to work with the Bureau,' replied the Sheriff, quickly. He and Doherty turned back to the Superintendent.

'I'm not being frozen out of my own jurisdiction, Mr Deputy Director, not by you or by anyone else. We'll go along with you, but I insist on being advised of any development that could lead to an indictment in this state.'

Doherty nodded. 'You will be so advised,' he agreed. 'But you will not move for any such indictment, nor release the identity of any person who might be a suspect. My director was confirmed in office by a political colleague of your state governor; remember that.' Weston's eyes blazed at his blatant threat, but she said nothing more.

'Fine,' he said, looking around the table once more. 'Let's move forward. Brand, Kosinski, you are seconded to this investigation, until otherwise advised by me. Troy, you will remain in New York as I have said, and will co-ordinate things here, advising me, Sheriff Dekker and Superintendent Weston of progress made. You will concentrate first and foremost on putting a name to our killer.'

'How are we going to do that, sir?' asked the Special Agent.

'Bob?' Doherty's invitation took his friend by surprise. 'Come on, don't hold back. You are the senior detective here. I've been out of the field for years.'

'You probably won't, Mr Kosinski,' Skinner answered, bluntly. 'Like I said earlier, this guy's been covering his tracks pretty carefully. So all you can do is to concentrate on the basics, and hope he's made a mistake. You have to look out for the use of a stolen credit card, but that is not going to happen. No, I would send the forensic team back out to the cabin, and keep them at the house until they've been over every inch of it. Look for matches between the two locations; fingerprints, fibres from clothing . . .'

'Cigar butts?' murmured Barbara Weston sarcastically.

'Yes!' Skinner snapped at her. 'You never dismiss anything, until you've disproved it, or you're in neglect of your duty as an investigator.' He looked at the Erie County detective chief. 'Right, Mr Brady?'

'Absolutely, sir,' the man concurred.

'That being the case . . .' he continued. 'Leo loved cigars, but there were none in the cabin, so it's a real possibility that our man took them. He's a cool bastard this one, so maybe, just maybe, he smoked one while he was going through the house. If he did, then, just maybe, he left the stub. Criminals have been caught through simpler mistakes than that. There's a guy doing life in Britain who probably wouldn't have been convicted if he'd paid cash for his petrol on a few specific days, years before he was arrested.'

He turned to Schultz, who looked back at him, intently. 'Lieutenant, you should send your people back to that cabin and you tell them to look for cigar butts. Tell them to look in the garbage if they have to. If they find any, tell them to take saliva samples from every one, and do DNA comparisons against Leo Grace. If one doesn't match, that could be your killer.'

'It would be, surely, sir?' Kosinski said.

'Not necessarily, son. Leo was generous with his Monte Cristos; first Christmas after Sarah and I were married he sent me a box. He could have had friends for supper any time before he was killed and handed them round. I know that as part of your investigation you'll be trying to trace everyone who was in the cabin that last time they were there, to eliminate their fingerprints. If you find any, and if you find any butts, you should take spit samples as well as prints.

'However, as I said, that's a long shot. Back to the basics; if you find any matching traces at both locations, other than of Leo and Susannah, you're on a winner. But even if you don't, you should feed every wild print you have into your mainframe and see what you get. Fibre matches are more difficult, but you have to do them too. I'd suggest too that you make sure your teams take comparison samples from every garment, every towel, in the cabin and the house.

'You think this is overkill, Superintendent?' he asked, with a glance at Eddie Brady, the Erie County detective chief. 'Well it ain't. It's what you have to do when you're dealing with a man like this. You have to look closely at the scene, then closer and closer and closer, until you find that one tiny mistake, the one that's going to catch him. You also have to look in the right way. I had an inquiry in Scotland a while back that might have been written off as a suicide, had a young police constable not looked at the scene and spotted something that to her eye was wrong.'

He grinned at Kosinski, Schultz and Small. 'Sorry, lads,' he chuckled. 'You're in for some boring times, but that's what you signed up for.'

He leaned back in his chair. 'That's what I'd do, Joe.'

The Deputy Director nodded. 'That's what'll happen. Now,' he went on, briskly, 'let's look at the other crimes we're targeting. First, the murder of Sander Garrett: Special Agent Brand, you will go to Nevada, where you will interface with the City of North Las Vegas Police Department. I have already spoken to Chief of Police Hall, although I have not briefed him in detail on what this is all about. His is a small department, with fewer than two hundred officers, so he may well be glad to see you.

'Zak, I want you to examine the scope and structure of the investigation as it has been carried out so far, looking initially at the forensic reports on Mr Garrett's house. Chief Hall didn't say so, but I have a feeling that you won't find a hell of a lot. If you feel that it's necessary, and the crime scene is still reasonably intact, you have my authority to fly in a team of our people to go over the place with the same thoroughness that is being applied to the Grace residences. When you're satisfied that you have all you're gonna get, touch base with Troy to run comparisons on unidentified prints and fibre samples.

'Also, I want you to find out everything you can about Sander Garrett. Give me a complete report on his career after his Washington years. He was still a consultant to his law firm in Vegas, so you should interview the partners there and find out what he was into. Speak to any family members you can find and to any friends he had locally. Put together an up-to-date profile of the man and find out, if you can, just what he did in Washington. Make your own judgement about the local resources; if you have to, call me and I'll detach people from the LA Bureau to work with you.'

'Yes, sir,' Brand exclaimed. 'I'll leave as soon as this conference is over.'

'You do that,' Doherty agreed. 'That leaves us with the first-degree murder of Bartholomew Wilkins, formerly of Chicago, Illinois, now of Asshole, or rather, Helena, Montana.'

'Excuse me, sir.' Troy Kosinski raised a hand, his unlined, earnest face looking almost like that of a schoolboy. 'What about the political angle?'

'Leave that alone for now. It may be significant, it may not; let's just see what the co-ordinated investigation of the three locations has to throw up. Speaking of which . . .' Doherty's lean face creased in a mischievous grin.

'Like I said, I've been out of the field for years, and this whole business intrigues me. So I thought I'd cover that end myself. The Helena Police Department has only seven detectives, so the Montana Department of Justice Criminal Bureau has been advising on the investigation; I'm meeting their chief tomorrow.'

He glanced at Skinner. 'Bob, it'll be a couple of days before the scene-of-crime teams are finished at the Grace residence. When does Sarah plan to arrive?'

'We're looking at next Monday. She wants to get the kids used to the idea of the nanny living in before she leaves them.'

'In that case, you'll have nothing to do but sit on your hands . . . unless you'd care to accompany me to the Queen City of the Rockies, as she likes to call herself.'

24

The address which McGuire's DSS friend had volunteered proved to be a tenement flat in a cul-de-sac off Newhaven Road, not far from its junction with Bonnington Road. The detective drove past the narrow entrance door, parked as close to it as he could, and walked back. He glanced at his watch; it was ten minutes to six; even if George Rosewell was a betting man, the last race was long past the post.

There had been no call from Mrs Dewberry, but his instincts had told him not to expect one. His unwanted father-in-law was still an absentee from a job which he would find was no longer there if he ever thought to return to it.

He came to the dirty green door that closed off the tenement stairway. It was one of the few left in the city in which an entry-phone system had not been installed. It was stiff, but he shoved it firmly, wrenching it back on its dry hinges, hearing the squeal of wood on the concrete floor. A smell of urine and cabbage rolled out to greet him, reminding him of visits to prisons he had made in his younger days in the force.

'Nice, Daddy, nice,' he murmured.

Rosewell's address was F2, second floor; he trudged up the stone staircase, noting that each step was worn in the centre with over a hundred years of use.

There were three doors on each landing; left, right and centre. The one for which he was looking faced him as he reached the top of the stair. It was grey; the gloss of its paint was long gone, and it was scuffed and scratched; the name was there, though, on a cheap white plastic plate below the letterbox. A narrow opaque glass panel was set at eye level; no light shone through it.

He pressed the bell button, but heard no sound from inside. He did it once more, for luck; still silence. Bunching his right fist, he thumped the door hard, making enough noise to waken a deaf night-shift worker. 'Come on, you bastard,' he muttered. 'Make it easy; be in.' He listened in vain for sounds of stirring, before pounding once more, and waiting again, listening to the silence.

'Where are you, you old fucker!' He glanced to his right and left. 'Aye well,' he muttered. 'Family business after all.' The door was locked by a single Yale. He took out a bunch of skeleton keys and tried them, one by one, looking for a match; he had third time luck. The latch clicked and the door swung open.

It occurred to him afterwards that he had never considered the possibility that Rosewell might be lying dead in his flat; nor had Mrs Dewberry. As a young constable he had opened a few houses after neighbours had reported a pile-up of newspapers in the letterbox, or a line of milk bottles at the front door. He remembered the smell; too right he remembered it.

But there was no trace of it in Rosewell's two-apartment; only staleness, only sourness, the scent of a man on his own, one with no great regard for his surroundings. 'George,' McGuire barked, as he stepped inside. 'Surprise, surprise; it's your son-in-law, come to batter the crap out of you. Where the fuck are you, you old bastard?'

There were only three doors off the hall, and all of them were open. He glanced into them, one by one. The bathroom was to his left, toilet seat up, towel on the floor beneath the electrically heated rail. The bedroom was straight ahead, discarded underwear still on the floor, duvet thrown back to reveal a sheet which had once been white, but which now was grey and heavily stained. The living area was on his right; he stepped inside.

At once, the heat, which he had felt in the hallway, became almost overpowering. He looked round the door and saw an electric fire, set in the wall, its three radiant bars shining. He found the switch and turned it off. The room was furnished sparsely; one old fabric-covered sofa facing a television set, a small sideboard, a kitchen table, and two dining chairs. There was a sink under the one window, a cooker to the left and a small work surface and fridge on the other side.

A dirty plate and cutlery lay on the table. He looked at it; scraps of pastry from a round Scotch mutton pie, unmistakable, a few beans in their tomato sauce and a sad, solitary, greasy chip. 'You'll have had your tea, then, George,' he murmured. 'But when?'

The answer came to him from the newspaper, which lay beside the empty, tea-stained mug. It was open at the sports section; his eye was caught by an action shot of two footballers, green shirt and blue, squaring up to each other like street corner punks. Without picking it up he looked at the top of the page. 'The *Sunday Mail*,' he exclaimed. 'And you've been off your work since Monday.'

He scratched his head. It had been unusually cold on the previous Sunday evening, he recalled. 'You had your tea and you went out, didn't you?' he asked the empty room. 'And you left the fire on. Was that by accident, or was it on purpose, to warm your old Portuguese bones when you came in?

'Only you never did.

'Where are you, you old bastard? What are you up to? I guess I'd better ask around.'

He left the small flat, leaving the door closed but unlocked; and stepped over to the door on the right, through which light shone. The nameplate on the door read, 'Brennan'. He pressed the bell and as he did so, heard a child's yell from inside. 'Daddy!'

Somehow, he had been expecting a woman, but it was a girl who answered, fifteen, maybe sixteen, he guessed, not yet grown to full height, still no more than five feet tall. She held the door on a chain, and looked at him through the gap, suspiciously. *I would be too, dear*, he thought. *Good for you.*

'Miss Brennan?' he asked, giving her what he hoped was a reassuring smile.

'Ms,' she answered, her expression unchanged; there was something in her voice that struck him as strange. She was barefoot, he noticed, with blond hair that might just have been for real, and a waif-like look about her that would have pulled him in about two seconds flat . . . when he was sixteen years old. There was a toddler clinging to her leg, a boy.

'Sorry to bother you,' he went on. 'I'm George Rosewell's son-in-law, and I'm looking for him, only he's not in. I wondered if you had seen him lately.'

'You're a policeman,' she said.

'Maybe so,' he agreed, widening his grin, 'but I'm also George's son-in-law.'

'I don't believe you.' Her accent was unusual for the outskirts of Leith; he wondered if she might be English. 'George told me he doesn't have any family.'

'Sure, and he told you his name was Rosewell, but that's not true either. Listen, my name's Mario, and there's the proof. Can I come in?' He showed her his warrant card; she surprised him by reading it . . . unusually in his experience, a quick flash of the plastic was enough.

The youngster nodded and loosened the chain. 'Yes, okay,' she said, sweeping the child up in her arms.

His eyes widened as he stepped inside; the hall was bright and fresh, its carpet plush and relatively new. The living area had been modernised completely. Essentially the apartment had the same layout as the one across the hall, but the two were worlds apart. This was a home, adequately furnished and equipped, comfortable, and well looked after; by comparison, the other was no more than a doss-house.

'What's your other name?' asked McGuire.

'Ivy,' said the girl.

He reached across and tickled the toddler under the chin, as he had done, once upon a time, with Lauren and Spencer, McIlhenney's two children. 'Who's the kid? Your wee brother?'

'My son, actually. His name's Rufus.'

He stared at her. 'How old are you?' he blurted out.

Without a word, she turned, and walked over to a tall unit set against the wall. She opened a drawer, took out a photographic driving licence, and handed it to him. 'It's all right,' she told him, in a patient tone. *Yes. Definitely English*, he thought, as she spoke. 'I'm used to it. I'm twenty-two, and every time I go out for a drink I have to carry that to prove it. I'm walking justification for a national identity card.'

He looked at the plastic-coated licence. The photograph was unusually good; it was her, and she was indeed twenty-two.

'I'm sorry,' he said. 'Rude of me.'

'No, really.' She smiled for the first time. 'I am used to it. It can come in handy at times.'

'What about Rufus's father? Is he . . .'

'He's gone. I'm a lone parent.'

'Does he visit you often?'

'When he feels like it. But that's okay; we get along fine, although he's not really interested in his son. He just goes through the motions of being a dad, that's all.'

'Does he support you?'

'No. My parents do. I have a degree in film studies, and once Rufus starts school I'll begin my career, but until then, I'm okay.'

There was something about the girl-woman that fascinated him. 'What about this?' He glanced around him. 'It's very comfy and all that, but this building ain't the finest piece of architecture in Edinburgh.'

She laughed. 'Blame my father for that, or his stupid solicitor. The seller told them that there was an improvement grant in place, and that it was all going to be done up. Wrong.'

She sat Rufus on the floor, beside a large stuffed panda. 'So what were you saying about George? That isn't his real name?'

'No.' He took the school photograph from his pocket. 'That's him, yes?'

She looked at it, frowning. 'Yes, that's George . . . apart from the beard. He's got a beard now.'

'How well do you know him?'

'Just as a neighbour, that's all. He's the only one in here I do know. So what is his real name?'

'Go back twenty-three years and he was called Jorge Xavier Rose; he's a mix of Scots and Portuguese.'

'And what happened twenty-three years ago to make him change his name?'

'You don't want to know. Just you take my advice, Ms Brennan, if he shows up here again, don't ever let him into your house.'

'I won't, don't you worry. Do you think he's gone, then?'

McGuire shrugged. 'He hasn't been home since Sunday night, of that I'm sure; plus he hasn't been to work since then. Maybe he's had an accident. I'll need to check that out. Or maybe he's got second sight; maybe he felt my hot breath on his neck, and decided to leave town.'

'I don't think I'd like your hot breath on my neck,' Ivy said. She paused and looked up at him, narrowing her eyes. '. . . Or maybe I would.'

He felt heat on his own neck, and found himself hoping that it did not show on his face.

'Did you really mean that George is over sixty?' she asked him, stubbing out a fledgling fantasy.

'He's sixty-three.'

'Well that's something else he lied about. He told me he was fifty-five.'

McGuire shook his head. 'I don't think there's any truth in his life.' He looked at her, then around the room. 'Are you on the phone?'

'I use a mobile. Let me guess. You want me to call you if he shows up here again?'

'Got it in one. These are my numbers.' He gave her a card from the supply in his breast pocket.

She showed him to the door and out of her oasis, back into the smelly grey place outside. 'Nice to meet you,' she said. 'I will call you, I promise. Maybe I'll call you even if George doesn't show up.'

He heard the door close behind her as he stepped back across the landing and into Rosewell's flat. The living room had cooled a little while he had been gone, but it was still uncomfortably warm. He wanted to get out, to leave the place behind him, but there was something he had to do first.

He took a pair of surgical gloves from his jacket pocket and slipped them on. Other than the newspaper, he had touched nothing since he had been in the flat, and he wanted to leave the scene untainted. The sideboard had three drawers. The first contained cutlery, and the second was empty, except for a few tea towels. He opened the bottom drawer, the third, and saw what he was after; piles of bank statements and credit-card slips, laid side by side. He took them out and laid them on the table, then leafed through them, carefully. There was nothing exceptional about either group. The bank account showed Rosewell's salary paid in on the last day of each month, plus regular debits for council tax, and other withdrawals by cheque or cash card. It was always in credit with a minimum balance of one thousand pounds.

The other stack of bills showed that the credit card was used infrequently, but that when it was, the balance was always settled in full, before interest charges could accrue.

McGuire noted down the numbers of the bank account and the credit card, plus the address of his Clydesdale Bank branch, then picked up the piles, in the same order as before, to return them to the drawer.

He was about to put them in, when he saw what had been lying underneath, and froze in his tracks. It was a cutting from a newspaper . . . the *Scotsman*, he guessed, by the typeface . . . beginning to yellow with age. It was a report on a high court trial, and it carried a photograph of one of the crown witnesses.

He had no need to read the caption, but he did: *Seen leaving court after her evidence, Detective Chief Inspector Margaret Rose.*

25

'I guess this means you won't be at the football tonight,' Neil McIlhenney grunted. He stood in his living room with his sport bag in one hand, and the phone in the other. He had been on the point of leaving for North Berwick, only to be halted by its summons.

'You guess correctly,' Bob Skinner agreed. 'Give my apologies to the rest of the Thursday Legends and tell them I'll be back as soon as I can.'

'And when will that be, d'you reckon?'

'Jeez, Neil, I wish I could tell you for sure. The bodies will be released tomorrow by the coroner in Loudonville, and I've instructed an undertaker in Buffalo to collect them and make all the arrangements. Sarah's booked a flight arriving next Monday, but there's no certainty that we'll be able to have the funerals next week. Leo was an important guy so the service will be public; from what Brad Dekker tells me, half the city will want to be there.

'Not just that, the new senator and her husband want to put in an appearance. That will get the Secret fucking Service involved. I didn't break that news to Sarah when I spoke to her; I'm saving it until I see her, so keep it to yourself for now.'

'Of course.' McIlhenney hesitated. 'Boss, what do you think you've got yourself into over there?'

'I wish I knew, mate. All I do know is that these three murders are linked. As soon as I read the reports I was certain of that; so's Joe, now he's looked at them. Every one of them was a professional job; in every one of them the items taken were the same; mere bloody trifles. You do not put three bullets in the middle of somebody's forehead just to steal his Rolex. You do not ram a stiletto into someone's head just for his credit card. You do not garrotte a man and his wife because you want his cigars.

'On top of all that, you have the professional and political links, and the fact that the three killings have all taken place within a two-week period. I can't be wrong, can I?'

'Well . . . Motherwell could win the Premier League next year,' said the inspector. 'I think the odds would be about the same. No, you're right. But what makes you think it's the same man who did all three?'

He heard a soft familiar laugh on the other end of the line. 'That's a question none of my distinguished American law enforcement colleagues has asked as yet. Who says I do think that? We're talking in terms of one man, because that's the way the hare started running, but it's no certainty at all. Still . . .' There was a pause. 'We're into hunch territory now, but my feeling is that it was. Like I said, no one's questioned that assumption; not till you.' He paused. 'I'd expect no less of you, mate, but . . . My gut still says it's one man. There's been an efficiency about each murder that's like a trademark. If I'm wrong and there's a team of them out there, we're in real fucking trouble!

'On that basis, the FBI's flexing its muscles. Joe has agents checking all passenger movements through Greater Buffalo Airport, McCarran in Las Vegas and Great Falls International . . . that's around a hundred miles from Helena, and it's where we're going this afternoon. People go to Vegas from all over the States for all sorts of reasons, but if we find someone who's been there, been to Buffalo, and been to Montana, all in the last couple of weeks, he's going to be put under the microscope.'

'It's right up your street, all this, isn't it,' McIlhenney observed. 'I don't mean burying your father-in-law; I mean jetting across umpteen states with an FBI big-wig on an investigation. If it wasn't for the circumstances, you'd be like a kid with the key to an ice-cream factory.'

'You're not wrong there,' Skinner admitted. 'I'm glad Joe asked me to get involved, otherwise I'd have gone out of my tree just sitting here doing nothing. God, I might even have started my own investigation.'

'That's fine,' said his friend quietly, 'until Monday, when Sarah gets over there.'

'What do you mean?'

'I mean that when she does, you should only be thinking of one thing; that she's lost her parents. She's borne up very well in Scotland, but when she gets back home, it's going to hit her hard. She's going to want to see them. She's going to want to see where they died. She's going to have a lot to come to terms with.

'So, Bob . . .' it did not occur to either of them that McIlhenney had only once before addressed Skinner by his Christian name, '. . . you have to be with her, and completely focused on her personal and emotional needs, rather than tear-arseing around America on an inter-jurisdictional investigation which, professionally at least, is none of your business.

'I'm sorry to be so blunt,' he concluded, suddenly awkward, 'and if that didn't need saying I apologise. But, well . . . What the hell, I thought it did.'

Silence hung there for a couple of seconds. 'Aye,' said Skinner finally. 'And you were right. Thanks, pal, I appreciate it. The only thing is, I think that one of my big problems may be in keeping Sarah from getting herself involved in the bloody investigation!' He paused again.

'I do want to see her, though. I'd rather be with her than here, make no mistake about that, but that's how she wanted it. I'm sorry to leave you guys in the lurch too, in these times of change. Most of all I'm sorry to miss young ACC Martin's farewell party. Where's he having it? There was nothing arranged when I left.'

'We're going for a meal in La Rusticana in Cockburn Street, then we're off to listen to jazz in the Cellar Bar in Chambers Street. Kicks off at half eight; ambulances at one a.m.'

'What about Jimmy's senior officers' dinner tonight?'

'Postponed,' said McIlhenney. 'The Chief's going to wait until you're back.'

'Good for him. I feel better about that.'

'That leads me to something I have to ask you. What about my move to SB? It's supposed to happen on Monday, when Mario heads off to the Borders Division. Do you want to put a hold on everything, save Dan Pringle's move, and leave the deputy in charge in the Borders, pro tem?'

'No,' Skinner replied, firmly. 'I've thought about that. My private office is secondary in my absence; you go ahead with your move. Keep an eye on my stuff long distance, you and Ruthie can manage that between you. Take anything with a health warning on it straight to Willie Haggerty.

'But what I do want you to do,' he went on, 'is to appoint your own successor.'

'Eh? You serious?'

'Sure I am. You know better than anyone, bar Andy, how I think and how I work. Look at the available talent, either a detective sergeant or a recently promoted DI, and make a choice.'

'I'd pick Jack McGurk, right now,' said McIlhenney, 'but Mr Pringle plans on bringing him in as his own exec.'

Skinner thought for a moment or two. 'Listen, if you think big Jack's the man for the job, pull rank. Tell Dan I want him and that's that. He'll huff for a bit, but he owes me one, and he bloody knows it. Go on; do it. I'll hose down the new head of CID if necessary.'

'Okay, if you say so. Christ,' the Inspector laughed, 'you can cause bloody chaos from three thousand miles away.'

26

'Well my God; it's our Mario! It's not like you to frequent the family business. What brings you here?' Paula Viareggio grinned at her cousin across the counter, her dark eyes carrying a mix of mockery and challenge, as they had done since they were children.

'A packet of porcini mushrooms and some Seranno ham, actually,' he said.

As he looked at Paula, across the counter, he was struck by the contrast she presented to the girl he had just left. Ivy Brennan was locked in a sort of extended childhood, her life shaped by her diminutive size and her elfin features. Paula, on the other hand, was ageless, her silver hair, high cheekbones and velvet skin giving her the appeal of a work of art, of an old master oil painting.

For a time in his late teens and early twenties, Mario McGuire had lusted after his Uncle Beppe's older daughter . . . something which Paula had understood from an early stage. The challenge had been in her eyes from that time on, but he had been sensible enough to know that if he rose to it, he would be setting off down a dangerous path from which there would be no turning. There had been a couple of close calls though; one at a party at Beppe's, and another after he had left home, when Paula had turned up at his flat late at night with a couple of drinks under her belt and mischief on her mind. And in truth, there had been another night, another party at which everyone had been very drunk, after which he had never been entirely certain what had happened. He had never asked, and Paula had never mentioned it.

'Mushrooms and ham indeed,' she laughed, scornfully.

'Why not? We're having friends for dinner and Maggie's got this new recipe.'

'So she sends you here to shop for her?'

He glanced around the big, double-fronted shop. 'This is still a deli, isn't it?'

'For the moment, yes. Come on, cuz, this is Paula; you're not kidding me. Your office is just along the road, but in all the time you've been working out of it, you've never set foot in here. Now, the day after Aunt Christina drops her bombshell, here you are. This is an inspection visit by the new trustee, isn't it?'

He smiled at her; the full high-octane Mario smile, the killer leg-opener from his single days which he had always been careful, until then, never to flash in her direction, for fear of what it might unleash. 'No fooling you, eh. Okay I admit it; I thought I'd drop in for a chat.'

'I'll chat to you any time, Big Irish, but why here? You can come round to my place any time you like.'

'I don't like to drop in there unannounced; you might have company.'

'Not right now, I don't; the lady is on her own. Anyhow, I never used to bother about paying you a surprise visit.'

'I remember.'

'Much good it used to do me, too. So what do you want to chat about?'

It was his turn to throw her a challenging look. 'Now who's being coy? You know bloody well; I want to talk about you, our Paula, and your place in the family business. By the way, how's Uncle Beppe taking it? I thought he was uncharacteristically quiet after Mum made her announcement.'

'Dad's very sad that she's going. He's relied on her advice whenever a major decision has had to be made in the past, and he'll miss her greatly.'

Mario laughed out loud. 'Hah! That's a belter, that one. Whatever Mum said he did the opposite. Remember after Papa died, he left a plan to launch Viareggio fish and chip shops as a franchise? My mother was all for going ahead with that; she pleaded, almost, with Uncle Beppe to agree to it. But did he? Not on your life. I was only sixteen then, and more interested in birds than business, but I remember Mum coming home from that last meeting with him. I've never seen her so angry; before or since. At the end he'd laughed at her. "Franchised fish and chip shops," he'd said. "Never heard anything so fucking stupid in my life."

'He's a real business tycoon, is your dad,' he chuckled, sarcastically. 'If he'd relied on my mother's advice, he'd be the chairman of a plc right now. D'you know there's a Harry bloody Ramsden in Singapore? If Papa Viareggio hadn't dropped down dead twenty years ago, it would have been his name . . . and yours . . . over the door.'

Paula looked at him coolly. He had tried to rattle her, but he had failed. 'Do you think you're going to change things then, Mario? Because if you do, I have to remind you that my father still has the casting vote in the event of a disagreement between the two trustees. You've got no more power than Aunt Christina had. You'll be a figurehead just like she was.'

McGuire crumpled up his mask of false bonhomie, and threw it away. He looked at her without a flicker of humour in his eyes. 'Don't you believe that, cousin, not for one moment. You see, I'm not blind to my mother's only fault; she had this classically Italian thing against washing the family linen in public. That's why she let Uncle Beppe get away with it, that time and on every occasion since. But I'm not like that; if I believe as a trustee that the casting vote is being used in a way that's against the best interests of the beneficiaries, then I won't hesitate for one second to go to court to have it overturned. That's the truth, and your dad better believe it. You too, for that matter.'

A flame kindled in her dark eyes. 'Are you threatening me, Mario?'

He shook his head, firmly. 'No. I'm telling you, that's all. Paula, I've got my own life to lead and a career outside the family business, so I've got no wish to get involved in day-to-day management things. I have got one or two ideas that I'm going to air, but I don't think that Uncle Beppe will have a problem with any of them. There's contracts of employment, for example. As I understand it, our managers have none at the moment; not formally, at least. That's dodgy legally, and it's not right morally, so I'm going to propose that they have.

'They don't need to be fancy; just the standard rights and obligations, and the customary loyalty clause.'

'What's that?' asked his cousin.

'You know, the one about no additional like employment without approval. It just means that if one of our managers, like you are, wanted to take on a second managerial appointment in her spare time . . . let's say she ran a few saunas for example . . . she couldn't without the approval of her principal employer, the trust.'

He watched as her face seemed to set into a hard shell. 'Now,' he said, his smile back in place, 'about those mushrooms and that ham.'

27

'Are you serious, McIlhenney?' Dan Pringle growled.

'Oh yes, sir, I'm serious. My boss has asked me to put my successor in place by the time he gets back from the States, and Detective Sergeant McGurk is number one on the list . . . providing he accepts the job, of course.'

'So that's what it's going to be like at headquarters, is it? The DCC takes a fancy to my chosen exec and that's it. I don't know if I fancy this job after all. Aye, fuck it, I think I'll just stay on in the Borders Division. Big McGuire can get back in the queue and you can stay in Skinner's office.'

McIlhenney glanced over his shoulder to make sure that the door of the head of CID's private office was completely closed. 'Speaking privately, sir, you don't know how fucking near you were to staying on in the Borders. It was a toss-up between you and Greg Jay, in Leith, who got the head of CID job; you won partly because the Boss preferred not to have both Mario and Maggie based in the city.

'If you really want to stay in the Borders, I reckon he'd agree to let you make that choice; but you'll have to decide it right now.'

The superintendent glared at him. 'You know, son,' he said, 'you might look like a big amiable bastard, but you're really good at putting the boot in. No wonder you and Bob Skinner get on.'

'I'll take that as a compliment, then,' McIlhenney murmured. 'But just so's you know, the Boss didn't take a fancy to McGurk. He asked me to find the best man for the job, and I said that he was. Would you argue with that?'

Pringle lowered his eyes and shook his head. 'No, I wouldn't, because you're right; big Jack's got command potential. Okay, okay, if the DCC wants him, or if you want him . . . What's the difference? . . . I won't stand in his way.'

'That's good, sir. Mr Skinner thought you would agree when you thought it through.'

'Good for me. It still leaves me stuck for back-up, though.'

'Not necessarily. There's Ray Wilding, McGurk's old partner in Central; he's just been promoted to DS. You could have him.'

'Aye, but would I have to fight Maggie Rose for him?'

'No,' said the Inspector, quietly. 'He's yours if you want him. I'm off to tell McGurk he's got a new job.'

As he turned to leave, Pringle called after him. 'Was this personal wi' you, McIlhenney?' he asked.

'No, sir. I don't let personal issues cloud my judgement.'

'But you don't like me.'

'I'm entirely ambivalent to you, Chief Superintendent.'

'Aye, that'll be right. Are you still carrying a grudge over that time I wanted to lift your wife's doctor?'

McIlhenney looked him in the eye. 'How could I, sir? Stupidity's a condition, not a vice. We all have occasional lapses.'

He closed the door on the new head of CID, wondering how big an enemy he had made . . . but not caring too much . . . and walked the long corridor back to his old office in the command suite. He asked Ruth McConnell to find Jack McGurk for him, then cast an eye over the DCC's morning mail. Spotting nothing contentious, he took over the call to McGurk and broke the good news.

'Is Mr Pringle okay about it?' asked the young sergeant.

'He's very happy for you. Talk to him yourself and he'll tell you that, I'm sure. Report here on Monday morning; I'll be a bit schizophrenic for a while, jumping between this office and my new one, but between us, Ruthie and I'll show you the ropes, and get you up to speed in time for the Big Man coming back.'

'When will that be?'

'Not next week, that's for sure. See you Monday, Jack.'

Having cleared his desk, he asked Ruth to re-direct his calls to the Special Branch suite and headed off to meet up as arranged with McGuire. He found him, shut away in his private office, seated, hunched, at his desk with the phone to his ear.

'Look, Mr Gwynn, let's not be fucking coy about this. You've called me back through the switchboard, so you know that I really am a detective superintendent and that this is not a hoax. I know yours is only a wee branch and you're worried about being crapped on from way up there, but I promise you that isn't going to happen. I'm trying to conduct a discreet enquiry here. Now are you going to co-operate or do I have to make some waves?'

He winked at McIlhenney as he poured a coffee from the filter jug.

'Yes, I can promise you that. None of the information you give me will be disclosed and nobody will ever know that you provided it. What do you get from it?' He laughed. 'You get friends in high places and two unlisted telephone numbers that you can call whenever you're knee-deep in shit. That's a good swap, believe me.'

McIlhenney watched him, saw him nod quietly.

'Good, good. Okay the man's name is Rosewell, George Rosewell. He has a current account and a credit card, that's also operated through your bank. I need to know whether either of them has been used this week, I need to know the last time either was used, and in the case of the cash card I need to know how much money was withdrawn. Oh yes, and I'd like the current account balance.' He nodded again. 'Sure you can call me back; I'll be here for a while. Use this number, and keep a note of it for the future: emergencies only, mind.' He read out his direct line number.

'That's changed every so often, isn't it?' asked McIlhenney as he hung up.

'Aye, but he'll never use it. The boy just needed to feel important, that's all; a lot of these small branch managers are shit-scared of head office these days.'

'Why do you need that stuff anyway?'

'I'm still trying to find Maggie's old man, so I can beat his fucking brains in . . . or at least run him out of Edinburgh. He hasn't been at work all week, and his house looked like the *Marie Celeste*.'

'You went in?'

'You're dead right I went in. I was paying a family visit, Neil . . . and even if it hadn't been, in this job I could have justified it. The man has a history of violence and child abuse, he's living under an alias and he's in a wholly unsuitable job.'

'Child abuse?'

'Don't ask. Anyhow, there were the congealed leavings of pie, beans and chips on his kitchen table, with a half-read *Sunday Mail* beside them. I spoke to a neighbour. She hasn't seen him since then.'

'He's not in the nick, is he?'

'No. I've just checked that. Nor is he in any hospital in this area. Nor is he lying in a mortuary with a John Doe tag on his toe. All this week's stiffs are accounted for. He has either gone on a very last-minute bargain break to Shagaluf, or he's been kidnapped by international criminals and is being held for a multi-million-pound ransom, or he's done something or upset someone to the extent that he's decided to do a runner.'

'He's upset you.'

'Aye, but he doesn't know that . . . at least I don't see how he could.'

The phone on his desk rang; his hand shot out and picked it up. 'McGuire. Ah, Mr Gwynn; that didn't take long. Aye, sometimes I wish the millennium bug had been for real; the bloody things are ruling our lives now. Okay, just hold on a minute.' He picked up a pen. 'Right.'

As he listened, he made notes on a pad on his desk. 'That's excellent,' he said, as he finished. 'Now here's that other contact I promised you.' He glanced at a list on his desk, and read out a number. 'Thanks. So long.'

'What was that one?' asked McIlhenney.

'My new direct line in the Borders. You never know, the boy might be moved down there one day.'

'Indeed, you have been here for too long.'

'Just long enough.' McGuire glanced at his notepad. 'It was useful though. George drew thirty quid from his bank account on Tuesday of last week. Since then, neither his cash card nor his credit card has been used; his account balance is eleven hundred and forty-one pounds.'

'He can't have run far, then. Do you think he could be in the founds of a new building somewhere?'

'I'm beginning to wonder. If he is, I just hope it'll be heavy enough to hold the swine down.'

28

Bob Skinner had been several times to the USA, before and since his marriage to his American wife. He had been to New York City and State, to Florida and to the original California Disneyland with his daughter Alex, to Houston, Texas, on an exchange visit, and to Atlanta, Georgia, as a delegate to a security conference. However he had never been to the north-western states, and nothing had prepared him for their size or for the spectacle they offered.

The flight to Great Falls, Montana, was blessed with cloudless conditions all the way, across the pale blue of the Great Lakes, the green of Michigan, and the changing shades of the landscape below as they flew westward. Even Skinner, who tended to view the wonders of nature with a jaundiced eye, spent the entire journey looking out of the window of the aircraft.

The hundred-mile drive down Interstate Fifteen to Helena was no less dramatic; the first half of their route, through Cascade County, ran close to the great Missouri River . . . the Scot had had no idea that it originated so far north . . . past Cascade itself, then into the great open spaces of Lewis and Clark. Finally they drove into the Helena Valley, overlooked by its gently sloping mountain, with the small state capital nestled at its heart.

'Well, did you enjoy that?' asked Doherty, who had driven from the airport in a rental car, as they cruised past the State Capitol building, to arrive at the Investigations Bureau headquarters on North Roberts.

'Yes,' Skinner admitted. 'But enough of the tourist bit. Who are we seeing?'

'The Bureau guy's name is Tad Polhaus. The police chief is Chuck Harris, but he's on holiday, so we'll be met by the senior detective, Lieutenant Gordon Sumner.'

The Montana investigators were waiting for them in the Bureau Chief's office on the second floor of the building. Both were in their mid-thirties; Polhaus was big and beefy, his broad features proclaiming his German ancestry, while Sumner was lean and wiry, equally tall but looking like a welterweight alongside his colleague.

As they ran through the formalities of the introduction, and took their seats around a coffee table, Skinner looked for signs of one deferring to the other but found none. State cop and city cop seemed to treat each other as equals; there was no sign of the jurisdictional jealousy that he had found in Buffalo. However they were both visibly impressed by, and slightly in awe of, the Deputy Director of the FBI, and his Scottish companion.

'Welcome to Montana, gentlemen,' said Polhaus. He looked at Doherty. 'I don't suppose I need to tell you, Mr Deputy Director, that your call took us by surprise. Make no mistake though, we're hell of a glad you're here. We've run into a complete brick wall on this Wilkins homicide investigation. Any input you can give us will be more than welcome.'

Lieutenant Sumner nodded. 'I'll second that, Tad,' he concurred. 'But tell me, sir, what brought this case to your attention? You gentlemen haven't come to the Queen of the Rockies just to see the sights.'

'I have,' Skinner told him. 'I'm an observer here, just tagging along on Mr Doherty's invitation. A visiting fireman, I understand you'd call me.'

'Now why don't I believe that?' said the city detective. 'I did some research on you, Deputy Chief Skinner. I had a look at your force's website, and at a couple of files on Internet versions of your Scottish newspapers. I know who you are; I know what you've been into. You haven't come here for the fishing.'

Doherty laughed. 'Goddamn Internet. Pretty soon there will be no secrets left in this world . . . but we're not at that stage yet, otherwise, pretty as your city is, we wouldn't be here. Tell me about the late Bartholomew Wilkins.'

'There isn't much to tell,' Polhaus answered, 'as far as his life around here goes. He was sixty-eight years old but he had been among us for only the last three years, since he retired from legal practice in Chicago, Illinois. He and his wife RoseAnne bought a house here at that time.'

'Any family?' asked Skinner.

'They have a son named Arthur, who succeeded his father as senior partner in the Chicago firm, and two daughters, Annette and Merle.'

'Where's the body?'

'It was released to the family last Friday. Mrs Wilkins and her son flew back to Chicago on Saturday with the coffin, for burial in their family plot. She said that the services were scheduled for Wednesday. Is there a problem with that?'

'I shouldn't think so,' said Doherty. 'Were either of you two gentlemen at the crime scene?'

'We both were,' Sumner replied. 'When she found her husband, the lady assumed at first that he had fallen and cut his head; she thought he was unconscious, and she reported the circumstances as such, so a paramedic crew was sent. They realised that it was a fatality, so they called for a patrolman to attend. Fortunately one of our smarter guys responded. He saw that there was no obvious place for the victim to have cut himself and that there was no blood trail . . . indeed that there was very little blood. So he radioed in for detective back-up.

'When I got there I knew at once that this was no superficial head wound, and I knew that I was going to need Tad's resources as well as my own.'

'Going on the report that was filed, and logged on to the national database, you decided that this was a homicide committed in the course of a burglary.'

'That's what it was,' Polhaus exclaimed. 'We're in no doubt about it. There were articles removed from the house. Mr Wilkins' pocket-book was taken, containing Amex, Master and Visa cards and over four hundred dollars in cash. The man wore a ten-grand Breitling watch. That was gone; so was a heavy gold bracelet from his other wrist and a top specification laptop computer from his desk.

'If that doesn't constitute a burglary, sir, I don't know what does.'

'Neither do I, Chief,' Skinner assured him. 'No one's disputing that for one minute. How about signs of entry? The report I read didn't mention that.'

'There weren't any. Gordon and I believe that Mrs Wilkins left the back door open when she went out to the mall and that the guy just walked in. She recalled that she locked it, but she admitted that she couldn't be certain.'

'She's been eliminated as a possibility, I take it?'

'Yes she has, completely. We did consider that possibility, don't worry, but the autopsy ruled that out straight away. The knife wound in the victim's head was five inches deep. It went clear through his brain; if the blade had been any longer it would have come out the other side of the skull. That was a hellish powerful blow, Mr Skinner. She couldn't have done it.'

'Did the pathologist give you a picture of the person who did?'

'Yes. A right-handed man, he said; probably as tall as the victim, and he was six one. Mrs Wilkins is five two; we're looking for a big guy, not a little woman.'

'Granted,' the DCC agreed. 'How about location? Where did the attack happen?'

'In the victim's den; his study, I suppose you'd call it in England.'

Skinner smiled. 'I wouldn't call it anything in England, Chief; I'm a Scot, remember. I know what a den is; I know also from my father-in-law that quite often it's in converted cellar space. Was that the case here?'

'Yes, it was. It's accessed by a door off the hall leading to a flight of stairs.'

'Apart from the items you described, what else was taken from the house?'

Skinner saw the frown gather on Polhaus' broad face. 'Nothing, according to Mrs Wilkins.'

'What else was disturbed?'

'Nothing, but so what? Our theory is that the guy broke in, started his search in the den and was disturbed by the victim. He killed him, grabbed what he could, and ran for it. There was a home gym next door and a shower-room beyond that. Maybe Wilkins was taking a leak and came back in.'

'I don't deal in maybes. When you found him, were his pants wet?'

'Excuse me?'

'Did he void his bladder when he was stabbed?'

'I dunno. Gordon?'

Sumner nodded. 'Yes, sir, as I recall he did.'

'In that case he hadn't just taken a piss.'

The visiting detective looked from one of his hosts to the other. 'What forensic samples have you recovered from the scene?'

'None that have significance,' the Lieutenant answered. 'We've identified every print we found in the house; no wild ones left.'

'Fibres?'

'Nothing out of place.'

'Dirt from footwear?'

'None that we found.'

Skinner's right eyebrow rose, almost theatrically. 'Come on, gentlemen,' he exclaimed. 'The intruder comes through a door, which Mrs Wilkins said she locked, without leaving a trace. He comes straight down here and kills his victim, then leaves without disturbing anything in the house, without leaving a single print, or shedding a single body hair.

'Fine, he takes the dead man's wallet and jewellery, his laptop, and a clock off his desk. But none of the credit cards . . . I don't even bother asking the question because I know the answer . . . have been used, and none of the other items have been offered for sale to any pawnshop or known fence in the massive and great state of Montana. You guys have been close up to this investigation; I understand that and I respect it. But now, take a step back from it, look at those circumstances and tell me what you see.'

Polhaus looked at Sumner, then back at Skinner. He sighed, heavily. 'I'll admit it; there was something about this investigation that didn't sit right, almost from the start, but out here we don't have much experience of burglary homicides. Like I said back then, we welcome your input.'

'No one has much experience of burglary homicide, Chief,' said Doherty, gently. 'Even in the cities it's a relatively unusual type of felony. We're here because of three incidents within a two-week period, and this is one of them: three retired lawyers, with career histories going back to Washington in the sixties.

'Tell me, was Mr Wilkins active in Democrat politics in Helena?'

Polhaus laughed, unexpectedly. 'Sir, this is Montana. There ain't too many active Democrats out here. Sure, I knew that Bart was on that side, but it was in his past. You're not suggesting that's what got him killed, are you?'

'To be frank, Chief, we don't know for sure, but at this point we are not ruling out any connection. Past involvement in Democrat politics is one of the factors linking the three homicide victims. But let's go back there; you said you knew Mr Wilkins.'

The big investigator nodded. 'Sure I did, and so did Gordon here. We both have kids in junior high school; they have a football team . . . touch football only at their age, you understand . . . and Bart was one of the coaches. Football was his main interest in life, apart from politics and the law. I guess he was a pretty good player in his youth; you have to be, if you're a first-string line-backer for Notre Dame.'

Doherty was impressed, instantly. 'He played for the Fighting Irish?'

'Yes, sir; class of fifty-three. He had pro offers, he said, but he turned them down, and went on to Yale law school instead.'

'Mr Grace was at Yale, wasn't he?' the FBI man asked the Scot.

'Yes, but before fifty-three. He was back from Korea by then and starting out in practice.'

Skinner looked at Polhaus. 'Did you play at college?'

'I wish. I was good enough for high school, but I didn't make the team when I stepped up; too slow, the coaches said . . . and they were right.'

'Did Mr Wilkins talk much about those days?'

'College?'

'Well, yes, but afterwards too. Did he ever talk about his early career; his Washington days?'

'Not much. He told me once that his father sent him there to gain work experience outside Chicago. His law firm was founded by his grandfather and his great-uncle; Wilkins, Schwartz, Wilkins, it was called, at the beginning at least. There never was a Schwartz, though; the two brothers added the name on for, let's say, commercial reasons. They wanted the Jewish business as well as the Irish.'

The DCC nodded. 'I've come across that one before.'

'For the last eighty years, though,' Polhaus continued, 'it's been Wilkins, Schwartz, Wilkins and Fellini. The Italian bit was for real; Bart said that the original Mr Fellini was made a partner in the early twenties, when they saw the way things were going in Chicago. They couldn't pull the same trick with the Italians; for one thing, a lot of them would only speak their native language when doing business.'

'Are you saying the practice was Mob-connected?'

'No, and Bart never did either. But you're a smart man, Mr Skinner; you'll realise that back in the Roaring Twenties, in Chicago, it was bound to be.'

'And is it still?'

It was Joe Doherty who answered. 'No,' he said, emphatically. 'That was one of the first things I checked out when we became aware of the possible link between these three killings. The Bureau maintains a continuous investigation of organised crime in this country. We know just about all of the law firms who deal with the Mob, knowingly; Mr Wilkins' firm isn't on that list, nor is Grace, McLean, Wylie, Whyte and Oakdale, Mr Grace's firm, nor Gregory, Mozlowski and Harold, the former practice of Sander Garrett. These days, at least, they're all clean . . . although so much hot money is re-invested these days in legitimate business that it's possible to be connected without even knowing it.'

'That's true in Europe as well,' Skinner admitted. 'The Mafia investigations in Italy have thrown up plenty of names in other countries, the UK among them, who connect up to other things.'

'I guess we're best off out here in the wilderness, Tad,' said Sumner.

'There is no wilderness any more, pal. I know a man, an American, who owns a large piece of Scotland, where few people, even tourists, ever go. He's officially legitimate, but still, his FBI file reads like a novel; I know in my heart that he was behind a major crime on my patch, but I'll never prove it because we killed the people who carried it out.

'You've got a nice little city here, in the heart of a spectacular state, but make no mistake . . . the world is coming to get you. Now,' he said sharply. 'Back to the crime scene. Did Mr Wilkins keep any business papers?'

'There was a filing cabinet in his den,' said the State Bureau Chief. 'But we didn't check its contents. I reckon we better had now.'

'I reckon,' agreed Skinner. 'Come on, let's do it now.'

29

He could see as soon as he walked through the door that she was having a bad day; frown lines showed on her forehead, and her hair, which was normally perfectly arranged, was ruffled.

Mario braced himself for the outburst. 'You would think that in this day and age, cash payrolls would be a thing of the past; but no such luck. Honest to God, some of our employers are still stuck in a time-warp.

'We advise them, we warn them, we plead with them, and do they take a blind bit of notice? Do they hell as like!'

Maggie frowned at him. 'And you can wipe the daft bloody smile off your face. You won't be grinning when you have an armed hold-up in the middle of your division . . . as you will, sooner or later.'

'Anyone hurt?' he asked at once.

'No, thank goodness. They waved shotguns around, but no shots were fired.'

'Where was it?'

'At that massive private housing development up near Myreside; three guys sat round the corner in a battered old Ford, watched the cash drop-off, then just moved in and picked it up. They drove off with twenty-two thousand pounds. We found the car a mile away.'

'Who were they this time?'

She caught his meaning at once. 'Tony Blair, George Dubya Bush and Lennox Lewis.'

'Check the toyshops; maybe whoever bought them used a credit card.'

'Teach Nana Viareggio, McGuire; that's already being done. As it happens, we found a school-patrol woman who saw them change cars; she told us that they headed east in a dark blue Peugeot saloon, plus she gave us a pretty good description of one of them. He's medium height, she said, with grey hair, a broken nose, and a birthmark on his cheek.'

'Bluey Scott to the life.'

'That's what I reckoned; I've sent Ray Wilding and a DC round to his house, with an armed response team because there were firearms involved.'

'I wonder which one he was?'

'Lennox Lewis, I'll bet. He used to be a heavyweight boxer, after all.'

'No, dear, he used to be an opponent. They took his licence away in the end. I saw him in the ring, twice; the two fights lasted a total of five rounds and Bluey was knocked down a total of seven times.'

'That could happen again, if he's still got the shotgun.'

'Nah,' McGuire drawled, 'Bluey won't give them any trouble. He might be punchy, but he's not suicidal. I lifted him once myself, and he came along quietly enough.'

'You're more scary than Wilding.'

'I'm not more scary than a Heckler and Koch carbine, though.'

'Let's hope so. There's always hell to pay when a police officer shoots a suspect.'

'Especially if he's carrying a table leg at the time, and he's on his way home from hospital.'

'Let's not go into that,' she said, ending the discussion. 'Now, get to the point. What's brought you here? If you thought you'd pick me up so I could get ready for Andy's do, I'll be a while yet. It's barely gone five.'

Her husband shook his head. 'No, it isn't that. Sit down for a minute, will you.'

'Why?' She threw him a puzzled look, but did as he said.

'It's about your father.'

'I told you, Mario,' she blurted out, urgently. 'I don't want to know.'

'Yes, but you have to; as a police officer.'

'What do you mean? Has he been up to ... Has he committed a crime?'

'Not lately, not one that I know of, at any rate. But he may just be a victim of one.' He told her about his discovery of her father's new identity and of his fruitless search for him.

'You're saying that my father's a missing person?' she asked. 'If you are, he can bloody well stay lost. That would be best all round, in fact. Jesus Christ, what sort of background checks does the education authority run on the people it employs to work with children?'

'Very careful checks,' he answered quietly. 'And in this case, what could it possibly have thrown up? Your father might be the worst sort of beast, but the fact is, he's never even been charged with anything, far less prosecuted, far less convicted. To everyone but you and your sister, he's clean.'

'There's been no trouble at the school?'

'None to speak of; certainly none of the sort you mean.'

119

'And you say he's just vanished?'

'That's how it looks.' He told her again about the scraps of supper and the Sunday newspaper that he had found in his flat. 'He's a missing person, love. You have to treat him as such.'

'But who's missing him?'

'His employer, for a start. And I am too. I want to find this man, to make bloody sure that he stays out of your life; our lives.'

'Mario, he probably has no idea where I am, or what I am.'

'Don't you kid yourself. He reads the tabloids.' He told her about the press cutting in Rosewell's sideboard; reading surprise and pain in her face.

'All right,' she conceded at last. 'I'll circulate his details round all the divisions and enter him on the national register.'

'In that case, you'll need this.' He took the photograph from his pocket and handed it to her.

It took a great effort of will by Maggie before she could look at the likeness of her father. Yet when she did, to her great surprise she felt nothing; his was just another face, just another of the many that had lain on the same desk. Some of those had been missing, as he was now, others had been dead, victims . . . as she had been, and in her mind, still was . . . while others had been criminals. George Rosewell fitted two of those categories; and for all she knew, perhaps he belonged in the third as well.

She looked at the photograph again. There was a familiarity about it . . . on occasion, the man still appeared in her nightmares . . . but that was all. She laid it on the desk, face down. 'Okay,' she said. 'I'll see about having it circulated. If he turns up . . . well, let's just hope it's after Manny English comes back.'

30

If Doherty and Skinner had driven around eight hundred miles down Interstate Fifteen from Helena, Montana, down across Idaho and on south, through Salt Lake City, and St George, Utah, skirting Arizona and into southern Nevada, they would have come to Las Vegas.

They would have come also to the aid of Special Agent Isaac Brand.

Thompson Hall, Chief of Police of the City of North Las Vegas, had been less co-operative than Doherty had hoped or expected. At four p.m., almost five hours after he had touched down at McCarran Airport, Brand was still seated in his outer office, waiting with growing impatience for the conclusion of what he had been told was a meeting with the mayor. He was staring at Hall's smoked glass door when his cellphone rang.

'Zak, how goes it?' Joe Doherty sounded as amiable as ever; until the young agent told him how it went. 'You been sat there for four hours?'

'Not quite, sir. The chief took a lunch break at one p.m.; his secretary suggested that I do the same. I know, sir,' he admitted, 'it's almost intolerable, but what can I do?'

'You can drop the "almost", son. It's completely fucking intolerable. You've never had a detail like this before, have you?'

'No, sir.'

'Then blame me. I should have made sure you got a better welcome. Is Chief Hall's secretary close to you?'

'Yes, sir. She's sat across the room.'

'Then here's what you do. Don't ring off; just give her your cellphone, and tell her . . . do not ask her, instruct her . . . to take it into the chief's room and, mayor or no mayor, to stick it in his fucking ear. You understand?'

'Yes, sir.'

'So go do it.'

He rose from his chair and did what Doherty had told him. The secretary, a frosty brunette who fitted every description of a Vegas showgirl that he had ever read, protested at first, but Brand, knowing that the line was still live and that his boss could hear him, stuck to his guns. 'Miss,' he said, slowly and with emphasis on every word, 'the Deputy Director of the FBI is on the line and requires to speak with Mr Hall. Do as I say.'

She gave in, took the cellphone from him as she stood, and disappeared into the chief's room, without, he noticed, bothering to knock. He looked at his watch as he waited, watching the second hand as it swept steadily round.

It was just short of completing its second revolution when the door opened, and a man appeared. He was short for a policeman, five eight at most, several inches shorter than Brand, with a spreading waistline, emphasised by a belt which was cinched at least one notch too tight, from which the hem of his blue short-sleeved shirt was escaping. He held the cellphone in his left hand; the other was stretched out in greeting. 'Hi, I'm Thompson Hall; welcome to North Las Vegas.

'Son, son,' he said, with the forced heartiness of a Texan governor on the stomp, as the agent accepted his handshake, 'why have you been sitting here in silence for all this time? Goddamn, if you had only said how important this thing is, Rosalie would have broken up my meeting, mayor or no mayor. Come on, come on, let's waste no more time. Rosie, fix us up with coffee and doughnuts.'

He handed back the cellphone then led the way into his office and walked round behind his desk. Brand looked around; there was no sign of any other visitor, but, at the back of the room, he saw what could have been an exit door, and so he gave the chief the benefit of the doubt. Nevertheless, the last of his diplomacy had evaporated around an hour before, and so, as soon as he was seated he launched into the reason for his visit.

'Sander Garrett . . .'

'Yes, son. I understand from your boss that the Bureau's got a burr up its ass about this guy. To me this is just a run-of-the-mill homicide, so what's the story?'

'What do you know about the man, chief?' the agent asked.

'Zilch,' the man replied, abruptly. 'I know that this is only North Las Vegas, the poor sister of the big city, but this place is still full of retired geezers come here for the golf, the gambling and the girls. Garrett paid his taxes and didn't get into trouble so we had no dealings with him till he got his head blown off.'

'Mr Garrett may have been retired, chief, but as I understand it he was

no newcomer to the area. He was a partner in a law firm on the strip, and
still went in there occasionally.'

'Is that so?'

'Yes. We've done some follow-up investigation, through the American
Bar Association; he's practised law here since nineteen sixty-eight.'

'Goddamn, you say?'

'Goddamn I do, sir. Can you tell me, how was Mr Garrett killed?'

Hall picked up a bound file from his desk and tossed it across to
Brand. 'See for yourself.'

The policeman watched with malicious amusement as his earnest
young visitor opened the file. What he had given him was a close-up
colour shot of Sander Garrett, taken on a mortuary table. He saw Brand
look at it, then, in what seemed to be an involuntary reflex action, close
his eyes. When he opened them again, he seemed to focus on the man's
small moustache and on a gold filling on one of his front teeth, as if to
help him cope with his revulsion. Where the centre of Garrett's forehead
should have been, there was a dark jagged hole, speckled with white
dots, which he knew had to be bone fragments.

'Kinda grabs you, kid, doesn't it?' said the police chief. 'That's what
a soft-nosed forty-five bullet will do on the way out, if you put the barrel
against the skull. Doesn't leave any room for doubt, you might say.

'Garrett was in his kitchen when he was killed, fixing his supper. The
way my guys read it the shooter just walked in through the back door,
which wasn't locked, pulled out a cannon and shot him through the back
of the skull, spreading his fucking brains all over the malted milk and
cookies. Then he got on with robbing the place.' Halfway through his
graphic description, Rosalie came into the room with coffee and
doughnuts, which she laid on the desk; Hall did not pause, nor did she
flinch.

As she left, Brand closed the folder. Hall offered him a doughnut, but
he declined. 'Did the back door open directly on to the kitchen?'

'No. It opens into a laundry; then you have the kitchen.'

'Was the front door locked?'

'Hell, I don't know. Why you ask?'

'Because we are not convinced that this was an opportunistic burglary,
as you have described it. We believe that it ties in with two other recent
killings. If that is right, the killer had the skill to come through the door
whether it was locked or not.' Brand tapped the folder. 'Are your forensic
reports in here, chief?'

'No, that's just the photograph book. But the guy didn't leave any traces. There were no prints, other than the ones left by Garrett, his cleaning lady, and a forty-year-old blonde called Charlene Stacey. Garrett was widowed; Stacey was his lady-friend. We thought about her for a while, but we couldn't tie her to it. She's a sales rep and she was out of town at the time.'

'Who claimed the body?' asked the agent.

'She did.'

Brand opened the folder once more; he flicked past the morgue photographs and turned to those taken at the crime scene; several showed Garrett face down across his kitchen table, slumped in the middle of a lake of blood. 'The guy didn't exactly barge in,' he said, quietly.

'How do you work that out?'

'The victim was shot through the back of the head. If he had heard the door open, he'd have turned around. How about the gunshot itself? Did any neighbours hear anything?'

'Nope. The lab said he used a muffler.'

'Just like your average burglar,' murmured Brand. 'He goes out on a job carrying a silenced forty-five.' If Hall picked up his irony, he said nothing.

'So what was taken from the house?'

'Money, Garrett's watch, credit cards and other valuables.'

The FBI agent spun the folder around and pushed it across the desk. 'See the display cabinet in that photograph?' Hall nodded. 'It's full of Meissen pottery; collectables, very expensive. Those are valuables, yet they were left.'

'Okay,' the chief grunted irritably, 'but they are also very identifiable. This wasn't no collector. It was probably some spic crack-head out to feed his habit.'

'So where did he sell the watch? Where did he use the cards?'

'He ain't done that, so far.'

'Let's hope he does,' said Brand, maintaining his patience. 'Those other valuables: what were they?'

'According to Ms Stacey, he took two items. An Apple laptop computer, plus ... wait for this ... he took a box of very expensive Cuban cigars.'

31

'Come on, Andy.' There was a challenge in Mario McGuire's voice. 'Tell us the truth. Are you really looking forward to Dundee?' The jazz quartet was on a break, and so the question carried to everyone in their alcove, some of them seated at two tables pulled together, others standing.

As he spoke he glanced around them all: Maggie, Willie Haggerty, Brian Mackie, Dan Pringle, the two other divisional heads, Detective Superintendents Greg Jay and Willie Michaels, Neil McIlhenney, Sergeant Sammy Pye and his fiancée, Ruth McConnell, and Karen, the outgoing head of CID's heavily pregnant wife. The Chief Constable had joined them for supper in La Rusticana, but had ducked out diplomatically, to allow the serious business to begin.

Martin leaned back against the wall of the Cellar Bar, his pint glass almost disappearing into his big hand. 'You know, Mario,' he said easily, with a grin, 'you always were a cheeky bastard.'

He slipped an arm around Karen's waist. 'As I think about your question, I can only reply with three of my own. First, how have I stood you lot for so long? Second, what the hell's going to happen if there's a serious crime tonight, since the entire CID command structure's in the process of getting rat-arsed? Third . . .' He spun his fingers and his glass appeared, empty. '. . . Who's going to fill this up? It's Deuchar's,' he added, 'in case you've forgotten.'

Sammy Pye picked up the mug containing the remains of their kitty, and the note of the round, and headed off to catch the attention of the big, red-headed manager. 'Are you going to give us the serious answer now, Andy?' asked Maggie Rose. 'Or is it too late for that?'

The newest member of the Association of Chief Police Officers looked back at her. 'One more pint and it will be. One more pint and I'd be too maudlin to say this, or probably I'd do something very embarrassing if I tried.' He started to put his glass to his lips, before remembering that he had drained it. 'I've been in the trenches with you guys . . . and gals. I include my beautiful wife in that, and young Pye up at the bar there, and you too, Ruthie, since you know where most of the bodies are buried, and of course our absent friend, who, even as I speak, is probably scaring the living shite out of some poor rural polisman in wild Montana. I love every last one of you.' He paused and ran his eyes around the group.

'These have been the best years of my life . . . so far . . . and for them, I thank you all. Mind you, I suppose I should extend that vote of thanks to all those villains who over the years have been so fucking stupid that they've let the likes of us catch them.'

Up at the bar, Sammy Pye looked over his shoulder, wondering what the laugh was about.

'So,' said Martin, out of his earshot, 'you want the serious answer, Mags? Well here it is. Through those years, I've had some close calls . . . the last one closer than most of you know. The truth is, I don't want any more; I've used up all my luck. I couldn't even trust myself to go out on an armed situation any more, because I know that if I did I would pull the trigger at the first hint of a threat.

'I'm looking forward to Dundee because it takes me out of the line of fire. I'm not saying that our job's life and death every day, because we all know that it isn't. But it can be. It has been for me, and for some of you, and we can all remember a couple of colleagues who aren't around any more. It's not getting any less dangerous, either; we'd an armed robbery this afternoon . . . brilliantly cleared up inside two hours by Super-intendent Rose and her team. Round of applause, gentlemen, and thanks, Mags, for letting me sign off without any red marks on the crime figures.' He raised his empty glass in his colleague's direction, while the others nodded agreement.

'So yeah,' he went on, 'I'll put on my ACC's uniform on Monday without the slightest qualm or pang or any of those things. I'll miss you all, of course; but I'll have the consolation of a new job. I'm going to be responsible, believe it or not, for community policing, traffic patrols and public relations, among other things. And if any of you lot are caught speeding round the Dundee ring road, don't think I'll pull the ticket. Far from it, I'll put on my PR hat and make sure you wind up in the *Courier*.'

He took his replacement pint of Deuchar's Ale from the tray that Pye had brought back. 'There is one other thing I should say. As some of you may know also, I have been round the block a couple of times and more in a personal sense. Well, finally, I've found what was meant for me all along. I'm looking forward, God willing, to many years of coming home safely at night to Karen, and our daughter, when she's born. I think she deserves that security. I think they both do.'

He took a long swallow from his glass. 'Right, that's it. Speeches over, let's get on with the business of the night.' The others, rendered silent for the moment by the frankness of his admissions, took their drinks from Pye's tray, as the musicians wandered back to their corner of the bar and picked up their instruments.

They had reached the third bar of 'Stormy Weather' when a mobile phone sounded in the middle of the detectives' alcove. 'Gonnae no dae that!' said Martin, theatrically, looking round for the culprit, and smiling as an embarrassed Greg Jay took his handset from his pocket. 'Be firm with her, Greg,' he called out.

The Leith CID commander turned his back on the group and held the phone to his ear. The rest could not hear what he was saying, but they saw his body stiffen slightly in his chair, a reaction that killed the smiles and stilled the laughter. Jay ended the call then turned back to face the table, his eyes picking out a colleague. 'Mario,' he said. 'Beppe Viareggio's your uncle, yes?'

McGuire nodded.

'In that case, I think we should have a talk outside.'

32

'What do you have for me, Special Agent Kosinski?' asked Joe Doherty.

'I don't have anything new, sir. The forensic specialists still haven't secured a positive result from their sampling.'

'How about our interview with the man who succeeded Mr Grace as senior partner of the Buffalo firm? Have you set that up yet?' The link flickered for a second, forcing the deputy director to repeat his question.

'Yes, sir, that is arranged. The man's name is Jackson Wylie; he says he recalls meeting Mr Skinner, at a party at the Grace mansion, in his and Dr Sarah Grace Skinner's honour. Since it's Saturday, he's asked if you'd mind meeting him on board his cabin cruiser in the Bayview Marina; he told me that he always spends Saturdays on the boat doing maintenance tasks. I said okay, sir; I sort of assumed you wouldn't mind, given that Deputy Chief Skinner has met the man.'

'Sure, that's no problem. What time have you set?'

'One o'clock, sharp, sir. Your flight from Montana is due in to Buffalo at eleven forty-five, but I left you a little leeway. Mr Wylie said he'd provide some lunch on board. There will be a fax for you at the airport showing the route to his mooring.

'I fixed the meeting through Mrs Thorpe, Mr Wylie's personal secretary; she also worked directly for Mr Grace when he was at the law firm. I asked her if she recognised the names Bartholomew Wilkins or Sander Garrett. She didn't, sir, but she has undertaken to check through his personal files . . . they're still held at the firm's offices . . . to see if either name comes up, but she wasn't hopeful. She's very efficient, sir; I don't expect results.'

'No; and neither do I, but I'm not beyond the age where I can take pleasure from a surprise, so let's just wait to see what she finds. While she's doing that, Troy, I want you to book yourself on a flight to Chicago on Monday. I want you to interview Mr Arthur Wilkins; he's the son of Bart Wilkins and he succeeded him as senior partner in the family law firm, Wilkins, Schwartz, Wilkins and Fellini.

'I want you to find out what he knows about his father's business and political life and about what he's been doing since he retired.'

'Yes, sir.' Kosinski seemed to hesitate. 'Eh, sir,' he continued, tentatively, 'about the weekend?'

'You done all you can there?' asked Doherty.

'Yes, sir, I believe so.'

'Then go home to New York, son. Just keep your cellphone switched on, so that Special Agent Brand or I, or your area SAIC can reach you.'

'I will, sir. Thank you, sir.'

The Deputy Director ended the call, shaking his head. 'These young guys,' he murmured to Skinner. 'I love 'em. They come out of the Academy these days trained as well as the guys in special forces, and as committed. I worry about my country sometimes, then I think fifteen years down the road, to a time when the director and I are gone and goodhearted boys like Brand and Kosinski are running the show.'

The big Scot shrugged. 'You may not be too good at running elections . . . I like the old-fashioned way, where voters put a cross on a piece of paper and they're all counted by real people . . . but usually you wind up with the right guys at the top.'

Doherty held up a hand, index finger pointing in the air. 'Ah, but now we live in an age when the outcome can depend in part at least on how funny the candidates are on fucking television chat shows. Now it really has started to get dangerous. Now if the wrong guys had the power . . .'

'In that case, my friend, it is all the more important that you and your director get hold of the young guys like Troy and Zak, and the young girls too, and teach them the things they haven't learned at the Academy. Teach them your values, and teach them that patriotism really can be the last refuge of the scoundrel.'

'We haven't got all that many years left to do it,' said Doherty, lighting a cigarette.

'Fewer, if you keep doing that.'

The American smiled. 'Christ, you're getting to be a zealot yourself on that subject.'

'No one has so many friends that he can afford to lose a single one to those things.'

'Blah!' Doherty exclaimed, but he dropped his Marlboro, crushed it under his foot and kicked it into the gutter.

Skinner looked back up Bart and RoseAnne Wilkins' driveway. 'So what do we do now?' he asked. 'We're done here, I reckon, and our return flight isn't until half seven tomorrow.'

'Ah hell, we'll see the sights of Helena, eat some prime beef and try to drink the Napa Valley dry. But first, let's see if the other young soldier's getting better treatment in Vegas than he was when we spoke last.' He dialled Brand's number.

Skinner watched as his friend spoke to the Special Agent. His expression was serious, matter-of-fact, as he listened, until all at once it broke into a wide grin. 'You say?' he exclaimed. 'Kid, you've made my day. Thanks, I'll see you Monday, back in Buffalo. Meantime, if you want to spend the weekend in Vegas continuing your investigation, that's all right with me . . . just don't let me see any roulette chips on your expenses claim.'

He pushed the 'end' button and put the cellphone back in his pocket.

'Well?' Skinner demanded.

'You're going to love this, pal,' said Doherty. 'Superintendent Barbara Weston will not, but you will. The guy who iced Sander Garrett stole his Cubans, Bob. He took his Goddamned cigars!'

33

Mario McGuire, clad in a white scene-of-crime suit, looked at the sheet in the corner of the room and shivered at the recent memory of what lay under it. To escape it as much as anything else, he rose from his seat by the wide window and walked through to the apartment's main bedroom.

His aunt lay on her bed, fully dressed; she was staring at the ceiling. He sat beside her and took her hand. 'How you doing, Sophia?' She turned her head to look at him; her eyes were rimmed all round with red, made all the more vivid by the paleness of her face.

'Mario . . .' It was a whisper and it was all she could say.

'Yeah, yeah.' He stroked her arm, doing his best to soothe her. 'Listen,' he said, his voice not much louder than hers, 'the doctor will be here soon. She'll give you a shot, and then I want you to go with Maggie, back to our place. She's downstairs in a patrol car. You can't stay here.'

She frowned, her eyes almost crossing as she tried to focus on him. She raised herself off the pillow, bracing her weight on an elbow. 'But will the police not want to talk to me?'

'Yes, we will, but no one's going to do that until you're fit and ready for it; and the guy who'll decide that is me. You're my auntie and no one's going to impose on you.'

'But who's going to tell the girls? Who's going to tell Nana? Who's going to tell your mother?'

'I'll do all that, don't you worry.'

She nodded, and lay back on the pillow once more, staring upwards again. 'Why, son, why?' she murmured. 'Why would anyone . . .'

He had no answer for her, not so soon. He was about to tell her as much, when the silence of the big flat was shattered by a scream. He jumped up from the bed, his foot slipping for a second on the plush carpet, and headed back to the great open-plan living room, almost at a run.

His cousin Paula was standing, with the sheet in her hands, staring down at her father's body. She was wearing a designer trouser suit, and most of her long dark-skinned back was bare as he looked at her. 'Jesus!'

he gasped, crossing the room to her side in four long strides, as Detective Superintendent Jay, drawn by the commotion, emerged from the kitchen. 'Greg!' McGuire roared at him. 'Are your people asleep out there?'

He turned her round forcibly, twisting her away from the sight on the floor. 'Who let you in here?' he asked.

'A guy outside tried to stop me,' she hissed, 'but I kicked him on the knee and came in anyway. Mario, what is this? What's happened?' She wriggled in his grasp; she was big and, in her heels, almost as tall as he was, but still he was much too strong for her.

'We're way short of being able to answer all of that,' he said, quietly, 'but your father's been shot, and he's dead. Aunt Sophia found him when she came in from the theatre; she and my mum took Nana Viareggio to the show at the Kings.' He paused, letting it sink in. 'What brought you here at this time of night?' he asked her.

'I was out for a meal at the Malmaison; when I was leaving I looked across the water and saw the ambulance outside the building. Then when I got here, I saw Maggie sitting in a patrol car. Oh, Mario . . .' Finally, Paula's hard outer casing seemed to crack. She laid her forehead on his shoulder and cried like a baby. He released his grip on her, and enfolded her in his arms, hugging her to him; as he did so, something came to him, a fragment of memory from a very drunken night many years before.

'Okay, kid,' he whispered, feeling her tears dampening the front of his tunic. 'Let it out, let it out.' As they stood there, embracing, his own grief for his dead, clownish, clumsy, but ultimately likeable uncle came to him. He buried his face in Paula's silver hair, kissing it gently. 'Okay, okay, okay,' he murmured, over and over again, feeling her hold tighten on him, feeling the warmth of her all the way down his body, feeling himself reacting, involuntarily, to it.

The weight of Greg Jay's hand on his shoulder brought him back to the time and place. 'Mario,' said the superintendent, gently, 'the doctor's here.'

He blinked and nodded. 'Paula.' She looked up at him, her face a mess of smeared mascara and eye shadow. 'Go see your mother,' he told her. 'She's in the bedroom.'

'Okay,' she agreed, beginning to gather herself together once more. 'Thanks, cousin. Look, take care of things, will you? Viola's going to be out of it, that brother-in-law of mine will be no better, and Mum's going to need me. Can you do that?'

'Of course. I'll handle everything.'

She kissed him on the cheek. 'Thanks,' she murmured. 'Love you for it.'

He turned, steering her towards her parents' room; as he did, he saw Sarah Grace Skinner standing in the doorway, waiting for him.

'Sarah,' he exclaimed, 'thank Christ it's you. I'm so glad you were able to come.'

'No problem,' she assured him. 'I haven't retired you know. The nanny's living in, for now at least, so I could leave the kids.'

She frowned at him. 'This is your uncle, Mr Jay told me.'

'Yes.'

'Should you be here?'

'Try to keep me away,' he grunted. 'Should the Boss be with the FBI?'

'You got me there,' she admitted. 'Let's get to work, then.'

'Okay, but first, could you talk to my aunt? She needs a sedative; then Paula and Maggie can take her out of here.'

'Paula? Oh yes, that was your cousin; I remember her now, from your wedding reception, a striking-looking woman, isn't she. How's she taking it?'

'She's made of solid steel inside; she'll be all right.'

'I'll decide that; I might just stick a needle in her anyway. You wait here.' She turned, medical bag in hand, and followed in Paula's footsteps, going into the bedroom after a gentle knock on the door. Mario heard the sound of his aunt's sobbing as she entered.

He stood in the living room for several minutes, watching Inspector Arthur Dorward and his crime-scene team beginning their task of gathering all the tiny pieces of potential evidence that the room might hold, watching the photographer as he took picture after picture of Beppe's body.

Finally, Sarah reappeared, looking sombre. 'This is unusual for me,' she confessed quietly to McGuire. 'In fact it's unique. Invariably, when I arrive at a scene the grieving relatives are long gone, but not this time.'

The detective looked at her with a trace of alarm in his eyes. 'You want us to get someone else?' he asked.

'Oh no. I'm ready to go to work . . . once your aunt and cousin have gone.'

'Okay. I'll see to that. Meantime you really should talk to Greg Jay; this is his division, and his investigation.'

'Sure. But isn't Andy here?'

'No. He ruled himself out of this one; technically he might still be in post, but that's only for another day or so. As for his successor, he'd had a couple of pints too many at the leaving do. Please, go and talk to Greg.'

Sarah did as he asked, while he went back into the bedroom to take charge of Sophia and Paula, and escort them down to Maggie in the waiting car.

When he returned, she had put on a white overall suit and was waiting for him, standing beside Beppe's body with Detective Superintendent Jay. She looked at McGuire. 'You absolutely sure you want to see this?' she asked him.

'Absolutely certain.'

'In that case, to business, gentlemen.' She took a small tape recorder from her pocket and switched it on. 'First of all, I need to know if the body has been moved.'

'No,' Jay replied.

'I understand that Mrs Viareggio found her husband. You're sure she didn't touch him?'

'No way,' Mario volunteered. 'My aunt's a nervous woman; she's scared of her shadow. She told me that she took one look, screamed and ran to the downstairs neighbour.'

'How about him?'

'Her. She's a single lady; her name's Dr Alexander, and she's a civil service medical adviser. She came up and took a quick look to verify that Beppe was dead, then closed the door and called the police.'

'She didn't touch him in checking for life signs?'

'No,' said Greg Jay. The Leith divisional CID commander was tall and pear-shaped, with shoulders that appeared narrower than his waist, and a small round head. His manner was as ponderous as his appearance. 'She didn't need to, doctor. Take a look.' He pulled back the sheet from the body.

Beppe Viareggio lay on his stomach, with his backside sticking up in the air, and his arms by his sides, palms facing upward. His forehead was on the birchwood floor, in the centre of a small, round pool of blood, which had run in streaks down both sides of his face. Sarah whistled quietly. 'This was not a suicide,' she murmured.

'No gun at the scene,' Jay told her.

'You could have found an arsenal here, and still that couldn't have been self-inflicted, not from that angle. Look at that.' She knelt and pointed with her tape recorder at a great wound, just at the point where the spinal column descended from the skull. She peered at it closely, taking in a mass of congealed blood, hair and bone matter. 'To shoot yourself there you'd need to be a contortionist, not a fat man on the threshold of the third age.' She pushed herself up and walked around the body, slowly looking at it from every possible angle.

'Okay,' she said finally. 'Has the photographer finished?' She looked across at the red-haired Inspector Arthur Dorward, who was lifting fingerprints from the front door. He nodded in reply. 'Then turn him over, please, gentlemen.'

McGuire and Jay did as she asked, Mario flinching slightly as he rolled his uncle on to his back, expecting to see a grotesque exit wound. But there was none; apart from the blood on his forehead and his cheeks, Beppe's dead face was unmarked.

Sarah read his thoughts. 'Whoever did this used a hollow bullet, and probably a large calibre firearm. This was an execution, pure and simple; very similar to a case we had a couple of years back. I'd say from the way he's fallen that the victim was forced to kneel and was shot once through the base of the skull. The bullet flattened out on contact with the first and second cervical vertebrae, shattered them and passed on through into the brain, pulverising it. I wouldn't look to get ballistic markings when it's recovered; it'll be pretty much destroyed.

'This wasn't a contact wound, or else it might well have blown the man's head clean off. The killer probably fired at a distance of two or three feet.'

Sarah looked at Jay. 'Was Dr Alexander in all night, do you know?'

'Yes,' McGuire answered her.

'And did she hear anything at all that could have been a gunshot . . . or hasn't anyone interviewed her yet?'

'I spoke to her, and I asked her that. No, she didn't. The only unusual sound she remembered was a thud coming through the ceiling at around nine thirty, as if something heavy had been dropped in the flat above.'

She leaned over and touched Beppe's waxy face. 'He isn't stone cold, and there's no rigor as yet, so that may well be the time of death. The thud could have been your uncle falling forward as he was shot, Mario. Big gun like this, he must have used a silencer, otherwise she would have heard it.

'There's no doubt in my mind, gentlemen,' she said, firmly, 'that this has all the signs of what the media love to call a gangland-style killing, or a contract hit. For what it's worth, I haven't had anything like this on my autopsy table.'

'What about that other case you mentioned, the one a couple of years ago?' asked Jay.

'There were two of those, in fact, but that investigation was solved at that time. In any case there are some significant differences here. In those murders a rifle was used, a lower calibre, higher velocity weapon, and there was another signature, a very distinctive thing. No, this isn't related.'

'I'll trust your judgement on that . . . especially if the person involved is locked up,' the superintendent said.

'He's dead, actually.'

'Couldn't have been him, then,' McGuire grunted, from the side.

'When can you do the post mortem on Mr Viareggio, Dr Skinner?'

'Tomorrow morning, Mr Jay; first thing, if that's good enough for you.'

'Yes, that'll be fine.'

She looked at the other detective. 'Mario, can I ask you something? Are you aware of any health problems your uncle might have had, anything I should look out for in my examination?'

'No, none at all. Beppe might have been a bit on the plump side, but he took his health seriously. He had regular BUPA medicals and came through them all with flying colours. Come to think about it, he had one a few weeks back; he was crowing about it at our family party on Wednesday night.

'Why do you ask?'

She grinned at him, wryly. 'Thoroughness, that's all.'

'Convince me of that.'

'You're too suspicious by half, McGuire. Okay,' she confessed. 'I saw a case like this back in the States once, when I was working there. It was similar to this, a prominent man shot dead in his home, and the cops tore up half of gangland over the next couple of days. Then the coroner found that the man was riddled with cancer. Subsequently, the police spotted a large cash withdrawal from his bank, made just a couple of days before his death.

'They never did find the shooter, but they started asking different questions, and came up with the answer. The man knew he was dying, and had actually chosen to put a contract on himself. But if your Uncle Beppe was physically fit, and financially sound . . .'

'Which he was,' Mario confirmed.

Sarah glanced down at the body once more; her smile had disappeared. 'Then that can't apply here. So how did your uncle come to have upset someone badly enough for them to do that to him? Do you know much about his business?'

'Not as much as I'm going to. As of three hours ago, control of it passed to me.'

'What? I thought your mother was the co-trustee.'

'My mother's retiring,' he explained. 'I'm taking her place, and with Beppe dead, I'm the senior partner, with the casting vote.'

'God, won't that make things difficult for you?'

'I guess it will. I didn't ask for this, Sarah, I assure you, but it all goes back to my grandfather's will; I can't walk away from it, however messy it is.'

'Not even if there was a conflict of interest with your duty as a policeman?'

'Not even then.'

'Couldn't you persuade your mother to stay on for a while?'

He gasped. 'After this? What if Beppe's murder is connected to the business? Do you think I'd put her in the firing line?'

'No, of course not,' she replied, quickly. 'I'm sorry, I wasn't thinking straight.'

'There is one up-side, though,' he told her. 'Greg Jay won't have any trouble gaining access to the books and records of the Viareggio Trust.'

34

'You ever been in an air terminal that you really liked as a place?' asked Joe Doherty.

'Barcelona.'

'Lucky you. I hate 'em, all of them, whether they're monsters like Heathrow and O'Hare, or small-town operations like this one. And when it's dark outside, I hate 'em even worse.'

'Bollocks!' Skinner laughed. 'What you're really saying is that you hate flying.'

His friend's lip curled into a sneer. 'Show me a man who says he actually likes it . . . especially since September 11 . . . and I'll show you a liar.'

'You don't have to like it, Joe; you just have to do it. Personally, I cannot see how heavier-than-air machines ever make it off the ground, but they do, so I take it on trust. Now if you were talking about sailing, that would be different.'

'Uh? You don't like boats?'

'The smaller they are, the more I dislike them. I'll go on cross-channel ferries when I have to, like when I take the kids on holiday, but that's it.'

'You get sea-sick?' Doherty's sallow face was lit by his broadest smile. 'The great Bob Skinner gets sea-sick?'

'No. I've only ever felt sea-sick once in my life, and that was on the waltzer at Portobello funfair with Alex when she was a kid. All I could think about was how wide it would spread if I actually did throw up. I made it to the end of the ride . . . just. But boats; I don't like them, that's all.

'It's a childhood thing; my mum used to tell a story about a time she and my dad took me to Millport for the weekend, when I wasn't much more than a baby. Somehow, my old man managed to miss the last ferry on Sunday night, and since he had to be at work next morning, he hired a local bloke with a motorboat to take us across to Largs. I've got no conscious memory of it, but Mother said that it was a hell of a choppy trip, and that she was terrified. I suppose that communicated itself to me and that it's stayed with me ever since.'

'Oh,' said the American. 'In that case there's something I'd better share with you: the location of our meeting with Jackson Wylie, your father-in-law's ex-partner.'

Skinner stared at him. 'Not his fucking boat! Christ, when I met the guy at Leo's place I had to dredge the bottom of the barrel to find an excuse not to go out fishing with the two of them. Joe, tell me Kosinski hasn't booked us on to his fucking boat!'

'Wylie calls it his cruiser, but you got it, buddy; that's where it's at. You want to duck out?'

The stare became a glare. 'Duck out? So you can tell your pals in Washington all about it? There's two things in this life I don't like; small boats and looking at dead bodies. From time to time, I have to do the one, and I'll fucking well do the other if it's necessary. Not liking is a human feeling; not doing is a human weakness. I'll go across Wylie's gangplank, don't you worry.'

'In that case, the good news is that it'll be moored in the marina. This ain't no fishing trip . . . other than for any information the guy might have.'

The airport announcer broke into their conversation, calling them to the boarding gate for their flight to Buffalo. Skinner glanced up at the departure hall clock; it showed twelve minutes after six. Through the glass walls he saw the lightening sky, realising that already it was breakfast-time at their destination, and that further east, Sarah and the children should be having lunch. A wave of homesickness washed over him; he took out his cellphone and called home.

Trish, the nanny, answered; she was a friendly girl, the daughter of a Barbadian mother and a Yorkshire father who had met on a county cricket tour of the West Indies. 'No, Mr Skinner,' she told him. 'Sarah isn't here. She's up at the Royal, doing a post mortem on a murder victim.'

He laughed. 'She can't resist, can she. I'm married to a workaholic, Trish.'

'I guess you are, although she did say there were special circumstances involved with this one.'

'Wonder what she meant by that?' he mused, aloud. 'She'll tell me, I expect. Meantime, let me have a word with Mark.'

He had a brief conversation with his son as he walked to the gate, catching up on school news, then switched off the cellphone and put it away as his boarding card was checked.

The flight was even and uneventful; after a while, Joe Doherty almost relaxed. This time there was no view, other than of a cloud blanket that lasted all the way to the Great Lakes. So, instead of sightseeing, Skinner passed the time thinking, searching in vain through his sketchy knowledge of his father-in-law's business and personal history for any pointers to the mystery of his death.

The flight to Greater Buffalo International ended with a textbook landing and a sigh of relief from the Deputy Director of the FBI. As they stepped out of the aircraft they were hit by the warmth of the morning, a contrast from the Montana chill.

'Nice day for a sail,' Doherty remarked.

'Fuck off,' Skinner grunted, grimly.

They collected Kosinski's fax, in a white envelope, from the airport information desk, and returned to the rental car in the long-stay car park. Doherty climbed in and turned the ignition. Nothing happened. 'Shit!' he swore. 'Dud battery.'

Luckily, they were parked close to an exit booth; within ten minutes, an airport worker arrived with a fully charged start-up pack, and they were mobile once more. Still, they had lost time and were tight for their scheduled water-borne meeting with Jackson Wylie.

The Scot took the Special Agent's map as they set off; as soon as he looked at it, he realised that the drive would be longer than they had anticipated. The airport was around ten miles north of Buffalo, and Bayview, on Lake Erie, where the marina was located, looked to be the same distance to the south. The route that had been plotted for them took them round the outskirts of the city, but nonetheless, the Saturday traffic on Lakeshore was heavy.

Fortunately Bayview was a small community; the signs were poor, but still the marina was easy to find. They found a space at the rear of its dedicated car park, and set out to find Wylie's cruiser.

The marina was a bustle of activity; Skinner guessed that most of the boat-owners were strictly fair-weather sailors and that the fine spring day had drawn them in droves to ready their vessels for the summer to come. 'Says here that we're looking for mooring number two-seven-three,' Doherty muttered. 'The boat's called the *Hispaniola*.'

'*Treasure Island*, eh. D'you think our man fancies himself as Long John Silver?'

'Maybe so. Robert Louis Stevenson spent some time in New York State.'

'Ah, come on, next you'll be telling me that John Logie Baird was an

American.' Skinner paused. 'Hey, wait a minute.' He pointed along a boardwalk jetty not far from the gateway to the marina, where they stood. 'See that cruiser there; about ten boats along. A big bugger of a thing with an awning on top. There's a guy on deck, and I'm pretty sure that's Jackson Wylie.

'Fuckin' hell,' the policeman chuckled, 'he's got a barbecue going. He's on a boat, and he's got a barbie lit.'

'You should be pleased then; it means he really ain't planning to sail anywhere.' Doherty glanced at his watch. 'Come on then, let's go see him. It's not too bad; we're only just over five minutes late.'

Skinner nodded, looked down automatically to check his footing among the ropes and paint-pots that littered the wide walkway, and set out after him. He had taken two steps when, with no warning, he felt his head swim, and his knees buckle. The strangest sensation swept through him; it was as if he had stood in that spot before, had played the same scene in a parallel life. He felt as if he was in a throng of rushing, relentless people. 'Joe,' he heard himself call out, hoarsely.

The American stopped and looked over his shoulder, frowning as he caught sight of his friend's face. 'Bob, you okay?' he asked.

But Skinner's spell had passed, as suddenly as it had come upon him. 'Yes, yes,' he said, quickly.

'You sure? You look as though you'd seen a ghost.' He walked back towards him.

'For a minute I thought I had; it was . . . Shit, I don't know. For a second there, I thought I was going in the drink. You know what I reckon it was? The water; the way it moves as you look through the planks. I know I said I don't get sea-sick, but I think I was pretty close to it there.'

'Listen,' said Doherty. 'Go back to the car if you want. I won't tell anyone, honest.'

'Don't be daft, man. I'll be all right.' They waited for a minute or so, until Skinner nodded. 'No, it's gone; I'm okay. Come on. Let's not keep the man waiting any longer.'

He took a step along the boardwalk . . . and then the whole world turned orange, and red, and black, all in the same instant.

A great invisible force seemed to pick the two men off their feet and hurl them backwards, sending them crashing on to the jetty. They lay there, stunned, until the noise caught up with them, followed almost at once by the awareness of great heat. A second explosion sounded; not so fierce, but closer this time.

Skinner propped himself up on an elbow and looked along, focusing his blurred eyes. The *Hispaniola* was nowhere to be seen; not in its original form. It was at the centre of an inferno; in the midst of which he thought he could see a figure, staggering jerkily around, a human torch, its arms waving in slow motion, and then seeming to sink into itself.

The boat next to it was on fire too; that had been the second explosion, he guessed, since it was closer to them. Its flames, in turn, were licking another large cruiser, even nearer to where they lay. If its tanks went up . . .

He scrambled to his feet, looking at his friend as he did so. Doherty was unconscious, stunned either by the blast or by the force of his impact with the boardwalk. Skinner knelt beside him; grabbed his left arm and his right leg, and in a single powerful movement, stood once more, heaving the American over his shoulder.

And then he ran, as if Doherty weighed nothing at all; as far and as fast as he could. Hearing the crackling of the flames and feeling their heat as they crept towards him, Bob Skinner ran, carrying his friend, for their very lives.

35

Mario had always been slightly in awe of his grandmother. As a child, he had loved Papa Viareggio almost to the point of worship, but Nana had inspired something different in him. She had never been forbidding, but there had been something about her that had marked her out from the norm, an inner strength that at times could make her seem aloof, even from her children and grandchildren.

She had always dealt with the world on her terms, and never in his life had her grandson seen her give an inch in the face of misfortune.

And so he was not surprised when he went to visit her, in the terraced house not far from Murrayfield Stadium that had been her home for sixty years, to be greeted at the front door with a steely look which betrayed not a sign of frailty.

'Well?' she demanded. 'What have you come to tell me, son?'

He did not answer her; instead he kissed her on the cheek, and allowed her to lead him into the living room, where his mother and Aunt Sophia sat, stunned by the loss of a brother and a husband.

'Where are the girls?' he asked.

'Our Paula's in the kitchen, cooking something or other for our supper. Viola's gone home to her family, where she should be. So, come on, laddie; out with it. Have your policemen caught the evil man who murdered my son?' Her voice was full of controlled rage; he read it at once, for he felt the same way himself.

'We're doing all we can, Nana,' he began, but she cut him off.

'I know that,' she snapped. 'I trust you not to let them do any less. But that's not what I asked you.'

'In that case, the answer's no. We haven't caught him. The truth is, Nana, we don't even know where to begin to look. We've got not a scrap of physical evidence. We recovered the bullet that killed him, but as the pathologist predicted before she did the p.m., it was too distorted for us to have a chance of identifying the gun that fired it. If the weapon had been used in another crime, you see . . .'

'Ach, I know that, Mario,' the old lady retorted. 'I watch *Quincy*.' She looked away from him for the first time. 'Can you tell me this? Did he suffer?'

He could see, out of the corner of his eye, his mother and his aunt tense as she asked the question.

'No,' he answered, as firmly as he could. 'Not a bit. It was instantaneous; I doubt very much if he even heard the gunshot.'

'Paula heard a policeman say there was a silencer.'

He glanced at his cousin as she came into the room. 'They just muffle the noise, Nana,' he said. 'And this was a big gun.'

'So what have you been doing all day?'

'I've been helping my colleague Detective Superintendent Jay. You have to realise, Nana, that I'm a witness in this investigation, not a participant. I've spent most of the day so far in Uncle Beppe's office with two specialist detectives, going through all of the books of the business in the hope that we might find something that pointed to a reason for the murder.'

'You mean you were trying to find out if Beppe had been up to no good?'

'No, Nana, I didn't mean that.'

She patted him on the arm and settled stiffly into her high-backed armchair, throwing him a faint smile. 'Of course you did, son; but you don't need to soft-soap me. I could have told you you'd be wasting your time there. Your poor uncle might not have been about to win the Businessman of the Year award, but he wasn't a crook.

'And remember, even if he had been that stupid, your mother was there as the second trustee. She'd have stopped him in his tracks.'

'I know, I know,' he agreed. 'But this is a police investigation, and things can't be taken on faith. They have to be looked at. We've done that now, and of course there was nothing there. In a way I wish there had been, it would have given us a bloody lead.'

'Aye,' the old lady said sharply, 'and dragged our name through the mud at the same time. I would rather that you didn't catch the man who shot Beppe, than for that to happen.'

'Oh, we'll catch him, Nana, don't you worry about that. The man's not walking away from this. As for the family name, I'll keep it as safe as I can. I may carry my father's surname, but I'm as much a Viareggio as anyone in this room.'

'Mario.' His mother called to him, from across the room. He turned to face her; she was as red-eyed as her sister-in-law, and at the sight of her the memory of his father's death flooded into his consciousness. 'I've been thinking all day about this, ever since you told me about Beppe. I think I'd better stay for a while; stay in the trust, I mean.'

He shook his head; there was a slow finality about the gesture. 'No,' he said. 'That's not going to happen. I've been thinking about it too, don't worry. This day was always going to come, one way or another; Beppe's gone and you're gone. Paula and I are in control of the businesses now, and that's how it's going to stay. It's Papa's will, and you can't fight that.'

'But won't it conflict with your duties as policeman?'

'It's unlikely, but if it did, there's a way around it. I have a lawyer, someone I know and trust. On Thursday, I had her look at the trust provisions; they allow for me to appoint her, or someone else suitable, as my proxy, to exercise all my powers on my behalf. If I'm advised that it's necessary, I may well do that, but first . . . we're going to find the bugger who made my Aunt Sophia a widow.'

36

'Of all the fatally stupid things I have seen, sir,' said the sheriff's marine patrol lieutenant, 'they don't come any more stupid than that . . . or any more fatal. Lighting a charcoal barbecue in the middle of a crowded marina, with all that fuel around . . .'

Dwayne Traylor shook his head and looked at Skinner. 'So far, in addition to Mr Wylie's cruiser, we've lost four other boats, and had serious damage to three others. There are no dead . . . other than the guy himself, and he's as dead as you can get . . . but one lady has gone to the emergency room with burns to her arms and face, and with most of her hair frazzled.'

The young man glanced into the treatment bay, behind the yacht club's reception area. Joe Doherty lay on a long leather-topped table; a doctor was leaning over him, putting stitches into a long gash on his cheekbone. 'How's your buddy?' he asked.

'Okay, I hope,' the Scot answered. 'He was out for three or four minutes after the explosion. I told him he should go to hospital; he told me I should go to hell.' He glanced at the officer. 'Did you call Sheriff Dekker?'

'As instructed, sir. He was on the tennis court, but when I gave him your names and told him what had happened, he said to give him ten minutes to shower and he'd be on his way.' Traylor frowned. 'He called you Deputy Chief Skinner, sir. From where, exactly, may I ask?'

'Edinburgh.'

'As in Edinborough, Scotland?'

'More or less.'

'Deputy Chief of what?'

'Well, I'm not a fucking visiting fireman, however you put it here,' Skinner snapped, irritably. He stopped, then apologised. 'I'm sorry, son. No need to bite your head off. I'm a policeman; deputy chief constable.'

'And your buddy, Mr Doherty there; is he Scottish too?'

'Son of a bitch!' came a shout, from the treatment table.

'Does that answer your question?'

Lieutenant Traylor grinned. 'I guess so.'

'Tell me,' the Scot asked, 'do you have many incidents involving moored boats?'

'Not like this one, sir, I'm happy to say. Last Thanksgiving I arrested a guy who was drunk and launching fireworks from his boat in a marina complex a little further down the lakeside. He told me they were distress flares. They may have been, but I still charged him with public disorder and breach of half-a-dozen county ordinances, and took him into custody, for his own safety, and everyone else's.

'That was an exception, though; most boat-owners are responsible people. They have to be. They're indulging in a very expensive hobby. Apart from the capital cost of these cruisers, the berths in places like this are expensive, and marine insurance doesn't come cheap.'

'So what Jackson Wylie did was exceptional too?'

Traylor hesitated. 'Cooking on deck on an open fire, rather than in an enclosed galley, is stupid, sir, like I said, but truth be told, it's common enough behaviour.'

'Have you seen many accidents like this one?'

'A couple of small fires, maybe, but nothing on this scale. Do you know if there's a Mrs Wylie?'

'I don't believe so. I heard she died a few years back.'

'Children?'

'None that I know of.'

'In that case, the executors, whoever they are, had better pray that the insurance company takes a sympathetic view, otherwise the other boat-owners, and especially that lady with the frazzled hair, will sue the ass off the estate. If that happens, Mr Wylie better leave a hell of a lot of money to pay off all the claims.'

The lieutenant was looking over Skinner's shoulder as he spoke, towards the door to the marina reception. Suddenly he stood, and came to attention. 'Good afternoon, Sheriff,' he exclaimed.

'Afternoon, Dwayne,' said Bradford Dekker, barely glancing at him. Instead he looked anxiously at the big Scot. 'Bob, how are you? How's Mr Doherty?'

For a second Skinner's inbuilt cynicism came to the surface, and he wondered whether the sheriff's concern was for his friend or for the potential fall-out from the FBI if its deputy director had been injured seriously in a sloppily managed facility in his territory.

'I'm fine,' he answered. 'Joe's got a hole in his head, but they're stitching it up right now.'

'What happened? Traylor gave me the outline, but . . .'

'There wasn't much more than an outline, Brad. We were walking towards Wylie's boat when it went up like a fucking candle.'

'There wasn't any warning?'

The DCC shook his head. 'Not that I can remember. All I saw was the fireball.' He frowned as the recollection of his dizzy spell came back to him. For a second he thought he was about to have a recurrence, but the feeling passed. 'I can't really swear to anything.'

'Me neither,' said Joe Doherty, from the doorway to the treatment room. 'I remember turning to talk to Bob, then coming round in here. Was there anyone else on Wylie's boat?'

Traylor sucked in his breath. 'We have no reason to think that there was, sir. None of the other owners saw anyone else. However, we won't be able to say for sure until we've been over what's left of the *Hispaniola*.'

'You mean it's still afloat?'

'Just and no more. They have pretty good fire-fighting equipment here, and the local volunteer crew responded quickly. They got the fire under control before she burned down to the waterline.'

Doherty raised his eyebrows as he looked at Skinner, wincing as the gesture tugged at the fresh stitches along the side of his head. 'That's a break, eh, Bob?'

'Maybe, but if it is, it'll only be a small one . . . and none at all for Jackson Wylie.'

'What . . .' The young lieutenant looked at them, puzzled.

'Tell your technical people to stand down, Sheriff,' said Doherty to Dekker. 'I'm bringing my best team up from Quantico to go over that wreck.'

'You think there's a connection to Mr Grace?' exclaimed the police chief.

'God preserve my country from elected public officials,' Skinner bellowed. 'Of course there is, Brad. They were partners in the same law firm, they're both bloody dead, and neither from natural causes!'

37

His cousin's house was a bit like the lady herself; all designer chic and soft furnishings on the bits that showed, but rock-solid underneath . . . or so Mario McGuire had thought until that moment.

The Paula Viareggio who sat in the passenger seat as he drew up outside the converted warehouse just off Great Junction Street was someone he had not seen since they were children, after her pet rabbit had been eaten by the cat next door.

She was sobbing quietly into the handkerchief that he had given her not long after he had driven away from Murrayfield, leaving Nana to comfort her daughter-in-law, and her daughter.

'We're here,' he said, gently; not knowing what else to do, he reached across and patted her on the shoulder. 'Come on; I'll see you inside.'

'Okay,' she mumbled, through the handkerchief, and then waited . . . *Un-Paula-like again*, he thought . . . as he walked round the car to open her door.

She took his arm as they walked towards the building. Normally he would have driven into the courtyard, but it was Saturday, and he had guessed, correctly as it happened, that the car park would be full and that manoeuvring would have been difficult.

As they turned in off the street, two figures were waiting, both young men, one of them holding a camera, the other what looked like a small tape recorder. They turned to look at them, and as they did McGuire heard the reporter exclaim, 'That's her.'

Before the photographer could fire off a single frame, the big detective stepped slightly in front of his cousin. 'Don't do that, mate,' he warned. The man moved to his right, hunting for Paula with his lens, but he was too slow. Mario's hand shot out, grabbed the camera and ripped it from his grasp.

'Hey, gimme that! You can't do that!'

'I just did. Now stop shouting or I'll give it back to you piece by piece.'

'Want me to get the police?'

'He is the police,' said the reporter quietly. Close to, he looked a few years older than the photographer, as if he had left his thirtieth birthday behind him on the road. As he turned back to the couple, the evening sunlight seemed to glint on his designer jacket. 'You're Chief Inspector McGuire, aren't you? I'm Christian Sanderson, of the *Sunday Mail*. I'd like to talk to Miss Viareggio about her father's murder. We've just come from Mr Pringle's press conference at Fettes. Are you involved in the investigation, Chief Inspector?'

'That's Detective Superintendent, Mr Sanderson,' Mario told him. As he looked at him he could see the front page of the following day's Sunday tabloid, but he knew that if he held back the truth and Sanderson found out, the headline would be that much bigger. 'And the answer's no; I'm not part of the CID team. This is a family matter; Beppe Viareggio was my uncle.'

He heard the reporter's gasp above the sound of a van roaring past on the street outside. 'Mr Pringle and Mr Jay never told us that.'

'Why should they? I'm as entitled to privacy as the rest of the family.'

'Aye, but now it's known, can I talk to you about it?'

'No!' McGuire bellowed. 'Don't be daft. I might be family, but I am still a copper, and I couldn't tell you anything about my colleagues' enquiries, suppose I knew anything.'

'It's been suggested that this was a contract killing,' said the journalist. 'Is that right? Was Mr Viareggio involved with the Mafia?'

'You . . .' He heard his cousin, standing beside him now, begin to explode, but he squeezed her arm hard enough to silence her outburst.

'What bright spark suggested that?' he asked.

'My news desk had a phone call half-an-hour ago. A guy rang in and told us that it was.'

'And did he leave his name and number?'

Many a journalist would have looked sheepish at that question, McGuire knew, but Sanderson kept a straight face. 'No. It was anonymous.'

'Surprise, surprise.' The big detective laughed, but only for a second. 'Right,' he said, abruptly. 'I will give you a statement, but it's not from the police, it's from the victim's family, represented by my cousin and by me as the Viareggio trustees. My uncle was an honest, upright, well-respected businessman, as was his father before him. Anyone who suggests otherwise in the press or elsewhere, will find themselves dealing with our solicitors.

'You give that to your news desk, word for word.' He looked Sanderson in the eye. 'Now the policeman's back; this is private property and my cousin is asking you to go.'

'Fair enough,' said the journalist. 'But what about my colleague's camera?'

'Sure, here you are.' He held out the Nikon to the photographer, pressing the shutter button as he did so and hearing the whirr of the motor drive as the rest of the film inside was exposed. 'By the way,' he called after the two men as they left, 'don't approach any other members of my family. You've been fairly reasonable so far, but you don't want to piss me off.'

'Thanks,' Paula whispered as he took her key and opened the door to the building. 'I don't know what I'd have done if I'd come in on my own.'

Mario grinned. 'Probably the same as you did to that copper on the door last night. It would have made a great photograph.'

'Bloody vultures,' she muttered.

'Nah,' he countered. 'Just guys doing a job.'

'What? Acting on an anonymous phone call?'

'No, just checking it out. The police get anonymous tip-offs all the time. Do you think we don't follow them up just because the caller doesn't leave his name? To tell you the truth, cousin,' he said, 'the thing that worries me about the call to the *Mail* is that it was bloody close to the mark. Your father's murder did look like a professional job.' They stopped at the elevator and he pressed the call button; the doors slid open at once. 'I think I'll come up with you; there are a couple of calls I should make.'

Paula's flat was on the top floor, not unlike her parents' in that the living space was open plan. Mario had never been inside in the two years she had lived there; he looked around, taking in the fabrics wound round the pillars, the tasteful modern paintings on the walls, and the expensive lighting which hung from the high ceiling.

'The sauna business must be good,' he chuckled.

She bristled at once. 'Not bad, thank you very much. God, you sounded just like my dad, there.'

'Never in my life have I sounded like your dad, rest his soul.'

'Well, stop going on about it, then. I saw a chance to get a wee business for myself, and I took it. What's wrong with that?'

'In principle, nothing; it's the "wee business" you chose to get into that I don't like. You know what these places are, Paula; they're knocking shops.'

'They're all licensed by the city council,' she protested.

'Which turns a blind eye to what goes on in them because it gets the girls off the streets. Tell me this. Do you pay the girls who work there, or do they pay you?'

'They don't pay me a penny, and they get decent wages! The punters pay for their saunas, cash or credit card. What happens between them and the attendants is their business, but I do not take a cut.' She stepped up to him, her dark eyes flashing, with real anger. 'I'll tell you what I do, though; I insist that they use condoms and I make them have monthly blood tests ... not just for the clap, but for drug use. If someone's working just to feed a habit, she won't get through the door. If someone's working to feed her kids, she's welcome.'

'That's very moral, cousin, very moral,' he flared back, his gaze as fiery as hers. 'You're a madam with a heart of gold! But what about the guys whose kids go short because they spend their dough getting blown on your massage tables? What about them, eh?'

'Would you rather have them prowling the streets looking for it? Better they pay for it, otherwise even some of those kids you're talking about might not be safe.'

'You . . .' He stopped himself short, as a vision of his wife filled his mind; until then he had been at pains to keep it at bay, but in the heat of the argument it managed to sneak under his defences.

Paula turned away from him. 'Let's call a truce, Mario. Just make your phone calls, then you can go.'

'Fine,' he agreed, 'but tell me this. Did Uncle Beppe know about those places?'

She paused. 'I never told him,' she answered. 'You only know because you're a clever bastard copper. But my mum doesn't know, nor does Nana.'

Mario smiled at her. 'The latter goes without saying. I'll tell you this too; if she ever finds out she'll boil you down for soup.'

'That's your hold on me.' She grinned back; her olive skin had a weary, yellowish tinge. 'Who're you going to phone anyway?'

He walked over to a big soft armchair, sat down, and picked up the mock-fifties telephone that lay on a table beside it. 'Listen in.'

He made two calls. The first was to Greg Jay, to advise him of the anonymous tip-off to the *Sunday Mail*. The second was to John Hunter, a trusted veteran freelance journalist, to whom he repeated the statement that he had given to Christian Sanderson. 'There,' he said as he put the big black handset back in its cradle. 'John'll put the word around. If that bastard's called any other papers, he won't go unanswered.'

She stood in front of him, laying her hands flat on his broad chest, running them up under the lapels of his blazer. Raising herself slightly on her toes, she kissed him, quickly, on the lips, then again, longer, then a third time, drawn out, her tongue flicking his teeth.

At last he gripped her by the elbows and held her away from him. 'Hey,' he whispered, 'what was that for?'

'It was for not being such a bad guy after all.'

'Don't tell anyone else, though.'

'I promise. Would you take me to bed, please, cousin?'

'We've been over this before . . . and I was single then.'

'We have indeed,' she murmured, pressing her body against him. 'And I wasn't as drunk as you either. You do owe me one, you know. There is absolutely nothing worse for a girl's morale than when a guy fucks her and can't remember it next morning . . . unless it's when they're in bed together and he doesn't fuck her at all.'

'So which was it then?' he asked, eventually. It was a question he had put off asking for years.

'Actually . . .' She gave a deep throaty chuckle. 'Truth be told . . .' She looked up at him with laughter in her eyes. 'It was more a case of me fucking you, big boy . . . or as I remember, very big boy.' She slid her right hand down, searching for him: he did nothing to stop her. 'Oh yes,' she hissed. 'That's the fella, all right.'

She gave him a quick squeeze then slid her arms around his waist. 'Come on. Find out what you snorted and mumbled your way through last time. Who was Bridget, by the way?'

He frowned. 'She was the barmaid in my local. Why?'

'That's what you kept calling me.'

She took his hand in hers and turned, pulling him towards a door off the big pillared room. He stepped into her bedroom, but then tugged her back towards him. 'Don't play games, Paula. All right, we gave each other one when we were youngsters, and I'm sorry I wasn't more up for it . . .'

Her laugh cut across him. 'What do you mean? Even in your sleep, you were as up for it as you could get.'

'Maybe so, but it isn't going to happen again, and you know it. Listen, it's been a hellish twenty-four hours, I know. Why don't you just have a big drink and get some sleep?'

She looked up at him, and he saw that her eyes were glazed with tears once more. 'Just stay with me, Mario. Please. I won't threaten your virtue if you don't want me to, but don't go. I can't get the sight of my father out of my mind. Whenever I close my eyes, I can see him lying there, with his arse sticking up in the air and the back of his head blown out.'

'You'll see that whether I'm here or not, love. So will I. I wish I could tell you different, but you'll see it for a while. When someone's murdered, there's usually more than one victim.'

She seemed to slump against him. 'It's not just that, though,' she cried into his chest. 'What if there is something about the business or about Dad, that we don't know? What if it passes to us now? You're a policeman; no one's going to threaten you. But what about me? What about me?

'I don't want to be next!'

38

Bob Skinner and Joe Doherty stood on the gangway beside Jackson Wylie's mooring, looking at what was left of his boat. All of the superstructure and the deck had gone, save for the twisted metal framework of some of the fittings; below, virtually all that was left was a black, soggy mess, where the firefighters' hoses had pounded the blaze into extinction.

The exception was a rectangle of Day-Glo yellow, a tarpaulin laid by the sheriff's deputies over the remains of Leopold Grace's former partner.

'Well, Bob,' asked Doherty, 'what do you think? Was it a stray spark from the barbecue and it's hooray and up she rises?'

'It's possible,' the big Scot murmured. 'So, I'm told, are interstellar travel, miracle cures for terminal illnesses, and peace in the Balkans. As a friend said to me the other day, it's also conceivable that Motherwell Football and Athletic Club could win the Scottish Premier League in my lifetime. But I don't believe that any of those things is actually going to happen, any more than I believe that this was a fucking accident.

'If our theory of a link between the murders of Leo, Wilkins and Garrett is correct, then that thing lying under the sheriff's groundsheet, done to a cinder, is number four. You're not going to tell me any different, are you?'

'No, sir, I am not. We'd better find out all we can about him, quick as we can. How much do you know? You met the guy, after all.'

Skinner shook his head. 'I know nothing about him. Yes, we met one time at my father-in-law's but we didn't exchange life stories.'

'Did Mr Grace ever talk about him?'

'Very little. He mentioned once that he had brought Wylie into the law firm back in the early seventies, and that he had appointed him as senior partner on his retirement on a sort of caretaker basis, a safe pair of hands while the younger guys were gaining more experience.'

'How old was he?'

'About ten years younger than Leo, I'd have guessed. He'd have been looking towards retirement himself now.'

'Married?'

'Widowed. His wife died a few years back. When we spoke he mentioned a son in Florida, a journalist with the *Miami Herald*.'

Doherty touched his head wound, gingerly. 'Gotta take another painkiller,' he muttered, taking a small bottle from his pocket. 'Let's go back to the office; I can't take these damn things without water.'

They walked silently along the gangway. Eventually the American gave a heavy sigh. 'Guess I'd better break into the guys' weekends.'

'To do what?' asked Skinner. 'They can't make any progress on Garrett or Wilkins till Monday. We're on the ground here; we can get Dekker's men moving on this new investigation, and we can do a couple of things ourselves.'

'Such as?'

'Well, eventually, we can sit down and think, but first we should find Mrs Thorpe, Wylie's secretary. We need to find out who might have known that he'd be on that boat. Brad Dekker's digging up her address for us.'

'Yeah. Who knows, maybe she can tell us a lot more than that. She worked for both him and Grace; maybe she can tell us what this is all about.'

The Scot grunted. 'I hope not, for her sake. If she could, I have a hell of a feeling we're going to find her dead. Come on, take your pill and let's get moving.'

39

When she saw the woman standing in the hall, holding a blue leather overnight bag, Maggie could not keep a flash of surprise from crossing her face; but it was suppressed almost at once, to be replaced by a welcoming smile.

Mario stood behind his cousin. 'I've invited Paula to stay the night,' he explained to his wife. 'She's still a bit shaken up. Nana's got a full house with Mum and Auntie Sophia, and Viola's is full of weans, so she's best here.'

'Of course,' she agreed at once, standing aside to allow them to pass into the living room. 'Come on in. Mario, put Paula's bag in the spare room, and stick a sheet on the bed while you're there. The duvet's okay, I think.'

'Yes, boss. We got enough grub for three, or will I get a takeaway?'

'No, we've got plenty. I raided Marks and Spencer's food hall this afternoon, big time. I decided we should invite the whole family for lunch tomorrow; I've spoken to Nana and Stanley, and it's all set up. Just as well you're here, Paula; it'll save you a drive tomorrow.' She looked at her husband. 'That's okay with you, isn't it?'

'Sure it is. Man U are on telly tomorrow afternoon; that'll keep the kids quiet.'

Paula laughed softly. '. . . And their father, and their uncle. Maggie,' she asked, 'can I use your bathroom?'

'Of course. Down the hall, first on the left; your room's the one beyond.'

'Fine. I'll drop my bag off myself while I'm there.'

Maggie waited until she heard the bathroom door close, then gave Mario a long appraising look. 'You're being very solicitous towards your cousin, aren't you? I thought you didn't even like her.'

'No, that's not true. I don't trust her,' he said, 'and I don't like some of the things she's done, but we were kids together, she's family and she's scared.'

'Scared? Paula?'

He nodded. 'Even tough girls . . . other than you, my dear . . . can get their knickers in a twist sometimes. Some nutter phoned the papers saying that Beppe's murder was a Mafia hit. Paula's afraid that might be true, and that she might be next.'

'And might she?'

'I doubt it. But the shooting was premeditated, that's for sure. It was efficient and there was nothing random about it.'

'And might you have something to worry about?' she asked, quietly.

Mario put his hands on her shoulders and looked her in the eye. 'I'm a police detective superintendent, love, and on top of that I'm quite a formidable bastard. Who's going to come after me?

'Honestly, I think Paula's worrying unnecessarily; once she's had a day or two to get over the shock of seeing her father like that, she'll come to realise it. Somewhere there's a reason for Uncle Beppe's murder, but I can't see it having anything to do with the business.'

'Have you spoken to your mother?'

'Not about that; anyhow I don't have to. She'd never have tolerated any nonsense within the trust, and she's too good a businesswoman for Beppe ever to have been able to hide anything from her.'

Maggie dropped into an armchair. 'This thing seems to have exposed a big gap in my knowledge,' she mused aloud. 'There's a lot of stuff you've never really told me, isn't there, Mario?'

He looked at her, from beneath raised eyebrows. 'Such as?'

'Your papa's will for a start, and your place on the trust in succession to Christina.'

He shrugged, as if it was no matter. 'I didn't want to think about it myself, I suppose. And you've kept a couple of things from me, remember.'

She flinched for a second, but ignored his comment. 'Okay, but there's more than that. I have a rough idea of the family's interests but no more than that. Exactly what does this trust control?'

It was Paula who answered her, as she came back into the room. 'We own a classic mix of Scots-Italian businesses,' she said. 'They're up and down east central Scotland, in strong retail centres. There are ten cafés doing tea and coffee catering, each selling our own-brand ice-cream, which we also supply to co-operative food stores. Then we have five takeaways, two in Edinburgh, one in Dundee, one in St Andrews and one in Falkirk. Originally, they were big chippies, with sitting-in areas, but when fish prices started to rise, we started doing pizzas and roast chickens as well, and took the seats out. My dad wanted to do kebabs as well, but my mum said no, because they'd stink the shops out.

'There are eight delicatessens in the chain, in Edinburgh, Dundee, St Andrews, Dunfermline, Dalkeith and North Berwick. We specialise in imported Italian food and wines, from suppliers that Papa Viareggio set up years ago.

'That's all the retail side; alongside it, there's our property holdings. We own our own premises, and in several cases the buildings in which they're located, the other shops and the flats above. That's the side of the business that's grown in recent years; Stan's started making investment purchases outside our traditional areas of operations. He's been buying office property around Edinburgh, outside the city bypass, with good solid tenants and the potential for expansion.'

'Stan?' Maggie asked, surprised.

'Yes,' said Mario. 'You know; Stan Coia, Viola's husband. He's a surveyor by profession, and he manages the property side.'

'I thought Uncle Beppe ran everything.'

'He had overall control, sure, but he had help. Aunt Sophia looks after the cafés, Viola supervises the takeaways, Stan, like I said, handles property, and Paula, although she works in the Stockbridge deli, is general manager of them all. They all reported back to the trustees.'

She looked at him, her mouth hanging open slightly. 'I knew hardly any of this; I didn't have a clue that Stan and Viola were in the business too. And now you're the senior trustee?'

'I didn't ask for it, love, honest; nor did I expect that it would happen for a while, possibly not till I was ready to retire from the police force.'

'And how are you going to handle it?'

'Maybe by appointing a proxy; I don't know. That's something Paula and I are going to have to sort out between us.'

'But not tonight, eh?' There was a tired plea in his cousin's voice.

40

To the immense relief of Skinner and Doherty, Mrs Lucinda Thorpe came to the door of her small suburban Buffalo home, alive and well, if slightly hysterical. She was a tall, sturdily built, middle-aged black woman, with an imposing presence, and so the white Kleenex with which she dabbed at her puffy eyes seemed entirely out of place.

'This is not a good time to be calling, gentlemen,' she told them in a strong, deep voice.

'We know, Mrs Thorpe,' said the Scot, 'but it's necessary. I guess you've seen a news bulletin on television.'

Mrs Thorpe shook her head. 'No, but I had a call from my husband. He's at his golf club, and he saw something there. It really is true? Oh my, poor Mr Wylie. My friend told me that the police are saying that he lit a barbecue on the deck of his cruiser boat and it blew up.'

'That's all true; but what they still have to prove is that the explosion was actually caused by a spark from the charcoal.'

Her eyes narrowed slightly. 'And let me guess: you don't think it was.' She paused. 'Who are you guys anyway? You're cops, but you ain't the local police, that's for sure.'

'No, we're not. Mr Doherty here is with the FBI.' As he spoke, the American pulled out a laminated identity card from his jacket and held it up for the woman to see. 'Let's call me a consultant in his investigation; I'm a detective from Scotland. I'm also Leo Grace's son-in-law.'

'Ah,' said the secretary, flicking through her memory banks, 'the guys Mr Wylie was meeting. So you're Miss Sarah's husband. Yeah, I heard she married an older guy.' Skinner heard Joe Doherty stifle a chuckle. 'But I heard it didn't work out.'

'It's working fine now, I promise you. Look, can we come in? We need to talk to you.'

She held the door open for them and ushered them indoors, through the living room and out into a sunny back garden, complete with a small blue-tiled swimming pool. She pointed to it. 'That was a personal gift from Mr Grace, when he retired. Nice man; what happened to him and his poor wife was just awful. And now, with Mr Wylie . . .' She paused, as they settled into white plastic chairs, set around a table.

'Of course,' she murmured. 'You guys think there's a connection.'

'Let's just say that we're blessed with the cynicism for which the FBI is famous,' Doherty answered.

Mrs Thorpe looked at him, almost for the first time, her eyes drawn to the gauze that had been taped to the side of his head, over the stitches.

'What happened to you?' she asked.

'I got a shade too close to Mr Wylie's boat when it blew up. It was as well I was with this big old guy here; he hauled my ass out of there.'

'You were actually there when it happened?'

'Yup.'

Her curiosity broke through her shock. 'So what did it look like?'

'Like the biggest bonfire night you've ever seen,' Skinner answered. 'Mrs Thorpe,' he continued, over her puzzlement, 'after Agent Kosinski arranged our meeting with Mr Wylie, who would have known about it?'

'Just about anyone in the firm,' she told him. 'Yesterday, we had our monthly lunch for partners and associates, and Mr Wylie mentioned there that the FBI wanted to talk to him about Mr Grace's murder. There were around thirty-five people present, so he might as well have run an ad on television.'

Doherty gave a soft moan. 'Superb,' he muttered.

'Ah, but he didn't say that it had been arranged.'

The deputy director's face brightened. 'Mrs Thorpe, do you know if Mr Wylie had been in touch with Mr Grace recently?'

'Depends what you mean by recently. The deer hunting trip was in January, but I'm not aware of their having spoken since then. Of course that doesn't mean that they hadn't. I don't know absolutely everything that my boss did; as well as his office engagement book, he kept a private diary on that laptop thing he had.'

'Laptop?' Skinner repeated.

'Yes, sir. An Apple Mac iBook; he's had it since the beginning of the year. It has a plum-coloured casing, and a built-in modem; everywhere he went, he took that damn thing with him.'

'Would he have had it with him on the boat today?'

'For sure.'

The Scot looked at Doherty. 'Wilkins had a laptop, remember. It was stolen.'

'I sure do remember.'

Without another word, the deputy director took out his cellphone and called the FBI lab. 'Alan,' he said, quietly, 'I want you to contact the team we have heading for Buffalo, and ask them to look specifically for the remains of a laptop computer.'

As he replaced the pocket phone he turned back to Skinner. 'Did Leo Grace have a laptop?'

'I wouldn't know.' The DCC paused. 'Sarah used to get e-mails from him; his address is in the book on our computer at home. But there's a desktop in his house, down in his den, so he probably used that. Still it's possible that he had a laptop as well; it's possible.'

'Mrs Thorpe,' asked the American. 'The names we mentioned, Wilkins and Garrett; Agent Kosinski told us you were going to look through Mr Grace's files for references to them. Have you done that?'

'Yes, sir, I did that yesterday afternoon; and I told Mr Kosinski the result. There is no mention of either of those gentlemen in Mr Grace's papers. There's nothing on the firm's computer files either. I ran a check on them at the same time. I even asked Mr Wylie if he had heard of either of them. He just shrugged his shoulders and gave me a blank look.'

'In that case, that completes our business. Thank you for your time, and our condolences over your loss.' He stood, with a sideways glance at Skinner. 'Bob.'

'Yes. But there's just one thing. You mentioned a hunting trip earlier.'

She smiled, and her pleasant ebony face seemed to light up. 'Sure, the deer hunt. That was back in January, like I said. Mr Grace and Mr Wylie decided to take themselves off down to the Appalachians for a week, blowing the hell out of those poor animals. Didn't your father-in-law mention it to you?'

'I can't say that he did. Never mind. Thanks anyway.'

She showed them out, and down the path to their car. As they stood on the sidewalk, Doherty took out his cellphone, and dialled in a number. 'Zak? Good; something I need to know. Was there a note on the Garrett inventory of a missing computer? A laptop. There was? Excellent. Thanks.'

He ended the call and nodded to Skinner. 'The kid confirmed it. Garrett had one too.'

As he closed the passenger door of the saloon, the Scot turned to his friend. 'Joe, there's something wrong with Mrs Thorpe's story. Leo Grace was a Korean War hero; he saw a lot of action. It affected him so much that after he got back, he never picked up a gun for the rest of his life. He detested the National Rifle Association, and I never met anyone who was more strongly opposed to blood sports.

'No fucking way did he go shooting deer in the Appalachians or anywhere else.'

'So I wonder what he did in that backwoods week? Maybe Sarah'll know when she gets here Monday.'

'Maybe. Roll on the day.'

Doherty smiled. 'Do I take it from that, that you're not looking forward to a quiet Sunday in Buffalo?'

'You take it right.'

'Well, that's good, because I have another day trip planned for you. We are heading, my friend, for the show that never ends, Our Nation's Capital. It's time we took a look at the politics of this thing.'

41

The gathering was sombre; even Ryan and David were subdued, although they were barely old enough to comprehend the meaning of death. Maggie wondered if they were simply behaving as instructed, or if their mother's near-paralysing grief had scared them into silence.

She asked their father as much, as they stood together in the conservatory, salad plates in hand, looking out on to the McGuires' neat and orderly garden.

Stan Coia sighed. 'It's a bit of both really; they were well warned not to upset their grandma, or Nana or anyone else, by screaming and shouting like they usually do. But the way Viola's taken it . . . Aye, you're right; the poor wee guys are frightened. She's excitable at the best of times, but this . . . I'd to get the doctor to her, you know. The emergency call-out service, I'd to get them out in the middle of the night, after Mario came by to tell me what had happened. The poor lass, she was hyperventilating; I thought she was having an asthma attack, and you can die from them.'

'How is she now?' Maggie looked back into the living room, where Viola stood, black-eyed, white-faced, beside her Aunt Christina.

'Doped up to the eyeballs, if you really want to know. It was touch and go whether she came today, but I managed to persuade her that her mother and her nana needed her.' His eyes flicked quickly around the room.

'The Viareggio women are a funny lot, you know. You must see that too, as an in-law like me. There's old Nana, at the top of the tree . . . if you leave out old Auntie Josefina, who doesn't know whether it's breakfast time or Easter, and never did, from what Beppe said. Then look at Aunt Christina, and at Paula; they're just like her, the pair of them, big, attractive women, very feminine, both of them, but as tough as teak underneath.

'On the other hand, there's Viola and her mother, complete contrasts to the other three, nice and good-hearted, but soft-centred where the others are hard.

164

'You could explain it away as coming from Sophia's side. The Rossis are a funny lot; her father was a lapsed Catholic, a real outcast, apparently. Only you can't, because it's not just the women that are mixed up. I mean, God rest poor Beppe's soul, but where the hell did he come from?

'I never knew Papa Viareggio; he was dead years before I met Viola. But from everything I've heard he was some man. Yet he and Nana managed to produce Beppe as well as Christina. I mean, he wasn't a bad man, and he didn't squander the family fortunes; but he was weak and if he hadn't had Paula and me and Aunt Christina around him, he might have. As it was, that business with the franchising, when he cancelled it after his father died, that was a fiasco.

'It's funny; isn't it,' Stan mused, unknowingly giving voice to Maggie's own thoughts. 'The Viareggio clan's a real matriarchy, and yet it's set up so that ultimately there's always a man in control. It's a real Italian thing, isn't it. There was Papa, then there was Beppe and now there's Mario, who's a throwback to his old grandfather, so they say.'

He grinned at Maggie, his eyes distorted by the thick lenses of his spectacles. 'Genetics, eh; a load of crap.'

She smiled with him, looking over at her husband, who was installing Ryan and David in front of the television set, in the far corner of the living room. 'What about you, Stan?' she asked him. 'Do you see yourself as part of the family, or still as an outsider, as I do for all that Mario's done to make me feel like one of them?'

'I'm a wage slave, pure and simple,' he answered at once. 'I don't know if I'd even be that, if Nana hadn't insisted on it. Okay, I've got my chartered surveying practice, and the Viareggio Trust is my most important long-term client, but that's it. More than that, when I'm ready to chuck it, that's all my boys will have . . . assuming that they're interested in coming into my business. The way that Ryan talks about his Uncle Mario and his Aunt Maggie, I think he's halfway to being a detective already.

'I resent that a bit, I have to confess. Not about him being a policeman,' he added quickly, 'but I resent the fact that the way the old man's inheritance was set up, my lads will miss out. Who are the beneficiaries of the Trust? Nana, Christina, Beppe and Sophia and their children; there's no right of succession after that. For all that he was a very clever and successful man, old Papa didn't, or couldn't, think more than two generations ahead.'

'I see what you mean,' Maggie conceded, 'but it would have been very difficult for him to do more. As I see it, he trusted Beppe, overseen by Christina, to carry the business on for a bit, until Mario and Paula were ready to take over. They were his real heirs, those two; and you're right, the Italian in him made sure that there would be a man in overall control.

'They're the future of the business, those two, and there are no restrictions on them, other than looking after Nana and Aunt Josefina. They can consolidate, they can expand, or if they choose they can liquidate, sell the bloody lot and distribute the proceeds. I'll promise you this though, Stan. Whatever happens, Mario will take his nephews' interests into account, and I'm sure Paula will go along with that too. She has no kids yet, and neither do we . . . nor will we, unless we adopt . . . so your boys could have quite a rosy future.'

'That's good to know; thanks. Mind you that assumes that any of us have a future. I saw the *Sunday Mail* front page today. What is this Mafia stuff, Maggie? I know that Uncle Beppe used to joke about it all the time, but should we take it seriously?'

'No more than Beppe used to take it himself; it was always a joke with him, even if it did wear thin from time to time. There is no organised crime in Edinburgh, not any more. We finally broke that a couple of years ago, when the last of the big drugs barons got sent down for most of the rest of his life. Even when it did exist, it wasn't Italian.'

'What if this came from outside Edinburgh? The deli side of the business has all sorts of Italian suppliers.'

'No it doesn't. We went over this with Paula last night. The deli suppliers are all wholesalers, and most of them are public companies, or part of public groups. The business deals with them and nobody else; it doesn't pay off middlemen and it never has. There are no supply problems just now, and no arguments with anyone over prices. Like most businesses, the biggest threat comes from the VAT man.'

'So who killed old Beppe then, if it wasn't gangsters?'

'We'd have told you if we knew. Now stop fantasising; off you go and watch the game with the rest of the boys.' She glanced at the women gathered around the table. 'I've got to stop Nana from pouring any more Chianti into your wife. God knows how it'll mix with the sedatives.'

As it transpired, the combination proved as effective as any sleeping pill. Viola was put to bed by her mother and slept solidly until seven thirty, when Stan decreed that the boys had to go home. The others decided to leave at the same time, Sophia and Christina going back to

Murrayfield with Nana, and Paula, her courage restored, returning to her warehouse apartment in Leith, uttering threats against the person of any journalist who might be lying in wait for her.

As soon as they had gone, Mario began to clear away the debris left over from the extended lunch. He had just loaded the last of the crockery into the dishwasher, and selected a programme, when he noticed, through the open kitchen door, that his wife was seated at the dining table, making her way through a stack of papers.

'What the hell's that?' he called to her, as he strolled back towards her.

'Stuff I brought home from the office yesterday. It's the first chance I've had to look at it.'

'Bloody hell,' he laughed. 'You're not turning into Manny English, are you?'

'Hardly; it's just that I feel that while I'm filling his shoes, I should try to do things his way.'

'Like spending every weekend shovelling shit?'

'No,' she said, severely. 'Not every weekend; only those when I find myself giving short-notice lunch parties for your family.'

'We won't make a habit of it, I promise. Anyway, I don't have any more uncles.'

Maggie winced. 'Sorry; that was a bit crass. I was glad to do it, honestly, and I think it did everyone a bit of good . . . apart from Viola, that is. Nana fed the best part of a bottle of Chianti into her before I could stop her.'

'Stan could have stopped her before you did,' Mario pointed out, 'but he wasn't bothered.'

'True. I don't think it's his style though. He loves his boys, but I get the impression that he and Viola aren't all that happy together.'

'They're fine. You're not seeing either of them at their best, that's all. Anyway, a couple of drinks and a few hours' sleep were exactly what she was needing. Trust Nana to spot it, too.'

'Oh yes, trust her.' She paused. 'Paula seems to have got herself together.'

'Aye, she's fine. I've asked Jay to keep an eye on her place, but she doesn't need to know that.'

'You don't really think she's in any danger, do you?'

'No, but I know a bloke that won the Lottery last year. You can never be quite certain.'

He saw her frown. 'Who did it, Mario? Who could have?'

'I don't know, but . . . My Uncle Beppe always had an eye for the

167

ladies. It's got him into bother more than once. I just wonder . . .' He paused, as his eye was caught by a sheet of paper on the table. 'Here, what's that?'

She handed it to him. 'It's the missing person poster on my dear father.'

'Oh shit,' he muttered. 'Sorry, I forgot to mention something. He's grown a beard since this was taken. This isn't a current likeness.' He laid the flyer on the table, picked up a pen, darkened the jaw and top lip on the monochrome photograph and handed it back to her.

Maggie gazed at it. 'He's still an evil-looking bastard. I'll have a revision issued though.' She laid it on top of her 'out' pile, then hesitated. 'That's funny; looking like that, he reminds me of someone. But who the hell is it?'

'Search me, love. Nobody I know, that's for sure. Damn!' As he spoke, he was interrupted by a distant, muffled tone.

'What's that?' his wife asked.

'My mobile. I left it in my jacket. I must have forgotten to switch it off.'

He strode through to their bedroom. His wardrobe door was open, and as he approached, the ringing tone grew louder. He snatched the cellphone from the pocket in which it lay and pressed the receive button.

The voice at the other end was light, teasing, and very female. 'Mr Superintendent?' it began. 'This is Ivy.'

'Uhh?'

'Ivy Brennan. George's neighbour, remember?'

'Oh yes. What can I do for you? Has he shown up?'

'No, it's nothing to do with him. I saw the *Sunday Mail* today, about your uncle.'

'Then don't talk to me. Call the Leith office and ask for the incident room. Ask for Superintendent Jay; tell him I said you should call.'

'No,' she said, firmly. 'I need to see you, now. The thing is, I might know who killed him.'

He hesitated, picturing the doll-like girl in his mind's eye. 'Where are you?' he asked, at last.

'My place.'

'Stay there; I'll be half an hour. Oh, and by the way, you'd better not be kidding me on.'

He took his jacket from its hanger and walked back through to the living room, wondering how much he should tell Maggie and, in particular, whether he should tell her that he was going back to see her father's neighbour. What if she wanted to come with him, to see the place where he lived? Would that be good for her?

His worries were academic. 'Let me guess,' she exclaimed as he appeared in the doorway. 'You have to go and see an informant. It's okay, I know by now what it means when that phone rings when you're off duty. You might as well; I've still got a bit to do here.'

He smiled at her, more gratefully than she realised. 'Never mind, love; once Neil gets bedded into the SB job it'll all pass to him.'

'And how will Louise take to that, I wonder.'

He leaned over and kissed her on the forehead. 'With the same understanding you've shown over the years,' he whispered.

'Get out of here,' she laughed, slapping him on the shoulder. 'Just don't be late, that's all.'

42

'It's like stepping into history, Joe,' said Skinner, a man not normally impressed by his surroundings, especially if they were late twentieth century and architect designed. But ugly or not, the Watergate Building was something else, having been the centrepiece of the biggest inter-national political scandal of his life.

'That's all it is now,' Doherty told him. 'The Democratic National Committee ain't here any more; it's on South Capitol Street. I just thought you'd like to see where all that started. Head on down there, Max, please.'

'Yes, sir.' The deputy director's driver nodded and slipped the anonymous black car into gear. The Scot had never seen his old friend on his home patch before; he sensed the difference at once. He was more formal, and had seemed almost to grow in stature from the moment their flight had touched down, an impression confirmed by the deference of the chauffeur when he had picked them up.

They moved south, away from the heart of government, and came quickly into South Capitol Street. 'Should you be seen going in here,' Skinner asked, 'with there being a Republican administration these days?'

'Ahh shit, it's Sunday afternoon. Look around you.'

It was true; for any capital city the streets were exceptionally quiet. There seemed, almost, to be more tour buses than cars.

'Anyhow, Congress has been GOP for years,' Doherty added. 'It's only the White House that's changed hands. But suppose this was a weekday, there'd be nothing exceptional about me going to meet with Rusty. I do it fairly often, just as I keep in touch with the Republican Party organisation.'

'Who?'

'Rusty Savage; he's the guy we're meeting. He's deputy chief of staff of the DNC organisation, and he's been around for years, almost as long as me.'

'Does he normally work weekends?'

'When there's an election, yes he does, but not right now. He's here because I asked him to meet us in his office.'

The car drew up at the entrance to 430 South Capitol Street, and the two passengers stepped out. Sunday or not, there was a receptionist on duty in the foyer. She recognised Doherty at once. 'Good afternoon, sir,' she greeted him, with the same clear show of respect that Skinner had seen from Max, the driver, at the airport. 'How good to see you again. Mr Savage is in his office; if you'd like to go on up in the elevator, I'll let him know you're on your way.'

Rusty Savage was waiting for them as the lift doors opened. Doherty greeted him warmly, and introduced his companion as they walked towards an office across the hall. 'It's an honour to meet you, sir,' said the American, taking the Scot by surprise. 'I know who you are, and I know what you did at that conference a couple of years back.'

Skinner looked at him, a touch warily, wondering how much he knew; most of the detail of that incident had been kept away from the media. 'It's okay,' Savage grinned. 'I heard the whole story at the time from the former White House chief of staff. The Man Himself is in New York for the weekend, otherwise I know he'd have wanted to meet you.'

'He might not have wanted to hear what we want to talk about, though,' muttered Doherty.

'Yeah, what is that, Joe? You were damned mysterious when you called me.'

'I had to be; I know that the Bureau isn't bugging your communications, but I can't be a hundred per cent sure about anyone else.'

'Wow,' Savage whistled. He looked around his modest office as he closed the door behind him. 'You can relax in here, though. We have these offices swept for devices once a month; there's nothing recorded here, unless we want it to be. Sit down, guys.' He poured three mugs of black coffee from a jug by his walnut desk and handed one each to his visitors.

'Now, what's so red-hot that it's come between me and my Sunday golf game?'

'A double homicide,' the deputy director answered. 'A week or so back in the Adirondacks National Park in New York State.'

'Leopold Grace and his wife,' said Rusty Savage at once. 'I heard about it. Tragic altogether, that such an eminent couple should die like that. Mr Grace was a Democrat from way back, and a personal friend of the former first family too. Matter of fact I had a call from one of the new senator's aides a couple of days back, asking me if I could let her know about funeral arrangements.'

'Still, how come the Bureau is involved? And what's your interest, Mr Skinner?'

'Mr Grace was Bob's father-in-law.'

Surprise flashed across the official's face. 'Ahh,' he exclaimed. 'So that's why you're here. When Joe said he was bringing you along, I didn't ask why. I just assumed you were on some sort of an exchange visit.'

He looked back at Doherty. 'That doesn't answer my first question, though, Joe. How come you guys have picked up on this? The man wasn't a public figure any more; although he was a former chairman of the New York State Democratic Committee, and his word was still the law, when he offered an opinion on something or someone.'

'Do the names Bartholomew Wilkins and Sander Garrett mean anything to you?'

Savage leaned back in his chair, sipping his coffee as he thought. 'Bart Wilkins,' he murmured at last. 'Chicago, Illinois, I think; he was head of a law firm, like Mr Grace, and retired, like Mr Grace. But his involvement in active Democratic politics ended way back, when Governor Dukakis was adopted as candidate to fight Bush the Elder in 1988.

'Wilkins thought it was a disastrous choice . . . he was right, as it happened . . . and withdrew from the Illinois party executive.

'Sander Garrett? Yes, that name rings a bell; I remember meeting him in Los Angeles a while back, probably in the mid-eighties. He wasn't a Californian, though; he was from Nevada as I recall, and involved with the Party as a volunteer fund raiser.'

Doherty nodded. 'That's very interesting. Let me throw another name at you; Jackson Wylie.'

'Leo Grace's former partner,' Savage replied at once. 'He worked for him in the attorney general's office nearly forty years ago, and followed him into the law firm in Buffalo. He's still an active Democrat, and a member of the State Committee.'

'I think you'll find he's less active from now on,' the deputy director drawled, with a trace of a wry smile playing at one corner of his mouth.

'How come? Who's upset him?'

'The guy who blew up his cruiser yesterday afternoon, with him in it. He's dead. My team confirmed this morning that the explosion was no accident.'

'Dead?'

'As a fucking doornail, Rusty; and so are Wilkins and Garrett. They were both murdered in their homes within the last month. Their killings made to look like they happened in the course of burglaries; but they were pro hits, both of them, as were the Graces' deaths. The Wylie homicide wasn't disguised as anything; there was enough C4 explosive in one of his cabin lockers to have made a good-sized hole in the battleship *New Jersey*.

'So that's why we're here, my friend. We have a problem and so have you; there's someone out there who's making serious inroads into the roll of registered Democratic voters. If he isn't stopped, you could start to run out of them.'

'How can I help?'

'We're looking for connections,' said Skinner. 'We have several already from the backgrounds on the victims, gathered by the police officers who originally investigated their killings. We know that these men were all active members of your Party. We know that they were all lawyers. We know that they all worked in Washington in the sixties, during the Kennedy administration.

'But that's as far as it goes. There's something we don't know, something that links all four men together, something that's got them killed. There's nothing in the files of my father-in-law's old firm. We have people asking similar questions about Wilkins and Garrett, but if there's nothing in Buffalo, there's unlikely, in my view at least, to be anything in Chicago or Las Vegas.

'So we're here. You're the end of the road, more or less. We need to go as far back as we can into your records, to see whether they got involved in something through the Party that's led to this.'

The Democrat official took a deep breath and pushed himself up from his chair. He walked over to the window and looked out over the city, back up towards the seat of national government. 'You tried the State Department?' he asked. 'Or the attorney general's office?'

They were questions that Skinner himself had not asked, but Doherty answered. 'Of course I have. There's nothing that helps us.'

Savage turned back to face them. 'In that case, guys, I'm sorry, but I'm don't think I'm going to be able to help you, either.' He paused.

'You are correct to assume that we do store biographic material on our activists, usually going back to the earliest days of their work within our movement. However, these days we keep very few long-term paper records; just about everything we have is on computer. Last week, when I heard about Mr Grace's death, I went into our mainframe and called up his file. It wasn't there; I asked our head of information technology what had happened to it.

173

'He looked into it, and reported that it had been erased; we've lost all the bios beginning with the letter G, and all of the Ws, too. We interrogated all our users, but nobody admitted to doing it, accidentally or otherwise. His conclusion, although he couldn't be certain, was that someone had hacked in and done it.'

He frowned down at them. 'Looks like now we know for sure.'

43

'This is a mistake,' he whispered to no one, as he stood on the dark landing. He had knocked on George Rosewell's door, just in case; there had been no answer but he had decided against taking another unauthorised look inside. He had almost gone back downstairs, but instead, against his instincts, he had rung Ivy Brennan's doorbell.

'Hello, Mr Detective.'

She was taller than she had been, the first time she had looked up at him in that doorway. He glanced down and saw that she was wearing thick-soled shoes, with high heels. She was better dressed too, in a close-fitting blue dress, and this time, there was none of the waif about her.

'Come in,' she said, holding the door wide for him.

'Are you going out somewhere?' he asked, as he followed her through to the living room.

'No. I was expecting someone, so I thought I'd get dolled up for him.'

'Who? Rufus's dad?'

'No, thicko! I was expecting you.'

'Now listen, Ivy . . .'

She laughed, a sound as gentle as wind chimes fanned by an opening door. 'Don't get all heavy on me, now. I could have stayed the way I was; no make-up and all smelly, like the first time you came here. Would you have preferred that?'

He smiled, in spite of himself. 'No; this version's more to my taste.'

'Oh,' she murmured, turning and stepping close to him. 'Do you fancy a taste, then?'

'Ah, Christ,' Mario exclaimed. 'I knew I shouldn't have come here!'

'Ah, but you did, though. In spite of all your better judgement, you did.'

His grin was gone; he glared down at her. 'You know fuck all about my uncle, do you, girl.'

'I know that he's dead, because I saw it in the *Mail* today. That's how I knew he was your uncle, because you're mentioned in the story, you

175

and your cousin, Paula. I know her, though; she owns a sauna, round the corner from here and along the road a bit.'

McGuire gasped with surprise. 'Are you on the game?'

'Certainly not!' she laughed, in a tone of mock protestation. 'I'm a good mother, I'll have you know, and I'm not a junkie.'

'I've met many a working girl who was a good mother,' he told her. 'As for being a junkie, you're acting like you're on something.' He seized her wrists and turned them, looking for needle tracks along the flat of her pale forearms and in the folds of her elbows, but they were unmarked.

When he let her go, she took a pace back from him, and hoisted up the blue dress, showing him the inside of her thighs. 'D'you want to check there as well?' she challenged. 'D'you want to check anywhere else?' She slid the dress higher; she was wearing a G-string, but he could tell that she was blonde, for real.

'Just chuck that,' he warned her, 'or I'm out that door right now.'

'Are you really?' She reached behind her and, in a flash, pulled down a long zip, and wriggled her shoulders. The dress fell in a circle at her feet. 'See? Not a needle mark anywhere.' Her tiny body was almost classic in its proportions; a little wide in the hips, perhaps, after Rufus, but otherwise perfect. Small, bud-like pink nipples seemed to wink up at him. 'Want to make certain?' She slid her thumbs inside the black thong and began to roll it down.

Suddenly he was aware that every muscle in his body seemed to be tensed; he could feel them bunched under his shirt and jeans. He could feel them, and more. With an effort of will he turned, and headed for the door.

'Okay!' she called after him. 'Okay, I'll behave myself. Just don't go.'

He stopped in the doorway. 'Get dressed, then.'

'I'm doing it; I'm doing it. There.'

When he turned, her back was to him. 'Zip me up.' He did as she asked, drawing the dress closed and tight to her.

'One thing you should know about me,' he told her. 'I love my wife. Anyone who harms her, or who even threatens it . . . in any way . . . is in big, big trouble. Understand me?'

She nodded. 'Yes. That's why you want to find George, isn't it? He hurt her before he went away. Now he's in bother with you.'

'Is he ever.'

'So you haven't found him.'

'Not a trace. He's either gone back to Portugal or he's in the Water of Leith.'

'I don't think the fish would fancy him.'

And then she grinned up at him. 'You have to admit, though, I did give it a good try. Did you like the quick flash? Just a bit?'

The girl-waif-woman look was back in her eyes; somehow, he found it disturbing, as if the poisoned apple had been offered and he had begun to reach for it.

'A work of art, Ivy,' he said, acidly, 'but a bit small for me. Never mind, though; one day you'll make some guy a fine desk ornament.'

'Ohh! We do have a way with the insults, don't we. Although that's not what that lump in your jeans was saying, a minute or so back. Still . . . far be it from me to come between a man and his wife. Want a coffee?'

'No, thanks. But if you have any mineral water, I'd take some.'

She nodded and went through to her small kitchen, returning with a bottle of San Pellegrino and two tumblers. 'That's how I got to know Paula, by the way,' she said, holding up the bottle as he took one of the glasses. 'I shop in her deli; I go in there quite a lot with Rufus. She likes him; she's very fond of children.'

'She's very fond of men,' he grunted, 'but I'm not so sure about kids.'

'She is; take my word for it. Anyway, she's my pal. She told me about the sauna; that's how I knew where it was. And that's where I saw your uncle.'

'You really did know him?' Mario exclaimed. 'That wasn't just rubbish?'

'Well, I wouldn't exactly say I knew him. I did exaggerate a bit when I phoned you. I was passing the place one day, and I saw him. The door was open and he was standing, framed in it.'

He looked at her, doubtfully. 'Are you sure it was him? Beppe had nothing to do with those businesses. There was no reason for him to go there.'

'Most men go to places like that for a pretty good reason.'

'Not Beppe.'

'I'm pretty sure,' Ivy assured him. 'That was a good photograph in the *Mail*, and when I saw him, he was dressed much the same.'

'Okay, you saw him once. But how does that tell you who killed him?'

'I didn't just remember him because I saw him. Like I told you, he was standing there, and he was having a screaming argument with someone.'

'Beppe? He wasn't the screaming type.'

'He was when I saw him.'

177

'And who was he screaming at?'

'Ah well, I laid that on a bit thick too, when I called you. The other person was inside the place, I couldn't see who it was and I couldn't hear their voice, other than that it was raised. But I can tell you this, your uncle was shouting at whoever it was as if he wanted to kill them. If the other person was as mad with him as he was with them, all you have to do is find him.'

44

'Well, Sauce, what do you have for me this morning?'

'Weekend reports, ma'am,' the probationer replied. 'The front desk said that Mr English normally checks them over first thing on a Monday morning.'

I'll bet he does, thought Maggie.

'Just put them in my in-tray,' she said, leaning back in her chair and looking up at the young man. 'Did you have a good one, then?'

Haddock stared at her, bewildered. 'Good what, ma'am?'

'Weekend, son; did you have a good weekend?'

'Oh, that. Yes, ma'am, it was okay. Went out wi' my girlfriend on Saturday, like. Watched the fitba' on telly yesterday. Just ordinary, like. What about you, ma'am?' he asked, emboldened.

'Mine? Family stuff, mainly.'

'Ahh,' he said. 'I suppose.' He paused. 'They were saying downstairs, about your husband's uncle, like. That must have been an awful shock for him.'

She grimaced. 'A bullet in the back of the head usually is.'

Haddock gasped at her response, and Maggie saw him go pale. 'Sorry, son,' she exclaimed. 'That was a bit blunt. But you do know what you can come across in this job, don't you?'

'Aye, ma'am,' the probationer replied, 'but you don't, do you, at least no' very often?'

'Potentially, every day you pull on that uniform, you're going to see something very unpleasant. The second week I was out on patrol, I was called to a traffic accident out on Queensferry Road; three young girls, all pissed, in somebody's daddy's Rover. All pissed, like I said, and all very dead. I picked one kid's head off the road and put it back in the car, then I was sick in the gutter.

'Two weeks later, my partner and I answered a call to a flat in Morningside. One of the neighbours had complained about the smell. As it happened, it was coming from an old lady who'd died of a heart attack, in front of her electric fire, about a week or so earlier.

179

We had to break into the house.

'I don't want to sound hard, Sauce, but if you're squeamish about this job, you'd better get it out of your system. Have you been out in a patrol car yet, or on the beat?'

'Not yet, ma'am.'

'How long did you say you've been with the force?'

'Four weeks now, ma'am.'

'It's about time you had some outside experience, then. I'll arrange it with Inspector Wright.'

'Yes, ma'am, thank you.' Haddock left, looking significantly more serious than when he had arrived.

Maggie shook her head, sighed, then drew her in-tray across the desk towards her. She had just picked up the first of the weekend reports, from the Oxgangs police office, when there was a faint knock on her door.

'Come in,' she called, but it was opening as she spoke. Chief Superintendent Dan Pringle's lugubrious form stepped into the room.

'Hello, sir,' she exclaimed, surprised.

'Aw, come on, Maggie,' the new head of CID protested. 'Don't start wi' the "sir" bit, not after pouring me into a taxi last Friday night. I hope that sitting in for Manny English isn't turning you into a book operator too.'

'Sorry, Dan,' she said. 'But you might be right. Our new ACC's a clever so-and-so, you know. I've only been doing the job for a couple of days, and part-time at that, but already it's got me thinking like management.

'I've just had a probationer in here, the lad who's acting as my runner; the boy's nice, and willing, and all the rest, but doesn't understand what the job's really about, or what it can involve.'

'So you've told him.'

'Too right. I'm going to make bloody sure he sees what it can involve, too. Young Sauce has potential, but he's got to get his feet on the floor and his head out of the clouds.'

'Sauce?'

'Nickname.'

'Bet you Manny English doesn't know his nickname,' Pringle murmured.

Maggie shrugged her shoulders. 'So?'

'So, for all that he's the very model of a modern divisional commander, that's something missing in him. Guys like him think they have to be aloof from the people under them. I'll bet you know the Christian name of everyone in this office.'

She thought for a moment. 'I probably do,' she conceded. 'Most of the nicknames too.'

'Manny doesn't though. I used to sit in this very office, so I worked with him, and I know that for a fact. He's a decent man, you can't fault his motives, and he never puts a foot wrong, but he doesn't know his officers. He'd never call your lad "Sauce", to his face or behind his back. I doubt if he even knows that the Chief's called Proud Jimmy, or that Bob Skinner and Andy Martin used to be Batman and Robin, or that you and Mario are . . .' He stopped short, as he saw her eyes widen.

'Oh yes,' she said, trying not to smile. 'And what do they call my husband and me, behind our backs?'

Pringle grunted. 'As if you don't know. You two are Clark and Lois, to just about the entire force . . . apart from Manny English.'

'I must tell Mario to stop wearing that bloody cape,' Maggie retorted. 'Anyway,' she continued, 'all that and Willie Haggerty's deviousness aside, what's brought you in here?'

The big, middle-aged detective tugged his moustache. 'I'm the new Head of CID,' he answered, blandly. 'I can come in here any time I like. I will, too.' She leaned back and waited. 'Ach, it being my first day in the job and all that, I thought I'd get out and about.

'I did think about calling in all the divisional CID heads for a round-table session, but then I thought better of it. Nothing against Andy, but I'm not going to run things quite like he did. I'll still have the odd headquarters meeting, but not every Monday; maybe one every three months, something like that. No, my idea is that I'll come to see you, rather than the other way around.

'I figure I might learn more that way. If someone's got a problem, he . . . or she . . . might be more likely to come out with it in a one-to-one session than across the big table with everyone listening in.' He looked her in the eye. 'You're the newest in the rank, but don't tell me you haven't picked up on the politics of it.

'Every one of us at those meetings knew that Andy wasna' going to be in that job long. He'll be a chief constable by the time he's forty, maybe in Dumfries and Galloway, maybe somewhere else; he was bound to move on up the ladder.'

'Why didn't he get the job here?'

'Us humble mortals can only guess at that, Maggie. Mine would be that it didn't fit in with Bob Skinner's plans . . . but you'd know more about that, having worked for the Big Man. Anyhow, those Monday sessions used to amuse me, watching certain people grinding their axes and jockeying for position, fancying themselves up as Andy's successor. Big McGrigor, he was near retirement, so he didna' give a stuff. As for me, I thought I'd been passed over for good when Andy got the job, then I was sure of it when I was shifted down to the Borders.

'The others, though, they all had ambitions, and two of them, Jay and Michaels, don't even like each other. They never offered an opinion; they said what they hoped Andy wanted to hear.'

'That's not true of Brian Mackie,' Rose protested.

'Even Brian was careful before he stuck his neck out.' The chief superintendent laughed suddenly. 'God, it was funny, though, when you came into the meetings. That changed the whole thing around, wi' you being so close to the Boss, and everything. When you were promoted straight into the Central Division job, Greg and Willie were really rattled.'

'I can't say I noticed.'

'Well, by Christ I did!' He laughed softly. 'Anyhow, I don't fancy listening to any more of it. And I'd have to. I won't be here all that long myself, and wi' Mario in the mix, those two's jockeying will be even worse. No, I'm going to do it my way.'

'Mmm,' the red-haired superintendent murmured. 'Just remember who started those meetings. It wasn't Andy, or Roy Old, it was Mr Skinner himself.'

'Oh, I remember that all right. There was no bullshit in those days though; they were all too scared of the Big Fella to take any chances wi' him. There's no problem there, anyway; the DCC's told me I can run things any way I like.'

'So this is the start of it, then. You're going to be peering round my door every Monday morning from now on.'

'No, no, no, no,' he assured her, quickly. 'This is just to tell you how things are going to be from now on. There'll be no surprise visits after this.

'But how're you doing anyway? And how's your man taking his uncle's death? That was a hell of a shock. Half-ratted as I was at the time, I remember thinking I've never seen him so rattled.'

'He had a rough weekend . . . the whole family had, as you'd imagine, and that crap in the Sundays didn't help . . . but he's okay now. He headed off down to Gala at half-six this morning. It's his first day as well, remember.'

The Head of CID rose to leave, but as he did so, his eye was caught by a paper in her out-tray He picked it up; it was the flyer on George Rosewell, on which Mario had doodled a rough beard. 'Who's this ugly bugger?' he chuckled.

In spite of herself, she felt a cold tug at her stomach. 'He's a missing person. It's got to be re-circulated, since he's thought to have changed his appearance since that photo was taken; hence my husband's artwork.'

Pringle gave his moustache another tug. 'You know,' he murmured, 'this looks a hell of a lot like someone whose mug turned up on my desk this morning. It came through from Strathclyde, a notice about a guy they're looking for through there. It's the sort of thing where you'd say he's just done a runner, but they're taking it seriously, since the guy's a parish priest.'

'Could you send me a copy?' asked Maggie.

'Sure, if you like. Why?'

'I don't know. I suppose I'd just like to see a priest who looked like him!'

45

'What do you think of the Borders so far, sergeant?' Detective Superintendent Mario McGuire asked his new assistant, as they strolled around the main thoroughfare of Galashiels, enjoying the midday sun.

Sammy Pye ran a hand over his dark hair. 'Come on, sir. I've only been here for four hours.'

'Come on, nothing. You make up your mind about a woman in about half a minute flat, so give me an instant opinion about our new surroundings.'

'If it's an order, boss; I know we haven't been out of Gala yet, but if this is the hub of the division as far as population's concerned, what's the rest going to be like? Even in comparison to Dalkeith and East Lothian, where I was before I was in Mr Martin's office, it's quiet.'

McGuire smiled. 'Maybe so, but your predecessor in this office got a lump shot off his ear not that long ago. There was no danger of that while you were working for the head of CID.'

'Maybe not, sir, but is it going to be that much different here? That thing they had last year was a one-off, and everybody involved got such heavy time that there won't be any repeat performances. Don't get me wrong, I jumped at the chance to get out to a division again, but my role's going to be much the same, isn't it? I was Mr Martin's exec; now I'm yours.'

'It'll not be the same, though, because my job's different . . . at least the way I do it will be. After doing my stint in Special Branch, I was as keen as you to get out in the field again. I'm not going to drive this division from behind a desk; I'm going to take the lead on most investigations as they come up, and you'll be there with me. We've got a small team here, I know, but even if I'd been given an Edinburgh command, that's the way I'd have handled it.

'The downside of SB is that it doesn't let you do any conventional CID work. You spend all your bloody time gathering and exchanging intelligence, unless you're Alec Bloody Smith, and look what happened to him.' He reached out a shirt-sleeved arm and punched his sergeant lightly on the shoulder. 'So you and I, Sammy, we're going to make this place sing. And don't you worry; the Borders might be quiet, but there are people here, and where there's punters there's crime. There's also a substantial amount of moneyed folk down here; it follows that there are also less-moneyed folk, some of a mind to do a bit of redistribution.

'We've also got colleges, and where you have colleges you have young people. Where you have young people you have discos and stuff, and where you have them you have guys peddling class A drugs. You get my drift, Sammy?'

Pye nodded.

'Good.' The superintendent stopped, in front of the police office. 'I don't like to speak ill of my predecessors, and I won't to anyone else bar you, but this division was a problem for a while. When Mr Skinner became Head of CID he inherited John McGrigor as his commander down here, and John was a problem. He was a former rugby international; that made him revered down here, and got him his job, but he was a piss-poor detective nonetheless.

'The Boss couldn't move him anywhere else; that would have been a disaster. He couldn't stick him back in uniform, because he wouldn't have been any better there. So effectively, he, and later Roy Old and Andy Martin, commanded this division from Fettes. When John took early retirement, the sigh of relief was heard all over headquarters.

'Dan Pringle started to get this place up to the same standard as the other divisions, but he'd tell you himself, as he's told me, that there's still work to be done, especially on pushing crime prevention down here. We haven't been sent down here for a rest, Sam, I promise you that.'

They walked back into the grey stone building, past the front desk and through to the CID suite; the outer office was manned by a lone detective constable. 'Message for you, sir,' he said to McGuire as Pye resumed his seat behind his new desk. 'Would you call Mr Jay in Leith, as soon as you can.'

'Aye, okay, Bert. Thanks.'

He went back to his room without a view, and called the Leith divisional office. 'Mario, old son,' Greg Jay greeted him down the line, when, eventually, his call was put through. 'Sorry to keep you hanging on. How are things in the Borders?'

'Warm and sunny thanks, Greg. I'm just getting the feel of my new office.'

'You'll be having a visitor in it soon; Dan Pringle's doing the rounds and he'll be heading your way this afternoon. I just thought I'd call to warn you.'

'Thanks, but I know that already. Maggie was second on his list; she phoned me after she had her official visit. Good for Dan; if that's how he wants to play it, that's fine by me. I couldn't see him chairing a formal meeting anyway: not his style.'

'You might find a flea in your ear after he's gone. When he was here, he asked me if I was happy with everything. He caught me at the wrong moment, 'cos I told him that as it happened, I was a bit pissed off with you. I saw the report you faxed in about your meeting with the Brennan woman. I know you've got a personal interest in the Viareggio investigation, Mario, but if you thought she had information, you should have passed it on to the investigating officers. I wouldn't even have minded if you'd called me at home. Seeing her yourself was a bit out of order, son, and I'm afraid I told Dan Pringle as much.'

McGuire felt the fuse of his temper burning away fast. As he fought to control it, he held the phone away from his ear for a second or two, and stared at it, noticing that he was gripping it so hard that his knuckles were white. Finally, he put it back to his ear.

'There's a couple of things I should tell you, Greg,' he said evenly. 'To begin with, please don't call me "son", ever; I don't like it. Also, next time you try to score points off me with Dan Pringle or Bob Skinner or anyone else, then, whether we're senior officers or not, I'll take you somewhere quiet and do something serious to your head.

'For the record, Ivy Brennan's on the fringe of something else I'm involved in, something personal. When she called me last night, I didn't really think she knew anything about Beppe or his murder. I'm still not sure she didn't make up that story about the argument in the sauna, but she volunteered it, so I passed it on to you, informally.

'She's a funny one, is Ivy, but she does know my cousin Paula. I've checked that out. If you're running your investigation properly, you'll send a couple of officers along to re-interview her, for the record. Or are you going to surprise me? Have you made an arrest already?'

'If I had, you'd have been the first to know,' Jay replied, stiffly.

'Have you got any new leads, then?'

'We might have. We found a taxi-driver who said he dropped a couple off on the corner of the street that leads to your uncle's place, just before nine.'

'Descriptions?'

'She was late twenties, he was older; that was the best he could do. You know how many fares these guys have on a Friday night.'

'Anything else?'

'We've been looking at the property side with your other cousin's husband, Stan Coia; to see whether your family might have had any tenants with a grievance against the landlord.'

'I doubt it. Stan's a good bloke; he keeps the portfolio in first-class shape. Maintenance can be a good investment, in terms of lower insurance premiums. I can't see anyone having grounds for complaint, not to the extent of wanting to put a bullet in Beppe.'

'Maybe not.' Jay paused. 'Did you know that the Viareggio Trust owns a bonded warehouse?' he asked.

'Yes, I do know that, as a matter of fact. We use it to bond wines from Italy for the deli chain, and we rent out space there to other importers.'

'Yes, that's right. There was one funny thing that Mr Coia mentioned. A firm rented space, but never used it; they didn't pass a single case of wine through there. A few months back, your uncle wrote to them . . . well, Coia wrote the letter, but Mr Viareggio signed it . . . and said that he intended to terminate their lease so that it could be made available to someone who actually needed it. There's a clause in the agreement that lets him do that.

'The tenant's response was very angry and aggressive. It was so threatening, in fact, that Mr Coia was going to back off, but your uncle Beppe insisted that they go ahead. So legal papers were served a couple of weeks ago.'

'What was the name of the firm?'

'Essary and Frances Limited; it's registered at the office of its solicitor, and the directors are named as Mr Magnus Essary and Ms Ella Frances.'

'You following it up?'

'I've got people on it as we speak. Oh, and by the way, Mario; this time I'd be grateful if you left it to them.'

McGuire slammed the phone back into its cradle. He was still scowling when Dan Pringle walked into his office.

46

'You set it up right here in the heart of the city,' said Detective Chief Inspector Mary Chambers; as she gazed at the young man, her plain square face was lit with a mix of incredulity and amusement. 'Excuse my use of industrial language, but did you clever boys really think we're as fucking stupid as that?'

'Well yes, actually,' he replied.

'They think that in Malaysia too; I was there last week at a conference. There's a queue of guys like you in prisons out in south east Asia, all waiting to be hanged.'

She sighed. 'Not just in the heart of the city, mind you. Oh no, you two have to set up your Ecstasy lab less than half a mile from a divisional police office.' She paused as the midday train rattled by outside, and looked around the windowless space of the small industrial unit which had been turned into a chemical factory.

'Where better to hide than the heart of a city?' the tall youth asked.

'Just about anywhere,' Maggie Rose told him. 'We've got a concentration of manpower here that you won't find anywhere else.'

He looked at her scornfully. 'You didn't catch us. We were grassed up.'

'You know all the slang, too,' said Chambers, shaking her head. 'You poor lads. All those brains and no common sense; you made the tabs locally, you sold them locally, and you used stupid bloody students like yourselves to peddle them for you. Of course you were grassed up! Did you really think those two kids were going to do time for you, once they were offered the chance of being Crown witnesses?'

'It's their word against ours.'

The chief inspector looked at the second young man; there was raw fear in his voice and his chin was trembling. 'No, son,' she said, wearily. 'It's your word against ours, mine and Detective Superintendent Rose and DS McConochie and DC Guthrie, who's taking photographs of your equipment *in situ*, just as he's been taking shots of you two and the others, coming in and out of this place for the last week.'

'There's that, and then there's the name on the lease for this place. I have got that right, haven't I? I'm not mixed up between the two of you, am I? You are Brian Litster and he's Raymond Weston.' The boy nodded.

'Right, that's enough, Beano,' snapped the other. 'No more talk. Arrest us and caution us, if that's what you're going to do, Inspector.'

'Too right that's what I'm going to do, Mr Weston.'

'Good.' He took a phone from his pocket. 'Then I'll be entitled to call my father.'

Chambers shrugged her broad shoulders. 'You can call him right now, if you want. Tell him you're being arrested and taken to the Torphichen Place police office.'

Raymond Weston looked at her in surprise for a moment, then dialled a number. 'Dad,' he said, and as he spoke his voice took on an urgent, frightened tone that had not been there before. 'I've been picked up by the police. They've set me up. I told you that guy Martin would have it in for me, and I was right.' He paused for a few seconds. 'Torphichen Place, they said. No, I won't say anything till you and he get there.'

He put the phone back in his pocket. The head of the Drugs Squad shook her head and smiled. 'I see we're in for a busy day. George,' she called to Detective Sergeant McConochie. 'Go through the formalities with these two, and then get them round the corner. I don't imagine that this one's dad will be too long in getting there.' She turned to Rose. 'Will you come back to the office in my car?'

'Fine,' the superintendent replied, a frown on her face, and followed her outside.

'Who's his father, I wonder?' Chambers mused as she slid behind the wheel.

'I can tell you that. He's Professor Nolan Weston, and he's a surgeon at the Western.'

'And what was that stuff about? The bit about us having it in for him?'

The superintendent took a deep breath, then blew it out. 'Potentially it's a mess, if Weston goes to trial. There was an investigation a while back into the death of his girlfriend's uncle. Dan Pringle was in my job then, and he thought Weston might have had something to do with it. He offered an alibi; he told Dan that he'd been in bed with someone at the time; not his girlfriend, someone else. It turned out that he was telling the truth.

'The other woman was Andy Martin's fiancée.'

'What? Karen?'

'No, this was before Karen. At the time, Andy was engaged to Bob Skinner's daughter, Alex.'

'Oh Jesus!' exclaimed Chambers. 'Weston's not still seeing her, is he?'

'Not a chance. Alex is working in her firm's office down south; the last I heard she was going out with an actor guy she met at Neil McIlhenney's wedding.'

'Still, if his defence alleges that we've got a down on him because of that, and we've fixed him up, you never know with juries. At the very least, it'll be all over the tabloids; I can see the headlines . . . and the pictures . . . even now.' She flashed a quick, engaging smile. 'By the way, did you know that Elvis Presley's song, "One Night with You" was originally called "One Night of Sin"?'

Rose chuckled. 'No, I did not. I was never into Elvis . . . or much into nights of sin, for that matter. But before you go offering Weston a deal to preserve the reputation of the force, there's something else you should take into account.'

'What's that?'

'The Bob Skinner factor. There aren't too many people who'd fancy throwing mud at his daughter. If you'd like a wager on how this will turn out, I'd say that Litster will catch the lot, since his name was on the lease, and that Ray Weston will plead to a reduced charge; being involved in manufacture, but not supply.'

'Fiver?'

'Done.'

'I'd better get on with it then,' said Chambers. She drove round the twisting Haymarket junction and drew up outside divisional headquarters to let Rose out of the car, then pulled away again, heading for the park at the rear.

The red-haired superintendent was frowning as she strolled back into her office. On impulse she picked up the phone and called the Special Branch number, the one that had been her husband's until the previous Friday. 'DI McIlhenney,' a familiar voice answered.

'Hi, Neil. How are you settling in?'

'Rushed off my feet, Mags. Is this a wish-me-luck call?'

'Not exactly. Something's come up that the Boss should be aware of, but it's far too delicate for Jack McGurk to handle on his first day in the job. And now that Andy's gone, you're the only man I can talk to about it.' Quickly, she explained what had happened at Weston and Litster's Ecstasy factory.

'I see what you mean,' the big inspector muttered. 'You don't think the lad would really be that stupid, do you?'

'I'm betting he isn't, but I've been wrong before.'

'Not very often, you haven't, but I agree, the Big Man needs to be told; Alex too, in case his lawyer gets cute and starts leaking stuff to the tabloids. Leave it with me; I'll take care of it.'

'Thanks. You know I wouldn't have figured on Alex getting into a jam like this.'

'Why not?' Neil drawled. 'Her father did . . . not that I'd be daft enough to remind him of the fact.'

She laughed as she hung up. Finally, she turned back to the papers on her desk, able to give them her full attention for the first time since Mary Chambers' urgent call two hours before. The photograph of her father still lay on top of the pile. She thought of Dan Pringle's comment, and then another recollection came to her, the memory of another face she had seen, a week before.

She picked up the phone once more, and dialled the general office extension. 'Sauce,' she began, as Haddock answered, 'I want you to dig out a file for me, if it's still there. It relates to an incident reported on night shift up in Oxgangs.' She gave him the details, then waited. Her door opened in less than five minutes; the gawky Haddock appeared, slightly breathless, and laid a file on her desk. 'Thanks,' she said. 'You don't need to wait.'

As the door closed behind him, she flipped up the folder and took out Charlie Johnston's Polaroid of the late Magnus Essary, then laid it on the desk before her alongside the amended likeness of George Rosewell. She stared at them for over a minute, looking from one to the other, then back again. There was no doubt about it; the likeness was remarkable.

The night-shift constable was a truly bad photographer; the snapshot of the body was fuzzy, but he had caught all Essary's essential features, save for the eyes, which were closed in death. The balding head, the sharp nose and the heavily bearded chin, they were all there.

She snatched up the phone again and dialled. 'Sauce, I've got another job for you. I want you to ring around all the undertakers and find out which of them has made funeral arrangements for a man called Magnus Essary. Get a couple of people out there to help you if necessary. When you find the right one, then even if they're in the act of lowering the coffin into the ground, I want the thing stopped.

'I want to take a look at the body.'

191

47

The risen sun was still low in the sky, bathing the 737 shuttle in a soft yellow light as he watched it taxi in from the runway. The jetties were filled by outgoing commuter flights and so the passengers disembarked using roll-up stairways, boarding a long bus for the transfer to the terminal.

Bob felt his heart jump as his wife stepped out of the Boeing's door, into the bright morning. She was dressed entirely in black; boots, jeans and tee-shirt, with her big leather bag slung over her shoulder, and she carried herself tall and upright, her auburn hair shining as it fell about her shoulders.

For a moment, he was overcome; his head buzzed, and he felt his knees weaken. He leaned against the glass wall of the terminal building, steadying himself, gripped again by an odd feeling that somewhere else, in another place, time, or even dimension, he had played this scene before. It passed in a moment, and when it did, he realised for the first time just how much he had missed her.

Brad Dekker had pulled strings at Buffalo International; Sarah had cleared customs at Boston, and so, when the bus arrived she was met by a ground-crew member and brought straight to the reserved VIP room where he waited, alone.

'Hello love,' he said quietly. 'Welcome home.'

She crossed the room in three strides and threw herself into his arms; the tears came then, sudden and uncontrollable, taking her by surprise. He held her to him until they were spent, feeling his collar dampen, stroking her soft shining hair, feeling for her in her explosion of pent-up grief, yet perversely and guiltily happy that it had brought them back together.

'Oh, Bob,' she murmured, eventually, 'I've needed you so much; I wish now I had asked you to come home.'

'Well, you've got me now,' he answered, smiling as she looked up at him, stroking the wetness of her face with his fingers. 'And for the avoidance of doubt, I've needed you too.'

'Have you been bored, waiting here alone for me?'

'I haven't had time, my darling,' he told her, honestly. 'I've been chumming Joe Doherty around America, talking to people who might have been able to tell us something about Leo and Susannah's murder. In the last few days, I've been upstate, I've been to Helena, Montana, and I've been to Washington, DC.'

'And did you learn anything?' Sarah asked, urgently.

'We learned that they still haven't found all of the Ws that the Democrats swiped off the computer keyboards, and that the new people still don't see the funny side of it. But did we learn anything positive? No, love, I'm sorry, but we didn't.'

'Bob, why's Joe involved? He's back with the Bureau now, isn't he? And homicide's State business. What have you been stirring up? Have you been upsetting Sheriff Dekker?'

He looked at her, innocently. 'Me? No . . . well, not much, anyway. Brad laid on this room for us, so he's okay. The State cops got a bit precious, at least their boss did, but Joe sorted her.'

'Look,' she demanded, 'let's cut to the chase. Do you have any idea who did it?'

Bob frowned. 'No, but . . . Sarah love, I have a lot to tell you, but not here, okay. Your luggage should have been picked off the carousel by now, so let's grab it and get going.'

'Where are we going, exactly?'

'Home, like you asked. But if you've changed your mind, and you feel it would be too much to go straight back into the house, we can check in to a hotel.'

'No, let's not do that. It would be worse for me to be anywhere else in Buffalo, I promise you.'

'That's fine, then. I should warn you, the place is still in a bit of a mess, after the FBI technicians dusted every imaginable surface looking for a usable print, but I've booked a cleaning service to come in this morning. Come on, we'd better get going or they'll be there before us.'

The airport staff member who had brought Sarah to the VIP room was waiting outside the door with the single large Samsonite suitcase that held the clothes she had brought with her. Bob thanked her, took it from her and wheeled it behind him as he led the way to the staff car park, in which he had been allocated a space.

'I brought Leo's Jag from the garage,' he told her. 'I wiped the powder off that though.'

'They printed that?'

'Honey, this is the Bureau we're talking about. They even printed all the toilet roll holders, in case the guy took a dump while he was searching the place.'

'My God! But Bob, what were the Bureau doing at the house in the first place? Dad and Mum were killed up at the cabin.'

'Later, love; I'll tell you all about it later.' He loaded the case into the boot of the dark blue Jaguar and walked round to the passenger door, to open it for his wife. He settled into the cream calfskin driver's seat, switched on, and pulled smoothly out into the exit roadway. As they drove out on to the highway, heading south, Sarah stroked the smooth leather of the console between them. 'Dad always liked to have a good car,' she mused. 'I remember the smell of newness coming off them, from when I was a little girl. It was the only way he spoiled himself, really.' She flipped up the lid of the compartment and looked inside, then took out a pair of Ray-Ban sunglasses, in their case. 'Do you need these?' she asked.

'Not right now.' She replaced them and closed the central console.

'Do we have a date for the funeral?' It was as if she had been avoiding the question, but finally had plucked up the courage to raise it, to make herself part of the process.

'Friday,' he told her. 'It's fixed for Friday morning; there's a memorial service in the Lutheran church, and a burial after that. I left all the arrangements with the undertaker, once release of the bodies was confirmed. He's fixed the time to suit the Secret Service.'

'The what!'

'You heard. The new senator wants to be there, and she's bringing her husband.'

'You mean that?'

'I'd hardly kid you about your parents' funeral now, would I?'

She whistled. 'You know, Bob, all my life I sort of knew that my dad was an important man, beyond Buffalo. But I never really understood how important.'

'Did he ever talk about his interest in politics?'

'No.'

'Or about his time in Washington?'

'He used to say that Teddy Kennedy was the best of the brothers, and that he'd have made the best president, but that was about it. There was a time, in my late teens, when I kept trying to get him to talk about it, but he always shut me down.'

'What did he think of JFK?'

'I once heard him say that he was shot at the right time, to ensure that he would be sanctified rather than vilified after his death. I think he approved of him. I recall once hearing him say to Jack Wylie that if adultery in office was a ground for impeachment, Congress would have been too busy with that to do any legislating. Make of that what you will.'

She paused. 'Have you seen Jack since you've been in town?'

'I was supposed to see him on Saturday, only . . .' Bob hesitated, then decided to economise with the truth. 'He had an accident, on his boat.'

'Oh no. Poor Jack, was he badly hurt?'

'That was something I was going to tell you when we got home. He was killed.'

She seemed to sag into her seat, as she buried her face in her hands. 'Oh no,' she moaned. 'What next? I've known Jack all my life. He was like an uncle to me; and he was as close to my father as Andy is to you. What happened?'

'The gas tank blew up. He was barbecuing on deck.'

She sighed. 'That was Jack all right. He was at his happiest when he was wearing an apron, or playing around on that boat of his.'

'Or both.'

'Yeah, or both.' Suddenly she reached out for the radio controls. 'Goddamn it, let's have some music in this car; anything to lighten the atmosphere.' She pressed the button, and a heavy classical piece boomed out through the speaker system. 'I don't think so,' she murmured, and changed channel; Wagner was replaced by a nasal Country voice. 'Not you either, Emmy Lou.' She switched again, to hear Jon Bon Jovi going down in a blaze of glory. 'This is a conspiracy,' she shouted. 'Hold on; maybe Dad had some CDs here.'

She opened the console again, took out the Ray-Bans, laid them on her lap and began to rummage in the deep compartment. She felt around for a few seconds until, in an instant, her expression changed, her frown of irritation replaced by something much deeper. From within the box she withdrew a gun; a dark, metallic, well-oiled automatic pistol.

'What the hell is this?' she gasped, holding it up for Bob to see.

He stared at it, oblivious for that moment of the straight road ahead. 'Jesus,' he murmured. He took it from her, slowing his speed as he did, and looked at it for a few seconds, before handing it back. 'That's no replica, and it is loaded. Now just do what I say. The safety catch should be on the side, at the top of the grip. Check that it's on, then put that thing back where you found it.'

195

She did as he had told her, then closed the console lid, slowly and carefully. She looked up at him, at his grim profile as he drove along. 'Bob, you know my father hated firearms; he wouldn't even watch a Charlton Heston movie, because of his NRA connection. So what was he doing with a loaded automatic in his car? What the hell was he into?'

He shook his head, slowly. 'I wish I knew, love, I wish I knew; for I'm damn certain that it got him killed.'

48

Often, during Mario's Special Branch days, he and Maggie would meet for lunch. The venue usually depended on the weather; sometimes it would be the canteen, on other occasions a restaurant or a pub. But occasionally when the weather was warm and fine, they would buy sandwiches and eat them at a table at the piazza in Princes Street Gardens, watching the children on the roundabout, and talking above the noise of the traffic up in the busy thoroughfare.

She went there again on his first day in Borders Division, feeling lonely already without him, and tried to remember her life before they met, before they got together on that crazy stake-out in Fife. She had been wary of him at first, of his big, outgoing personality, of his smile, and of his bedroom eyes, all of them so much in contrast to her own make-up. Yet when the time came, it had been she who had made the move.

She had been a private person until then, showing a reserved and, often, a severe face to those around her. She had had few interests outside the Job, and even fewer friends. Once, she had tried to break the mould by placing an ad in the dating column of a Sunday newspaper. It had led to a few encounters, and eventually, when she had plucked up the courage, to her first adult sexual experiences, clumsy, fumbling affairs in drab hotel rooms, for she had refused to take her partners home with her, or to go with them to theirs. Quickly she had come to the conclusion that she was very bad at sex, and had given it up, virtually, until her big Irish-Italian detective had come along to stir genuine lust within her, for the first time in her life.

Yet, for all that she had developed as a person since her marriage, Maggie knew that many of her work colleagues could still see only her old self. They did not know the social animal she had become; they could see only the severe, strict, senior officer on her way up the ladder. She had heard her 'Lois' nickname long before Dan Pringle had let it slip, but she knew that she had another, one she still bore in the eyes of some resentful colleagues. When she had overheard a Special Branch typist ask Ruth McConnell, the DCC's secretary, in the ladies' room at Fettes, 'How are you getting on with Rosa Kleb?', she had known about whom the woman was talking . . . even if her loyal friend Ruth had ignored the question.

She threw the wrapping of her sandwich into a bin and walked up the steps and out of the gardens, then along Shandwick Place towards her office. All the time, her mind was gnawing away at her concern that a few days earlier a probationer constable had actually been afraid to come into her office. For all the encouragement of Willie Haggerty and Dan Pringle, she knew that someone with aspirations to chief officer rank should inspire respect, not fear, in their juniors. But the question that Maggie still had not answered, even in her own mind, was whether she actually had such aspirations.

Walking briskly in the sunshine, without stopping to window-shop, she reached Torphichen Place in less than fifteen minutes. She had only just hung her jacket in its usual place on the back of her chair when there was a knock; she called and young PC Haddock entered, wearing his diffident expression.

'Excuse me, ma'am,' he began.

'Okay, you're excused.' He stopped and stared at her. 'Oh, go on, Sauce,' she exclaimed. 'We don't need the preamble every time.'

'Very good, ma'am. Well, it's like this . . .' She sat behind her desk and waited for him to come to the point. 'We've found the undertaker, ma'am; the firm that made the arrangements for Mr Essary. It was the Co-op, up at Fountainbridge.' He paused again. 'The only thing is . . . the funeral was on Saturday.'

'Damn,' she hissed. 'That makes it difficult. Where's he buried?'

'Aye, well, ma'am, that's the other thing. He was cremated, down at Seafield.'

'Oh damn!' she snapped. 'Just our bloody luck. Ah, well, that was good work, son, to come up with an answer so quickly. What was the undertaker's name?'

'Mr Jaap, ma'am; Walter Jaap.' He held out a piece of paper, torn from a notebook. 'That's his number; I thought you might want to talk to him.'

'You thought right. Thanks. Anything else?'

'Sergeant Wilding, from the head of CID's office, dropped in an envelope ten minutes ago, ma'am. It's in your tray, there; apart from that, there's nothing else.'

'Okay, on you go then.'

As Haddock left, she flattened out his note on her desk and dialled the number he had written on it. 'Funeral services,' a solemn voice answered.

'Mr Jaap, please.'

'This is he. How can I be of assistance?'

'I want to talk to you about a funeral.'

'Certainly, madam. Shall I call on you?'

'No, that won't be necessary. This is Detective Superintendent Rose, Edinburgh CID. The funeral I want to ask you about took place on Saturday, in Seafield Crematorium; the guest of honour was a Mr Magnus Essary.'

'Yes,' Jaap replied. 'I attended that one myself.' He paused. 'But everything was in order, I assure you. The body was released from the mortuary with a cremation certificate, issued by medical staff at the Royal Infirmary.'

'I'm sure it was. I'm not questioning your procedures, sir. I'm interested in the funeral itself. For example, I'd like to know who was there; how many mourners, the names of the pall-bearers, anything else you can tell me.'

'Ahh,' came a sigh. 'But that's the pity of it. The poor man had no one to see him on his way.'

'No one?'

'Not a soul, other than myself, and my staff.'

'But who instructed you?'

'A lady; a Miss Ella Frances. She phoned me and asked me to collect the deceased from the mortuary and bring him to our chapel of rest, here at our salon. I did so that very day, and next morning she came to see me. She showed me all the necessary paperwork, by which I mean the cremation certificate and the death certificate itself. She told me that the late Mr Essary was her business partner, and that he had no relatives. She asked me to book a cremation; I did it there and then; she chose a simple coffin and reserved a hearse. I asked her if she wished me to place an intimation in the press, but she declined.'

'Can you give me an address and telephone number for Miss Frances?'

Jaap sighed again. 'Alas no, superintendent. She gave me neither.'

'But what about payment?' Rose asked. 'How are you going to invoice her?'

'I don't have to. She asked me what the bill would be. I told her that her requirements would cost just under nine hundred pounds, and she paid me there and then, in cash; she gave me one thousand pounds, the balance being a gratuity for my staff.'

'And then she didn't turn up for the funeral? Is that what you're saying?'

'That's right. She told me to proceed as instructed; she said that the late Mr Essary had been a humanist, and had wished no formal ceremony. She also told me at that time that she would be unable to attend herself, as she had to be in France, unavoidably, on business. She did lead me to expect that there would be mourners from Mr Essary's circle of friends, but on the day, there were none.'

'This stinks!' the detective exclaimed.

'I agree,' said the undertaker. 'I must admit I was concerned by the circumstances; I had it in mind to discuss it with my chief executive. I have an appointment to see him this evening, and I intended to tell him about it then; your call has anticipated that.'

'Give me a description of this Ella Frances woman.'

'She was small, in her twenties, I'd have said, but I'd hate to put an age to her. She was dressed in mourning black . . . nothing unusual in that, given the circumstances . . . with a wide-brimmed black hat and heavily tinted glasses which she never removed during our meeting.'

'Voice? Accent?'

'She was quietly spoken; I can't recall whether she had a particular accent of any sort. But people often sound strained when I meet them, so it can be hard to tell.'

'Okay.' Rose paused, thinking. 'Thank you for that, Mr Jaap. Listen, if by any chance Miss Frances should contact you again, get a number for her. I may have to speak to you again, but for now, that's all.'

She hung up and pulled the Essary folder across to her. Charlie Johnston's note was all right, as far as it went, but it stopped well short of being comprehensive. She snatched up her phone once more and dialled Haddock. 'Sauce, I want you to get someone for me. He's a doctor, Dr Amritraj, and he practises up at the health centre in Oxgangs. Find him, and make an appointment for me to call on him.'

Maggie was aware of a long, awkward silence. 'This is not a personal matter,' she added, heavily. 'I want to talk to him about a death he certified . . . but do not tell him that.'

She sat back and waited, and as she did her eye fell upon an envelope on the top of the pile in her in-tray, with her name scrawled across it; Dan Pringle's package, she guessed. She picked it up and tore it open. Inside there was a two-page Missing Person report, circulated by Strathclyde Police: the man Pringle had thought looked like her father. She looked at the name on the heading, reading it aloud. 'Father Francis

Donovan Green. A turbulent priest, I wonder . . . probably done a runner with a married parishioner.'

She scanned the report. Father Green was a fifty-one-year-old parish priest, in the appropriately named district of Holytown, in Lanarkshire. Ten days earlier he had gone off on a weekend's leave, to visit his spinster sister in Crieff. Maggie was struck by the adjective. *Spinster, eh. I could have been one of those*, she thought. She read on; the priest had been due back on the following Monday, ready to take confession, but he had not reappeared. On the following morning, his curate had telephoned his sister, who had told him that she had not seen her brother since Christmas, and certainly had not expected him that weekend.

The police had been informed; the curate and housekeeper had been interviewed, but Father Green had given no hint as to where he might really have been headed.

'Mid-life crisis, maybe,' the superintendent mused. And then she turned to the second sheet of the report.

The photograph seemed to become almost holographic as it jumped off the page at her. 'Jesus,' she shouted, involuntarily. She laid it on the desk, grabbed the Polaroid of Magnus Essary, and laid the two side by side. This time she had no doubt; what she needed was confirmation.

She snatched up her phone once more and dialled Haddock. 'Sauce,' she barked, 'have you got that doctor yet?'

'Sorry, ma'am,' he answered, fearfully. 'I'm having trouble finding the right number.'

'That's okay. Put a hold on that for now, anyway. I want you to get me someone else; PC Charlie Johnston. He's stationed up at Oxgangs, too. I don't care what shift he's on: suppose he's still on nights, and in the Land of Nod. Find him and tell him to be in my office inside an hour.'

49

Bob handed the keys of her parents' house to his wife. 'You do it, love,' he said. She took them from him, and unlocked the big front door, then stepped, slightly hesitantly, into the hall. The heat of the day was building up in the morning sunshine, but inside it was still cool.

Sarah looked around the familiar entrance; Bob had done as much as he could to clean up after the technicians, but she could see that the rest was a job for the professionals. Much of the panelling on the walls, and the woodwork on the stairway, were still streaked with their powder. Once more it got to her: she knew that there would be many such moments over the next few days, but it was comforting to know that with her husband at hand, she enjoyed the luxury of being able to yield to them, from time to time.

'Excuse me,' she whispered, and walked upstairs into the bedroom that had been hers as a girl, and in which she guessed that Bob had slept the night before. The sound of her crying carried down to him in the hallway; for a moment he thought of going up to her, but instead, he left the suitcase at the foot of the stairs and walked back out to the drive. He found a cloth in the Jaguar's glove compartment and used it to wrap the pistol, which he retrieved from its hiding place, and carried into the Graces' spacious reception room. Indoors, he was able to give the weapon a thorough examination. He recognised it at once as the double of several owned by his own police force, not his own firearm of choice, but one which was popular with his colleagues, because of its reliability: a 9mm Glock 19, compact model. He slid the fifteen-shot magazine from its housing in the butt, and saw that, indeed, it was fully loaded.

He laid pistol and ammunition on a side table, then reached into a pocket of the cotton jacket he had bought a few days before, and took out a small notebook, searching through it until he found the number he needed. He sat in his father-in-law's armchair, picked up the phone and dialled.

'Schultz,' a strong voice answered.

'Lieutenant, good morning, it's Bob Skinner here. I hope I'm not interrupting anything.'

'No, sir, I have this morning off. I've just been running and I'm about to step into the shower, but otherwise, I'm clear. How can I help you?'

'Leo and Susannah's car,' the Scot began. 'The Ford Explorer they had up at the lake; where is it now?'

'We have it in the park at my office. Would you like it delivered back to Buffalo? I could have Toby drive it down, with a patrolman following to bring him back. No big deal.'

'Thanks; maybe I'll take you up on that. But first, there's something I have to ask you. Have you searched it? The Explorer, that is.'

'No, sir.'

'Okay, I'd like you to do that, first chance you get. I haven't had a chance to check my copy of the inventory you took at the cabin, but I don't recall seeing any mention of any firearms being found there.'

'You're correct; there were none.'

'In that case, I'd like you to look in the car; in the glove compartment, central storage box, under the seats. My wife and I have just found a loaded Glock in his Buffalo car. If Leo was carrying a gun, it was unusual behaviour for him; so if he had one in Buffalo, it stands to reason . . .' He paused. 'There isn't another in the house here; the Bureau have been all over it, and they'd have found it for sure. So search the car, please. I'd just like to know.'

'Sure, sir,' Schultz responded. 'I'll go in soon as I'm showered. Apart from anything else, we have occasional thefts from cars, even in the police park. If Mr Grace had a second gun, it should be under lock and key in my desk, for safety's sake. I'll get back to you.'

'Thanks.' Skinner hung up, and leaned back in the comfortable chair, thinking. After a few minutes he picked up the phone again and called Joe Doherty's Washington number.

'Tell me about the registration of firearms in the US,' he began, when finally he was put through to the deputy director.

'You won't be here long enough,' his friend replied, tersely. 'Be specific.'

'My father-in-law had a gun, maybe two. Would there be a record of where and when he bought them?'

'For sure,' said Doherty, quickly. 'Federal law requires all dealers to be registered, and also it requires them to keep a record of every sale made. But if someone buys two guns, the dealer has to report their sale to the ATF . . . that's the Bureau of Alcohol, Tobacco and Firearms.'

203

'I know what the ATF is.'

'You wanna find out whether Mr Grace is on their list? It'll take me one call.'

'Yes, please, Joe, if you could. And if he did buy two firearms, would you find out when. The automatic Sarah found in his car looked more or less new.'

'Gimme your number there; I'll call you back.'

Skinner replaced the phone, then reached out and picked up the unloaded pistol once more. He was used to guns; he had been a qualified marksman since his earliest days on the force. He felt the weight of the Glock in his hand, admiring its balance. He worked the slide mechanism, silent and smooth, sighted along the barrel and pulled the trigger.

'I can understand why McIlhenney likes this baby,' he murmured; to himself, he thought.

'Nothing but the best for my old man,' said Sarah, behind him. 'It didn't do him any good, though, did it. Are you ready now to tell me what this is all about?'

He opened his mouth to reply, but the phone rang, silencing him. 'One call, just like I said,' Doherty drawled. 'Leopold Grace bought two identical Glock 19 automatics from a dealer in Buffalo just over two months ago. In accordance with federal law, the transaction was reported to the ATF two days later, on form number 3310 point 4.' The American laughed. 'If you think you have a bureaucracy in Britain you wanna get a load of the paperwork our government can generate.'

'At least we've taught you something,' Skinner grunted. 'Have you heard from Kosinski yet?'

'No. He's due to see Arthur Wilkins around now; he said he'd call me straight after. I'll let you know if anything fresh comes out of the interview.'

'Okay.'

He hung up and turned to Sarah. 'Your father felt under threat, love,' he began. 'I don't know why, but he did . . .' He stopped in mid-sentence as the *déjà vu* feeling he had experienced earlier that morning, and before, swept over him once more. He had become used to it, and so this time, he simply made himself wait it out. When it cleared after a few seconds, it was as if a door had been opened in his mind.

'Bob, what is it? For a second there you just glazed over.'

'Wait.' He waved her to silence, snatched up the phone, and dialled Doherty's number again. This time, he was put straight through.

'Joe,' he snapped. 'I must have had a bang on the head as well as you on Saturday. The device on Wylie's boat: have your people found any traces yet of a timing mechanism?'

'Yeah, they did. I just got the report. So what? It stands to reason there was a timer.'

'Sure, but think about this. If you and I hadn't been delayed in transit, and if I hadn't stopped for a few seconds on the boardwalk, we'd have been on that boat too. Suppose, just suppose, Jackson Wylie wasn't the only target.'

'Yeah?' the deputy director responded, slowly.

'So who knew we were seeing him there, and at that time? Who set up the meeting?'

'Fuck!' The single hissed syllable took about five seconds to form. 'Hold on a minute, Bob! He's one of mine!'

'Sure, but suppose, just suppose . . .'

'Shit, shit, shit!' Skinner had never heard his friend raise his voice before. 'Yeah, okay, okay, I get the picture. I don't believe it, but I'll have him intercepted and brought to me for questioning.'

'Before he sees Wilkins, Joe, yes? You'll do it right now.'

'Yes, Goddammit; right now.'

Sarah was staring at him, hard, as he put down the phone. 'The device on Jack Wylie's boat?' she exclaimed. 'What device? You mean someone planted a bomb on board? And you and Joe were meant to be there when it went off?'

He held up his hands, as if to ward her off. 'I don't know,' he said. 'Yes, there was a bomb, but it might have had nothing to do with us. It's just a possibility, but it has to be checked out.'

'Who's being checked out? This Kosinski guy you mentioned?'

'Yes.'

'Who is he?'

'An FBI agent, one of Joe's team on the investigation.'

He looked at her. 'To go back to what I was saying before, Joe's confirmed for me that your dad bought two guns a couple of months ago. He kept one in the Jag; the other, I'd guess, he kept around the house, and took with him to the cabin. Either the guy who killed him stole it, or it's still in the off-roader they had up there.

'I want to ask you something,' he said, 'and I want you to think long and hard about it. Do the names Sander Garrett or Bartholomew Wilkins mean anything to you, either or both of them?'

She frowned, and sat on the chair facing his. 'No,' she answered, slowly. 'I don't think they do. No, I'm certain; I've never heard of either one of them. Were they associates of my father?'

'So it seems. Let me tell you the whole story.'

She nodded, looking at him intently.

'Bart Wilkins and Sander Garrett are both dead,' he began. 'They were both murdered, shortly before your father; they were lawyers, Democrats, and they both worked in Washington at the same time as him and Jackson Wylie.'

Suddenly her eyes widened, and she sat up in the armchair. 'Hey, wait a minute, wait a minute!' she cried out. 'Bart and Sandy, Bart and Sandy: I know those names. When my dad was in Washington, a bunch of the guys used to play touch football every Sunday. Dad said it was the most exclusive club in DC at the time, because the star player was You Know Who.'

'I do?'

'You sure do. The president himself; he turned out on most of the Sundays he was in DC. Bobby played too, sometimes. Two of the guys in the squad were called Bart and Sandy; I remember that now, although he never mentioned their surnames. Jack Wylie was in it too.'

'How did they get together?'

'Through their jobs. The president himself invited Dad to join them, but all the others were in the Secret Service.'

50

Looking across the room at his new boss, Sammy Pye was surprised by the gleam of satisfaction that was written on his face. Dan Pringle had gone, back to Edinburgh, and they had been in the middle of a team meeting with the available divisional CID staff when the phone had rung. McGuire had frowned at the interruption at first, but had taken the call when he had heard who was on the line.

'Yes, Greg,' he murmured, pleasantly. 'What can I do for you?'

'Company business, Mario,' his colleague replied, in a tone that was just a shade too affable. 'You could say that this is an interview, rather than a conversation.'

'Oh aye. Do I need a lawyer then?' He grinned at the reactions of some of his seven-strong squad, sat around the conference room table. 'Greg,' he continued, 'I'm just coming to the end of a meeting here. Hold on for a minute while I wrap it up.' He wrapped a massive hand around the mouthpiece and looked at Pye. 'Sammy, take the lads across the road to the pub, and buy them the last beer they're going to get out of me till next Christmas. I'll square you up when I join you.' He waited while they filed out of the room then put the phone back to his ear. 'Okay,' he resumed briskly, 'what's this interview about, then?'

'Joking, Mario; I was joking,' said Detective Superintendent Jay. 'Actually, I was sort of hoping you could help me.'

'Indeed. Tell me, that crunching sound I hear in the background; could that be a portion of humble pie being eaten?'

'With salt and pepper.'

'Good. So what's your problem?'

'It's that company I told you about; Essary and Frances, the wine importers who rented space in your warehouse, the lot your uncle was trying to turf out. My people can't find hide nor hair of them.'

'How hard have they tried?'

'As hard as they can. The company has no listing in the telephone directory or in Yellow Pages; nor are there any private subscribers named Magnus Essary or Ella Frances. We checked with the solicitors who registered the company; they're a small firm out in Corstorphine.

'They know virtually nothing about them; they took all the instructions at a single meeting which was attended only by Ella Frances, handled the set-up for them, sold them one of the shell companies they keep for the purpose and registered the name change with Companies House, in Castle Terrace. They sent them a fee note and it was paid in cash. They haven't heard from them since then; no one could even recall an occasion, since that first meeting, when either one has called at the office.'

'Where did they send the invoice?'

'To the address they gave, 46 Leightonstone Grove, Hunter's Tryst. A couple of days later, a woman handed in an envelope to their reception desk with the exact amount in cash. The office was just closing, so she didn't wait for a receipt; it was posted out to them, same day.'

'You've been to the house?'

'Of course. No answer; the place was locked up.'

'Who's the registered owner of the property?'

'A Mr Lyall Butler; we've checked with the City Chambers. He's retired and shown as being normally resident in Portugal, and getting a fifty per cent discount on his council tax.'

'Have you contacted him?'

'He's not on the phone there. It would mean asking the local police to interview him ... if he speaks Portuguese, or they speak English. Chances are they'd need to find an interpreter. If I did that, it would take a long time to get a result. No, what I was hoping, was that you might ask around for me within your family to see if anyone has actually met these people, and knows where or how they can be contacted, other than at that address.'

'Didn't Stan tell you that?'

There was a silence, then a sigh. 'We didn't actually ask him,' Jay admitted. 'I just tried to call him back myself, but he's gone out. His secretary said that he'd gone for a meeting with a client and that he didn't take his mobile.

'I don't really want to send officers to his house in the evening, so I wondered . . .'

'It's all right for me to get involved when it suits you, eh, Greg,' said McGuire. 'Okay, I'll have a word with Stan. And I'll ask my mother about them. Beppe might have discussed the tenancy with her, you never know.'

'Thanks, s . . .' Jay stopped himself just in time.

51

Charlie Johnston was none too pleased to have been summoned from the betting shop in the middle of his day off, but the big career constable knew better than to show it to the acting chief superintendent. He stood to attention in front of her desk, in his hastily donned tunic, all too aware, suddenly, that it was covered in fine cat hairs.

'You wanted to see me, ma'am?' he began, his speech as stiff and formal as the rest of him.

'Yes. Relax and sit down, please. I want to talk to you about something that happened a week or so back, when you were on nights, minding the Oxgangs office. You were called out to a sudden death, I understand; in a doctor's surgery.'

Johnston nodded, vigorously. 'Aye, that's right, ma'am. Dr Amritraj.' Then he paused, as if it had dawned on him that for all young Haddock had said, he might be on the carpet after all. 'Ah didna like leaving the office, like,' he assured Rose, 'but a'body else was busy, and the paramedics were gettin' bolshie.'

She read his thoughts. 'It's all right; I'm not questioning your judgement, Charlie, don't worry. No, I just want you to tell me what happened when you got there.'

The constable leaned back in his chair and scratched his head. 'Well, ma'am, there wisna much to it really. There was this bloke, and he was deid.' He chuckled, grimly. 'No doubt about that right enough. He was as deid as he's ever goin' tae be.'

'Tell me about the doctor.'

'There's no' much tae tell about him either. He was an Asian bloke . . . nothing unusual about that these days . . . and he was in a hurry tae get home.'

'Did you question him?'

Johnston looked offended. 'Oh aye, ma'am. It's all in my report.'

'Fine, but tell me. How did he explain the man being there in the middle of the night?'

'He said the bloke had called him, complaining about chest pains. He

209

said the guy was feart of hospitals, so rather than upset him, he took him tae his surgery to give him a check-up, put him on a machine, like, and he had hardly got there when the fella took a big coronary and popped off. He said he was ten minutes trying to bring him round, but it was nae use.

'So he just called the ambulance tae take him away.'

Rose looked him in the eye. 'Not the police? Only the ambulance? You're sure about that.'

'Dead sure, ma'am. It was a wee paramedic lass that phoned me.'

'And how did the doctor react when you arrived?'

The middle-aged officer cocked an eyebrow. 'Ye mean was he pleased tae see me like?'

She nodded. 'That'll do.'

'Naw. He was just wantin' hame, like the ambulance crew were wantin' back tae the Royal.'

'Had you ever met him before?'

'Who? The deid fella, like?'

'No,' Rose said, patiently. 'The doctor.'

'Naw, naw, naw, naw, naw. Never in ma life. He was a new one on me, like.'

'Do you know many of the doctors up in Oxgangs, Charlie?'

'Ah thought Ah knew them a', ma'am, but like Ah said, no' this one.'

'Have you seen Amritraj since then?'

'No, ma'am.'

She leaned across her desk and pulled her in-tray towards her. 'The dead man, Essary,' she said. 'You'd remember him if I showed you a photograph, would you?'

'Oh aye, ma'am. Ah've got a good memory for faces . . . especially if they're deid.'

She ripped off the second sheet of the Strathclyde memo, and slid it over to him. 'Is that him?'

Johnston picked it up and gazed at it for a few seconds. Then he nodded, slowly. 'He looks a bit better there, ma'am, a bit mair life about him, ken; but that's him a'right: no doubt about it.'

52

'I always meant to ask your father about this thing American men have with their dens,' Bob murmured, as he and Sarah looked around the converted cellar space beneath the mansion. It was a big room, with walls and ceiling panelled in pale beechwood, comfortably furnished, and geared to play rather than work.

'Simple; they express the part of them that never grew up. That was well over fifty per cent in some men I've met, I can tell you. In my father's case, probably about five, but he wasn't exempt, as this place shows.'

Like the rest of the house, the den bore the marks of a thorough sweep by the police and Bureau technicians. 'This photograph you remember,' asked Bob, 'he would have kept it here, would he, rather than in one of the public rooms?'

'Here, for certain,' she said, without a moment's hesitation. 'My dad wasn't showy; he met presidents and senators, and he had been one of those himself at state level, but he never talked about it unless he was asked, and he never displayed any photographs from those days. All those, and his few bits of memorabilia, were down here.'

Skinner laughed. 'I was in a guy's office once and you could hardly see the walls for pictures of him with the rich and famous. They were arranged in a sort of pecking order. The actors and pop stars were on the bottom rung, then politicians, then up one more to the royals, and right at the top of the ladder was him and the Pope.'

'Whom you'll be meeting yourself, quite soon.'

'Yes, but don't let's go into that. Where did Leo keep his photographs?'

'They were in albums. Let's see.' She pointed to a sideboard against one of the walls. 'In there, I think.'

Sarah stepped across to the cabinet, knelt beside it and opened a door on its right. 'Yup. Here they are.' She reached in and withdrew a stack of red leather-bound volumes. She passed them to Bob, then reached into the small fridge in the corner, took out two bottles of Budweiser, uncapped them with a tool fixed to the wall and handed one to him.

'Wassup,' he muttered, as he sat in a rocking chair, the albums on his lap. He glanced at the covers and saw from their labels that they were in decade order, from the thirties on.

Laying the others on the floor he opened the 1960s volume and handed it to his wife. 'This is where it should be,' she muttered, sitting on a three-seater couch and wiping a line of foam, back-handed, from her top lip. He watched her as she looked at the first few pages, smiling at some photographs, passing others by quickly. She had reached only the seventh page, when she stopped and turned the album towards Bob. 'Look.'

Skinner had only known his father-in-law as an old man; even then he had been strikingly handsome. The photograph that his wife showed him filled a page of the book. Leo Grace smiled out at him, in his early thirties, with movie-star looks that made even the man by his side seem ordinary. The man by his side; Bob had been a child on the twenty-second of November, 1963, barely halfway through primary school, yet the memory of his parents' shock when the news-flash confirmed his death had remained vivid. The president must have been at least fifteen years older than Leo, a veteran of the war before his, yet an innocent looking at the two of them, razor-sharp in their evening dress, could have been forgiven for wondering which of the two was the leader.

'They seem to be fairly chummy,' he murmured.

'They were; it was Bobby whom Dad never liked. No, it was really the other way round; the Attorney General didn't get on with him. My father didn't care about him one way or another. He never talked about it, though; that was the way Jack Wylie told it.'

'What else did Jack say?' he asked, as she turned back to the album.

'He reckoned that Bobby was jealous of Dad, and that he was afraid the New Yorkers would pick him for the senate vacancy when it came up.'

'I can see why they might have. But your father never ran, did he?'

'No. He decided against it.'

'Was he warned off?'

'You're kidding. If anyone had tried that he would have gone for it. The truth, for it was one of the few things he did tell me, was that he felt it would have put the president in a difficult position, if he had run, having to choose whether to endorse his brother or his friend. So when the offer to join the firm was made, he decided to accept, thinking that he might give it a run when he was a little older, and a little richer.'

212

'He never did, though. Did he tell you why?'

Sarah nodded. 'Yes, he did,' she answered. 'It was the assassination; the effect it had on him. He wasn't afraid,' she added, quickly. 'He wasn't afraid of anything after Korea; he said he left all his fear out there. The thing that horrified him was that when they shot the president, the first lady was in the car. She could have been hit rather than him; as well as him.

'Dad said that he'd only have gone into politics with the intention of making it to the top of the tree. But when he saw what happened in Dallas, he decided there and then that he could never put my mother in that position.' She stopped, as she realised that he was gazing at her with a faint, curious smile on his face.

'You said "they", just now. Did you realise that?'

'Did I? Well if I did, that's what my father said; because I remember having that discussion with him, as clearly as if it was only an hour ago. I was barely in my teens and President Reagan had just been shot.'

'Are you sure? Think again.'

She closed her eyes for a second or two. 'No. I don't need to think again. That's what he said.'

'He didn't say, "When the president was shot"?'

'No, Goddammit. He said, "When they shot the president." But so what? It's a colloquialism, almost. Lots of Americans say that.'

'I suppose so,' he admitted, letting the matter drop as Sarah went back to the book.

She had not gone much further when she stopped, staring at the pages that lay open in front of her. 'Look here,' she exclaimed. He jumped from the rocking chair in a single easy movement, and sat on the arm of the couch, looking down at the album. He saw two photographs, one on each facing page. The image on the left showed Leo Grace and another, older man . . . Bob realised with a start that it was J. Edgar Hoover . . . with the vice president of the United States; in the other he stood alongside Dr Martin Luther King. But it was not the photographs at which his wife was staring; beneath each one was a rectangular shape, whiter than the rest of the backing page. 'Two photographs have been taken from here,' she said. 'The corner fixings are still in place, even.'

'Go through it and see if any others have been removed.' She did as he asked, no longer studying the photographs, only flicking from page to page looking for what might not be there.

'No,' she said at last. 'Only those two.'

'Still, you should check the rest of the book, just in case Leo took those two out, and they're not the ones we're looking for. The photos you remembered could still be there.'

She seemed to nod, then shake her head all in one movement. 'Yes . . . no . . . wait. There was something else.' She turned to look behind her, at a series of shelves, fixed so that they seemed part of the panelling. 'Dad had a football,' she exclaimed. 'It was signed by the president and by all the guys; they gave it to him after the last game he played with them. He kept it on a shelf up there . . . and now it's gone.'

He sensed her hesitation. 'Bob, I hate to say this . . . but this has been done by someone with access to all sorts of files and places; someone who knew about the connection in the first place. Are you sure about Joe Doherty? Can you trust him in this?'

Bob drew in a deep breath. 'I hear what you're saying, honey. This could be coming from inside, and Joe is inside, very high up, too. Except . . . Joe didn't hold us back on Saturday, when we went to see Jack Wylie. I did. If it hadn't been for me stopping on the boardwalk, we'd both have been on that cruiser when it went up.

'On that basis alone, I can trust him. I trust my own judgement too. Joe's straight.'

'If you're sure of that, it reassures me. But even at that, where do the two of you go from here?'

'Good question. If we go anywhere, we go very carefully, however important Joe might be. But we do have a couple of leads; for a start there's the mysterious hunting trip.'

'What?'

'Exactly. Your father and Jackson Wylie took themselves off on a trip to the Appalachians last January, ostensibly to shoot deer.'

'Dad? Never!'

'Maybe not, but the two of them did go off somewhere and that was the cover story. I'd like to know where they stayed and who else was there . . . although I can make a pretty shrewd guess. Then there are the laptops,' he added.

'What?'

'Computers. Wilkins, Garrett and Wylie all had portable computers; the first two were stolen from the crime scenes in Montana and Las Vegas. We think that Wylie's went up with the boat. Do you know if your father had a computer, apart from that thing over there?' He pointed to the Compaq on a table beside the television set.

'If he had, I've never heard of it. But . . .'

The ringing of the phone on the computer table interrupted her. Bob walked across and picked it up. Lieutenant Dave Schultz was on the other end. 'No gun in the car, sir,' he said. 'I've just searched it, as thoroughly as I've ever searched a vehicle without cutting open the panels. There is no firearm there. Also I've rechecked the crime scene inventory, and there is definitely nothing of that nature listed. Do you want me to check with AT and F?'

'I've done that,' the Scot answered, 'or at least Mr Doherty has. Mr Grace bought two matching Glock 19s a couple of months back. He kept one in his Jaguar; my bet is that the other was for the house, and that he'd have taken it to the cabin.'

'You want me to run another search?'

'No, it would have been found by now if it was still there.' As he spoke to the detective, the cathedral tones of the doorbell boomed out in the hall above: Sarah ran upstairs to answer its summons. He thanked Schultz and hung up, then followed her out of the den.

He had assumed that the cleaning service had arrived, finally, and so he was slightly surprised to see a youngish man in the doorway, following his wife into the house. Taken off guard, Skinner gave him the classic enquiring look of policemen everywhere.

'Bob,' said Sarah, with the faintest hint of sharpness, 'this is Ian Walker, our Lutheran minister. I've told you about him. As well as being our pastor, he's an old friend. Ian and I were at high school at the same time, then later at college.'

'Yes,' the newcomer concurred, 'for a while. I graduated two years before your wife.' He was a medium-sized man, with dark, crinkly hair, and round, piercing eyes, informally dressed in a sports shirt and slacks . . . sure confirmation in the circumstances, Bob thought, that they were old friends. Indeed, there was something in the way they looked at each other that made him wonder, for a moment, just how friendly they had been. 'The mortician told me you were due in town this morning, Sarah,' the clergyman continued. 'I had to come right away, to express my condolences and to pay my respects.'

'Thank you, Ian; that's much appreciated. We'd have called you later today, in any case; we need to discuss the arrangements for the funeral service. Come through to the drawing room. Will you have coffee?' She realised that she had brought her Budweiser upstairs with her. 'Or a beer?'

Walker smiled. 'Coffee will be fine. You know how it is with us guys; we can't be breathing fumes over the faithful . . . not even us Lutherans.'

'I'll make it,' Bob volunteered. 'You go on through.' He headed for the kitchen, as his wife ushered the minister through to the reception room.

'I can't tell you how appalled I am by what's happened,' he said, as the door closed on them. 'Babs is distraught too.'

'How is she?' asked Sarah. 'How are the kids?'

'She's very well; she still looks like a teenager, just like you knew her in school. And Matthew and Daniel are growing by the day. And yours?'

'Mark, our adopted son, is turning out to be a mathematical whiz; the other two, James Andrew and Seonaid, are just ordinary, peaceable children; even if Jazz is built like an outhouse, and eats more than his brother, who's twice his age. I'm happy to hear that Babs is just the same; I couldn't imagine her any other way than just as she is. I must see her. Can you get a sitter, tomorrow or Wednesday maybe, and come to us for dinner?'

'No,' said Ian, 'we've thought of that. Much better if we do it the other way round. We thought that you might like to come to us on Wednesday, a couple of nights before the funeral service, to talk about the running order, as well as to catch up.'

She yielded to his logic. 'Okay, that's a date.'

'Good; I have to tell you that we're getting in first. If you see all the people who've asked me to pass on condolences, and ask if they can call on you, then you'll have little or no time to yourself. I have a list of all their names.'

'Thanks.' She smiled at him, but as she did, she read something in his eye.

'There is one in particular, though. When you and the baby were back home a couple of years back, that time that you and Bob had troubles in your marriage; remember you came to see me, and we had a heart-to-heart about a guy you were dating? The guy you were with when we went out on that foursome?'

She smiled at him. 'Heart-to-heart, indeed; that's a sweet way of putting it. Truth was, I used you like a confessor; I told you that I had had sex with him.'

'Sure, and I didn't have any problems with that. I'm one of your new-fangled clerics, Sarah; you know that as well as anyone. But the thing is, you'll find the name Terry Carter on that list. He called me last week and said that because he knew that I was your friend as well as your family minister, he'd like to ask me a favour. He said that he'd like to meet you when you got here, to express his condolences in person.'

'Damn,' she whispered. 'Is he in Buffalo?'

'No, he told me that he works in New York, and he gave me a cellphone number for you to call, should you decide to.'

'Should I decide to? Yes, should I?' she asked herself. 'Not if I've any sense, but . . . Fact is, Ian, I've always felt just a little guilty about the way I treated him. I know he probably didn't want any more than to get himself fucked . . . Pardon my language, padre . . . but I didn't even want that, not really.' She shrugged her shoulders and flashed him a quick grin. 'Okay, I can't lie to you of all people; sure I wanted it, but I had other things in mind too.

'I used him deliberately as a counter-balance against Bob, not to get even with him as such, but to put us on the same footing for the future. Afterwards, I tried to hate myself for it, but I couldn't, not like I did after you and I had our college fling, when I knew all along how Babs felt about you, even if you didn't.'

Walker looked at the floor. 'Yeah,' he murmured. 'But we were just kids then, and we didn't do anyone any harm. I've never felt guilty about that, and I've never seen why you should, any more than I see why you should feel guilty about Terry Carter, or hate yourself for having a relationship with him, given your circumstances at the time. To lapse into professional language, I don't see the sin in it.

'As far as you and I went, Babs and I weren't dating then; that's in the past and it can stay there. You and Terry, though; I'm not advising you, understand, but from what you're saying, it sounds as if there's some closure lacking there.'

The phone rang, beside her, but she made no move towards it, knowing that Bob would pick it up in the kitchen. 'Maybe,' she conceded, as it fell silent once more. 'I'll have to think about it.' She looked up at him. 'You got that list on you?'

53

Skinner reached out and took the kitchen phone from its cradle on the wall. 'The Grace residence,' he answered.

'You sound like the fucking butler,' said Joe Doherty, tersely, with none of his usual dry humour sounding in his voice.

'Kosinski?'

'If only I knew for sure. I tried to call him myself, on his issue cellphone; but it was unavailable for connection. So I sent two guys from the Chicago office to intercept him at Arthur Wilkins' office, but by the time they got there he'd already been and gone. They weren't briefed to interview Wilkins, so they left and reported back to me. I called the guy myself and had him call the switchboard back to verify me. I spun him a story that I'd wanted to catch Troy at his office, and with more than my usual subtlety asked if their meeting had gone okay. He said that it had; that Kosinski had asked him about his father, whether he had done or said anything strange recently.

'He told him that last time he saw his father, before he died, he had given him an envelope. He knew from the feel of it that it had a computer disk inside, and he asked him what it was about. His father replied that it was a copy of something on a new laptop he had bought, a memoir of his time in the Secret Service. He asked Arthur if he would keep it in the office safe.

'Kosinski told him that the computer had been stolen when he was murdered, but that if the disk did contain material relating to the Service, that might make it a matter of national security. So he asked Wilkins to give it to him, and the guy, after some thought, did so. Troy thanked him and left.'

'Interesting,' said Skinner, 'but it sounds on the up-and-up.'

'I'd agree,' replied Doherty. 'Except for two things: Kosinski's cellphone is still out and I can't locate him, plus this. Less than half an hour after I spoke to him, Arthur Wilkins left his office to go home for lunch. He was shot dead in its private parking garage, just as he was climbing into his Lexus. My Chicago guys heard the police department alert and called me.

'And you guess right: no, the police didn't catch anyone.' Suppressed fury exploded from the deputy director. 'Bob, I have a renegade; a fucking renegade within the Bureau. When I trace this bastard, he's as good as dead.'

'Hey, cool down, man. Who says you're going to have to trace him?' asked Skinner. 'You may be jumping to a big conclusion.'

'You kidding?'

'No, I'm not kidding. Whether it's Kosinski who's been taking these people out or not, the killer is a very clever guy. He also has access to files and information that I suspect are beyond even you. We suspected Kosinski because of the timing of the explosion, and the theory that it could have been set to kill us as well. But this guy has the resources to hack into sophisticated computer systems and delete records. Do you think he couldn't have bugged Jackson Wylie's office, or the Wilkins firm in Chicago?'

'So why can't I contact Kosinski now?'

'Maybe his cellphone battery's gone soft; maybe his pager's lying on the bathroom shelf. Maybe by now he's been taken out himself, if that envelope Wilkins handed over is significant. You see? Your man may be a suspect, but by now he may also be a victim. If he's either, the odds are that you'll never see him again.'

'Oh no, why not?'

'If Kosinski killed these people, then after Wilkins, he's blown, and he'll disappear back into whatever outfit planted him in the Bureau in the first place. If he didn't, and that envelope contained what I think it might have, it made him a target as soon as he left the Wilkins building. If he has been killed, they'll make him disappear, so that you, being essentially a dumb copper like me, will assume that he was the bad guy all along.'

'I wish I was a dumb copper like you,' Doherty grunted. 'Any way we can tell which is which?'

'No, but if you find that Wilkins was killed by a bullet from Kosinski's Bureau-issue firearm, you'll know that he's gone, one way or another. He either killed him, or they made it look as if he did.'

'They?'

'The same people who killed the president.'

'What!?' The word escaped as a cut-off scream. 'Bob, what the f . . .'

Skinner laughed. 'Okay, okay, okay. Calm down, Joe; I'm about seven steps ahead of myself. But here's what I know from Sarah. Wilkins, Garrett and Jack Wylie were all members of the Secret Service back in the early sixties, sharp kids straight out of law school looking for something extra on their *curriculum vitae*. Leo Grace wasn't, but he was one of their circle; they all knew him because they all played on the president's Sunday football team, and so did Leo. According to Sarah he was the only guy there who wasn't in the Service.

'When Leo left Washington, eventually, they gave him a football, signed by the Man and all the guys. That's been stolen from the house up here. So have two photographs of the squad.'

'Shit!' Doherty squealed.

'Aye. Anyhow, he settles in Buffalo, and a few years later he invites Jackson Wylie into his firm. They all live happily ever after. There's no mention of Garrett or Wilkins, and no contact we know of, either through the law, or through their shared political interests. Then last January, out of the blue, Wylie tells his secretary that he and Leo Grace ... who hasn't shot anything since Korea ... are going to kill deer in the Appalachians. This is peculiar also, since Leo doesn't own a rifle.

'I'd like to know who else went on that trip, and where exactly they went. I'd like to know also about the purchase by one of the four, somewhere, of three, possibly four, identical Apple Mac iBook laptop computers. Most of all, I'd like to see the Secret Service duty rosters for November 22, 1963; it would be interesting to know whether Wylie, Garrett and Wilkins were on duty that day.'

'Why, for God's sake?'

'The only time Leo ever talked to Sarah about those sixties years, he referred to "them" shooting the president. Sure, I know it's just a word, but Leo weighed every word he used. Joe, when all else fails, I go by hunches. In this case, my nose tells me that these three guys either knew who killed the president, or ... they did it themselves.'

Doherty sighed. 'I don't know if I want to hear this, Bob. If you're crazy, I'm crazy for listening to you. And if you're right ... I'm still crazy for listening to you.' He paused. 'But what about Leo? How did he know?'

'My guess is that Jack Wylie told him at some point; maybe not that he'd done it, but that there had been a plot and he knew who was involved. I guess too that with old age looming, and all it brings with it, the three of them, Wylie, Garrett and Wilkins, may have decided that at the very least they had to make a record of the truth. But they needed someone else, someone from that time who could vouch for them all; so Wylie approached Leo.

'They met up, in the Appalachians or wherever ... and from that point they were done. I'll bet you, Joe, that these guys have been watched, from the day they left the Service.'

'Watched? By who?'

'By whoever set up the assassination. The CIA, the Mafia, another agency, I don't know; but they've been keeping tabs on these guys for the last thirty years and more.'

'Why not kill them back then?'

'Then kill the guys who killed them? Where would it end? How long before the last gullible American died and there was no one left to believe that Oswald did it? No, you don't take that risk till you have to. But when those three guys, plus Leo Grace, the president's friend, got together, that time had come.

'They must have realised the danger, though; or at least Leo must have. Straight after that trip in January, he went out and bought those two automatics.'

There was a long silence. Skinner let it run its course. 'Kosinski,' said Doherty, after fully two minutes. 'If it was Kosinski, why him, why someone in the Bureau?'

'Deniability. The organisation that planned or commissioned the hit wouldn't, then or now, use someone who led back to its door. But like I said, it may not have been Kosinski. He may be dead himself. Wait till they dig the bullet out of Wilkins: see if it's FBI issue.'

'And if it isn't?'

'Then there's a fair chance it'll have come from a Glock 19. Leo's second gun is missing.'

'What will that tell us?'

'Fuck all, except that it'll mean Kosinski could still be in the game.'

'Jeez. So how do we investigate all this?'

'You want to investigate it?'

'Sure as hell, I do. I guess I'd better brief the director, though.'

'Can you trust the director?'

'Bob!'

'Could you trust Kosinski?'

'Aw hell. Okay, what do I do?'

'Use Special Agent Brand. Have him go through the bank and credit card records of the other three guys. I have access to all Leo's stuff. See if they tell you where they were in January. See what they tell you about those laptops. That's all for now.'

'Okay, I'll do that, and I'll ask for a copy of the Wilkins autopsy report.'

'No. You do the Wilkins autopsy through your own people. You have the authority; father and son murdered in different states makes it your business, yes?'

'You're catching on. I'll get Chicago on to that; be back in touch.'

'What about the Secret Service rosters?'

'Now you are being crazy. That stuff's off limits.'

'Tell me, Joe, aren't all records in the US computerised by now?'

'Pretty much.'

'And is the Bureau the only law enforcement agency in the US that doesn't know how to hack into a computer?'

'Bob, you didn't say that. I could have you deported just for thinking it, never mind suggesting it to a federal civil servant. I'll call you.'

Skinner hung up. The coffee filter had completed its programme, and the jug lay steaming on the hotplate, but he had forgotten his task entirely.

'Honey?'

Sarah's voice from the kitchen doorway brought him back into contact with his surroundings. 'Yes, sorry.'

'Bob, are you all right? You didn't seem with it there, and it's not the first time it's happened since I've arrived. I'm getting worried about you.'

'I'm fine, honest. I just had a call from Joe, that's all; I got wrapped up in it. I'll bring the coffee through now.'

'Forget it,' she said, lightly. 'Ian had to leave. We thought you'd gone to Colombia for the beans.' She walked across to the work surface and picked up a mug. 'I'll have one now, though. You?'

He shook his head; unusually, he found that he had no taste for coffee.

'Did Joe speak to his agent?' asked Sarah.

Bob looked down at her. When they had been reconciled after their split, part of their deal had been that there were to be no secrets between them, none of any sort. Yet something held him back from answering, held him back from telling her the whole story of Arthur Wilkins' murder, on the heels of Kosinski's visit and Doherty's phone call. Instinct told him to protect her from that knowledge, to protect her from it all . . . yet he did not know why.

'Not yet,' he answered, and left it at that; better to be economical with the truth than to bend it.

Even as he spoke, he saw something on her face that told him that she had a preoccupation of her own. He said nothing, leaving her to spit it out in her own time. He had to wait for little more than a minute, watching her as she sipped her coffee, holding the mug in both hands.

'Bob,' she began. 'Remember when I was over here with Jazz . . .'

'How could I forget?' he chuckled. 'Much as I'd like to.'

'Yeah, me too; but that won't happen. I'd just hoped that it would all stay in the past.'

His smile turned into a frown. 'Yes?'

'The guy,' she said quietly, 'the man I had an affair with when we were apart.'

'The guy you worked beside in the hospital?'

'I didn't work beside him, exactly. He was a visiting consultant in another department; one that had nothing to do with me. But yes, the guy you mean, the guy I told you about; Terry. The thing is, he wants to meet me.'

'Does he now,' Bob murmured, his face unreadable.

'He called Ian when he read about the murders. He knew that he and Babs are the best friends I have in Buffalo, and he asked Ian to pass on his condolences. He said also that he'd like to express them in person, if I'd be prepared to meet him.'

'And do you want to?'

'No, I don't; I hoped I'd never see him again. But . . .'

He held up a hand. 'Listen, Sarah,' he said, firmly. 'You told me about you and him; you hit me over the head with it, in fact. Yes, you told me why you let it happen: you did it to put us on an equal footing in the infidelity stakes, you said, and I've always forced myself to see it that way. Yet when you boil it all down, that's just an elegant way of saying that you did it to get even with me. To be dead honest, I wish you'd put it that way from the start.'

She looked away from him. 'If that's the way you want to see it, fine,' she snapped.

'Okay, let's cut away the soft words and tell the truth of it. You wrecked our marriage because you were wrapped up in your job and your obsessions, and eventually, wrapped up in screwing your lady detective sergeant. You didn't have the guts to tell me that at the time though; you just froze me out of your life.

'So I came over here; I missed you every moment, waking and sleeping, and worse, my self-esteem was in pieces. Then someone took an interest in me. He wasn't pushy, he wasn't devious, he saw me as an attractive, unattached woman and he told me so. Better than that, he made me *feel* attractive again. When I slept with him, I had decided, more or less, to go back to Scotland, but yes, you're right, I did feel that it evened the score between us, whether you want to put it bluntly, or gently, as I tried to.

'But if you want it straight, here it is. I also felt that I owed him, for being there when you weren't, and for picking me up after you had knocked me down. I felt that it was right to give him something of me, and, truth be told, I wanted to. I hadn't had any for a while, since way before I left you, as you'll recall, and I was missing it, so why the hell not!'

'Just the once, you said,' Bob murmured.

'Just the once, I said, last time I saw him. The fact is, I thought about spending the whole night with him, but I'd have had to call and tell my mom where I was. I felt guilty when I left him, knowing that I wasn't going to see him again, and knowing that I'd used him for mostly the wrong reasons. I've always felt sorry that I didn't say goodbye properly.'

He gave a short fierce laugh. 'Seems to me you couldn't have said it better!'

Sarah shot him a quick glance. 'Why? Do you feel the same about Leona McGrath?' She bit her lip almost as soon as she had said the words. 'Sorry. Cheap shot.'

'Yes, but so was mine.' He reached out, put his hands on her shoulders and turned her to face him. 'Anyway, so what? All that's in our past and we've owned up to it, both of us. Look, love, I'm not going to jeopardise what we've rebuilt by getting uptight over this . . .' He grinned at her. '. . . Even if I've got double standards, just like most blokes, and regardless of what I've done myself, my natural instincts are to kick the shit out of anyone I catch screwing my wife.

'If you feel you need to see this guy Terry to sign off, so to speak, that's up to you. I don't want to know, and I sure as hell don't want to see him.

'Don't call him direct; contact him through Ian, and arrange to meet him. Just don't do it anywhere that could compromise you, and don't do it in too public a place either; nowhere you could be seen and talked about.' He grinned, grudgingly, but to her enormous relief. 'Oh yes, and don't go kissing him goodbye again, either.'

54

'You going to like it here, d'you think, Ray?' the Head of CID asked his assistant as they sat in the office that had been Andy Martin's until the previous Friday.

'Headquarters, sir? It's a nicer building than Torphichen Place, I have to say that.'

'Actually, son, I meant are you going to like it in my office: is the job going to be exciting enough for you?'

'I'd have said "no thanks" when I was offered it if I'd thought that, sir. It's always been a wee bit exciting around you; I don't see why it should change just because you're in this job.'

'Jesus,' said Dan Pringle, vehemently. 'You think that? And here's me hoping for a quiet couple of years up to retirement.'

'You've got a foot in every division now, boss. I don't see how that could happen. You were hardly in the job when we had that murder down in Leith.'

'Aye, but that could be our quota for a while. We might not have another major investigation this year.'

Rising to leave, Detective Sergeant Ray Wilding paused to throw the chief superintendent a sceptical look, implying that a flight of pigs was passing the window. As he did so, there was a soft knock on the door, and Maggie Rose came into the room, not waiting for a summons.

'Got a minute, sir?'

'Aye, sure, Mags.' Pringle nodded to Wilding. 'On you go, Ray. See you in the morning.' He waited as the visitor took the seat vacated by his assistant. 'What can I do for you?'

Rose laid a brown A4 envelope on his desk. 'Remember that flyer you sent me from Strathclyde?' she began. 'The missing priest? Well he's not missing any more.' As the head of CID drew out the report, she took Charlie Johnston's Polaroid from her pocket and laid it alongside it.

'He died just over a week ago, in a doctor's surgery up in Oxgangs. Death was certified by a Dr Amritraj, an officer from my division

225

attended and took that photograph, and the body was removed by ambulance to the Royal Infirmary mortuary.'

Pringle beamed with pleasure. 'Magic,' he exclaimed, reaching for his phone. 'We'll just call Strathclyde now, and tell them to come and pick him up.'

'Ah well, Dan,' said Rose slowly, 'it's not going to be quite that easy. The man I'm certain is Father Green was identified, by Dr Amritraj, as Mr Magnus Essary, of 46 Leightonstone Grove, Hunter's Tryst. The body was claimed next day by a woman named Ella Frances, who said she was his business partner; it was cremated at Seafield last Saturday morning.'

'Aw, shite,' Pringle cried out. 'Why the hell did I not stay in a division? The Frances woman; what do we know about her?'

'Next to nothing. Dr Amritraj gave PC Johnston . . .'

'Charlie Johnston?'

'That's the man.'

'It'll be right then; big Charlie's a chancer, but he's a sound copper. Sorry, Mags, on you go.'

'Okay; Amritraj named Ella Frances as the personal contact listed with the practice. He gave Johnston a mobile phone number. I've checked with the practice already; they had Magnus Essary listed all right, but he had a fictitious NHS number. The entry in their records was made by Dr Amritraj.'

'Lift him,' said Pringle, immediately.

'I wish I could,' Rose countered. 'But he doesn't work there any more. He was a locum, hired on a two-month contract. He didn't appear for surgery on Tuesday and they haven't seen him since. He lodges with an Indian family out in Livingston; I've got officers going out to see them now. You know the chances of him being there.'

'Bloody hell! What about Frances?'

'The mobile number she gave was a pre-paid type. It was bought in the name of Ella Frances all right, but the address given was as phoney as Essary's NHS entry.'

Pringle tugged at his moustache, so violently that Maggie wondered that he had any left. 'What have we got here?' he muttered.

'Time will tell,' she answered, 'but once my people confirm that Amritraj has gone from his digs as well, I'll put a trace out for him right across the NHS. Since nothing else is as it seems in this business, it's a pound to a pinch of shit that Father Francis Donovan Green didn't die of natural causes.'

'I agree with you, but how the hell did he come to wind up in a doctor's in Oxgangs in the middle of the bloody night?'

'Good question, Dan. We'll need to involve Strathclyde in that end of the investigation. Father Green came from North Lanarkshire. I've got a contact in CID there, so if you're happy, I'll call him quietly and start them to work building up a profile of the man.'

'Do that,' Pringle exclaimed. 'There's another thing you should do as well; unless Amritraj is stupid enough still to be in Livingston, you should get a warrant to search his digs, and the surgery in Oxgangs, just in case the landlord and the doctors don't co-operate. We're no' going to be able to do a post mortem on a pile of ashes, so we've got to look everywhere we can to see if we can find out how he was killed.

'I don't fancy the Crown Office's job in this one, Mags. Once we catch this fella, someone in there's got to decide what the bloody hell we can charge him with.'

55

'Mario, I'll search my memory banks all night if that's what you want, but I promise you, I never met either of those people. Stan reported to your uncle and me that he had been approached by a new importer wanting to rent space in the bonded warehouse; we agreed, and later he told us that a deal had been done. He needed the signature of one trustee. Beppe said he would do it, and that was that.

'Later, I heard from Stan that there was some difficulty with them, but he said they were dealing with it, and that I shouldn't bother.'

He sighed, partly out of relief that his mother had taken no part in the family's business with the elusive importers. All afternoon, since Greg Jay's second call, he had felt a growing unease, a detective's sense that something was very wrong with the firm of Essary and Frances.

'Okay, Mum,' he said. 'I'm waiting for Stan to call me when he gets in. I'll get chapter and verse from him, I'm sure.'

'Yes, I'm sure you will; Stan's very efficient. What's the fuss about anyway?'

'Nothing, really. I'm just doing a favour for Greg Jay.'

'Why? Is he interested in these people? Does he think they might have been involved in your uncle's murder?'

'Nah. He just wants to eliminate them from his enquiries, that's all.'

Christina McGuire snorted down the phone. 'Mario! This is your mother you're talking to, not the crime reporter from the *Evening News*. Don't give me any of your official police language. Are these people suspects or not?'

He laughed, reproved. 'No, not exactly. Beppe had a dispute with them over the tenancy; that's all. Greg needs to check them out, but he can't find them.'

'I see. You might have said that in the first place. Your colleague must be scraping the barrel; that's all I can say. Who's going to resort to murder over a few feet of warehouse space?'

'You're absolutely right. It has to be done, though, Mum.'

'If you say so. Just make sure it doesn't distract your friend from pursuing the real criminal; Sophia and Viola are at their wits' end.'

That's not very far, Mario thought, but he knew better than to say it. 'We'll catch him, don't you worry.'

'Hmm. Now you're talking like a policeman again. Good night, darling.'

'Night, Mum.' He cradled the phone and checked his watch; it was pushing nine, yet Maggie still was not home. She had called him to say that she would be delayed, and that she would bring in a takeaway. He was hungry enough to eat a bear, but there was still no sign of his wife, or of the chicken Madras, or the naan bread.

The phone rang. 'Stan's late back too,' he muttered, thinking it would be his cousin's husband. But he was wrong.

'Is Detective Superintendent Rose in?' a man asked.

'No, but I'm a detective super as well. Will I do?'

'I suppose so, sir,' the voice was smooth, confident, with a hint of a laugh in there. 'This is DI David Mackenzie, N Division, Strathclyde Police. Ms Rose called me this afternoon, and asked me to make some enquiries about a priest off my patch who's turned up dead on hers. She said I should call her whenever I'd something to report.'

Mario had heard of Bandit Mackenzie, from Maggie. 'Flash' was how she had described him, but beneath that too-self-assured exterior, she had also said, there lurked one very good detective. And that was not her view alone; Bob Skinner seemed to rate the guy, too.

'Fine. Do you want to tell me, or leave a number for her to call you?'

'You'll do, sir. It's my wife's birthday today, and I'm in bother as it is. Would you tell her that I've spoken to Father Green's curate, Father Tomkinson; I put him in the confessional, so to speak. I didn't tell him his boss was dead, but I did lean on him a bit, and he was a bit more forthcoming than in his first interview. He admitted to me that the late father wasn't exactly celibate. He liked the ladies, and he liked them youngish and attractive. Naturally, he was discreet about it; he never fished in his own river, so to speak. He used to go cast his line through in Edinburgh; whenever he went off to visit his sister, that's where he was really going.'

'How did the curate know this?'

'Father Green told him. Whether it was in formal confession, or a casual conversation, I don't know; I didn't ask and the lad didn't say. Green said that he used to go down the pubs in the Royal Mile in his dog collar. Never failed, he claimed; his experience was that there's any number of women out there who'll jump at the chance to shag a priest.

It's an interesting thought that, eh, sir? Any time you fancy an illicit leg-over, all you need to do is put on a dog collar.'

'I'll bear it in mind, Inspector. I'll give your message to my wife. You'd better hurry off home to yours; I just hope you don't find her dressing up like a nun when you get there.'

Mackenzie laughed. 'Nice one, sir. I'll be in a bit late tomorrow, if Ms Rose wants to talk to me about what the curate said.'

'Did he mention any specific pubs?'

'No. But now you mention it, he said the busy pubs; yes, he did say that, the busy ones.'

'Thanks; that cuts a few out. Good night, Inspector.'

He hung up, then made a brief note of Mackenzie's information on a pad beside the phone. He had barely finished when it rang again; this time it was Stan Coia on the line. Mario told his cousin's husband, briefly, about Greg Jay's problem. 'Murder investigations are about talking to people and knocking them off one by one as potential suspects. That's all Greg wants to do with Essary and Frances, but we can't find either of them. There's no answer at their registered address, and no trace anywhere else. Have you got a contact for them?'

'I've got the address on the lease, but I don't remember having any other details.'

'I can guess what the address is. How did you set the tenancy up? Can you remember?'

'Ella Frances phoned me; she said that she and her partner were starting an import business, and they needed to show Customs and Excise that they had the facility to bond stock in the UK. She asked if we rented out space; I said yes we did, she asked how much per square metre, I told her and she said "Fine", and asked to lease some for a year, with an option for a further twelve months.

'I sent her a standard draft agreement, and told her we'd want payment in advance.

'She called me back a couple of days later; I said that I'd draw up the official document, and fixed a date for us to meet them to sign it. I insisted that both of them had to sign it, in person, on the premises. She huffed a bit, but eventually they met Beppe at the warehouse; they did the business there and they paid up.'

'So you've got bank details?'

'Cash, Mario. They paid in cash. I remember Beppe bringing this wadge of money back to my office, and asking me to bank it in the property account.'

'When did all this happen?'

'Last September.'

'And when did Beppe write to them about terminating the lease?'

'A couple of weeks ago.'

'Mmm.'

He stood with the phone in his hand, aware vaguely of the living-room door opening. 'Is this significant, Mario?' asked Coia. 'Could those two have been behind Beppe's murder?'

'I can't say yes, Stan,' he answered, 'and I can't say no. All I can tell you is that Greg Jay and I want very much indeed to speak to Mr Magnus Essary, and his partner.'

From behind him, there came a crash as a chicken Madras takeaway, still in its carrier bag, hit the floor.

'What did you say?'

He turned and surveyed the scene, incredulous. 'Is that our dinner on the floor?' he asked, irrelevantly.

'Never mind that. What did you say there? What was that name you used?'

He realised that he still had the phone in his hand. 'Sorry, Stan,' he said, 'got to go.' He hung up and turned back to face her.

'Magnus Essary. He and his partner rented space in our bonded warehouse a while back; Beppe wanted to terminate their lease and they were kicking up about it. Greg Jay wants to talk to him but he can't find him.'

'I'm not surprised,' Maggie exclaimed. 'Magnus Essary was identified as having died of a heart attack, just over a week ago, in a doctor's surgery in Oxgangs.'

'Ah shit. Greg can take him off the list then.'

'Oh no he can't. We're one hundred per cent certain that the man identified as Essary was actually Father Francis Donovan Green, a parish priest from Holytown in North Lanarkshire.'

'. . . Who liked to cruise the Royal Mile pubs looking for friendly ladies with an eye for a new experience, like screwing a priest, so they could tell their pals about it.'

'How did . . .'

He cut her off in mid-exclamation. 'Bandit Mackenzie phoned a few minutes ago. Green's curate told him the whole story. Who certified the death?'

'A doctor named Amritraj; a locum.'

'Who's now missing?'

'Of course; leaving a mountain of debt in his wake. I was late home because I had to dig up a sheriff to give me warrants to search his digs and the surgery.'

'Where's he from?'

'Goa, in India.'

'He won't be Goa-in' back there, then.'

She groaned at his bad joke. They both became aware at the same moment of the odour of spilled Madras. She bent to pick up the bag, and carried it into the kitchen. Mario watched her as she scooped the curry into a Pyrex bowl, then transferred it to two plates, laying a naan bread on each one. He pulled up two stools and they ate, hungrily, at the breakfast bar.

'What do you think all this business is about, Mario?' she asked.

He smiled, his cheek bulged out with a chunk of sauce-dipped bread. 'Money,' he answered, when he could. 'Two people go through all the motions of setting up a company; they register, they take commercial space, they have a business address. But they never use the space, and they can only be contacted by mail, through the address.'

'A rented house near where Amritraj worked,' she interposed.

'Why would they do all that?'

'As a front, of course. Smuggling?'

He frowned at her. 'How about insurance? We've got an Essary, dead, only he isn't really.'

'And who, it turned out, never existed in the first place ... not as Essary, anyway.'

'But what if there's a bloody great policy on his life, the kind small companies take out to cover the death of directors, so that their shares can be bought in?'

Maggie nodded. 'What if, indeed.'

'Where's the body?'

'Up the chimney at Seafield; it was claimed by the partner of the so-called deceased.'

'Ella Frances?'

'The same. She had him cremated on Saturday.'

Mario laughed out loud. 'First thing tomorrow, love, you'd better check with all the main corporate insurers.'

'A day in the rank,' she snorted, 'and you're telling me how to do my job?'

'Funny, Greg Jay said much the same to me today. Here, that's a point. Whose investigation is this anyway, yours or his?'

'It's Dan Pringle's. And you know what? I'm going to see him, right now.'

He looked at her, his frown back in place. 'You do that,' he murmured, 'and while you do, I'm off to visit our Paula. No one else but Beppe has seen Essary, that I know of at any rate; but she was close to her old man. You never know, maybe she can shed some light.'

56

'I made that call to Ian,' said Sarah.

'I told you. I don't want to know anything about it.'

'Okay, I just thought . . .'

'Don't start thinking about this at this stage,' Bob snapped. 'You'll only confuse yourself.'

She looked at him across the bedroom, angered and hurt by his retort. He softened at once and moved towards her. 'Hey, I'm sorry, love,' he said, wrapping his arms around her in a great bear-hug. 'You do what you have to do. It's just that this is going to be a difficult week for you as it is; I'm not sure you need this added complication.'

'You ain't kidding there,' she murmured, her voice muffled by his chest. 'But I have to deal with it, if I'm ever going to feel right about that time. I won't mention it again, I promise.'

'Fine. The main thing for you, for us both, indeed, is to get through Friday.'

'I know. The meeting at the law firm, whenever it happens, is going to be tough too. And there's something else I have to do before that.'

'What's that?'

'I have to see them, Bob. I have to say my goodbyes. I called the mortician and arranged it for this evening.'

'Now I do understand that, love. Do you want me to come with you?'

She looked up at him, her eyes glazed. 'Take me there, please, but give me some time on my own.'

'Sure.'

The phone beside the bed began to ring, softly at first, then growing in volume. 'You'd better take that,' said Bob. 'Just in case it's your Reverend pal calling you back.'

She nodded and went to answer the call. He was on his way into the en-suite bathroom when he heard her speak. 'Joe. Hi, how are you? That's good. Yes. He's here. Hold on.'

He was already by her side. 'Hello, mate,' he said as he took the phone. 'What you got?'

'You want the interesting news or the really interesting news?' Doherty answered.

'Work me up to really.'

'Okay. I'll begin in New York; Troy Kosinski, large as life, called me half an hour ago from the Bureau office there. He reported on his meeting with Wilkins and he told me about the floppy he took from him. I told him to send it to me by courier, pronto.'

'Did he know Wilkins was dead?'

'When I told him he whistled and went "Wow". Read into that what you will.'

'Have you recovered the bullet yet?'

'Fast work, but yes I have. I commissioned a trusted pathologist in Chicago, rather than send someone in. It was a nine millimetre; could have come from a Glock, but it'll take specialist testing to prove that. It didn't come from Kosinski's standard issue piece; that's for sure.'

'Okay, but if he didn't do it, and Wilkins' office was bugged, how come he was allowed to get back to New York with that disk?'

'Good question; maybe we'll find out when it arrives at my home this evening.'

Skinner frowned. 'Joe, your daughter lives with you. If that thing is hot . . .'

'Not a problem; Phil's out of town with the airline.' Skinner had forgotten that Philippa Doherty was a flight attendant. 'She won't be back for a couple of days.

'Anyway,' the deputy director continued, 'you wanna hear what's really interesting?'

'Okay.'

'You know, Bob, I'm always amazed by how open our so-called Secret Service really is. Goddammit, it even has a website, with the director's résumé on it and every detail of its operation. It has several functions, but the one everyone knows about is presidential protection.

'This openness doesn't extend to its personnel records, though; they are not for public consumption. Still, I have some clever researchers here, and sometimes I don't ask how they go about their work. They tell me that Wylie, Garrett and Wilkins were indeed all on the presidential security team during 1963. But the really interesting thing about them is that November twenty-second of that year was the only day on which they were all off duty at the same time.

'What do you make of that?'

There was a long silence. 'Nothing,' said Skinner, at last. 'I don't think I want to make anything out of it. And at this point, I don't think you should either, Joe.'

'Too late to stop me now, as Van the Man used to say. Hey, you got me started on this thing, buddy. Come on, look at the circumstances; the only day of the year, Bob, the only day of the year when these three guys were off duty at the same time, was the day when their man, the president, was shot. Now, nearly forty years later, they all get together in secret; and a few months later they're all dead. Now come on, copper; do you believe in that kind of coincidence?'

'No,' sighed Skinner. 'No, I don't.'

'That's good; don't want you going coy on me when it's starting to light up, my friend, 'cos there's a twist. My very clever researcher took things a little further; he looked deeper into the careers of these three guys. They were all still in the Service five years later; but they were no longer on the president's team. No, on the fifth of June, 1968, when Bobby was shot, Wylie and Garrett were working out of the Los Angeles office, and Wilkins was in San Francisco.'

'You going to tell me they were off duty that day too, or were they guarding him when that guy walked up to him and shot him?'

'The Secret Service didn't start to protect candidates until after Bobby was hit, so it doesn't matter whether they were on duty or not; but two out of the three were based in LA where it happened. And, Bob, there have always been conspiracy theories around that shooting, just like the other one. Come on, man, don't tell me your detective's pulse isn't racing at the very thought of uncovering them.'

Skinner took a deep breath, as he pondered what Doherty had told him, then let it out in another long sigh.

'Joe, my friend,' he said, 'I'm more than just a detective; as you know. Back home I have connections to a national organisation that deals in secrets, and I know the steps we're prepared to take to protect them, when they're important enough. But this isn't back home; this is your country, and I don't know what your people are capable of in the same circumstances.

'What I do know is this; if we have stumbled on to what you're suggesting, then six people have died so far because of it. As for my pulse, it isn't racing. As a matter of fact, it's beating nice and steady, and I want it to stay that way. I can see what's happening, and I can also see that it could have been sanctioned very far up your national chain of command.'

'But it's a crime, Bob,' Doherty protested. 'And I'm sworn to fight crime and uphold the federal law.'

'Sure, I know that. So listen; I got involved in something like this a few years back, and I ended up killing someone. I shot him in cold blood . . . well no, that's not quite true; actually, I was fucking angry with him at the time. That was covered up too, and so was he, very quickly. Nasty things happen in the dark, Joe; sometimes it's better to leave the light off so you can't see them. Hear what I'm saying?'

'Loud and clear.'

'So what are you going to do with that floppy when you get it?'

'If it turns out to contain what I think it does, I'm going to print it and take it to my director.'

'What if he tells you to burn it?'

'Then I'll resign and give it to the *Washington Post*.'

'And what if your floppy turns out to have nothing on it? If Kosinski is clean, and he still had the thing when he got it back to New York, what's the betting that before it gets to you, someone manages to run a strong magnet over it and wipe it?'

'Then, my friend, I'll still have my ace in the hole. This is the rest of it. Two days before he went off to meet up with Leo Grace, Jack Wylie, and Bart Wilkins in a small lodge in Altoona, Pennsylvania, Sander Garrett went into a computer store in Vegas and purchased four identical Apple Mac iBooks; he used MasterCard, incidentally. We know that his and Wilkins' computers were stolen by their killer, and we can assume that the same happened to Leo Grace's.

'I have no doubt that those machines were used to make four copies of a declaration, a confession, it may be, of their knowledge of the Dallas assassination . . . and maybe Los Angeles as well. I'd guess it may cover how they were recruited to the plot, what the plan and layout was, how the patsy, Oswald, was put in place, and also, most important of all, who gave them their orders.'

'Why was Leo there?'

'You said that yourself; to legitimise the whole deal; as an independent witness, a person of standing who was around at the time and who could verify, in the event of official denial, that these guys were who they said they were.' Doherty paused; Skinner thought he heard a chuckle.

'So back to those computers; three were stolen, like I said. The fourth went up in the explosion on Wylie's boat. Only . . .' This time there was no doubting the laugh. 'Those boys at Apple Mac make a damn fine computer, you know. It's amazing what it . . . or at least, its central core, the hard disk . . . can withstand. Today we recovered what was left of

Jack Wylie's iBook; my technicians reckon that, with care, they can recover the data that's stored on it.

'One way or another, Bob, the floppy or the hard disk, I've got it.'

The big Scot sighed, as Doherty finished. 'Cowboy,' he exclaimed, 'have you any idea how far this shit's going to fly off the fan?'

'Have I ever!'

'What about your career? Do you think you're going to get a medal for this?'

'Maybe; unless the director decides to grab all the glory for himself when I tell him.'

'If I were you, pal,' said Skinner, heavily, 'I would let him.'

57

'You don't need to ask me how close to my father I was, Mario. You know quite well. I inherited his pushy gene, while our Viola takes after my mother all the way. They're both classic types; keep outa ma kitchen,' she mimicked in harsh Scots Italian, 'but keep me outa the rest of the world.'

He looked at his beautiful cousin; her silver hair glinted in the flickering light of the candles arranged around the spacious apartment. She was seated in a deep armchair, barefoot, her long legs tucked up under her, with a goblet of red wine warming in her hands.

'You know something else? I've never asked my mother about it, mind you, but I think their marriage was arranged, by Papa or Nana, or maybe even both of them.'

Mario laughed, quietly. 'Sure, kid, I know that; I've known it since I was fifteen years old. Papa Viareggio told me himself. He said that when Beppe was a lad they didn't trust him an inch, and even less when it came to fixing himself up with a wife. So the two old devils looked around for a nice quiet girl from a suitable Italian family . . . in other words, one with no money, folk who would just be grateful for the match and wouldn't try and influence the family business . . . and they found Auntie Sophia, from the Belmontes in Dunfermline. Nana knew your other granny as a girl; she made the approach and a meeting was set up between your dad and mum.

'They both knew the score; plus, your mother was a very attractive girl . . . as she still is.'

Her mouth gaped open. 'Is that right?' she exclaimed.

'That's what our grandfather told me. You know, Paulie, it's a shame that you never really got to know the old man, but you were just too young for him to take you under his wing, the way he took me. Plus, of course, you're a girl. That's why the trust was set up as it was; with Beppe in ultimate control, then me.'

She smiled; in the candle-glow, she looked devastatingly beautiful. 'So Papa was an old chauvinist, was he?'

'Yes, but no more than your father was. They were both wary of women with ambition . . . which is ironic, since Papa was ruled by the most ambitious woman I've ever met.'

'Nana?'

'Too right; our granny is the archetypal matriarch. That's why my mother made her way outside the family; she knew that our hive could only support one queen. With every respect to Beppe, my mum's forgotten more about business than he ever knew, yet Papa only gave her the minor role in the management of the trust, and he ensured that ultimately it passed to me, rather than you, regardless of how we grew up.'

'You're just like him, you know,' said Paula. 'I looked through my dad's office today, and I found an old piece of cine film that had been transferred to video. It was a family thing, a holiday in Italy when Dad and Aunt Christina were kids; Papa must have been around the age you are now, and honest to God, Mario, it could have been you. I was a bit scared of him when I was a kid, and of you, too.

'I imagined all sorts of things about him; I really did think he was a Godfather type, and I thought that you were a sort of apprentice.'

'He wasn't, though,' Mario told her, 'he was one of the most honest men I ever met, even if he was one of the craftiest, too. You were wrong about him, and you're wrong about yourself as well. You're just like my mother; you've got Nana's blood flowing in your veins too. That's why she doesn't trust you.'

She stared at him in amazement that might just have been genuine. 'What! My own granny doesn't trust me?'

'It's true, she doesn't, because she knows she can't control you. She even told me to keep an eye on you.'

'Hah! Doesn't she know that you've been keeping an eye on me for years?'

'Only discreetly; and I haven't really been keeping tabs on you. I'd rather you thought that I've been looking out for you. I was worried when I heard that you'd gone into the sauna business; especially those ones. The guy who used to own them was the biggest fucking hood in Edinburgh, until he got topped.'

'Are you happy now?'

'Now that I understand why you did it, yes, I am.'

He flashed her a smile. 'Where did you get the money to buy them anyway? Go on, tell me.'

Paula sipped her wine; the air between them was sizzling, and they both knew it. 'If you insist,' she said. 'But don't blame me if you don't like it. Your mother gave it to me.'

It was Mario's turn to gasp in astonishment. 'You what?'

'Sorry, but it's true. Are you imagining the headlines? *Detective's Mammy Bankrolls Brothels*. Is that it?'

'Could be,' he retorted.

'Well relax; there's nothing to connect her with the businesses.'

'So how did you talk her into it?'

'I didn't have to. Your mother and I aren't strangers, you know. She's my favourite aunt, and we talk. We were sharing a bottle in a restaurant in Leith one night and a prostitute walked past the window. Auntie Chris gave one of her classic humphs; I thought she was disapproving, until she started on about a society that forced women to walk the streets like that, and about how anyone who thought you could make prostitution disappear by outlawing it was off their head.

'She said that what we should really be doing was giving women like that decent working conditions and regulating what they did, rather than arresting them for it. I said that to an extent that was what was happening in the saunas, but that the danger there was that the wrong sort of people might get to own them. I mentioned Tony Manson's saunas being for sale, and she said why didn't I buy them then, and run them the way they should be run.

'I said, "Buy them with what?" And that's how it came about. She put up most of the money, and I bought them through a shell company. No one knew about it but Auntie Chris and me, till you started sniffing around.'

Mario's eyes narrowed slightly. 'You mean you really didn't tell your father?'

'No way did I; he'd have raised merry hell if I had done, and got my mother all worked up too. My dad might have liked a bit of skirt, but he was prudish too. All right, he did find out on the grapevine, eventually; he wasn't best pleased, to put it mildly. He said I was on my own, that he'd never set foot in such places, and that if I came a cropper he wouldn't bail me out.'

'Then why the hell . . .' He frowned. 'Paulie, remember that wee girl I asked you about, the one who said she knew you?'

'Ivy Brennan? Yes, she asked me straight out one day what I had to do with the Bonnington sauna. She said she'd seen me going in there a few times. At first I thought she was implying I was on the game, but actually she asked me if there would be any chance of a job there.'

241

'What did you tell her?'

'The truth. I told her that she looked about fifteen, and that she'd attract the wrong sort of customer. You know what I mean; there are guys out there who have a physical need to get their ashes hauled every so often, and my places cater for that. But there are other guys too, perverts, and I won't have any truck with them. Anyway, what about Ivy?'

'Maybe nothing; only I'm trying to work out why she told me she had seen Uncle Beppe having a shouting match in the doorway of the Bonnington place with someone inside.'

'You're kidding.'

'No.'

'Then she was. Not only would my dad not have set foot in one of my places; he wouldn't have had an argument in public either.'

'No,' Mario mused, 'he wouldn't, would he; not Uncle Beppe. Yet that's what she told me; she called me yesterday and said she had to see me. That's what it was about.'

Paula smiled. 'Is that all it was about?'

He took a deep breath and grinned back at her. 'Well, no. She did have something else in mind.'

'But she had to tell you something to get you to see her, so she made up that story, knowing that the place was mine.'

'I suppose so.'

'Hey, Mario . . . you didn't, did you?'

'Certainly not. The fact is, with her kit off she still only looks about fifteen.'

Gradually, his frown deepened; he sat in the chair facing his cousin, but staring into the far corner of the room.

'What's up?' asked Paula, breaking the silence. 'Do you wish you had now?'

'No, just a thought that occurred to me, that's all.'

She shook her head. 'Bloody policemen; you never stop working. I went out with a copper for a while, a bloke called Stevie Steele. He was exactly the same; in the middle of God knows what, he'd be away in another world.'

'Mmm,' he murmured. 'Our Stevie, eh. He never told me that when we worked together.'

'Probably because I told him I still fancied you something rotten.'

'What else did you tell him?'

'Nothing that didn't happen,' she answered, mischievously.

'Are you kidding me?'

She raised an eyebrow and smiled. 'Maybe yes, maybe no.'

'Well if you're not, he's discreet: I'll say that for him. But back to this world; did Uncle Beppe ever mention to you anyone called Magnus Essary?'

'Never.'

'Sure?'

'Certain.'

'Or Ella Frances?'

'No. Why?'

'We're trying to find them, that's all.' He saw her stiffen momentarily.

'Are they suspects?'

'No. They're just a lead we're having trouble following up.'

'Sorry I can't help then.'

He stood up from his chair. 'Never mind. But if you do find anything to do with either of them, let Greg Jay know.'

'I will do, promise.' She gazed up at him, and candle-flames twinkled in her eyes. 'You sure you have to go?' she whispered.

He took a step towards her, leaned down and kissed her, long, slow, soft, breathtaking, until eventually she broke off, with a cross between a gasp and a sigh. 'Yes, Paulie,' he murmured, wickedly. 'I'm absolutely certain.'

58

Dan Pringle sat with his face buried in his hands. 'Where are you when I need you, Bob Skinner?' he exclaimed, in a muffled grunt. The coffees on the dining table had grown cold in their mugs as Maggie had explained the remarkable appearance in two investigations of the late Magnus Essary, a man who, it seemed, was not so dead after all.

He looked up and across at her. 'You're telling me that this Father Green was picked up in a pub by some young tart, killed in some way or another, and certified as a heart-attack victim by this bent doctor, Amritraj.'

'Who's now done a runner himself,' Rose added.

'You're also telling me that this same Magnus Essary and his partner Ella Frances . . .'

'Who claimed the body and had it cremated.'

'. . . set up a wine-importing company together and rented space in the Viareggio family warehouse, which they never used. And when the deal was done, the only guy who saw either of them was Beppe Viareggio himself.'

'That sums it up.'

'And your theory is . . .'

'That it has to be an insurance scam. It's got nothing to do with the wine business. That was a pure front; there's no evidence that they imported a single bottle. My bet is that if we trawl round the major companies we'll find a large term insurance policy written on the life of Magnus Essary.'

'Why would they set up a company to do that?' asked Pringle.

'I can think of a couple of reasons. Better rates for a start; also, it's common practice for small businesses to have big policies on the lives of key people, but an individual doing it might attract more attention.'

'And if you're right, how quickly would they pay out after a death?'

'I have no idea. That's one of the many things we need to find out; which is why I'm here tonight. Who does the finding out? This man Essary is central to a crime that's been committed in my territory, but

Greg Jay's looking for him as well. We don't want to duplicate effort, so . . .' She let the rest of her question hang in the air.

'He's yours, Maggie,' the head of CID answered at once. 'You picked the ball up, so you run with it. I'll brief Jay in the morning. Do you need anything from me, other than that decision?'

'I don't think so, but if I do, I'll give you a shout, don't worry.'

'What do you plan to do, then?'

'Ask around the major life offices, first thing in the morning; that's top priority. But I'm also going to find out as much as I can about Essary, starting at the General Register Office.'

'Good idea,' Pringle muttered. 'Do we go public on this?' he added, almost to himself.

'Please no, Dan,' said Rose, quickly. 'The real Essary is still out there, thinking he's got away with it. I've already got Strathclyde to agree not to release the news that Father Green's been traced. I need him to think that he's in the clear.'

'Okay, you play it that way. But don't be surprised if he's no' just in the clear, but in the bloody Bahamas by now.'

59

'Are you going to be able to talk to me about your new job?' she asked.

Neil McIlhenney propped himself on an elbow and looked down at her, then reached under the duvet and pinched himself on the right buttock, hard enough to make himself wince.

'What are you doing?' she asked again, amused.

'Making sure I'm awake,' he answered, 'and that I really am in bed with Louise Bankier, actress. I'm surprised you've never caught me at it before.'

'You're in bed with your wife, my darling. What my day job used to be is irrelevant. It's yours that matters now.'

'Not to the kids, it isn't. Have you any idea how many Brownie points they've picked up at school since you and I got hitched? Lauren's become a sort of icon among her pals, and as for Spencer . . . I've told that wee bugger that if I ever catch him selling your autograph again, I'll ground him for a year.'

He reached over and flicked a strand of hair away from her eye. 'Anyway, you're not completely out of your day job. They haven't even finished the edit of your Edinburgh movie, and there'll be the premieres and all that other stuff.'

'Well, the kids will love that too. But once it's over, I'm out of the business, for at least five years. That's what I promised you and I will stick to it.'

'It's a promise I never asked you to make.'

'I know. That's what makes it all the more important to me. I'm your wife, Neil; and I've never been so happy in any role, honestly.' She looked him in the eye. 'Remember what I said about me having a baby?'

He gasped. 'You're not, are you?'

'No . . . not as far as I know, anyway. However I have been to see a specialist, up at the Murrayfield Hospital, and she assured me that, physically, everything's fine and that there's no reason why I can't. We know you're in good working order . . . you've just proved that . . . so . . .'

He laughed. 'I'll keep my efforts up, so to speak. But remember, it's pot luck at the end of the day.'

'I know. Look at Maggie and Mario. How long have they been married now?'

His expression changed. 'Ah, but that isn't a matter of luck . . . well, maybe it is, but it's bad luck on Mario's part. Randy big sod that he is, he's unfortunate in that respect. Don't tell him I told you, though.'

'As if I would! It's bad luck for Maggie too, though. I know she maintains her career-woman image, but the truth is, I think she'd like to have a baby.'

'She tell you that?'

'Not exactly; it's just a feeling I have. But don't you mention it to her.'

'Of course not.' He ran a finger round the edge of one of her big brown nipples. 'Speaking of keeping secrets, I know this sounds a bit silly in this day and age, but when you're doing the publicity interviews and stuff for the new movie, if any journo asks you about me, and about what I do, tell them I'm a copper, that's fine, but don't get specific, okay? I mean I will talk to you about my job, but it is a bit sensitive, and I wouldn't hold it long if it was mentioned in *Hello* magazine and the like.'

'I understand. I promise, my angel; you will remain a man of mystery as far as my public is concerned.' She gave a shiver under his touch. 'Hey,' she murmured, 'do that some more. I'm approaching peak fertility just now, you know.'

Neil moved closer to her. 'I'll have to see what I can do, then.'

He was about to show her, when the bedside phone rang. 'McGuire,' she heard him growl as he picked it up. 'This is just like the old days when you were single and used to phone me at all bloody hours.'

'Perish the thought,' his friend answered. 'I'm sorry, pal . . . and say sorry to Lou as well . . . but this is important, and I didn't want to call you about it from home.'

In the background Neil could hear soft music. 'Where the hell are you, then?'

'I'm at Paula's. We'd some business to discuss.'

'You just watch it there, son. I remember her from the old days, as well.'

'Aye, but we're grown up now, though. Listen now; you got a pen handy?'

'As always.'

'Right, get it; because there's some stuff I need checked out on the QT, and I can't do it myself without making waves. It's the sort of thing that's best handled through your office, not mine. I need chapter and verse and I need it damn quick.'

60

Bob Skinner sat in the waiting room of the place that morticians, or undertakers, around the English-speaking world describe discreetly as the chapel of rest; the showroom for their skills, as he thought of it. He had seen his parents-in-law in death, and although he knew that they would look vastly different when presented to their daughter, he did not wish to repeat the experience.

He had been in similar places before in his life; for his parents, for his maternal grandmother, who had died when he was twenty-two, and for Myra, his first wife, whose death in a speeding car had haunted him for almost twenty years, to a point at which it had become the catalyst for his brief separation from Sarah.

No, he had sworn, and he had meant it. The next time he would be in another of those soft-lit, well-ventilated rooms, the serene, made-up face in the white-lined coffin would be his own.

He sat alone with his grim thoughts for twenty minutes; for most of that time he pondered the chain that he and Doherty had uncovered, connecting the four men who had met a few months before in Altoona, Pennsylvania, and who had all died violent deaths. If the FBI hackers had indeed uncovered the truth about their Service past, then, circumstantial or not, it was dynamite. And if their record of those days did exist, and said what Doherty believed, it could go nuclear. Yet Skinner was wary. He was an experienced detective, with the hunting instinct of a jungle animal, but he was in someone else's forest now, a place where the prey had sharp teeth too.

He snapped back to the present when the waiting-room door opened. Sarah's freshened make-up just failed to hide the blotches around her eyes, but she was composed. 'Okay?' he asked.

'Okay,' she replied.

They walked through to the reception area of the funeral home, where Mr Poe, the splendidly named mortician, was waiting for them. He handed Sarah a white envelope. 'That is a note of the timings which we agreed for the funeral service and for the burial. The hearse and your limo will call at your residence at ten after ten precisely on Friday morning.'

'We'll be ready,' said Skinner.

'I'm sure, sir. There is one change of which I have to advise you. The senator's office just called me to express her profound regret that she and her husband will not be able to attend after all. There's a confirmation hearing that may come to a vote on Friday, and it's essential that she be there. He feels that it would not be appropriate for him to come alone.'

'That's a pity.'

'Yes it is, sir. However, if I may say so, it may be a blessing in disguise; I once officiated at a funeral where President Nixon was a mourner, and the requirements of the Secret Service left me in no doubt as to who was really in charge of proceedings. It's unfortunate for you, though, in that it denies you the opportunity of meeting our former president.'

'I've met him,' Bob told him, casually.

Mr Poe was lost for words . . . for a micro-second. 'Ah,' he exclaimed. 'In that case . . .'

Sarah kept her face straight until they were outside, in the car park, where her smile escaped. 'That was wicked. The poor man was only being an American; you could have gone along with him.'

'Maybe,' he replied, straight-faced. 'But I don't like politician worship, at any level. I don't like politicians, period. Anyway, it's true; I have met him. He offered me a cigar. Okay, he's got more charisma than all the Hollywood A-list put together, but he's still a politician.'

'As far as I'm concerned, they should be an endangered species.'

'In this country, honey,' she said, quietly, 'they are.'

A small shiver ran through him; he was on the brink of telling her about Doherty's discoveries, but stopped himself. Instead, he reached into his pocket and switched on his cellphone. It showed one call unanswered. At first he thought it might be Joe, but when he checked the log he found that it was from the private handphone of Sarah's lawyer, Clyde Oakdale, interim successor to Jackson Wylie as senior partner of her father's firm.

He made the return call, and handed the phone to Sarah, as it was put through.

'Clyde? You're working late,' he heard her say, as he opened the Jaguar with its remote, and walked towards it.

He was in the driver's seat, with the engine running, when she ended the call and slid in, lithely, beside him. 'The meeting?' he asked.

'Yes. He wants to do it tomorrow; he says it'll take him that long to complete the audit of Dad and Mum's estate.'

'What time?'

'Five,' she answered; he heard an awkwardness in her voice. 'Bob, I know you're named as joint executor, but Clyde said that he'd like to see me alone for the formal reading. It's the way Dad wanted it, apparently. You don't mind, do you?'

He smiled and shook his head. 'I never questioned anything Leo did when he was alive. I'm not going to start now. We'll be a bit tight for the Walkers, though. Aren't they expecting us around six?'

'Yes, but how about if you go there on your own and I'll join you once I'm finished with Clyde? You can walk to their place from here; it's only a couple of blocks.'

'Yes, I suppose I could do that.'

'That's good.' She reached over and patted his hand. 'Okay, that's all today's difficulties over. What are we going to do now?'

He grunted. 'I reckon it's about time you got some sleep. Then tomorrow, I'm going shopping.'

'Shopping?'

'Too right: I left home with a case packed for a few days in Malaysia. I have to buy a suit that's appropriate for a funeral in Buffalo.'

61

'How quickly do you want this, ma'am?' Stevie Steele asked.

'Mmm?' Maggie Rose lowered her coffee mug from her lips and glanced back across the table at the recently promoted detective inspector. 'Sorry, I was away somewhere else just for a second.'

'Late night?'

'Does it show? I suppose it must; I feel bleary enough. Yes, I had to go and see Mr Pringle about this thing, and then Mario got in from Paula's at God knows when. To answer your question, Stevie, I want it to be exhaustive first, and urgent second. I've established that when this Ella Frances woman registered the death, she asked for five copies of the death certificate.

'That's more than the norm. Why would she need that many? It suggests to me not just that we're right and there was an insurance policy on Essary's life, but that there might have been more than one. So take as long as you need. She'd need at least one certificate for the undertaker, so don't stop till you've been round all the life insurers, or until you've traced four policies. Give it top priority, though; this is a key part of a murder enquiry and it's down to you.'

Steele nodded. 'Understood, ma'am. I'll get on it right away.' He stood, then paused. 'By the way, ma'am,' he asked, 'is there anything on the Viareggio case yet?'

'Nothing I want to talk about, even to you. Why do you ask?'

Suddenly, the detective, normally confident, looked awkward. 'I thought you might know. I went out with Paula Viareggio for a while. It never got too serious; we were friends as much as anything else.'

'No,' the superintendent answered, truthfully, 'I never heard about that. Did you know Beppe?'

'Yes, I met him. Almost by accident it was; we were out for a meal and he came into the place with a couple of pals. He came over and she introduced us. He was not at his most charming, I have to say. He'd had a drink, and when Paula told him what I did, he said, in this loud voice that the whole restaurant could hear, "Oh dear, no, I'm not having another policeman in the family" . . . or words to that effect. And then he said to me, a lot quieter, confidential like, "You want to watch her, son. She's an effing pimp, you know." Nice man.'

Rose nodded. 'Uncle Beppe had his faults, I'll agree. How did Paula take that?'

The inspector whistled. 'I never knew she had a temper until then. She went dead white, and the look she gave him scared even me. There was a steak knife on the table; she picked it up and started out of her seat. I grabbed her wrist, quick, and forced her back down. I told her father it would be a good idea if he went somewhere else, and he did. She scared him sober, I'll tell you.'

'Was that the only time you met him?'

'Yes. It was never the same after that between Paula and me. About a month later, we decided to pack it in.'

'You both decided?'

'Well, she said it first, but I didn't argue.'

'Did you know what Beppe meant by his remark?'

'No. I never asked, and she never said.'

The superintendent sighed. 'I almost wish you'd never told me that story, Stevie. But you have, so I have to ask you whether you think you have to tell it to Detective Superintendent Jay, as well.'

Steele sat back in the chair he had just vacated. 'I've been asking myself that, ma'am. That's probably why I brought up the subject; to get a bit of guidance.'

'You don't really need it, though, do you?'

'No. I'll go to see Mr Jay today.'

'Like hell you will. You'll concentrate on our investigation; get Greg to send a couple of officers along here to take a statement from you.'

He stood once more. 'Very good, ma'am; but to tell you the truth, I don't see her having done it. There and then, maybe, but not in cold blood like that.'

'Why not?' asked Rose. 'She surprised you that night. Tell me, do you know anything about other men in Paula's life?'

Steele took a deep breath as he considered his answer. 'There weren't all that many, as far as I could tell. I remember she did say to me once that she was a one-man woman, but that there were lots of reasons why that couldn't happen. Actually, I was pretty certain that she was talking about her brother-in-law, Stan Coia.'

After he had left the room, Maggie sat for five minutes, staring at the wall. She thought about calling Mario, to tell him Steele's story, but decided that some news is better broken in person. Eventually, she stirred herself, looked at her private address book, picked up the telephone, and dialled a direct line number in the General Register Office. It rang three times before a cheery voice answered. 'Glossop.'

'Jim, hello. It's Maggie Rose here, Central Division CID. Remember me?'

'Of course I do. You were in Bob Skinner's office a while back, weren't you?' The statistician's accent had originated in the north of England, and had remained untarnished by decades in Scotland.

'That's right. I wasn't sure whether you'd still be in yours, though.'

'Hah! You just caught me: my bags are packed and I'm ready to go. I take early retirement next week.'

'Can you do me a favour for the road, then?'

'Sure. What do you need?'

'Everything you can tell me about a man named Magnus Essary. His death, aged forty-nine, was registered in Edinburgh just over a week ago. We have no leads to next of kin; the man's a mystery.'

'Is the body unclaimed, then?'

'No, it was claimed next day by his business partner, a woman named Ella Frances. But we can't find her.' She paused. 'Jim, I'm going to tell you something that's very confidential. The death was registered as that of Magnus Essary, but it wasn't him at all. We know whose the body really was, and it certainly wasn't his.'

'Bloody hell! The registrar general won't like that; it's a serious offence to make a false statement to a registrar.'

'It's a serious offence to kill someone, as well.'

'This man was murdered?'

'We're sure of it. But that's another problem. The body was cremated at the weekend.'

'Who signed the death certificate?'

'A locum doctor.'

'Why can't you arrest him?'

'Not for the want of trying, but he's vanished too.'

'How about the partner?'

'Her name's Ella Frances, but we know even less about her. Probably she's in her twenties, but Frances could be a married name, and Ella could be short for a few things.'

'Aye,' said Jim Glossop. 'It could, couldn't it. Essary was forty-nine, you say?'

'Yes.' She spelled the surname for him.

'Leave it with me. I'll get back to you.'

'Soon, Jim, yes?'

'Too bloody right,' he laughed. 'Remember I'm retiring next week. My first leaving do is tonight, and after that I won't be worth a stuff.'

She hung up and went back to her in-tray, cursing Manny English and Willie Haggerty for their combined roles in introducing her to the job of divisional commander of operations, yet interested, in spite of herself, in the different tasks and responsibilities which the role involved. Gradually she became immersed in the papers before her, considering each one, delegating most tasks but taking command decisions on a few. To her surprise, she was actually annoyed when the phone rang, interrupting her.

'Mags?' Dan Pringle's gruff voice enquired.

'Yes, sir.' There was background noise on the line; she guessed that the head of CID was on the move.

'I'm on the A1, on the way to Gifford. I want you to head out there and meet up with Brian Mackie and me at the Goblin Ha'. You know it?'

'Sure. It's right in the middle of the village.'

'Fine. As quick as you can, then, but I want you to bring Charlie Johnston with you. Brian's got another deid bloke up the Lammermuirs we want him to look at.'

62

'You know, sir, when I phoned you, I didn't expect you to come yourself.'

'Come on, son,' replied Detective Superintendent Gregory Jay, amiably. 'I'd hardly send a DC to interview a DI now, would I? I'm glad I did come too; that was a very interesting story you just told me.'

'Maybe so, sir,' Stevie Steele interposed, quickly, 'but I wouldn't read too much into it.'

'I would, though, Inspector; I surely would. You have to prevent the woman from attacking her father with a knife, and later he's found shot dead.'

'Two years later, sir.'

'Yes, and so what? That makes her a suspect in my book, and it would in yours too, if you hadn't been so personally involved.'

Steele said nothing, for he knew that Jay was right. 'What about this chap Coia?' the superintendent continued. 'What did you make of him?'

'Nothing much. I met him a couple of times, casually, but he didn't make any impression on me. His beard was his most interesting feature, I reckoned. I could see that he and Paula hit it off, though. They were comfortable together . . . or maybe she was just sorry for him, being married to her sister. She's an absolute mouse beside Paula.'

'You don't really fancy Coia and Paula for this, do you, sir?'

Jay smiled. 'Start thinking with your policeman's brain, son, and not with your dick. You slept with her, so she can't be a murderer. Is that what you're saying? The fact is I've got no one else to fancy for this, but a stray lead to this character Essary and his partner Frances. But where are they? Who said they ever existed? Maybe they were just a front for Coia and your bird, fictional culprits set up for when they did in her father.'

Steele hid his surprise; clearly, Dan Pringle had chosen not to tell Jay about the couple's involvement in the death of Father Francis Donovan Green.

'But why would they do it, sir? Beppe Viareggio's murder was

255

premeditated and planned. Okay, Paula's got a temper, but there's nothing cold-blooded about her.'

'Money, son. What else? The father controlled the business and they wanted him out of the way.'

'But Paula doesn't inherit control. She told me that when we were going together. Mario McGuire's mother becomes head of the family business, and after her, Mario does. Or are you going to tell me that Detective Superintendent McGuire's involved in this as well?'

Jay sat bolt upright in his chair. 'Certainly not,' he snapped.

'Well, that's where your logic's taking you,' said Steele quietly. 'Go with Paula as a suspect and you're bringing him into it as well. Are you ready to go to DCS Pringle, and to the DCC when he gets back, and tell them that?'

63

The drive to Gifford went by mostly in silence. Charlie Johnston sat in the passenger seat, content; he was back on day shift and did not mind one bit that he had been hauled off patrol to go on a jaunt with a detective superintendent. He liked the country, too, and spent the latter part of the journey staring out of the window, admiring the scenery on the winding approach to the village nestling at the foot of the Lammermuirs.

Dan Pringle was waiting for them, leaning against his car, when Rose drew up outside the Goblin Ha' Hotel. She rolled down her window as he approached. 'Where's Brian?' she asked.

'He's waiting for us. What he's got's no' here. It's up the Lammermuirs; a couple of backpackers found it this morning. We'll take your car up there; this used to be your patch, so you know the way.' Without waiting for agreement or invitation he opened the rear offside door and climbed in.

Maggie felt her blood run cold. She had been on the Lammermuirs before, and Pringle knew it; at the scene of a terrible air disaster, which had ended so many people's lives, and changed several more, irrevocably. She had never been there since. Nevertheless she clenched her jaw and drove off, out of the village and up the winding, undulating road that led to the great heather-covered moor. They seemed to go on for miles until they reached the junction offering a choice of routes to Duns, Cranshaws on the left, Longformacus on the right.

'Take right,' grunted Pringle, from the back.

'You got wellies on?' she asked as she followed his direction.

'No. Why should I? It's been fine weather for days.'

'That's right; so the adders'll be out, sunning themselves. There are a lot of them up here, you know.' She took a quick glance in her rearview mirror and was quietly pleased to see the head of CID's frown. Beside her, Charlie Johnston flinched; suddenly his day out seemed a little less cushy. She drove on, looking straight ahead, as they passed the crash site.

She guessed that they had reached the highest point to the road when they saw the vehicles pulled into a lay-by; a patrol car, an Audi estate, a Nissan saloon and an ambulance. On the other side of the single-track carriageway, a Land Rover was parked on the heather. As she looked towards it, the tall, dome-headed figure of Detective Superintendent Brian Mackie stepped out of the front passenger seat.

'Afternoon,' he said as they approached. It was two minutes past midday, but Mackie was famed for his precision.

'Hello, Brian,' Pringle answered. 'Where is it, then?'

'It's not far, but I'll take you in the four-by-four.' Rose followed behind the head of CID and the constable, looking on amused, as they picked their way through the heather to the waiting vehicle. They scrambled on board, awkwardly in the cases of Pringle and Johnston, and the uniformed driver set off up a steady incline. No one spoke as they drove; Johnston knew his place while the senior officers knew that the questions in their minds would be answered soon enough.

The terrain was rough even in the agile wagon; Maggie found it impossible to judge how far they had travelled, but as they drew to a halt she looked at her watch and saw that they had been travelling for around three minutes.

'We're here,' said Brian Mackie, superfluously, as he opened the door and jumped out. 'This way.' He nodded towards a group of white-coated men and women spread out in a line around thirty yards away, heads down, studying the heather intently. At their centre a big white frame tent had been erected; Mackie headed towards it, Pringle, Rose and Johnston following close behind.

As they reached it, the flap opened and a tall young man stepped out; Maggie recognised him at once. 'Hello, Dr Brown,' she said cheerfully. 'Haven't seen you since North Berwick.'

The medial examiner smiled, a touch ruefully. 'I'm sure you're very nice socially, Superintendent,' he replied, in a light Irish accent, 'but every time our paths cross professionally, you've got a real ripe one for me.'

'Cause of death, doctor?' Mackie asked, briskly.

'As it seems, I'd say. Gunshot wound from close range; in the back and through the heart; death would have been instantaneous.'

'Is the bullet still in situ?'

The doctor shook his head. 'Not a chance. You might find a fragment, but you'll be lucky; there's an exit wound the size of a golf ball in the chest. Heavy calibre weapon, undoubtedly.'

'Was he killed here?'

'I'd say not; there's very little blood around the body. No, he was shot somewhere else and brought here.'

'When?'

'I honestly haven't a clue. He's been dead for several days, but if I ventured anything more than that it would be pure guesswork. It's been warm so that would accelerate decomposition, and a few things have been gnawing at him. Too many variables; I'll leave that to the pathologist.'

'Fair enough,' said Mackie. 'Let me have your report as soon as you can.' He turned to the driver. 'Jimmy, give the ME a lift to his car and then come back.'

As the doctor left, he turned towards the tent, with a glance at Pringle. 'It's all yours, sir.'

'I want nothing to do with it,' the head of CID retorted. 'That's what Charlie's here for. On you go, Johnston, take a look.'

The big constable stared at him. 'Me, sir?'

'Aye, you; did you think Superintendent Rose brought you as her body-guard? Take a look at the deceased and tell us if you've seen him before.'

Johnston paled, visibly. 'Very good, sir,' he answered.

'On you go, Charlie,' said Rose, lifting the flap once more. 'I'll come in with you.' She had known since Pringle's phone call who, or what, they were likely to find.

It was breezy on the moor, and the air was redolent with the scent of heather. As soon as they stepped inside the tent, another smell over-whelmed them; the odour of recent death. Maggie steeled herself to ignore it, as she had done many times before. At her side she heard the constable's stomach heave.

The photographers had finished their work; the body lay on its back, staring upwards through sockets whose eyes had been supplanted by a mass of yellow movement. It was fully clad, but the shirt had been ripped open below the ribcage and so had the abdomen, the work of foxes, or carrion birds, Rose guessed. They had been at work on the face too, but it was still recognisable as a human being, possibly . . . for skin discoloration made it uncertain . . . of Asian descent.

'Well, Charlie,' she asked, 'do you know him? I know it's not pleasant but take a good look.'

As if she had pulled some internal trigger, the constable vomited voluminously against the side of the tent. Pringle must have been standing close to it, for his muffled curse floated in from outside. Rose waited until Johnston had calmed himself. 'Okay,' she said. 'Now that's out of the way...'

The big veteran sighed and leaned over, looking the corpse in the face. He stared at it for almost a minute, before straightening up.

'It's yon doctor,' he announced at last. 'The one frae up in Oxgangs.'

'Dr Amritraj?'

'That's the boy. It's him all right.' He looked down again. 'So what did you get yourself into, my mannie?' he pondered.

'More than he could handle,' Rose muttered, 'that's for sure. Thanks, Charlie; you've done your bit.' She held the flap open for him and they stepped outside, into the clean air once more.

She nodded to Pringle. 'It's him, all right. Looks as if Mr Essary's been cleaning house. He doesn't take any chances, this fellow, does he?'

'It was a bit of a chance leaving him up here, was it not?' the DCS grunted.

'Not really; this place is vast. We were very lucky that those walkers happened upon him when they did; another day or two in the open and he'd have been unrecognisable.'

'Fine,' Brian Mackie exclaimed. 'Are you two going to tell me what this is about now?'

'Aye,' said the head of CID, 'I think we can. The stiff is Dr Raj Amritraj; we were after him in connection with an investigation that Maggie has underway at the moment. As you can see, someone didnae want us to find him. You stand down on this one, Brian; it's part of the ongoing investigation and Maggie'll handle it. Send all the technical reports and witness statements to her, and tell the pathologist to do the same with the p.m. report.'

'With pleasure; I wish all my murder investigations were that easy.'

As he spoke, the Land Rover appeared at the top of the rise above them. 'Let's get back then,' Pringle grunted.

They were halfway to the vehicle when Maggie's mobile phone rang. She stopped in her tracks and took it out, leaving the others to go on ahead.

'Yes?' she answered, tersely.

'Miss Rose?'

'Yes, sorry.'

'That's all right; we can't be too careful these days. Jim Glossop here; I rang your office and a young lad there gave me this number.'

'I told him to do that, but I admit I didn't expect you to call back so soon.'

She heard a chuckle. 'Ah, the things we can do these days. It makes me sorry in a way that I'm retiring; maybe I can get some freelance work off your lot . . . compiling criminal stats and the like.' He seemed to sense her impatience. 'Anyhow, I've got a result for you. Magnus Essary, no middle name, was born on the fourth of August, forty-nine years ago, in Bathgate, West Lothian. His parents were Alexander and Margaret Essary, mother's maiden surname, Smith, residing at 28 Dundee Terrace, Edinburgh. No one else of that name registered in that year, or during the ten-year periods before or after.'

'That's great, Jim. At least it gives us somewhere to start looking.'

'I can probably tell you exactly where to start looking. I did another check, just out of curiosity. Your man Essary's going to earn himself a special place in our museum; according to our records this is the second time he's died. Poor little Magnus succumbed to meningitis, aged three years and one month.'

Maggie threw back her head and stared up at the blue sky. 'Now why doesn't that surprise me,' she murmured.

'In that case,' said Glossop, 'this won't either. I did another check off my own bat. This time I looked at infant deaths in the Edinburgh area over a fifteen-year period between twenty and thirty-five years ago, under the name Frances. Guess what? Little Ella Frances, of Prince Street, Polwarth, Edinburgh, died of leukaemia at the age of four-and-a-half, just under twenty-seven years ago. She'd have been about thirty-one now, had she lived.

'The two deaths were nineteen years apart, but they both took place in the same registration district in Edinburgh. I can't check this from here, but I'll bet you a pint of Guinness that both those children are buried in the same cemetery. Someone's gone round looking at gravestones, taken the details and then gone along to Register House and picked up copies of each of their birth certificates.'

'Can you check that?' Rose asked. Dan Pringle, looking back at her from the open door of the Land Rover, read the urgency on her face.

'I have done already. They were both issued to the same person, on the second of July last year. She said she was a research student doing some genealogical work. The clerk took a note of her name and address as usual.'

'And what was it?'

'Paula Viareggio, Penthouse One, Collier's Court, Leith.'

The cellphone slipped from Maggie's fingers, to land softly on the heather at her feet.

261

64

'You shouldn't be telling me this, Stevie,' said Mario McGuire. 'Mind you, when we worked together last year you might have mentioned that you'd been giving my cousin a seeing-to.'

'Maybe, but it was all over by that time, and I didn't want to dig it up again. As for the other thing I'm telling you, put it down to professional courtesy.'

'Appreciated; thanks. You don't really think that Jay's going to pull Paula in for questioning, do you?'

'It's hard to say,' Steele replied, evenly, down the line. 'But he's under pressure to come up with something; the new head of CID's got a hard act to follow, and he's not going to fancy starting off with an unsolved investigation.'

'Still, he'd better be careful; if he involves me in it, even by implication, I really will do the bastard.'

'That would sound really great if this call was being recorded, wouldn't it?'

'True,' McGuire muttered, ruefully. 'The sooner we find this Essary man the better. How are you getting on with your inquiries? Maggie told me what she was going to have you do.'

'Don't tell her I told you first,' said the inspector, 'but I'm finished.'
'Good news?'

'She won't see it that way. There were four policies on the life of Magnus Essary, each one with a major-league Edinburgh-based insurer, for a quarter of a million. Claims were submitted in each case on Tuesday last week; all four companies have paid out, two on Wednesday, one on Thursday and one on Friday. The cheques were all paid into a Clydesdale Bank account, in the name of Ella Frances. It was closed yesterday and the funds were transferred to a numbered account in a bank in Basel.'

'Can the money be frozen there?'

'That's doubtful, given the reputation of the Swiss. But chances are it will have been moved again by now; it'll be pretty well untraceable.'

'As will Magnus Essary and Ella Frances,' McGuire grunted. 'Have you put out an all-ports alert?'

'I wanted to talk to my boss first.'

'What's stopping you?'

'She's not here. I went to look for her but young Haddock, her gopher, told me that she had a call from DCS Pringle and headed off to meet him, with a big fat PC in tow.'

'If I were you, Stevie, I wouldn't wait for her coming back. It's too late to be coy about Essary now; you get that alert out, pronto. Mind you, it's a case of for what it's worth. If they're travelling as Essary and Frances, then my passport says I'm Cliff Richard.'

65

'I wondered how long it would take you to get to a loose end, Bob.' ACC Willie Haggerty laughed. 'Are you worried that Edinburgh's descending into lawlessness, with the Chief on holiday this week and you in the States?'

'I have no doubt,' Skinner replied, his voice echoing on the satellite link, 'that my city is safe in your hoary hands. But I just thought I'd give you a call to say hello, see how you're doing.'

'I'm doing fine, big fella, just fine. How's it with you? How's Sarah coping?'

'Simply "coping" is not a term you apply to my wife. She deals with life with a capability that's just . . . well, fucking awesome, as they say over here. We're more or less set for the funeral on Friday, the cleaners have done their bit here at the house, and now she's taking me out to find a caterer for a reception afterwards.'

'How about the investigation?'

'It seems to have run into a series of brick walls, from what I gather . . . not, mind you, that the police need to tell me anything. I'm just a civilian, you understand.'

'Aye, and so was Attila the Hun,' Haggerty barked. 'But still, if they're stalled and it's over a week, we know what that usually means.'

'We do, Willie, we do; it means they're stuffed. So how's it going over there anyway? Have I missed any action?'

The DCC heard a loud booming laugh in his ear. 'Have you ever . . . and I'm loving it! Pringle's taken over from Andy, and found himself in the middle of a right pile of shite. First, Mario McGuire's uncle gets his head blown off in his own living room. Next, Maggie Rose discovers that a parish priest from Lanarkshire who's on the missing persons list was actually certified dead of a heart attack in Edinburgh, under another man's name, and turned into ashes at Seafield last weekend. Then the man who's no' dead after all turns out to have been a tenant of Beppe Viareggio, who's well and truly fucking dead.'

'The faked death,' Skinner interrupted. 'An insurance scam?'

'A big one; there were four policies, adding up to a million, so Pringle just told me. They were written on the basis of an outstanding medical report by a GP, the same doctor who certified the phoney death. They've all been paid out and the money's been moved.'

The DCC's mind raced as he took in and analysed everything that Haggerty had told him. 'Have we gone public on all of this?' he asked.

'Only on Viareggio's murder.'

'Good; that's a help. Where's this doctor now?'

'Found this morning; up the Lammermuirs with a big hole in his chest.'

'Fucking hell! But what about Beppe Viareggio?' Skinner asked himself, aloud. 'He was just a harmless clown with a Marlon Brando fixation. Who'd want to kill him?'

'His daughter Paula,' Haggerty answered, 'or so Pringle's telling me; Greg Jay took a statement this morning from her ex-boyfriend, a DI no less, who said that he once stopped her from sticking a steak knife in her old man in the middle of a restaurant.'

'Who's the DI?'

'Steele.'

'Sound lad; not prone to exaggeration.'

'So I'm told. But this is where it gets nasty. I've just had Pringle in to see me . . . and not before time either. The couple in the insurance fraud had false identities, built around two birth certificates of long-dead people, obtained from Register House. Paula Viareggio's just been fingered as the person who obtained them.

'As it happens, Greg Jay's had her under observation since last weekend, in case whoever killed her old man had it in for her as well. His people reported that Mario McGuire's been seen with her twice since the murder; once on Saturday, then again last night. He arrived at her place about ten and stayed till after midnight.

'Now, Pringle tells me, Jay wants to lift McGuire for questioning as a suspected accomplice in the conspiracy, and maybe as the brains behind the whole thing.'

'What!!!' Willie Haggerty had the foresight to hold the telephone receiver away from his ear just before the explosion sounded across the transatlantic link.

'You tell him from me,' Skinner roared, 'that if he does, he'd better get his lawnmower sharpened, because he'll be spending a fucking long time in his garden from now on! And you can tell Pringle the same, while you're at it.'

265

'Relax, Bob, I have done already. Jay's been told to wind his neck in. I've asked Mario to come up to see me personally this afternoon; he's on his way now.'

The DCC's rage abated. 'Good for you. If the late-night visit means that Mario's having it off with his cousin . . . well, I'd be disappointed in him, but until it affects his work it's his business. Unlikely as that is, it's far more credible than the notion that the pair of them are involved in a conspiracy. I know Paula Viareggio, and I know about her sauna businesses too; Mario told me a long while back. She's a classic case, that one; her granny reborn. She didn't kill anybody, least of all her father.

'Tell me, Willie. Do you think it's occurred to Detective Superintendent Jay that if someone's going to acquire a couple of copy birth certificates for an illegal purpose, they'd be major league stupid to use their own name when they're doing it?'

'I don't know,' said Haggerty evenly, 'but I'm going to find out. It certainly hasn't occurred to him that if the money's gone, then so are the couple behind the fraud.'

'Yes indeed; so you'd suppose. Willie,' Skinner continued, after a moment, 'this con-man, how did he come to be Beppe's tenant?'

'It looks as if he and his partner set up a fake wine-importing company to show the insurance companies, so that they could take out key executive policies on his life. The names they used were Magnus Essary and Ella Frances.'

'Who's met them?'

'According to Pringle, Beppe signed the lease personally; he's the only one who actually saw the man who called himself Essary.'

'Then that's why he was killed; so that he couldn't identify him. But if the bloke and his partner are long gone with the money . . .'

'Why bother about that?' Haggerty exclaimed. 'I see what you mean, Bob.'

'Right. As an entity, Magnus Essary's dead and gone, no one's left to identify him, and the money's in the bank. Therefore this man and his lady accomplice can go back to being who they were before. If we haven't publicised the fact that we've identified the body, they'll be sitting there thinking they've committed the perfect crime.'

There was a silence. 'Or maybe, just maybe before he heads off to the sunshine with his woman and his million . . . he's got something else to do.'

66

'This is getting crazy,' Maggie murmured, almost to herself. 'What else did Haggerty tell you?'

'That was about it,' her husband answered. 'After your man at GRO came up with Paula's name, and you told Pringle, he went haring into Leith to see Jay. The two of them pulled the watchers' notes and saw that I've been to her place twice since the murder, and Greg just went crazy.

'I must really have upset him; he was for sending a couple of senior officers down to Gala to bring me up to Edinburgh for questioning. Old Dan was sensible enough to tell him to hold his bloody horses, while he went to see Willie Haggerty. The ACC ordered him to calm Jay down, and said that he would talk to me personally, which he duly did.'

Mario sensed her bristling, and saw her sit stiffly upright in her dining chair; that was as close as her icy control would allow her to come to full-blooded, exploding anger. 'The nerve of that man Jay,' she exclaimed. 'Just as well that Dan was there, or he might actually have done it. I tell you, love, if he had done that, it would have been him or me. I'd have gone to the DCC and told him that.'

'You wouldn't have had to. First of all, I'd have beaten you to it, and second the Big Man wouldn't have needed any threats from us. The ACC told me he had a call from him this afternoon. They discussed the case; Haggerty said that he sends us his condolences about Beppe. He also said that they've come to a conclusion about Essary.'

'That he's still around, even though the money's gone?'

'That's right, and that he's sitting there thinking he's a genius, having pulled off the perfect crime, and that we don't know that he's even done it, far less that we know who he is.'

'The second part of that's true.'

'Maybe so, but if Big Bob and Haggerty are right, he's still around for you to catch.'

Mario paused to slice off a strip of his fillet steak. 'There was something else, though,' he continued, forking it up. 'I wasn't late home because I was with Haggerty.' She looked at him, curiously, as he chewed.

'I was just leaving Fettes when I had a call from Paula, doing her nut. So I had to go back there again . . . another one for Greg Jay's book, no doubt.

'She was still shaking with anger when I got there. Apparently while Dan was off having his arse chewed by Willie Haggerty, Jay went ahead and lifted her. He had her picked up from the deli and brought to his office, then questioned her about the restaurant incident, and about those birth certificates.'

'What did she tell him?'

'She accepted the story about the restaurant . . . although Stevie Steele's had his last Christmas card from her, I can tell you . . . and she told Jay that she's never been in Register House in her life, far less gone there to pick up other people's birth certificates.

'He hammered away at her for over an hour, then he let her go, with a warning that when they found the clerk who issued the certificates, he was going to stick her in a line-up.' He paused to eat the last of his steak. 'He's wasting his time, though,' he added, at last.

'Why?'

'Because . . . although she was too shaken up to remember it at the time . . . on the day in question, Paula was on holiday in Italy.'

'Can she prove that?'

'Oh yes. It was a girlies' trip; she went for a week with her mother and her favourite auntie. I'll tell you something; Greg might have been within his rights in questioning Paula, but if he has my mother hauled down to Leith in a patrol car, he and I are going to have hard words again.'

'Mmm,' said Maggie. 'So Paula's well off the hook, is she? Yet someone used her name to get those certificates. Why, I wonder; why hers?'

'Thinking ahead, probably. This whole thing was planned in minute detail; I reckon that if Stan had gone to sign those leases rather than Beppe, he'd be dead now.'

'Or your mother,' Maggie murmured, and regretted her words, as she saw the look which passed across his face. 'I'm sure you're right,' she went on, quickly. 'Yet I wonder . . . maybe Paula's met Magnus Essary or Ella Frances, and doesn't even know it.'

He looked at her, darkly. 'Never mind Paula, love. Maybe we have. That's how clever these people have been.'

He was in the act of rising to clear the dinner plates from the table, when the doorbell rang. Grumbling at the interruption, he walked through to the hall to answer it. Neil McIlhenney stood on the doorstep. 'Glad it was you,' he said. 'I don't have to persuade Maggie to let you come for a pint.'

'But I don't want a pint,' McGuire protested. 'And you don't drink any more, remember.'

'Nonetheless, we're going for one. I'll wait; you get your jacket.'

'That quick?'

'That quick.'

McIlhenney's car was parked just along the road. 'What did you tell Maggie?' he asked, as they drove off.

'The plain truth; that you had turned up out of the blue with a pink ticket from Lou and were hauling me off into the night.'

'She'll be used to that, by now. Tell me some more truth. Are you screwing your cousin Paula?'

Dusk was gathering; so was the silence inside the car. At last, Mario broke it. 'Why are you asking me that?'

'Because I hear things; even more in this new job than I did before. A little bird . . . to be exact a woman DC in Special Branch whom you know well . . . told me this afternoon that she heard that you were, from a pal in Greg Jay's team.'

'So the word's got out, has it,' McGuire growled. 'I wonder who else Alice Cowan's pal's talked to.'

'Does that mean that you are?'

'What do you think?'

'I don't think you're that stupid; daft yes, but not stupid. Mind you, she's some piece of woman, your Paula. I can see how anyone who saw you go into her place at night and stay for three hours might jump to that conclusion.'

'Aye, well you tell Alice from me to let her pal know that if one more whisper of this reaches my ears, then I'll pull every string I've got to make sure that a few detective officers down in Leith wind up on uniformed night shift in Craigmillar, or worse, find themselves transferred down to the Borders under my command.'

'She needed no telling; that's exactly what she said to her pal. She's a fan of yours, even though she didn't fancy the Borders herself.'

'I'm touched,' said McGuire, sourly, as his friend drew up outside the Liberton Inn. 'Why here?' he asked.

'It's as good as anywhere else; plus, they know us here from the old days, and they'll give us a wide berth. It'll be as good as talking in a phone box.'

'You've got something for me, then?'

'Oh yes,' McIlhenney grunted as they stepped into the lounge bar. 'Have I ever.' A few heads turned as they entered, then looked away quickly. Neil went to the bar, while Mario found a table in the furthest corner.

'Well?' the big superintendent asked quietly, as his friend returned with a pint of lager and another, of orange squash.

'Tennent's.'

'Bugger the beer. What is it?'

'Okay; to business. I've done those checks you asked. You wanted to know all about your dear old dad-in-law, and here it is.

'For a start he has no criminal convictions, either here or in Portugal, where he lived from the time when he made his sharp exit from Maggie's mum, until about three years ago. When he went back there, he settled in Setubal, just south of Lisbon, where he lived with his parents, during the war. I spoke to the chief of the local police, who was very helpful.

'When he arrived in town, Jorge bought a bar and restaurant that had been pretty well derelict and turned it into a decent business, good enough to keep him in a degree of comfort, but not one that was ever going to make him rich.

'Like I said, he has no record of any sort, but that doesn't mean that the Portuguese police never took an interest in him. Some of his customers were pretty tricky; you know the sort, wide boys who find all of a sudden that London's too noisy for them. But not just English; Jorge Xavier's bar . . . that was the name he used over there . . . was a hang-out for ex-pats in general. There were suggestions that he was involved in more than alcohol: the place was raided a few times over the years, but it was always clean.

'The closest he came to being in bother over there came around twelve years ago, when a kid disappeared. She was a Portuguese girl, aged twelve, the daughter of a woman who worked in Jorge's kitchen, and she just vanished. She was never seen again. A lot of people were questioned about her disappearance, including him. The kid used to hang about the place, apparently; he was friendly towards her and he used to let her wait on tables.

'The Portuguese police didn't go as far as to say that he was a suspect, but he was the nearest they had. They had him in three times, and they gave the mother a hard time too, but she told them nothing that would have incriminated him.'

'Shit,' Mario growled. 'If only they'd asked over here.'

'And if they had, what would they have got? The guy's clean here too, remember. Anyway, it died down after a while, and Jorge's life got back to what passed as normal. Until, that is, three years ago, when he did another vanishing trick. He sold his bar to one of his German customers for a hundred and twenty grand's worth of D-marks, and he disappeared.

'But not alone, it seemed. For the daughter of one of the ex-pats, a widow named Baldwin, left home at the same time, without as much as a goodbye note to her old lady. The girl, whose name was Ivy, had worked in Jorge's place as well. She was a very striking kid, the locals said; very attractive. But the thing that made her stand out was the fact that she looked like a wee doll. When she left, she was eighteen, but she could make herself up to look mid-twenties, or dress down to look early teens. That was the way Jorge liked her to dress when she worked; he said it put the punters off groping her.'

'How did Ivy's mother take the news?'

'She raised the roof, apparently. She had a fancy man, one of the Londoners, and the word was that Jorge's card was marked if any of his old friends ever caught up with him. But like everything else out there, the excitement died down after a while.'

Neil looked across at Mario; he was grinning, from ear to ear. 'It's about to get stirred up again. George Rosewell lives down in a tenement in Bonnington, next door to a doll-like waif called Ivy Brennan, and her two-year-old son. George is the kid's father.'

'But he's sixty-three!'

'Ivy said he told her he was mid-fifties.' He snorted. '. . . Not that that makes a hell of a difference. But now to the killer bit. Did you drop that other name?'

It was McIlhenney's turn to grin. 'I did indeed. It's well seen why you're the superintendent, pal, and I'm only a scruffy DI. The police chief in Setubal recognised the name at once. He lives most of the time in Setubal; in fact he's officially resident there, although he still has his house in Edinburgh. And as far as anyone could see, Mr Lyall Butler was Jorge Xavier's best pal.'

'Yes!' Mario exclaimed, loudly enough for heads to turn once more.

'So what does that prove, then?'

The two detectives looked at each other. 'I reckon,' said McGuire slowly, 'that it means that my father-in-law killed my uncle; or at least, he's a prime suspect.'

'You mean that this Magnus Essary . . . the dead guy who wasn't . . . is really Maggie's father?'

'You know about Essary? That was supposed to be under wraps.'

McIlhenney looked at him. 'You're gone less than a week and you've forgotten what SB is like?'

'Not even I worked that fast. Yes, George Rosewell the janitor and Magnus Essary the non-existent wine importer are one and the same; he used Lyall Butler's house in Edinburgh as an accommodation address for his phoney business, and rented our warehouse space as premises just to have a lease to show anyone who asked questions about the set-up.

'I see it all now. He probably planned the scam out in Portugal; thought about it for years, maybe. Then he had a complication in his life; he was banging wee Ivy Baldwin in her schoolgirl gear, and he put her in the club. Rather than hang around in Setubal and wait for Ivy's mum's boyfriend to have him dumped off a trawler into the Atlantic, he sold up and came back to Edinburgh to put his plan into operation.

'So as not to look conspicuous, he bought two flats side by side, one for him, and the other for Ivy and the baby, when it came along. Her cover story was that her father had bought it for her. George got himself an ordinary job, waited for a while, then put the plan into action.'

'Why did he wait?'

'This is a pure guess, but I'd say he was waiting for Dr Amritraj to get set up over here. He must have been in on it from the start. The medical report for the insurance companies, so good that it was just accepted, was written by him. Then he certified the late Father Green as Magnus Essary, dead of a sudden massive heart attack.

'Raj Amritraj was from Goa, in India; not all that far back, Goa was a Portuguese colony, until the Indians booted them out. Check that out for me too, with the GMC, but I'm right, I know it; Jorge and Raj met in Portugal. The poor old doctor probably thought he was in it for half a million, but all he got was a bullet in the back and maggots in his eyes.'

McGuire stood, abruptly, and walked up to the small bar, returning with another pint of lager and another squash for McIlhenney. 'Don't let that go to your head,' he said, acidly.

'So,' his friend asked, 'does that make Ivy this Ella Frances, then?'

'That's what logic tells you, except for two things. Ivy's age is pretty flexible, but all the descriptions we have of Frances put her around the thirty mark, and that would be pushing it for the wee lass. Plus, when I showed Ivy George Rosewell's photo, she told me that he had a beard; that's what started this ball rolling in my head. Now why would she do that, if she was in on it?' He paused. '. . . Which begs another fucking big question.

'But meantime, pal, you and I better go and see Ivy in the morning.

No way I'm going to be alone with that one, not again, but I need to know everything she knows about old Jorge.'

Neil raised his eyebrows. 'Hey, hold your horses, McGuire. You're divisional commander Borders CID, remember. This is not your investigation; it's Maggie's first, and it's Greg Jay's second.'

'That's where you're wrong. I saw Willie Haggerty this afternoon . . . this thing's gone above Dan Pringle . . . about matters not unrelated to the story Alice Cowan told you. I told him what I suspected, and that I had you checking it out for me on the quiet. He told me I was a fucking chancer, and then he said I was dead right.

'As things stand now, Mags is in charge of an investigation which, if it succeeds, will lead her to her own father as the culprit. That can't be allowed to happen. At the same time, Greg Jay's compromised himself as far as the ACC's concerned. After Haggerty heard my story, he called the Big Man himself in the States. As of now, in the light of what you've confirmed, I'm ordered by him to take this thing forward myself, to trace Jorge Rose and Ella Frances, whoever she is, and to arrest them if they're still in our jurisdiction.

'I've also got discretion to choose my own team . . . and you, DI McIlhenney, are it.'

'Thanks a million. So who gets to tell Detective Superintendent Rose about this?'

'Haggerty's going to brief Jay, but that job is down to me, very definitely.'

'Fine. And when you break it to her, I'm going to be somewhere else.'

67

'You did what?' she screamed at him. 'Just run that past me again. You had Neil McIlhenney make enquiries that related directly to my investigation and you never told me. Then you told the ACC about it, not just over my head, but over Dan Pringle's head as well. And now, as a result, I'm being fucking well stood down!

'Is that it? Does that sum it up?'

He stood there like a schoolboy; their living room had become the head teacher's office and he was well and truly on the carpet. She was in a rage the like of which he had never seen before, not from her, and rarely from anyone else. Sometimes he had wondered what it would be like if his wife ever lost the self-control which, alongside her talent, was one of her twin trademarks. Now he knew; he could see the result, and, big and tough as he was, it scared him.

'Yes,' he replied. 'Baldly put, that sums it up. Now would you like to hear why?'

'No, I would not,' she yelled. 'I'm not interested. All I can see is the sneaking, conniving ambitious toadying bastard that you are. Three days it's taken you to trample my fingers on the ladder; that's all, three fucking days.'

'Listen, damn it,' he protested, his own voice raised for the first time. 'I didn't tell you because Neil's checks might have come to nothing. And if they had, all it would have meant was that your father had done yet another runner from his job and his life. I don't want that man to appear in your life one more time. If I had even floated the possibility that he might be involved in all this, far less behind it, I was afraid it would do your head in . . . as it has done.

'When I told Haggerty this afternoon, it wasn't just because I had to, it was because I was concerned about you, and about the position you might be in. He agreed with me; Bob Skinner agreed with me.'

'And where is my career now, alongside yours? Up shit creek, in their eyes, in mine, in yours and in the eyes of everyone who ever finds out about this. You've fucked me, Mario, just like he did; you're just the same.'

He recoiled from her words. 'I suppose you told Neil everything,' she hissed. 'Of course you did, you always do.'

'No, I didn't; I told him that the bastard knocked your mother about and left, but I didn't tell him why.'

'And he hasn't guessed by now? Don't make me laugh.'

'Don't you compare me to your father either,' he retorted. 'The man is a beast; he's a pederast, a thief and a murderer. When he was in Portugal he probably raped and murdered a child, only they never found the body. When wee Ivy came along he must have thought all his Christmas Days had come; she looked fourteen, she was willing, and it was legal. No, do not compare me to Jorge Rose.'

'Okay, I won't compare you to anyone. You are unique; I had complete trust in you and you betrayed it. You undermined my career as you were advancing your own. When I think of it, what have you ever given me? Jesus, you can't even give me a kid.'

She exploded into tears. He put a hand on her shoulder, but she shrugged it off, violently. 'Get out of here!' she screamed. 'Get out before I call my office and tell them you've been thumping me. That would look really good in the *News*, wouldn't it. Get out, God damn you!'

He was in the doorway when she called after him. 'You don't get it, do you? You don't get the worst part of it. Since I've been a police officer, I've wanted him. It's been my dream that one day I might arrest him; I wanted it so badly it hurt me. I wanted to see him in cuffs, humbled, being slippery and slimy, then scared, in the interview room. I wanted to leave the likes of Charlie Johnston alone with him for ten minutes or so. I wanted all of that, for my mother, for my sister, but most of all I wanted it for me.

'I was seven when he started on me, Mario. Seven.'

'Mags . . .'

'Shut up! Just get out, or I pick up that phone and start screaming into it.'

68

'Where did you spend the night, then?' asked Neil McIlhenney. 'Under the Dean Bridge, maybe? You look like death warmed up in the micro.'

'I thought about going to my mother's, but that would have involved her, and that's the last thing I want. So I went to Paula's instead. So now Greg Jay's lot really have got something to talk about.'

'Oh Christ, Mario, you didn't, did you?'

'Did I sleep with her, do you mean? Keeping it in the family, like? No I didn't, but if I had it would have been . . .' He stopped himself short, the word 'appropriate' frozen on his tongue. 'Not that Paula was offering, not last night, not with the mood I was in. She switched into mother-hen mode, instead. Even did me a cooked breakfast, whether I wanted it or not.'

'Have you called Maggie this morning?'

'Yup. The sound of the phone being slammed down is still ringing in my ear.'

'Aw shit. I knew she'd be mad, but not this mad. Do you want me to phone her?'

'That's very brave of you, pal, but there's no sense in the both of us being disembowelled, is there. No,' he pushed himself up from his seat in McIlhenney's office, 'let's go and see Ivy instead. We might do some good there.'

The two big detectives strode outside the headquarters building. 'My car,' said McGuire. 'I know where she lives. It's not that far, actually.' In fact it took less than ten minutes for them to drive up to Ferry Road, and along to the crossroads that led down towards Bonnington, on the right.

'I've seen better, I've seen worse,' McIlhenney murmured as he looked up at the shabby frontage of the tenement. 'You sure this girl will be in?'

'There's more chance of her being in than of Jorge. Mind you, we'll check his place just in case.' Mario led the way upstairs to the Rosewell apartment; without bothering to knock, he used his skeleton key to slip the lock once more. Nobody was in and nothing was different; the apartment had not been touched, nor as far as he could see entered since his last visit.

They stepped back on to the landing, closing the door once more, and across to Ivy's flat. McGuire rang the doorbell, then leaned down and shouted through the letterbox. 'Ivy! Miss Baldwin! Open up, it's the police.' He straightened up and waited for the sound of her coming to open the door, smiling as he imagined her face, in the knowledge that they knew her real name.

But there was no sound of Ivy; only a thin wavering cry, the tired wail of a child, rising to a scream of panic or even pain. He thumped the door this time, but still she did not come. Rufus' screams grew louder.

'Stand back,' said McIlhenney, 'I was always better at this than you, even when I was a fat bastard.' He jumped high, kicking out with the heel of his right foot, striking just below the lock, which gave at once under his violence. In a shower of splinters, the door swung open.

McGuire reached the living room first, but stopped at its entrance, filling it with his bulk. His colleague eased him out of the way and moved ahead.

Ivy was lying naked on the carpeted floor, in the middle of the room. Her tiny body was covered in contusions, and her face seemed to be one single bruise; her left eye was closed, and her nose had been broken. Great angry welts stood up round her throat.

'Strangled, the poor wee thing,' McIlhenney sighed. 'Beaten half to death, then strangled.' He turned to look at his friend, and saw him still in the doorway, tears streaming down his face.

'Too much, Neil,' he moaned. 'It's just too much. When I find this man, I'm going to kill him, nice and slow.'

'That's why we have to find him together, pal; so as you don't do that very thing.' The inspector reached for his phone. 'Better call it in; we can't deal with this one on our own.'

'Phone Haggerty,' said McGuire, pulling himself together with an effort. 'Not Pringle or Jay; I don't trust either of them. Tell him where we are, and what we've found. Let him decide who deals with it.' He turned and moved towards the bedroom, where Rufus screamed on. 'But tell him to get the childcare people here, pronto.'

69

Bob Skinner had sensed the tension building in his wife from the moment she had wakened. In a sense he welcomed it; she had been entirely too cool for his liking when she had viewed her parents' bodies, too composed by far, but this was the day when the tough stuff would begin again. She had her meeting with her lawyer, and then the funeral run-through.

Ian and Babs Walker were good people, to think of easing things for her with their supper invitation, but he knew that she would not relax again . . . any more than he would . . . until she had laid Leo and Susannah to rest.

He had that burden on his shoulders too, and more besides. He had told her nothing of Doherty's discoveries, and of the awful place to which they led. He did not know if he ever would, for all of his experience as well as his instinct for self-preservation told him that the secrets buried there had to be left undisturbed. Too much time had passed for any good to be served by the truth, whatever it was, being uncovered.

He knew that, and he only hoped that he had been able to bring Joe Doherty to agree with him. Whoever was behind the deaths of Leo and the others was not kidding, not at all, and besides, similar things had happened in his own country. He dreaded to think what would happen if his own story, and that of his friend Adam Arrow, ever found their way into the public domain. Few things ever worried Bob Skinner, but that was one of them.

He was relieved when Sarah told him, over breakfast, that she planned to spend the morning indulging in retail therapy, and asked him to join her; in fact, he jumped at her suggestion.

Buffalo is not the most sophisticated shopping city in America, but it had enough to occupy them. He had already bought his funeral suit, and so while Sarah shopped for clothes for herself and Seonaid, he concentrated on the boys.

He had just bought a New York Mets cap for Mark, and the smallest baseball glove in the store for James Andrew, when his phone sounded in his pocket. When he took the call, Willie Haggerty's gravel voice sounded over the satellite link. He checked the time; ten fifteen, mid-afternoon in Edinburgh.

'McGuire was right, Bob,' the ACC said, without pleasantries. 'McIlhenney's enquiries confirmed what he suspected. But it's worse; it looks as if the man Rosewell is still around. He's getting ready to move, though.' He told Skinner about the discovery in Bonnington, and about the dead girl's link to the man they were after.

'Who knows that he's Maggie's father?' asked Skinner.

'Only McGuire, McIlhenney and me; I didn't see the need to tell Pringle.'

'Good, keep it that way. When was the girl killed?'

'Yesterday afternoon, the doctor reckoned.'

'Do we know for sure it was Rosewell?'

'He's the only runner in the field. Plus, we can check. The lass put up a fight; they found skin under her fingernails, so we have a DNA trace. We're going to have to take a blood sample from Maggie Rose; if it matches, it's him.'

'Bloody hell. Who's going to ask her?'

'If it comes to that, it'll be down to me. Things are bad between Mario and her just now.'

Skinner sighed. 'I was afraid of that. Willie, I reckon we should take McGuire off this investigation as well.'

'Who else is there, Bob? He knows the case, he knows the people involved. If Rosewell's killed the girl, he's maybe gone already, but if not, he won't be here for long. My feeling is that we let Mario run, but have big McIlhenney at his side all the way, to keep him in check.'

'He's the only man I know who could do that,' the DCC admitted. 'Okay, do it, but keep tabs on it all the way.'

Sarah was frowning at him as he returned his phone to his pocket. 'Business at home,' he told her. 'Nasty, but you don't need to know right now.'

'Beppe Viareggio?' she asked.

'Partly, but let's drop it.' She looked as if she had no inclination to do so, but he was saved by the bell, or the tone, of his cellphone as it sounded again.

'Yes,' he answered, expecting Haggerty again.

'Mr Skinner?' It was an American woman's voice, low and even.

'Yes.'

'This is Philippa Doherty. I have some bad news for you.' Bob's head swam and his stomach lurched. He leaned against the store counter feeling the blood rush from his face. 'I got back from my flight this morning. When I let myself into the apartment I found Dad dead in bed.'

'Oh no,' he hissed.

'The doctor reckons he had a massive heart attack in his sleep.' He heard the girl catch her breath, keeping hold of her control. 'We've been warning him for years about his smoking,' she said. 'I guess it's finally caught up with him. I know you were in touch with him recently, and I found your number on his pad, so I thought I'd better tell you, along with his other friends and colleagues.'

As she spoke a wholly unreal feeling swept over Skinner; it was as if he was in a room full of people, everyone on the move, steadily, not rushing, but heading somewhere. He started to slide down the counter, until Sarah caught his arm. 'Bob!' she exclaimed. 'What is it?'

Slowly he realised that he had passed out for a few seconds, but his wife's touch, her voice and that of Philippa Doherty, asking if he was still there, seemed to have brought him back to the present. He nodded to Sarah, and spoke into the phone. 'Yes, yes. It's a terrible shock, that's all. Poor old Joe. I will miss him so much. My condolences to you and all the family.'

For a moment he was on the verge of asking if she had found a floppy disk in the house, but he realised that would have been pointless, and maybe even dangerous for her. There would be no floppy disk, and Jackson Wylie's recovered iBook would either vanish or yield nothing.

'Philippa,' he told her, instead, 'I'm still in the US as it happens, so please, let me know the funeral arrangements. And thank you for thinking of me; thank you for letting me know.'

For the second time in five minutes, he ended a call, but this time looking stunned, not just worried.

'Joe Doherty?' asked Sarah, incredulous.

He nodded. 'Coronary, they say.'

'You doubt it?'

'No; at least I'm sure that's what a post mortem will show. I've never yet heard of a cat that actually died of curiosity.'

70

Mario McGuire hated plastic coffins, the containers the mortuary guys brought with them to murder scenes. Whatever little dignity they allowed was more than offset by their odour; a mix of polyurethane and disinfectant, and by the brutal truth that they had been used on uncounted occasions in the past, to carry victims of all shapes and sizes.

He had seen people being crammed into these things. One corpse, that of a man stabbed to death in a pub fight early in the career of young PC McGuire, had been so gross that the crew of the meat wagon had simply left the arms hanging over the buckling sides as they had carried it away.

As they lifted her into her container, Ivy Brennan, who had been Baldwin, looked like nothing more than a broken doll. There was something especially tragic about her, the tiny, flawed innocent who had deserved so much more from life than to be the victim of George Rosewell, that even the black humour of the attendants was silenced.

Mario had banished his earlier weakness; grateful that only his friend had been there to see him overcome. It had been replaced by a huge, towering rage, which seemed to emanate from him in waves as he thought about everything that had gone wrong so suddenly in his life, and contemplated what he was going to do to the man who had brought it all about.

'Are you absolutely sure,' asked McIlhenney, forcing his way into his musing, 'that Ivy couldn't have been Ella Frances?'

McGuire turned away as a mortuary porter placed the lid on the coffin; he walked across to the window and peered through the slit between the drawn curtains. 'I'm as sure as she's dead,' he answered harshly. 'Ivy lived her odd life with her old sugar daddy next door, but she had no idea of what he was really up to.

'If she had, she wouldn't have pointed me at him with the tip about the beard, or made up that daft story about Uncle Beppe; no, she'd have done the opposite of those things. What she might have done, though, innocently, was set up the Viareggios.'

'Uh?'

'Maybe. I asked Paula some more about her last night. She started coming about the deli in Stockbridge when Rufus was no more than an infant. Talked nineteen to the dozen, according to Paulie; she asked all sorts of questions about the shop. She told her that she didn't just come to buy stuff; she said that she liked being there, she liked the smell of it. She said that she liked just to stand there and breathe in because it reminded her of where she used to live . . . although she never said where that was, and Paula never asked.

'She asked her about the special wines we stock as well, and whether you can buy them anywhere else. Paula remembered telling her no, that we imported our own, and that we owned a commercial warehouse where they were bonded.

'There was a man too,' said McGuire. 'She told me that once or twice, at weekends, a bloke came into the shop with Ivy; an older bloke, stocky, swarthy, hard-looking, with a grizzled beard. Paulie thought he might have been her father, but she never asked about that either. She said that she was happy to talk to the kid . . . she liked her well enough . . . but she didn't want to get involved in her life, so she always tried to keep her at arm's length. She never spoke to this man, and he never spoke to her.'

'But you think he was listening?' asked McIlhenney.

'Chances are that he was. Maybe he told Ivy what to ask, maybe not, but the likelihood is that's how he came to know about our warehouse and to know Paula Viareggio by name and sight.'

'I agree; that's probable. But you've still got to convince me that Ivy wasn't involved. Everything you've told me about her makes it seem that she was quite an actress.'

'Okay, I'll convince you. There's some more checking I want you to do, then a man I want you to see.'

'Who's that?'

'Walter Jaap, funeral undertaker. He's the only man alive I know who's actually met Ella Frances, as such.'

'Okay,' said McIlhenney, 'but I'm not doing it, we are. I've got orders from very high up not to let you out of my sight.'

'Is that right? In that case I might have to sleep with Paula tonight, if you're going to be on the sofa.'

71

It occurred to Sarah that Clyde Oakdale looked more like a lawyer than anyone she had ever known. He wore a three-piece, pin-striped suit, the jacket cut long, a blue shirt with a white collar, and he peered at her over half-moon spectacles as she laid the last will and testament of Leo and Susannah Grace on his desk.

'You're sure you understand all of this, now you've read it?' asked the interim senior partner of Grace, McLean, Wylie, Whyte and Oakdale.

'I think so, but perhaps you'd summarise it for me.'

'Of course,' he answered. 'Some time ago your father consolidated all his investments into a trust fund for his benefit and that of Susannah, during their lifetimes. With their deaths you inherit everything, other than his continuing interest in the law firm, which is distributed among the surviving partners; you and your husband are joint executors of the estate, and have absolute discretion over its disposal. You can dissolve the fund, or continue it in being for your own benefit. Alternatively you may appoint your children as beneficiaries.

'The will places no constraints upon you of any sort. It does not require you to resume residence in the United States, nor does it require your children to become American citizens as a condition of benefit. In case you're surprised by that remark, I have seen such conditions imposed in situations such as these.'

'What's the total value of the estate?'

'The current valuation of the fund is just under eight million dollars, and the two properties are worth in the region of one-and-a-half million. There are no borrowings attached to either.'

Sarah whistled. 'I always knew I had a rich daddy, but that surprises me.'

'I have to tell you that it would be to your advantage to continue the fund in being, for the immediate future at least,' said Oakdale. 'It is extremely tax-advantageous, and the firm would be happy to continue to manage it for you, through our associated brokerage, for the same fee arranged with your father.'

'I'll come back to you on that. Obviously, I'll have to discuss it with my husband. However in the meantime would you please proceed as soon as possible with the sale of the lakeside cabin. Neither Bob nor I have any wish to see that place, ever again.'

'I don't blame you; I'll instruct a real estate agent on your behalf, once the police give me the all clear to proceed.'

'Good,' she said. 'Now if that's all, I must be going. I have another engagement.'

Oakdale held up a hand. 'There is just one more thing.' He rose, ponderously, and walked towards the wall of his office. Behind a mirror, there was a wall safe, which he opened by dialling in a combination. He reached in and took out a long legal envelope, with a red wax seal on the back.

'A few weeks ago,' he announced, 'Leo gave me this, with the instruction that should he fail to reclaim it before his death, I was to give it to your husband; to no one else but him. I have spoken with him by telephone, and he said it was okay for you to receive it on his behalf, as long as you don't open it.' He handed it to her. 'I must say that I was surprised that he gave it to me rather than to Jack, who was, after all, my senior partner at the time.'

'Do you have any idea what it is?' she asked.

'No. All I can tell you is that, from your father's demeanour when he entrusted it to me, it is very important.'

72

Skinner was still dazed by the enormity of Joe Doherty's death as he walked along the tree-lined street in which the Walkers lived. He had stopped believing in coincidences when he was around eighteen years old.

'Why couldn't you take a hint, old pal,' he muttered, sadly. 'As if Wylie's boat blowing up when we should have been on it wasn't enough to give you the message.'

The thing that surprised him to an extent was that he felt no real threat to his personal safety. He was sure beyond any doubt that the explosion had now been reclassified as an accident, and that the remains of Jack Wylie's computer were as useless as they had no doubt looked when they were recovered from the hulk.

The secret was buried once more; there would be no sense in disturbing the ground by killing a foreign national, and a policeman at that. Yet he could not be one hundred per cent certain; that was why Leo Grace's Glock, all fifteen rounds in its magazine, was tucked into the waistband of his slacks, nestling cold but comforting against his back.

The day was still warm when he reached the clergyman's house, large by British standards but modest when set against Leo and Susannah's home. He crunched his way up the drive and rang the bell; after a few moments, the door was opened by a pert, blonde woman, around Sarah's age.

Until then, he had not been aware that he had met Babs Walker. He remembered only an encounter with one of his wife's friends, during the period of their separation, when he had been in Buffalo to visit his son, rather than with any hope of patching things up. The thing he recalled most clearly about that meeting was how frosty the woman had been towards him.

There was still a faint chill about her as she greeted him at the door. 'Bob. Right on time; won't you come in.' She held the door open for him, then escorted him through to their main reception room,

285

where her husband was waiting. From somewhere below, the den, he guessed, he heard a child's laugh.

'Welcome,' said the minister, 'it's good to see you again, but for the circumstances.'

'Yes,' Babs added. 'We never seem to meet in happy times, do we, Bob.' He had no doubt from her tone that she still disapproved of him. He guessed that there was little forgiveness in the preacher's wife.

He glanced around the room. The Walkers were keen collectors of family photographs; they stood in frames on every surface; parents, he supposed, children at various stages from birth, and the couple themselves, individually in high school graduation robes, and together on their wedding day.

'Nice,' he said, absently. 'I hope Sarah isn't too much longer. She said she'd get done with Oakdale as quickly as she could.' A glance was exchanged between husband and wife; he caught it, and Ian realised as much.

'She will be a little later, actually, Bob,' he confessed. 'She has another meeting to fit in.'

Babs Walker was out of his vision as he looked at her husband, but he knew that she was smirking at his discomfiture. 'That guy?' he asked.

'Yes. He called this afternoon, and said he was in town. I caught Sarah on her cellphone just as she was driving to meet the lawyer. She agreed to see him immediately afterwards.'

Skinner shrugged, feeling the gun move against his back. 'Fair enough. She's thought it through; she reckons it's the thing to do.'

'Will you have some lemonade while you're waiting, Bob?' Babs asked.

'No, thank you very much. But coffee would be appreciated.'

'Sure,' said Ian. 'I'll make it.' He headed off towards the kitchen, leaving his visitor with his wife.

She shot him a vixen smile as soon as they were alone. 'Please be seated,' she urged, indicating a deep blue couch. As he settled himself in she went over to a sideboard, took something from it that he could not see at first, then walked round to sit beside him.

It was an album. 'While we're waiting,' she said, 'I thought you might like to see some more of our photographs.'

'That would be nice,' he answered, insincerely.

She opened the volume at the start; the first page showed two girls; they were in their very early teens at most, but he recognised them both. One of them was by his side; the other was his wife. 'Most of these have

Sarah in them,' Babs told him, as she flicked through the pages. It was almost a montage of his wife's life; school student, prom queen, diploma winner, undergraduate. And then there were adult shots, the two of them together, Sarah and Babs, friends together at barbecues, on a ski trip, some with Ian and with other young men, boyfriends of the time, of whom he had heard, no doubt.

His hostess stopped to point one out. 'That's Ron Neidholm, the football player. He and Sarah had this red hot thing going while she was in med. school; they couldn't keep their hands off each other. But he went off to Dallas and she got bored. She was quite a girl in her youth, was my friend.' Bob kept an icy smile fixed on his face.

Finally, she came close to the end. 'This is the most recent one I have,' she exclaimed, as she turned the page, 'her last big fling . . . to which she was certainly entitled, since you were being a very naughty boy at the time.'

The photo showed two couples in evening dress, at a formal dance. 'Sarah's hospital ball,' Babs explained. 'She had one too,' she said, with a lascivious chuckle. He stared at the photograph, his smile gone, looking at the two Walters, at Sarah and at another man, young, confident, handsome, smiling, a big cigar held between the first two fingers of his right hand.

'That's him,' she said. 'The guy she's gone to meet.'

He was on his feet in a single lithe moment. 'Where?' he barked.

'What?'

'Where are they meeting?'

'I can't tell you that,' she protested.

He reached down and yanked her to her feet. 'You can,' he hissed, 'and you will.'

She looked at his face and realised that he was right. 'At Ian's church,' she croaked.

'Where is it?'

'Go left, to the end of the street, then right and it's about half a mile. But what . . .'

He shoved her back on to the couch and left her, speechless, as he ran out of the house, racing for dear life towards the meeting place of his wife and the man he had known until that moment as Special Agent Isaac Brand.

73

The two detectives stood at the door of the secluded, detached house in the East Lothian village of Ormiston. 'If we're wrong,' McIlhenney grunted, 'we're up to our armpits in shit . . . and when the tea-break's over we'll be back to standing on our heads.'

'We're not wrong,' Mario McGuire whispered. He flexed his shoulders to ensure that his pistol was loose and accessible in its holster. 'Your checking revealed that she's resigned her job. It turns out that George Rosewell's absence from work has never been reported to the council. Walter Jaap more or less identified her from her staff mug-shot as the woman who paid for Magnus Essary's funeral.'

'Aye, only more or less; I like my witnesses to be definite.'

'She didn't tell me about the beard, Neil. She gave me Rosewell's photograph but she didn't tell me that he had a beard.' His smile gleamed in the moonlight. 'It was enough for the sheriff to give us a warrant; be content with that.'

'My life in your hands, pal.'

'It was ever thus.' McGuire glanced at his luminous watch, then at the light in the bedroom window upstairs. 'Just after eleven; if he's there, they'll be tucked up by now.'

He reached out and rang the doorbell, keeping his finger on the button for at least ten seconds, hearing the strident call from inside the house.

Pat Dewberry came to the door, attractive in a long pink nightgown, even without make-up and with her hair ruffled from the pillow. 'Don't tell me. You've forgotten your . . .' she exclaimed, stopping with a gasp as she saw the two figures on the doorstep. She gave McGuire a look of pure terror, and in that instant even McIlhenney was convinced that they had come to the right house. He drew his gun as McGuire pushed the woman into the house and closed the door behind them.

'You take her,' he said. 'I'll get Rosewell.'

'There's no one here,' Mrs Dewberry called out. 'There's no one here.'

'Nevertheless,' said the big inspector. He headed upstairs.

'How did you kill the priest?' McGuire asked, once he was gone.

She was deathly pale, and shaking violently, like a tree in a gale. 'What priest?' she wailed.

'Father Francis Donovan Green. The man you had cremated as Magnus Essary was a Catholic priest. Didn't he tell you that when you picked him up?'

The woman's eyes seemed to glaze over; she started to buckle at the knees, but the detective caught her by the arms and held her up. She seemed to crumple into herself as he looked at her.

'I didn't kill him,' she whispered. 'George did; he used an electric stun-gun and then he suffocated him. It was horrible; I had no idea he was going to do that. He told me he just wanted to talk to him, that was all.'

'Don't make me laugh. Where did you pick up Father Green?'

'But it's true,' Pat Dewberry pleaded. 'We saw him at a pub called the Last Drop, in the Grassmarket.'

'Appropriate. How long did you have to trawl there?'

'We didn't trawl there; at least not that I was aware of. It was just one of the places we used to go for a drink. We chose pubs well away from the school, where there was little or no chance of bumping into parents. Then one night, George pointed out that man; he was on his own, and looking around. He told me that he was his brother, and that he hadn't seen him for years. He asked me to pick him up and bring him outside, so he could surprise him.'

'And you believed that?'

'Yes! They could have been brothers . . . twins, almost.'

'So you did what he asked.'

'Yes. It was easy, really; the man was only after one thing. In less than half an hour we were on our way. I took him across to the car, knowing that George would be hiding in the back. He got in and that was when George hit him with the stun-gun. That was when it all went crazy.'

'So why didn't you stop it? Why didn't you go to the police? Why didn't you tell me everything when I visited the school?'

'Because I was afraid by then,' she whispered.

'You didn't seem too scared when you opened the door just there.'

She looked at him, her eyes shifting around, as if she was searching for something in her mind. 'Listen,' she exclaimed in a voice that was suddenly stronger, as if she had glimpsed a ray of hope, 'I'll give evidence, I'll do anything you want.'

McGuire smiled at her, mocking her. 'I'm sure you will; but only if we let you,' said McIlhenney, appearing downstairs with a shake of his head.

'How did you get into this?' he asked.

'It was all George's idea,' she answered at once, 'you have to believe that. I fell in love with him. We had an affair; it began not long after he came to the school. He's an extraordinary man, mesmerising, charismatic; I've never met anyone like him. But there's another side to him . . .'

'We know,' the inspector growled. 'And it's pure evil. Yet you went along with him, just the same.'

'I thought the wine company was real,' she protested. 'He told me that he knew a lot of good Portuguese wines that we could import into this company and sell to private customers.'

'Some janitor!'

'It was only a job to him; he told me it was just something to keep money coming in while he set up the business. Then he asked me to be his partner.'

'Using false names?' McIlhenney exclaimed.

'He told me that he didn't want any hassle from the education authority; I thought that made sense, so I agreed. It's not illegal, after all.'

'What about the insurance policies?'

'George told me it was common business practice for partners to insure each other.'

'Why weren't there any policies on you?'

'He said we could do that later after the business was established. First, he said we had to set it up properly. I believed him, really, and then that awful thing happened, with that man.'

'When George shot my uncle, were you there too?' McGuire demanded.

'Your uncle?'

'Beppe Viareggio.'

She shook her head, violently. 'I drove him there. I thought he was just going to talk to him about the lease. I didn't know about the murder until I read about it in the papers next day. George told me that it had to be done, that with him out of the way we were free and clear and able to go and join our money without anyone ever being any the wiser.'

'Okay,' McGuire snarled. 'So where is he now, this charismatic devil? You were expecting him back, so where's he gone?'

'He said that he had one last thing to do, one last loose end to tie off. He muttered something about someone who had crossed him a long time ago, and before he could go anywhere, he had to get even with her.'

Suddenly, it was the big superintendent who was trembling. 'Oh Christ,' he gasped. 'Oh Christ, Neil. He's gone after Maggie.'

74

The knock at the door was gentle, almost apologetic. She was in the kitchen when she heard it, in her towelling robe and almost dry from the shower, making herself a cup of hot chocolate to take upstairs to bed. For a moment she thought about ignoring it; she had heard nothing from Mario all day . . . not that she would have taken his call if he had rung, but his failure even to try to contact her pained her, and made her wonder how much she had hurt him with her final withering remark.

She could guess where he had spent the night. It had been too late for him to go to Neil and Lou, and he had never in his life been one to run home to mother. So Paula's it must have been, and in the mood he had been in there was no doubting either what had happened. Still . . .

She can't be as good a lay as everyone imagines, she found herself thinking, *if he's knocking on my door tonight rather than going back for more.*

The gentle knock came again, a little louder but not much. 'Oh hell,' she said aloud, and headed for the door.

When she saw who was standing there, her mouth fell open, and she stopped herself only a fraction short of collapse. She had forgotten, or made herself forget, many things about him over the years. How blue were his eyes, how cold, how hard and how merciless. How deep was his tan, some of it complexion, the rest the result of years in the sun. How rough were his hands. How brutal he had been, as he invaded her. And most of all, she had forgotten, until that moment, just how much he terrified her.

He stood there with a terrible smile on his face. Not only was his beard gone, but his head was shaven, and gleaming, like a brown egg in the moonlight. He looked ageless; unchanged from the day he had left. She was frozen as he stared at her, and as he brought the massive automatic, made bigger still by its silencer, from behind his back.

'Well then, Margaret,' he murmured in the strange accent that had brought her terror then, as it did now, 'how you've grown. I've been watching you for a while, watching and waiting for that man of yours to leave you alone. And now he has. Ditched you finally, has he, for Miss Viareggio?' He moved towards her and she staggered backwards, helpless before him. 'Come on now, lass. Invite your daddy in.

'I've waited a long time to visit you again, you with your big mouth, you that couldn't keep a secret. I've waited a long time to pay you out.'

He moved into the darkened hall and closed the door behind him. Still she backed off, into the light of the living room, where the curtains were drawn. 'Superintendent now, I believe,' he murmured. 'It counts for nothing now, my girl, for nothing before me.'

He jabbed the gun at her, then laughed as she flinched. 'Let's see how you've turned out then, woman.' He reached out, fast, with his left hand and tugged at the cord of her robe, ripping it from its loops, then staring at her as the garment fell open. 'Not bad, not bad; bigger than your mother, for sure. And now, we'll see what else . . .'

She stepped away yet again as he moved towards her; her foot caught in the hem of the dressing gown. It slipped from her shoulders, and she fell backwards, full-length, on the floor. She lay there, paralysed, staring up at her monster of a father as he towered over her.

75

The vestry door was open when she arrived, as Ian had said it would be. There had been no other car in sight as she had parked the Jaguar, and so she assumed that she had made it there before him.

She was mistaken; there he sat in a wooden chair under the high vestry window, caught in the rays of the westbound sun, smiling as she entered the room, leaving the door ajar behind her. 'Thank you for coming,' he said, 'it's very important to me, much more important than you can guess.'

She looked at him, and that old feeling of lust swept over her. There had been so much she had not admitted to Bob, and never would. She could recall every one of the several lovers she had had in her life, since she and Ian Walker had deflowered each other in her freshman year at college, but none, not even Ron, her footballer, with such clarity as she remembered Terry Carter. The perfect, beautiful musculature of his body, the easy skill with which he had aroused her to frenzy, so often in their brief, energetic affair, his knack of entering her at exactly the right moment and his ability to stay there, all rock-hard velvet, holding himself back until she was absolutely ready for him to let go. Yes, she had been demanding of him. Yes, made bitter and revengeful by her husband's betrayal, for all the watered-down story she had told Bob eventually, she had demanded plenty. Now, once more, in the vestry of a Lutheran church of all places, she could feel herself moisten at the very sight of him. She laid her capacious black leather bag on the carpeted floor, and knew that if he asked her, they would probably join it there.

Yet lust was all it had been. For all of his beauty and grace as a lover, she had never felt herself falling in love with him. There was something about him that had precluded that from the start, a distance kept between her and the real man inside him. And so she had gratified herself with him, readily and frequently, in friendship and without shame. In fact she had felt no guilt over their parting, as she had pretended to Bob; she had simply wanted to see him again.

He rose and she went to him. They kissed, briefly, then again, for longer. 'Hello Terry,' she murmured as they broke off their embrace. 'This was probably a lousy idea, but I'm glad I agreed to it.'

'Me too,' he said. 'How are you, Sarah? Are you happy back in Scotland with your policeman?'

She nodded. 'Yes, I am. He's the foundation I've always needed in my life. Not that I didn't appreciate the time we had together. That's why I said I would meet you, I suppose . . . to thank you in a way I never did before.'

'You thanked me every time we made love,' he told her. 'I'll never forget you. And much as I'd like to reprise those days, they're over, I'm afraid. You have something I need; the package Mr Oakdale gave you.' He glanced at her bag and saw the long envelope, with its seal, sticking out of the open top. 'That's it, I guess.'

She frowned at him. 'Honey, what is this? How did you know about that?'

'Oakdale's office is bugged. I heard every word you said in there.'

Her look had become one of astonishment and confusion. 'Terry!' she exclaimed. 'What are you saying?'

'My name isn't Terry,' he told her, 'but you don't need to know what it really is. I'm afraid you have been unfortunate in your choice of father. Your old man was one of a small group of people who have been watched for a long time, by a succession of people like me. In Senator Grace's case it wasn't so much because of what he had done, but because of who his friends were; in particular, his friend Jack Wylie, the leader of the group.

'Those men were entrusted with one of the deepest secrets of our nation. Not I, nor any of the other men who have watched them over the years, know fully what it is. They were rewarded for what they did and for many years that kept them happy, but there was always the fear that, one day, one of them might have an attack of conscience. So they were kept under constant observation, in their places of work, in their homes, and in their recreation.'

Sarah stared at him, her eyes narrowing. 'And you and me? That was part of it?'

'Yes, I'm afraid it was. After your father retired it became difficult to keep him under complete surveillance. Then you showed up, back in Buffalo, his beloved only daughter. One of my superiors had the bright idea that you could be used as a conduit to him, so to speak. And so I was ordered to get close to you . . . an order which,' he added with a grin, 'if I may say so, I carried out to the best of my ability.

'Like I say, your father was included because of his links to those men. It was all a precaution, you understand; but as it turned out a precaution that was very necessary. For eventually, one of them did get flaky, and persuaded the rest to follow. Your father was enlisted to be their messenger, their most honest of brokers. In those circumstances, action had to be taken.'

She stared at him, incredulous. 'You are saying that you killed my father and mother, you bastard?'

'That is correct; them and a few others. And now, of course, since you are privy to all this, you have to go too.'

He reached into the jacket of his dark suit and took out a gun, a compact weapon that she recognised as the twin of the one in her father's car. He levelled it at her head. 'You may prefer to turn around,' he murmured.

'And you may prefer,' a rough, breathless voice said from the doorway, 'to lay that weapon very slowly and very carefully on the ground at your feet. No, don't even think about pulling the trigger, son. And don't get any other ideas either. I may be out of puff but you wouldn't get halfway round towards me before your brains were all over that wall.'

Very slowly, and very carefully, Isaac Brand did as he had been instructed. 'That's good,' said Skinner, 'now slip off your jacket so I can see you aren't carrying anything else.' He waited, as the special agent dropped his coat on the floor. 'Okay, that's good. Now turn, slowly, and face me.'

Brand inched round until he could see the big figure of the Scot, holding an identical Glock to the one on the floor. The barrel was a black dot and he was transfixed by it. Almost casually, Skinner took one pace forward and kicked him in the testicles, as hard as he was able. The American squealed and fell to the floor, clutching his crotch and squirming.

'That's for fucking my wife. I'm an unreconstructed caveman where that sort of thing's concerned. It's also out of frustration that I was so stupid, from the moment I told Joe Doherty to use you to check on Wylie, Garrett and Wilkins. I should have been suspicious from the moment you didn't tell Joe about the stolen laptop. We were all wrapped up in Kosinski, but it was you all along; you were the plant. Troy had nothing to do with it. That's right, isn't it?'

On the floor, Brand gurgled.

'It's okay,' said Skinner. 'I'll take a nod as a "yes".' Purple-faced, the man nodded.

'I wish I could kill you now,' the Scot told him, 'for Leo and Susannah and for all the others. You've no idea how badly I want to . . . or maybe you do. If this was my country, you'd be well dead by now; I'd have dropped you as soon as I came through that door and saw you with a gun on Sarah. But it isn't, and I don't want to import any shit to Scotland; so I don't want to take a chance on shooting you.

'I've been in your world, and so I know how it works. So my proposal is that we're going to go now, and we're going to leave you with the thing you came after.' He glanced towards Sarah's bag, on the floor. 'Is that it in there?'

'Yes,' she replied, a catch in her throat.

'Okay; take it out and leave it there. Then pick up the gun and come over here.' She nodded and did as he said, then moved over to the door behind him.

'I want you to carry a message from me, Brand, to whoever pulls your strings. I don't want to know who was behind it, or even how you killed Joe. The end of the story's in that envelope; I'm going to leave it for you, and I'm going to walk away.

'You have two choices, son. You either take that package and what's in it, and give me your personal word that you will never come near me or any of mine again, anywhere, or I'll yield to my basest instincts and put a bullet through your head, right where you lie.

'Which is it to be? Are you going to be sensible, or are you going to be dead?'

Zak Brand twisted his head to look up at him. 'Sensible,' he hissed, in an agonised voice.

'Just as well. Stay where you are until you hear us drive off. And don't think of calling any back-up you may have out there. If any vehicle as much as moves towards us as we leave here, or tries to tail us, I will turn right round, come back in here and kill you. Do you believe that?'

'Yes.'

'Then just keep on believing.' He put an arm around Sarah's waist and steered her through the door.

She said nothing until they were in the Jaguar; then she turned to him. 'Is that it?' she asked, with fury written on her face. 'That man killed my parents and we're just going to leave him there?'

'Do you really think I want to?' he snapped back at her. 'That's the way it has to be. But he hasn't got away with anything.'

'What do you mean?'

'I mean this. I can't shoot the bastard because I need him to deliver his message to whoever sent him. Much as I'd like to get them all, I never could, because wherever they're from and whatever their background, be it state, organised crime, or foreign government, their resources put them beyond even my reach. If I tried to track them, which I could do by tailing Brand . . .'

'Brand?' She frowned.

In spite of himself, Babs Walker's drawing-room tour of Sarah's past flashed through his mind. 'Your lover's real name is Isaac Brand,' he told her, coolly. 'He's a Special Agent of the FBI, and he was one of the two guys Joe Doherty assigned to me . . . only he had other loyalties.

'If I did tail him, I'd be putting you, all of us, at terrible risk; so I can't.'

Skinner looked at her, and a hard light flickered in his eye. 'But he's at risk himself now. Brand took his orders from someone, and even if he's only met that one link in the chain of which he himself is a part, now he's failed in his mission and been exposed.'

A look of blood-chilling satisfaction crossed his face; it might even have been taken for a smile. 'And that makes him . . .' he murmured '. . . the weakest link. Goodbye.'

He switched on the engine of the big car. 'I could have made him dead, but you could say I've done worse. He isn't a pursuer any more; I've made him a target. He's got two choices. Either he takes a big risk and tries to bargain for his life with that envelope, probably not even knowing what's in it, or he takes a big risk and runs. Either way he'll never know anything but fear for as long or as short as he lives.'

She looked at him as he drove off; for the first time he noticed how pale she was. 'And us. We'll be safe, you're sure?'

'I'm sure. When we get home I'll go to see a pal in Whitehall, just to make certain. I've already sent him by courier, via the British Embassy, the item that Clyde Oakdale gave me this afternoon when I passed by him by accident in a crowded shopping mall, out of shot of the video cameras and where we couldn't be overheard by any nearby microphones, like those which are undoubtedly planted in his office.'

She gasped with surprise, then frowned. 'But how did you set a meeting up, without that being overheard?'

'I sent him a text message on his cellphone.'

'You cunning so-and-so,' she exclaimed. 'So what did Clyde give you?'

'A copy of everything in the envelope we left back there. Do you think I'm completely bloody daft?'

'You mean you expected someone to come after me when Clyde gave me the original?'

'No. I knew that someone would come after it, not after you; I just didn't expect it would be so soon, or that the guy who would do it would be the same guy I asked to keep an eye on you after you left Oakdale's office.'

'You mean you asked Brand to look out for me?'

'That's how good he was . . . or how stupid I was.'

'And Terry's . . . Brand's people; how will they know about the duplicate?'

'They'll figure out that I wouldn't have given it up unless I had some sort of pretty good insurance.' He looked at her. 'Now trust me on this,' he said, 'with your life and the lives of our kids.'

Sarah was silent for a long time, knowing that he was the only man she had ever met, other than her father, whom she could trust to that extent. 'Since you put it that way, I must,' she murmured, grimly.

They drove on in silence for a while, back to the Walkers' home. 'How much did you overhear back there?' she asked him, eventually.

'Nothing. I got there just as he was getting ready to shoot you. Why? Did I miss something?'

'No,' she said. 'Nothing at all.'

76

She had no idea how long she had been sitting there, staring numbly at the wall. Somewhere in the back of her consciousness, she heard the door open again. Somewhere behind her she heard two men enter the room, one of them her husband . . . she knew the very sound of his footfall . . . and the other certainly Neil McIlhenney, for wherever Mario went in a crisis, his friend would not be far away.

But she made no move to turn; she simply sat there, on the edge of the armchair, her father's gun, and his body, at her feet.

'Oh my Lord,' McIlhenney murmured. 'Mario, here's where I disobey orders; this is for you to deal with on your own. If you need me, I'll be in the kitchen, doing something useless.'

McGuire barely heard him; instinctively, he snapped off the light and stepped into the living room. In the second before Neil turned away, she looked round and up, and he saw her face in the moonlight. Her expression made him shudder; it was that of someone he had never seen before, someone who, for all she knew, was fully dressed and greeting a surprise visitor, not sitting naked on a chair, looking up at her husband as if nothing untoward had happened. Whoever she was, she wasn't Maggie Rose, not as he had ever known her.

'I didn't appreciate . . .' he heard her begin in a chillingly calm voice . . . not hers, someone else's . . . as he left Mario to what he had to do.

In the kitchen, he filled the kettle, found three mugs and dropped a tea bag into each one; he had no idea why he was doing it, other than to pass the time. He stood there and waited, trying to imagine how Pat Dewberry would embellish her story, now that no one was left alive to contradict her.

They had had no time to arrest her formally; all they had been able to do was call two constables from the nearest patrolling car to sit with her until DC Alice Cowan from McIlhenney's Special Branch team could get there to relieve them.

'Neil.' McGuire's voice came from the hall. McIlhenney stepped out and found him on the stairs, one hand on Maggie's waist as if he was steering her. He had put her bathrobe around her shoulders, but it hung loose on her and he looked away, embarrassed. Mario tossed him a car key, on its dealer fob. 'I dug that out of his pocket. His motor'll be outside; find it and run it into the driveway, as close to the house as you can get it.'

'What are we going to do?'

'I'm going to take him somewhere else. You don't need to have anything to do with it.'

'Fuck off.'

The big superintendent's smile gleamed. 'Since you put it that way, I'd welcome your help.'

Neil nodded and headed off, out into the night. He looked at the key and saw that it was for a Ford. A Mondeo and a Focus were parked close to each other, less than fifty yards away. Squinting in the street light, he found the button which operated the remote central locking. He pressed the unlock sign as he approached the two vehicles, heard a 'clunk' and saw the courtesy light come on inside the Focus. He slid in behind the wheel, adjusting the driver's seat to give himself more leg-room, then started the car and reversed quietly up his friends' drive, positioning the front passenger seat less than six feet from the side door of the house. He glanced around as he stepped out. Mario and Maggie lived in the sort of neighbourhood where people kept conventional hours; all the curtains were drawn in both of the houses that overlooked the drive.

McGuire was back in the living room, waiting for him. He winced as he took his first close look at the body. 'Ouch! What did she shoot him with? A cannon?'

'More or less. Here, help me get him into this.' He held up an old parka he had unearthed from the depths of his wardrobe; it was a winter garment with a big hood. 'Come on,' he said. 'Kevin O'Malley the consultant shrink's on his way here and I don't want him to see any of this.'

'Where are we taking him?'

'Home.'

Together they heaved the dead weight of George Rosewell into a sitting position, forced his arms into the jacket, which was, fortunately, two or three sizes too large for him, and zipped it up. Then, pulling the hood as far over the ravaged face as they could, they pulled him upright, and hauled him out to the car, looking to any distant observer, had there been one, as if they were seeing off the last drunk to leave the party.

They wedged him into the passenger seat, where Mario fastened the safety belt as tightly as he could across his chest and round his waist. 'Last bloke I saw looking like that,' said McIlhenney, as they finished, 'was Dan Pringle after a CID dance.'

'This bastard's luckier than Dan; at least he won't feel like shit in the morning.' McGuire went back into the house and returned with the rolled-up, bloodstained rug, which he shoved behind the front seats. 'On you go now; you head off to Bonnington. Don't park, just drive around till you see me there. I'll be as quick as I can.'

Neil nodded. 'How's Mags?' he asked.

'In a trance; lying on the bed, staring at the ceiling.'

'What have you told Kevin?'

'That she's had a breakdown, and that I want it kept quiet. He's going to take her to his clinic and keep her sedated and under observation for a couple of days. He's used to working with us; he'll keep it under wraps all right.'

'Wouldn't she be better here? I mean, shouldn't you be with her when she comes out of it?'

'She may not want to see me when she comes out of it. And to tell you the truth, old pal; I don't know if I want to see her.'

77

The bathroom was lit only by the strip-light above the mirror, in which he had shaved less than a day before. He lay back in the great oval tub, in the middle of the night, more exhausted than he had ever been in his life. Paula sat beside him on the lid of a laundry basket, nursing a mug of coffee; with her hair tied in a ponytail and wearing only the long tee-shirt in which she had been sleeping when he had leaned relentlessly on the entry-phone buzzer, after McIlhenney had dropped him off.

'Is this going to become a habit?' she asked.

'I couldn't honestly tell you,' Mario sighed.

She stood, drew her makeshift nightgown over her head, and lowered her long olive-skinned body into the bath beside him. 'Come on then, move your bum,' she murmured. He made room for her; it was big enough and then some.

'It won't do you any good,' he murmured, 'you know that, don't you.'

'Maybe not,' she replied, 'but I know when a man needs a hug. It's been a bad day, then?'

'The worst of my life,' he told her, truthfully. 'Remember wee Ivy? She's dead; Neil and I found her at her place this afternoon.'

Paula sighed. 'Oh, no; the poor kid. What was it? An overdose?'

'An overdose of life.'

'And what about the man who killed my dad? Are you any nearer catching him?'

He nodded, sending ripples across the surface of the bathwater. 'We know where he is. We'll go and get him tomorrow.'

'You wouldn't kill him for me, would you?' She smiled as she asked, but he knew that she was deadly serious.

'I won't have to go that far.'

She pulled back an inch or two, focusing on his face. 'What do you mean by that?'

'Don't ask. Don't ask any more questions. In fact, shut your bloody mouth.' He turned half round towards her, drew her to him and kissed her. Even in the warm bath, she could feel him shiver.

'Here,' she whispered. 'I thought you said this wouldn't do me any good.'

'It won't,' he told her. 'We're going to hate ourselves in the morning.'

'You speak for yourself, big boy.'

78

They arrived outside the tenement building just after ten on Thursday morning; McIlhenney looked the fresher of the two, but it was marginal.

Mario had awakened in Paula's bed three hours earlier, to find her propped up on an elbow beside him, looking down at him with a smile on her face. 'You did it again, you big bastard,' she had chuckled. 'You fell asleep on me.'

'Oops, sorry,' he had murmured in reply, reaching up to draw her down beside him. 'But I'm half-awake now.'

'You really know how to make a girl feel wanted.'

He had barely finished shaving . . . the sign of the modern single woman, he had decided, was a Gillette Mach III, still in the wrapper, and a can of foam, in her bathroom cabinet . . . when his friend had arrived to collect him. He had asked no questions on the drive out to Ormiston, and Mario had told him nothing.

Pat Dewberry was cleaned up, made up and composed, when they walked into her living room, after Alice Cowan had let them in. 'He hasn't come home, you know,' she had said.

McGuire had simply shrugged. 'We'll have to look somewhere else, then.'

They had cautioned her and had told her that she would be taken into custody for questioning in connection with fraudulent claims from several insurance companies, and had called in a team from Detective Superintendent Brian Mackie's division to take her to their office in Lasswade.

And then they had headed for Bonnington, where they had found Willie Haggerty, Dan Pringle, Stevie Steele and four armed, uniformed officers, a sergeant and three constables, waiting for them.

'What's this about then, Mario?' asked the head of CID. 'Stevie said you wanted me here, and an armed response team, but that was all. I thought I'd better tell the ACC too, then I found you'd phoned him. You're fuckin' about with the chain of command here, Superintendent, and I don't like it.'

'Easy, Dan,' said Haggerty, calming the belligerent DCS. 'The lads have been operating under my orders. You want to shout at anyone, shout at me.' He looked at McGuire. 'Okay. Tell us all your story.'

The big, swarthy detective nodded. 'We have information that the man who called himself Magnus Essary . . . his real name is George Rosewell . . . may be holed up in a flat here; the one next door to where the girl was killed yesterday. We also believe that he killed her; we should be able to prove that when we get hold of him.'

'What else do you know about him?'

'He shot my Uncle Beppe. He also killed the priest Father Green, and the doctor who certified the death; we have his accomplice in custody. She's spilled the lot.'

Haggerty frowned. 'If he killed the girl, what the hell's he doing hiding next door?'

'We think he probably watched the place,' McIlhenney volunteered, 'and came back here after our guys had finished. Not entirely daft when you think about it.'

'And you think he's armed?'

'We must assume that.'

'Agreed; let's do it.'

The ACC nodded to the uniformed officers; weapons drawn, they led the way upstairs, moving silently until finally they reached the landing for which Ivy Brennan's taped-over apartment told them they had been heading. McGuire pointed to Rosewell's flat, and one of the constables stepped forward. He swung a heavy wooden bludgeon at the door; the frame shattered, it swung open, and the armed team rushed inside, their shouted warnings announcing their presence.

Inside a minute, the sergeant stepped out on to the landing. On floors above and below, they heard doors opening. 'He's in here, sir,' the officer told Haggerty.

The ACC led the detectives into the flat, following the armed sergeant. George Rosewell lay on his back, on a bloodstained rug, with half his face gone; a great silenced automatic hanging loosely in his right hand. Haggerty looked down at him. 'You've done us a favour then, pal,' he said, as if the man could hear him. 'Good idea, bad bastard that you were.'

'He's had two whacks at it,' Steele murmured, pointing at a shattered mirror, above the cold fireplace. 'His hand must have been shaking the first time he tried.'

'Made no mistake next time,' Haggerty grunted. 'Okay, that's it; call up the meat wagon, Stevie, and let's have him carted off for post mortem.'

'Are you not going to get Dorward's team in before we move him?' asked Pringle.

'Nah. No need for them. It's clear what happened; we'll do a residue test to prove he fired the gun. That'll be enough for the report to the fiscal.'

He looked at McGuire and McIlhenney. 'That's it all sorted then, lads, is it?'

'Everything.'

'What about the woman, this Dewberry?'

'She's co-operating, sir. We've got her for the insurance scam, and she'll admit to dropping Rosewell off at Beppe's place the night he was shot.'

'What about the priest?'

'That'll have to stay unsolved. The priest, the doctor, and Rosewell are all dead. No decent brief will let her incriminate herself.'

'True. Well, come on; let's get moving. I haven't got all day; I'm the only bugger in the command corridor this week.' The squat Glaswegian headed for the door, McGuire by his side. 'How's Maggie, by the way? I heard you called her in sick.'

'She's got flu, sir. She'll be off for the rest of this week, at least, I'm afraid.'

'Not to worry. Manny English is back tomorrow, a bit early, and you've just sorted her investigation for her. Tell her I was asking for her. In fact, you and McIlhenney take the rest of the week off yourselves. The pair of you look fucking knackered. Anyone would think you'd been up all night.'

79

He sighed inwardly when he saw her; she lay on the white single bed, on a mound of pillows, staring at the ceiling, as she had done almost two days before. 'Mags?' he whispered.

She turned towards him; she was deathly pale, her eyes were hollow, her red hair was lifeless. 'Well?'

'How much do you remember?' he asked.

Her face twisted. 'All of it,' she hissed. 'Every last bloody second; being paralysed with fear, thinking I was dead, him, the beast, getting down on me. I remember all of it, and I know for sure that I always will.'

She grinned but there was only bitterness in it. 'Kevin says I'm suffering from some sort of post-traumatic shock. He thinks it might go back to the plane crash. How gallant of you, not telling him what I did . . . or what he did, either.'

The brief smile became a scowl. 'You've stuffed me too, you realise, getting me out of there. Nobody took a vaginal swab, nobody went over me for body hair; there was no forensic examination, nothing. I'll have no defence now. Have they decided what they're going to charge me with? Are they going for murder, or will they accept a plea to culpable homicide? Or is Kevin going to certify that I'm crazy? Is that what this is all about?'

He sat on the bed and tried to take her hand, but she yanked it from his grasp. 'We recovered George Rosewell's body in his flat, yesterday morning. He shot himself. We believe that he saw a police car outside his accomplice's house and realised that we were on to him.'

She gazed up at him, her fuzzy brain trying to follow what he was saying. 'But he didn't.' Her voice was hoarse. 'I shot him; right in the fucking face.'

'We did a residue test which proved that he fired the gun. Would you like us to do one on you? It'll be clean, I promise. He committed suicide; that's what it says on Stevie Steele's report to the fiscal, approved by the head of CID in your absence. Accept what Kevin says.'

She resumed her examination of the ceiling. 'And suppose I do?' she

307

said. 'And suppose you're right and my father's death is written off that way? I still don't have a career left, do I?'

'You have flu, which will turn into viral pneumonia, which will require a period of convalescence. The ACC sends his best wishes for your speedy recovery.'

'Does Willie Haggerty know?' she asked him, her eyes suddenly sharp.

'Mr Haggerty knows what I've told him. He didn't get to be an assistant chief constable by asking the wrong bloody questions.'

'You are a cunning bastard, aren't you. I suppose I should be thanking you now.'

He shook his head. 'No, you shouldn't, not now, and not ever if you don't want to. If you want to thank anyone, thank Neil. He put his arse on the line for you and he really didn't have to. He had more to lose than me. I can walk away from the police if I want, and run the Viareggio Trust with Paula. If he was disgraced, all the shit would come down on Lou and the kids, and heavy at that, because of who she is.'

'Then thank him for me.'

'No. You have to do that yourself, when you're ready. Meantime, just get over that flu. While you're doing that, I'm going to give you something to think about.'

He left the room, only to return a moment later, carrying a toddler, a young, fair-haired boy. 'This is Rufus,' he told her. 'He's Ivy's wee lad. She's dead, and he's lost his mum, only he doesn't realise it yet. He has a grandmother in Portugal, but she doesn't want to know about him . . . not that I'd let her anywhere near him even if she did. That makes him our responsibility, yours and mine . . . because you see, Mags, he's your half-brother. Who said I couldn't give you a kid?' Mario said, bitterly, and sat the child on the bed, beside her.

If he had expected her eyes to fill with tears at the very sight of the boy, he was disappointed, for what she did was look at him with something akin to fear in her eyes. 'I don't know if I want this particular kid,' she whispered. 'If what you're saying is true, as I look at him, all I can see right now, is our father, his and mine. I don't know if I can handle that.'

'But you have a sister. Where's the difference?'

'Why do you think I don't see her?'

He lifted Rufus again, hefting him up on to his shoulder. 'Well, I tell you this, Mags. I'm looking after this boy from now on. I'm going to bring him up and teach him my values and beliefs, and I'm going to prove that when it comes to character, heredity counts for fuck all. But I don't have to do that really, because you're living proof yourself.

'Paula's helping me take care of him right now, until you're ready to play your part in raising him, with me or without me, however it works out.'

She shook her head. 'I don't know, Mario; I don't know.'

'No? Well I know this. If you stay huddled up in that bed then your old man's done for you right enough, because you'll have let him take away your strength, your self-belief and your pride. If you do that, you'll no longer be the woman I love, the woman I married.'

He looked at her, and suddenly he knew once more where he had always belonged, and he knew the one last thing he had to do to bury Jorge Xavier Rose. 'God damn it,' he exclaimed, 'I'm not going to let the bastard have that satisfaction. I'm overruling O'Malley, right now. So do what you're told, Detective Superintendent; get your shapely arse out of that bed and come home with Rufus and me.'

For a long time, Maggie looked at him, and at her brother. Then at last, she sighed, and with an act of will greater than ever before in her life, she threw back the covers.

80

The confirmation hearing had been postponed; the senator and her husband were there after all. Skinner and Sarah stood by the graveside as Ian Walker recited the words of committal . . . they had gone on to the minister's house after leaving Brand at the church. Nothing had been said about Bob's angry departure, and in the presence of her childhood friend, Babs had become the perfect hostess.

Now it was almost over, the journey which had brought him from the Far East to stand beside the coffins of his parents-in-law. Along the way, he had seen more than any of them knew, and had lost more too. He let his gaze pass over the congregation in the cemetery, unable to guess their numbers, noting the irony of the Secret Service presence.

He swept around the gathering, coming at last to Sarah . . . and as he did, his head began to swim, and he was back in that grey place, the one filled with faceless, hurrying people.

As she looked at him she saw his eyes glaze over. As he looked down at her, blankly, he was swept by that strange feeling of *déjà vu*, an instant certainty that he had played the scene before. And then . . . in slow motion, it seemed to Sarah as she watched . . . Bob Skinner pitched forward, falling face down, stretching out full-length on the green carpeting of the graveside, dead to his world.